WARLORD'S
GOLD

Also by Michael Arnold

Traitor's Blood
Devil's Charge
Hunter's Rage
Assassin's Reign

WARLORD'S GOLD

MICHAEL ARNOLD

HODDER &
STOUGHTON

First published in Great Britain in 2014 by Hodder & Stoughton
An Hachette UK company

1

Maps drawn by Rodney Paull

A CIP catalogue record for this title is available from the British Library

Hardback ISBN 978 1 848 54760 5
Trade Paperback ISBN 978 1 848 54761 2
Ebook ISBN 978 1 848 54762 9

Typeset in Bembo by Hewer Text UK Ltd, Edinburgh

Printed and bound by Clays Ltd, St Ives plc

Hodder & Stoughton policy is to use papers that are natural, renewable and recyclable products
and made from wood grown in sustainable forests. The logging and manufacturing processes are
expected to conform to the environmental regulations of the country of origin.

Hodder & Stoughton Ltd
338 Euston Road
London NW1 3BH

www.hodder.co.uk

For Joshua

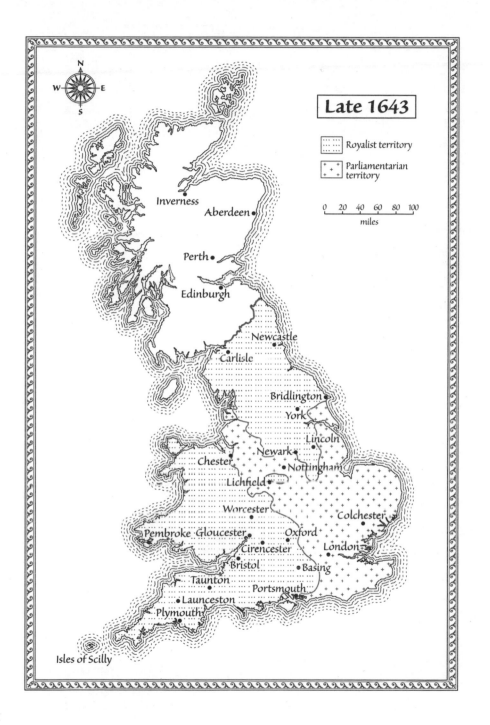

N
W ★ E
S

Late 1643

Royalist territory

Parliamentarian territory

0 20 40 60 80 100
miles

Inverness

Aberdeen •

Perth •

Edinburgh

Newcastle •

Carlisle •

Bridlington •

York •

Lincoln •

Chester • Newark •

• Nottingham

Lichfield •

Worcester •

Colchester

Pembroke • Gloucester •

Oxford •

Cirencester •

London •

Bristol •

• Basing

Taunton •

Launceston •

Portsmouth •

Plymouth •

Isles of Scilly

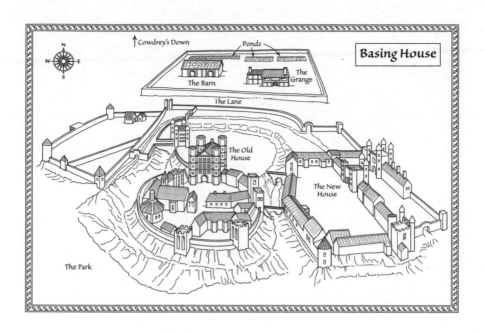

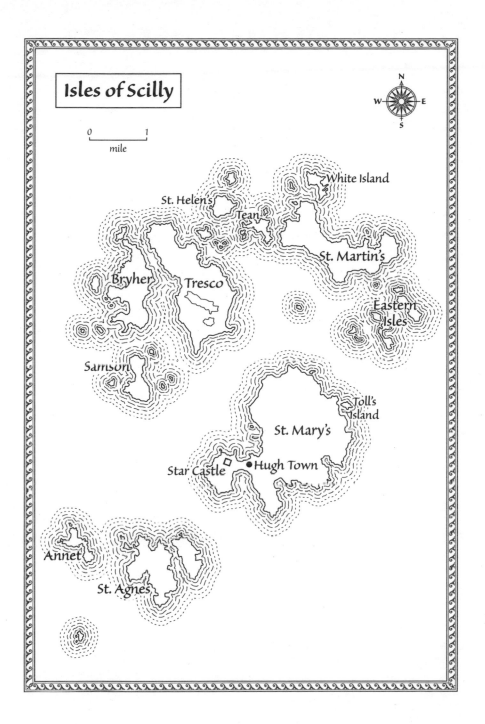

Isles of Scilly

0   1
mile

White Island

St. Helen's

Tean

St. Martin's

Bryher   Tresco

Eastern Isles

Samson

Toll's Island

St. Mary's

Star Castle   ●Hugh Town

Annet

St. Agnes

PROLOGUE

St Margaret's Church, Westminster, 25 September 1643

Sterne Fassett heard the echo of his own footsteps as he paced quickly along the nave. No one looked round, but he felt uncomfortable nonetheless. It had been many years since he had stepped inside such a place. Besides, he preferred to move in the shadows, and the notion that his every movement was being echoed by the beams above made his skin prickle with sweat. The first half-dozen pews were full of men. Black coats, white collars, sober and sombre, all staring at the big fellow pacing before the wooden pulpit, lantern jaw stiff with belligerence. It was very much akin to a Sunday service, except there were no women here, nor children. Indeed, there seemed to be no clergymen either. Even for a Puritan service this seemed strange, and the man addressing the well upholstered congregation did not seem like any preacher he had ever encountered. His belli-cose delivery might have been reminiscent of the ranting hot-gospellers, but his bearing was proud, his dark eyes were blazing, and his garments – though dour enough for a Puritan – were well cut and expensive. And in Westminster, this meant he could be only one type of beast.

'Politicians,' Fassett muttered as he reached the rear of the crowd, slipping behind one of the grand pillars to the right of the nave. 'Bastards the lot.'

'Have a care, sir,' hissed the man he had come to meet. Tall and thin, his face was hidden deep inside the grey hood of a cloak that fell all the way to his ankles.

Fassett looked him up and down and smirked. 'I know we are beside the abbey, but I thought the Benedictines had been run out of England.'

The cowled man kept his focus on the big fellow who yet gripped the assembly in thrall. 'Sir Henry Vane,' he said in a tone that carried the silk of privilege and education, a tone markedly at odds with Fassett's own coarse drawl. They were both, he knew, from London, yet their lives could not have begun more differently. 'Parliament's leading light.'

Fassett followed his gaze. 'Where is Pym?'

'Ailing. His body fails by the hour. Vane is his voice, though Pym yet tugs the strings.'

Sterne Fassett's jaw ached, and he opened his mouth to poke at the offending tooth. It wobbled at his touch, making him wince as a stab of pure agony lanced through his head. He caught an admonishing glance from one of the dour greybeards nearby and clasped his hands at the small of his back, exploring the excruciating molar with his tongue. It would have to come out, he thought with irritation. A good tooth, too. Free from decay, it had been the victim of a well-placed elbow in a tavern brawl that had ended in a welter of blood and three new widows. He let his tongue snake across the empty gum line at the front of his mouth. Christ, he thought, but he'd have none left at this rate. That, he supposed, was a necessary evil of the life he had chosen, but he by no means welcomed the steady corruption of his looks. He had been comely enough once, he reckoned. Dark-haired, bronze-skinned and quick to smile. Now the hair was retreating at his temples, the copper skin, the legacy of a blackamoor father, was blighted by scars, and the smile as empty of kindness as it was teeth. His wiry stubble was flecked with grey and his nose was blunt where the tip had been sliced clean off. And yet, he thought wryly as he let his gaze drift to the man at his side, there were those who had suffered more for their choices. He stifled a shudder.

'You summoned me. We have work?'

The hood quivered. 'I summoned you hours ago. Where have you been?'

'Gathering the lads.'

'You were successful?'

Fassett grunted. 'You mean, did any die in the night?'

'Your carousing clearly came with consequence.'

The cowled head turned, and Fassett saw a blue eye glint against lily-white skin. He lifted a hand to feel the lump on the edge of his jaw. 'Our carousing, as you put it, saw blood spilt, but not our own, praise God.'

'I doubt it is God you ought to praise, Mister Fassett. Your protection is down to another.'

Fassett smiled nastily. 'You are a man of faith. If I am so damned, why would you employ me?'

'To further His kingdom, Mister Fassett, one must, on occasion, treat with God's enemies.'

A ripple of applause swept through the pews, drawing the pair back to Sir Henry Vane. The powerful Parliamentarian held a piece of parchment aloft, his face tight with triumph. 'There you have it, gentlemen. The Solemn League and Covenant is accepted. All here at Margaret's bear witness. Six points to which we, in the sight of Almighty God, do solemnly swear.'

More claps chattered amongst the assembled men like a morning chorus of sparrows. Fassett glanced at his master, speaking quietly, 'Six points? I hear we're selling our souls to the Scotch.'

'We must all swear to preserve the Church of Scotland, and to reform the religion of England and Ireland.' The hooded man croaked a bitter laugh. 'The Kirk has us over a barrel.'

'Bent, legs splayed, arse thrust at the clouds,' Fassett added. 'And the Divines agree?'

'The Assembly of Divines was constituted to advise Parliament on religious reforms, and perhaps this is one reform too far for many. But they know they have little choice. Our daring enterprise teeters on the brink of catastrophe.'

'But Gloucester—' Fassett began. Everyone had heard of the city's stubborn stand against the Cavalier horde.

'Gloucester was a juicy apple into which the pamphleteers

sink their greedy teeth. Tales of courage and sacrifice are their meat and drink, and they have fed off Massie's unlikely heroism like sows at a trough. But Gloucester did not alter the war. It was a worthless town before the siege and is a worthless town now the soldiers have left. One heavy defeat. One daring attack by Rupert or Maurice or Newcastle and this great rebellion will be but a memory. The Parliament will agree to almost anything if it'll bring the Scots into the fray.'

'Like a game of chess,' Fassett said. He saw the hairless brow crease in surprise. 'I know such things,' he muttered.

The hood quivered as its wearer nodded. 'I forget you have a modicum of education. To use your analogy, the pieces are at stalemate.'

'King Pym would make an audacious move.'

The hood turned fully, the impossibly pale face within the sepulchral depths staring out like a creature from Fassett's child-hood nightmares. 'King Pym would change the rules.'

Fassett screwed up his scarred face. 'This League will take such an effect? It'll change the game?'

'The Solemn League and Covenant is an agreement between the English and the Scots, to further the cause of Presbyterianism and religious reform.' He lifted an arm, a brittle hand appearing from the voluminous sleeve, and counted each point on the end of a spindly finger. 'A guarantee by both parties to preserve Parliament and the person of the King. The suppression of religious and political trouble-makers, the preservation of the union of the kingdoms of England, Scotland and Ireland. And a pledge of mutual support and commitment to the League.' He turned back to stare at Vane, who was now engaged in private conversation with several of his peers. 'That last being the reason we're here, Mister Fassett. The Scots will give us their army, and together we will crush the malignants 'twixt our twin fists.'

'Still a big risk for them,' Fassett said, unconvinced. 'What if they get beat? Lose their army for the sake of an English brabble?'

'We will pay for it. The Parliament undertakes to fund the entire cost of this Scots expedition.'

4

'Jesu, how much?'

'Mind your tongue.'

'How much?' Fassett persisted.

Now the taller man turned back to him. He pulled back the hood just a touch, enough for Fassett to see the taut skin, pulled so tight it might have been the surface of a drum. The man had no hair on his face. No stubble, no eyebrows or lashes. His lips were purple, thin as a reeds, and just as tight as the rest of his features, so that it seemed as though it must be impossible for the man to smile or frown. But those eyes. They were so blue against such a pallid setting, like sapphires on a linen pillow. They seemed to bore into Fassett's very mind as the narrow lips moved. 'One hundred thousand pounds.'

Sterne Fassett whistled softly, drawing a few vexed glares from the nearest men who were now beginning to file out of the church. 'How will—?'

'Loans.'

Fassett laughed openly this time. 'Voluntary?'

The pale face dipped. 'To begin with. When that achieves nothing, they will take them by force, have no doubt. Either way, they'll find the money. They have to if they're to win the war. And there are always other avenues down which they may stroll.'

'Oh?'

'Have you not wondered why we are here, Mister Fassett? Why I have requested your dubious skills once more?'

Sterne Fassett had assumed a man – perhaps an important man – would need to be found dead in some filthy gutter or floating in the Thames. But the glint in the blue eyes told him there was more.

Just then a black-suited dignitary carrying a tall, buckled hat in the crook of his arm left Sir Henry Vane's side and marched a little way down the nave. When he was parallel to their pillar, he turned on his heels and lifted a hand in summons. 'Mister Tainton?' he called. 'Roger Tainton?'

The hooded man pushed the cowl back to his shoulders.

Most of the assembly had dispersed by now, but those left behind could not suppress gasps that seemed unnaturally loud in the cavernous interior. Fassett did not blame them, for his master was truly something to behold. The abnormally taut skin did not stop at his face, but covered his entire skull. No hair sprouted from his pate, and his ears were shrivelled buds, curled in on themselves like leaves left out in a searing sun.

Tainton bowed slowly, as though the movement was achieved with some effort. 'Sir.'

The man indicated the head of the nave where Vane stood. 'Will you come this way?'

'Gladly, sir.' With that, Tainton left the pillar, striding between two of the pews and out on to the wider path behind the suited man. He wore bright spurs on his boots, and their rhythmic jangle echoed loudly as he moved. He paused only to look back at Fassett. 'See to your men. I want them ready to travel immediately.'

'Where do we go?' Sterne Fassett called in his wake.

'That is what I am about to discover,' Tainton replied. 'But we are on a hunt, Mister Fassett.'

'A hunt? For what?'

Tainton's arm whipped out and he flicked something metallic towards Fassett. As it spun, it winked in the light that streamed in from the high windows. He plucked it from the air with one hand, abruptly snuffing it out, and looked down as he uncurled his fingers. It was a coin.

'For things that glitter, Mister Fassett,' Roger Tainton called as he walked away. 'Things that glitter.'

CHAPTER 1

Atlantic Ocean, 30 September 1643

The ocean broiled. It was deep night and the sky was blanketed in angry clouds that glowered when lightning forked in their midst.

Rain lashed the *Kestrel*, pulsing on the wind in diagonal sheets to whip viciously through her rigging and soak her deck. She was a lone island in the wild abyss, struggling, riding one impossibly huge swell after another, dipping and bucking like a raw colt, prow poised before sky and sea in turn.

The *Kestrel* was a fluyt, built by the Dutch and bought by the English, a curved beast of Baltic pine and sail, beautifully crafted and manned by some of the best seamen to navigate England's treacherous coastline. But now she was battered and bruised, tossed by the elements, her trio of square-rigged masts like winter trees, all shrouds bound tight against the howling wind. She was a trading vessel by design, fashioned with a wide hull that swept inwards up to a narrow deck. A ship to carry much cargo and few crew. But this night, aside from the score of grizzled seamen, the fluyt carried a compliment of thirty-six for this most special voyage, though the storm had chased most below decks to wallow in self-pity and vomit. The slop buckets, filled by those too unwell to move, had long since tipped, dashing slurry over the timbers as they rolled back and forth in a stinking parody of the water outside.

A stab of lightning turned the sky white as the lone figure struggled up the ladder and on to the deck. He was wrapped in a heavy cloak, one hand clutched at his breast to hold the greasy layers fast against the wind, the other gripping the voluminous hood tight about his skull, his head tilted down to let the rain drip from its edge. He took a broad stance as he reached the deck, lest the gale lift him clean off his feet, and leaned into the gusts, dipping his shoulder as he pressed forwards. Up ahead he saw the smudges of folk huddled at the bow and he went to join them. He was a soldier, and he felt his scabbard bounce against his thigh as though it taunted him. His weapons and skill were of no use to him here.

He passed two weathered seamen clinging to ropes as the rain lashed down. They were strong men, broad at the shoulder and well used to the cruel fury of the ocean, and yet their faces betrayed something disquieting. He paused, grabbed a loop of rope to keep himself steady, and stared at them. They were frightened and the knowledge made his guts twist. The soldier reached the steersman who wrestled manfully with a whipstaff that he could not hope to control. The tiller to which it was attached would be bucking with the waves, bending only to the will of the water beneath. The man squinted into his face, then looked hurriedly away; the soldier was accustomed to the reaction. His was a face of harsh lines and sharp edges, scored and scoured and beaten like the cliffs the *Kestrel* had left behind. It was long and narrow, beaten dark by the sun and given a feral aspect by the one grey eye that gleamed in the side of the face that might still be called handsome. The left side had gone. All that remained of eye and brow and cheek was a tattered mess of scar tissue, a tangle of pink and white, the legacy of some ancient horror. His nose was canted slightly to one side, swollen and crimson, recently broken, the mark of a man whose life was defined by violence. His hood was pulled up tight to shield him from the storm, but some of his long hair had broken free of the cowl, flapping about his temples like a headdress of raven feathers. He gathered the soaking strands with gloved fingers and brushed them back behind his ears.

'Where is the captain?' he called above the howl of the night.

The steersman nodded towards the ship's prow and the soldier moved carefully on. Somewhere nearby a single lantern clanged against its brace. Out beyond the floating fortress's pine breast-work he could see splashes of frothy white where the swirling torrent was kicked up and shredded by insidious rocks. He was not a religious man, but he prayed all the same.

The soldier found the ship's captain at the foremost point of the curved vessel, where plank and mast and rigging gave way to simple, sheer, endless darkness. Like his one-eyed passenger, he was swathed in a heavy oiled cloak with only his wrinkled face exposed to the elements.

'The Irishers call them banshees,' the ship's master shouted up at his passenger as he clung to a lanyard. He nodded out to sea. 'That unholy chorus.'

The soldier shrugged. 'It's the wind, Captain Jones.'

Jones looked up past the masts and rigging and the tightly lashed bundles of gathered sail. 'Ever heard a wind like this, Mister Stryker?'

The ship lurched suddenly to larboard, dipped into a valley between two gigantic waves, and bucked on the next swell so that the only thing the men could see was the pitch fastness of the sky. The vessel seemed to cry out like an injured whale, every timber groaning in dreadful unison.

Stryker gathered his cloak tighter. 'The truth, Captain Jones. We will survive this?'

Jones grinned wolfishly. 'Of course!' He patted the slick rail. 'My beauty's built to tame the oceans!'

Stryker was not so sure. He had always hated the treacherous unpredictability of the sea. A patch of foam frothed and seethed wildly in the inky distance, betraying a hidden point where the water's angry surface was torn like black cloth. 'More rocks?'

'Keep your nerve, Captain!' Jones brayed in dark amusement. 'It signals our success!'

'Land?'

'Land indeed, sir! St Martin's. Did I not tell you to trust me?'

A sheet of stinging spray jetted up off the bow to dowse the two men, and they hunched low. Stryker slipped, only just managing to right himself. He swore into the wind. 'I mean to make for St Mary's.'

'And I shall see that you reach it, Mister Stryker,' Jones said confidently. 'The Scillies are comprised of many islands.' But when the ship groaned again, the mirth melted from his eyes. He cocked his head to the side like a hound sniffing the breeze.

Stryker felt his pulse quicken. 'What is it?'

'Nothing, I am sure,' Jones said, but his voice was barely audible.

'I do not believe you.'

Jones swallowed thickly. 'The timbers should not sound like that. Something is amiss, that is all.'

The *Kestrel* rose quickly, as if propelled by the fist of God Himself, and they were staring at the sky again. When it dropped the groan was deeper, like the grinding of cogs that had fallen out of step. The deck vibrated.

'Jesu,' Jones murmured. 'Oh, Jesu.'

'Captain?'

Jones's eyes were suddenly wide, bright discs above the hedge of his beard. 'Oh, Jesus, help us!'

The impact began as a series of small cracks, like the felling of a dozen trees, one after another, rising in volume and force, each shaking the timbers at their feet. Stryker grasped the rail and looked to Jones for an answer, but the skipper was already backing away, staggering and sliding rearwards across the slippery planks. His hands raked down his cheeks, tugging at his whiskers, as though he suddenly witnessed a horror too awful for his mind to consider. 'We have been blown off course, sir!' he blurted as Stryker began to pursue. 'Rocks! My God, we are lost!'

When it came, the collision knocked both men off their feet. If the first cracks had been like falling trees, this was as though a building of stone had come crashing down in a single instant. Stryker sprawled on the watery deck, scrabbling for purchase as the vessel reeled. It screamed as the unseen assailant tore into its belly, the timbers splintering far below them, eviscerating the keel, exposing the *Kestrel* to a most terrible fate. As Stryker clambered back to his feet he could no longer see the ship's captain, but through one of the hatches further along the deck came the shapes of men. They were bellowing, snarling oaths and warnings, beseeching God for mercy, because they all knew what was happening to their ship.

More snapping and cracking and grinding. The timbers at Stryker's feet juddered as though some great fissure had torn open on the seabed immediately below the hull, and the black night came alive with a roar that was like nothing he had heard before. In his time he had stood in tight ranks of men and been pounded by batteries of vast iron cannon. He had stared up at the whirring arc of a mortar shell and witnessed the explosive power of a well-placed petard. Yet none of those horrors compared. The *Kestrel* brayed like a wounded beast as her very heart was broken, planks and ropes and spars all splintering together, her great frame pulverized by this invisible foe. She heeled violently to port. This time there was no swing in the opposite direction, no innate balancing act. She could not right herself but slewed about the rocky crag, as though pinned to the jagged shadow, glued fast by the foam that swirled in white patterns where stone shredded sea. And the first men screamed. They screamed because of the noise and because of the salty water that must surely be pouring unchecked into the *Kestrel*'s torn bowels. And they screamed for sheer terror, because most of them could not swim.

Stryker fell again, dashed about the deck like a rag doll, lost to the elements that had turned so maliciously against them. He needed to find his men. His team of musketeers who had accompanied him on this mission, and who now needed his leadership more than ever before. There was a hatch further back. He had used it countless times since they sailed out of the Bristol Channel, but now, in this clawing panic, he was blinded and vulnerable, his mind wiped blank by the sheer need to survive. The *Kestrel* shook again and slid further to port so that she seemed to hang at a steep angle. He found his footing once more, was thrown immediately back into the rail and only saved himself by clinging to a tangled mass of rigging that hung loose like ancient vines. The vessel was emitting a low, visceral mew, like a heifer catching the scent of a shambles, and he knew that he was pinned, doomed to hang in these sodden chains as the ship was swallowed by the cold depths. He gritted his teeth, stared up at the sky, and screamed impotent fury at the world.

And the *Kestrel* began to slip into the darkness.

Oxford, 30 September 1643

Captain Lancelot Forrester hated the noise of the ropes. The creak, gentle yet incessant, always made his teeth itch. It was a sound that frightened him the first time he had witnessed a hanging, and, he reflected morosely, might very well be the last thing he heard, should life take an unfortunate twist. God knew he had flirted with such a fate enough times. He felt his shoulders tremble a touch at the thought.

The bodies were still now, mercifully. They had been positioned on a cart, nooses looped about their necks and fastened to the thickest bough of an ancient oak, and then, quite calmly given the circumstances, each had fallen as the rickety vehicle had been pulled away by its pair of disinterested palfreys. There had been no drop to speak of, nothing that could snap a man's neck, and none of the condemned had died quickly, but at least the life had finally been throttled out of them. The kicking had stopped. The tongues lolled tantalizingly for the circling crows and kites.

Forrester sniffed the air. It smelled acrid, stomach-churning. Shit and piss. He noticed the steady drip of liquid from two of the five pairs of bare feet and turned away. 'Mister Jays?'

An earnest-looking youth in red coat and brown breeches appeared at his side. 'Sir?'

'Leave 'em for another half hour. Make sure they're gone, then cut them down.' Forrester glanced up at the mass of black dots that swirled below the grey clouds. 'And chase those buggers off, should they decide to break their fast on our friends here.'

Jays twisted the tip of his wispy moustache as he eyed the carrion birds from beneath the rim of an ostentatiously wide hat. 'That I will, sir. Pit'll be dug nice and deep. We'll get them in directly.'

'Good.' Forrester took off his hat, ruffling the sweaty strands of thinning, sandy-coloured hair with pudgy fingers, and took one last look at the swaying corpses. 'They may be mutineers, Lieutenant, but they're still men. Let us bury them with a modicum of dignity.' He shrugged. 'Or at least without their eyeballs pecked out.'

'I'll see to the digging party,' Jays replied, touching a gloved finger to the brim of his hat as he turned smartly about.

'And, Reginald,' Forrester called as his second-in-command scampered away.

'Sir?'

'I hope what remains of your birthday will be more agreeable.'

Lieutenant Jays grinned. He had been a Parliamentarian at the outset of the war, and, with a name to be made for himself, led a small detachment of men into an ill-fated assault on a tavern on Dartmoor's eastern fringe. Unfortunately for him, Lancelot Forrester and his company of veterans were resting inside, and the fight had been swift and brutal. But the Royalist officer had seen a spark of potential in Jays' reckless ambition, and had offered the youngster a position within his cohort, should Jays be willing to turn his coat. 'Fifteen today, sir.'

'I know, Reginald,' Forrester said with an exaggerated roll of the eyes, though he was secretly proud of how far the lad had come since that first bloody meeting. He pointed at the oak that had become a makeshift gallows. 'And your gift is five rotting cadavers. Do not thank me.'

He watched the lieutenant scuttle off towards a stand of trees behind which a burial pit had been scraped from the clay soil. The men would be left there, unmarked and forgotten. More casualties of an increasingly bitter conflict. On his way, Jays paused to speak to a musketeer who nodded briskly and moved to stand beside the hanging tree, evidently ordered to keep watch.

Forrester winced at a sudden pain in his right shoulder, and he rolled it gently, instinctively touching the aching flesh below his coat with his opposite hand. A musket-ball had clipped him at Newbury Fight. It had been fired at long range, but the blow had nevertheless knocked him backwards into the mud. And now, though ten days had passed, the skin was still bruised. Still, he chided himself, at least his skin was intact. Newbury had been the worst scrap yet. The Royalist high command might have felt the sting of humiliation after their abortive attempt to take rebel-held Gloucester, but the opportunity to redeem themselves had presented itself almost immediately. The Earl of Essex, commander of the Parliamentarian army that had marched so effectively through the obstructive cordon of Royalist cavalry to relieve the beleaguered city, had, by that very act, left London open to attack. Thus, the theatre of war had moved as soon as the siege had been lifted, the two huge forces promptly turning about in a race for the capital. Essex had a head start but was slowed by his artillery train and the sheer incompetence of some of his hastily raised regiments, and the Royalists finally cut him off at Newbury. The opportunity to destroy the rebellion had been handed to them on a platter. Even Forrester had felt the rush of blood in his veins as they hunted the Roundhead army down, the promise of rescuing glory from the ignominy of their failure at Gloucester sharpening their wits and bolstering their resolve. They knew that if they could defeat Essex decisively, London would be left defenceless. The war would be over in its first full year.

Forrester rolled his smarting shoulder again, picked a scrap of salted pork from between two molars, and stared about the sprawling encampment. His own regiment, Sir Edmund Mowbray's Foot, were five hundred yards to the south, and he could see some of them gathered in their usual groups, drinking tobacco smoke, gambling, tending to wounds or repairing weapons. Oxford was the capital of Royalist England. The ancient city had been commandeered by the king and his court; shops, homes and university buildings turned to barracks and storehouses, arms depots and powder magazines. But for all its size, it could not contain the vast army it now entertained, and most of the king's soldiers were bivouacked in the surrounding fields, a rambling warren of men and horses scattered below the city's great earthworks. He wondered when they would be on the move again. It was not good to keep an army static for too long, for such inertia bred lethargy and camp fever, a concoction that could only lead to mutiny. He looked again at the five wretches he had been ordered to hang this morning. He thanked God they were not members of his unit; he had not even known their names. But how much more hardship would it take for unrest to spread to his own ranks? It did not bear consideration, especially after the blood they had all shed just the previous week.

He gritted his teeth at the memory of stinking powder smoke, the acrid plumes of jaundiced white that had drifted sideways like a wind-blown fog to obscure the killing ground at Newbury. The battle had not unfolded as they were hoping. The rebels had held their ground after a day of carnage that saw three and a half thousand bodies left to bloat in the autumn sun. It had ended in stalemate, and, though the Royalists still blocked the road to London, King Charles had ordered a withdrawal. God alone knew why, for, as far as Forrester was concerned, they owed it to their fallen comrades to put down roots on the road, continue the battle the following day, and make that vital play on London. Instead they simply left the way clear for Essex, who wasted no time in high-tailing it home. It had been a bloody day of destruction and missed chances, and now here they were, skulking back in Oxford, no better off than they had been at the start of so costly a summer. And all the while the Parliamentarian news-sheets would be making merry with reports from Gloucester and Newbury. News that could only give hope to the hitherto wavering rebel resolve.

'How fare's the wound, Captain?'

Forrester turned to see a small man pick his way through the flotsam of the sprawling camp. He was an incongruous sight in this martial setting, his small, portly frame draped in a hooded cloak that gave him the appearance of a monk.

'I cannot gripe, Mister Killigrew,' Forrester muttered. 'Many did not see dusk.'

Ezra Killigrew pushed back his hood to reveal black hair scraped close along his scalp and gleaming with oil that stank of lavender. His fleshy face was sallow and his blood-shot eyes hung with thick lids. He offered a smile of small, white teeth and glanced up at the makeshift gallows. 'What was their offence? Spying?'

'Revolting.'

Killigrew wrinkled his sharp nose, putting Forrester in mind of a rodent. 'Mutineers are the scourge of any army. All five involved, were they?'

'Five were condemned,' Forrester said tersely.

The corners of Killigrew's little eyes creased. 'Oft times it pays to hang an extra two or three, Captain, as well you know. To press the point home, so to speak.'

Forrester sighed. 'If you seek Captain Stryker, he is not here.'

'I am very well aware of that, thank you.' Killigrew smirked and dropped his voice to a whisper. 'The Isles of Scilly. He was dispatched to recover a hoard of treasure.' He winked conspiratorially. 'Do not be so abashed, Captain, I have these rather delicate fingers in many a pie.' With a flourish, he shook his hand and thrust it into the folds of his cloak, pulling out a small bag. He opened it with a lick of his puffy lips and plucked free a glistening sugar plum. '*Nervos belli, pecuniam infinitam.*'

'The sinews of war are unlimited money.'

'Dear Cicero,' Killigrew said, though he was clearly a little surprised. He inspected the sugar plum as though it were a precious gem. 'Just as well Stryker is away, truth told.'

Forrester did not like Ezra Killigrew; the man was a weasel. A creature of politics and secrets. A man who seemed so insignificant, yet one who might have another's neck stretched on a whim.

He was a dangerous person to know, and to ignore, so Forrester chose to humour him. 'Enlighten me, Mister Killigrew, please.'

Killigrew crammed the sugar plum into the side of his mouth and shot him a crimson-gummed grin. 'Between you, me and those rather off-putting fellows,' he said, jerking a thumb at the hanged men, 'Artemas Crow is making something of a nuisance of himself.'

'Colonel Crow received only just reward for his malice,' Forrester snapped angrily, immediately realizing his mistake. He looked quickly away, though the rising heat in his cheeks was like bubbling lava.

Killigrew stared up into Forrester's face. 'Oh?' His tiny black eyes fixed unblinkingly on the captain's. 'I thought you refuted his claim, Captain. You bore witness that he fell from his horse.'

Forrester felt his throat thicken. 'Aye, that is what happened.'

'Strange, is it not?' Killigrew said, delving for another sugar plum. 'Crow is a dragooner. He spends most of his life in the saddle, yet topples quite inexplicably, landing on his face!' He chuckled at the image. 'The daft old curmudgeon didn't even think to put out his hands to break the fall.'

'Strange indeed,' Forrester echoed. His pulse seemed to be louder than his voice. 'Perhaps he was in his cups.'

'Of course,' Killigrew went on brightly, 'That must be it. Though, that is not what dear Artemas testifies. He claims his nose came to grief when it collided rather heavily with your particular friend's knuckles.'

'That is entirely untrue,' Forrester lied. Artemas Crow blamed Stryker for the death of his sons, and the grudge had festered like an open wound. Outside Gloucester's crumbling but defiant walls, the dragoon had drawn his pistol on the infantryman, and had received a broken nose and abject humiliation for his trouble. Only Forrester and Lisette Gaillard, Stryker's lover, had witnessed the altercation, much to Crow's rage.

'Still, the word of a colonel carries much weight,' Killigrew said. 'Stryker is fortunate he finds favour with the Crown.'

'As he should,' Forrester replied. The ghost of a memory

haunted him as he spoke the words. Llanthony Priory, outside Gloucester, had been the place where an assassin's crossbow bolt had almost ended the king's life. It had drawn blood that day, he remembered with a keen pang of sadness, but the life it had taken was that of Cecily Cade, whose body had stopped the poisoned quarrel, and in whose memory the mission to the Isles of Scilly was undertaken. But the sovereign had survived because Captain Stryker had recognized the killer, tackled him, and thrown off his aim.

Killigrew offered a shallow shrug. 'Nevertheless, he is safer away from court. Indeed, I am surprised you have not accompanied our sullen Cyclops on his latest sojourn.'

'I was not permitted,' Forrester replied, struggling to keep his temper in check.

'A shame,' Killigrew chirped smugly. 'Still, the battle was a thing of horror by anyone's standards. Colonel Mowbray was disinclined to lose you and Stryker both.' He dragged his gaze up to the hanged men. 'Not when spirits are at such low ebb.'

The pair paused while a heavy cart full of hogsheads trundled past. The driver screamed obscenities at the harnessed oxen that loped and bellowed and defecated, seemingly oblivious to his commands.

Forrester's snapsack was nearby. He stooped for it, suddenly craving his pipe. 'What do you want, Mister Killigrew?'

Killigrew gnawed the inside of his cheek as he chose his words. 'Times are troubling, I'm sure you'll agree. Newbury was all failure.'

'We were not defeated,' Forrester mumbled through teeth clamped around the clay pipe stem.

'Ah, but nor were we victorious. And we withdrew first, do not forget. We slithered off the field under cover of darkness.'

'That sounds very much,' Forrester said, beckoning the hanging-tree sentry with a wave of his arm, 'like something your young master might say.'

'And he *has* said it, Captain,' Killigrew replied as he watched the musketeer hurry over the trampled grass. 'He urged His

Majesty to hold the field overnight but he was not heeded. Faint hearts won out, as so often is the case. Prince Rupert's view is that our withdrawal turned stalemate into outright defeat. Essex returns to London like Caesar himself, and we find ourselves back in Oxford, licking our divers wounds.'

The red-coated sentry reached them, doffed his cap and set down his musket. Coiled about his forearm like a thin snake was a length of match-cord, the tip between his middle and ring-finger smouldering gently, for he was obliged to keep it alive should he need to make use of his weapon. He briefly blew on the embers and dunked it into the pipe bowl while his commanding officer sucked the tobacco into fragrant life.

'Newbury was certainly costly,' Forrester said once the sentry had returned to his post. 'I hear Lord Falkland fell.'

Killigrew's eyes narrowed through the pall of smoke. 'He did. Carnarvon and Sunderland, too.'

'That may prove a greater loss when all is tallied.'

Killigrew gave a rueful grunt. 'You are a shrewd man, Captain. More of our best leaders fall at each hurdle. Ever since Lindsey and Aubigny were lost at Kineton Fight we have felt that particular sting.'

Forrester sucked hard on the pipe, drinking in the pungent smoke so that his chest seared satisfyingly. 'Northampton at Hopton Heath,' he said on the billowing outbreath. 'Denbigh at Birmingham, Grenville at Lansdown.' A commotion ripped the calm afternoon as a ring of soldiers some hundred paces away bawled and crowed at two of their number – shirtless and wild-eyed – who were circling in what looked to be a prearranged wrestling bout. Forrester let his gaze shift to the fight, absently noting which of his men were in attendance. He smiled, pleased they were able to take their ease after the horrors of recent days. 'Grandison, Trevanion and Slanning all cut down in the streets of Bristol. There will soon be no good men left.'

'Save the prince,' Killigrew said pointedly.

'Indeed.' Forrester glanced down at the shrewish power-broker. 'And where is our dashing young General of Horse?'

'My master harries Essex's forces to the east.'

'You do not follow your master into battle, sir?' Forrester said, aware that needling the little man was not a good idea, but unable to resist. 'I am surprised. His other dog is always at his side.'

Killigrew's mouth split in a mean grin. 'Now, now, Lancelot, keep a civil tongue, I beg you.' He nodded at the executed men, gently swaying at the end of their taut ropes. 'You wouldn't wish to find yourself joining those poor fellows, I'd wager.'

Forrester drew on his pipe and blew a huge pall of smoke to conceal his fear. 'You threaten me, sir?'

'Never, Captain.' Killigrew stepped into the roiling cloud. 'I simply advise you that your burgeoning reputation does not negate the need for proper manners.'

There followed a moment's silence. The wrestlers met, torsos slapping together like two slabs of cold beef, and the watching crowd bellowed their appreciation. Occasionally flashes of white skin punctuated the ring of bodies as the fighters took to their feet, but they came together quickly, twisting and wrenching at each other, hitting the churned earth to a chorus of cheers.

Forrester watched in amusement before upending his pipe, tapping away the blackened debris to scatter in the breeze. 'If Rupert is away, and you know Stryker is elsewhere, what can I do for you, Mister Killigrew?'

Killigrew's face set hard. 'Word reaches us from London that the Parliament has made an alliance with the Scots.'

Forrester stared down at him, desperate to read some trace of jest. 'A—military alliance?'

Killigrew nodded slowly, hushing his tone. 'They do not concur on the ideal conclusion for this endeavour. That is to say, the English seek to win a war above all else, the Scots seek religious conformity. I suspect they will not remain friends for long, but for now they agree that the only way to achieve their objectives is to smash King Charles in the field.'

'Christ's beard,' Forrester heard himself mutter. His mind swam, tossed by currents whipped up by this new revelation.

'The Scots want Parliament to follow their lead in religious matters?'

'And in return they will give Westminster their army.'

Forrester blasphemed again, because the Scottish army was a truly formidable force. It would change the course of the war for certain. 'You are working against this impending calamity, I trust, Mister Killigrew?'

The intelligencer's eyelids flickered. 'In my own small way. I find myself attached to Lord Hopton's staff for the time being. I do his bidding while he recovers.'

Mention of Hopton, raised to the peerage as Baron Hopton of Stratton, caught Forrester's attention, for he had served under the general at the battle that had given its name to his new title. 'And he does recover?'

'Oh, yes, admirably so. The explosion burned him badly, but his skin heals with time, as does his hearing, thank the Lord.'

'Good,' Forrester said genuinely. He liked Hopton, and had been terribly shocked when news spread through the camp after the battle at Lansdown that the victorious commander had been severely wounded when an errant spark somehow found its way into an ammunition waggon.

'Yesterday there was a council of war,' said Killigrew.

'So I understand.'

'One consequence was Hopton's appointment to a new post.'

'Oh?'

'He was governor of Bristol after the prince took it last July, but he feels his recuperation moves on apace. Warrants a return to the field.'

'In what capacity?' Forrester asked. 'With what purpose?'

Killigrew dug at his raw gums with a sharp fingernail. 'He will command a new army. His Majesty tasks him with clearing Dorset, Wiltshire and Hampshire of rebellious elements.' The wrestlers rose briefly, entwined in a grunting, sweating, grime-caked embrace before crashing down once more. Killigrew grimaced. 'Once those counties are ours, Baron Hopton will strike at London itself.'

'So simple?' Forrester said, neither willing nor able to keep the incredulity from his tone.

Killigrew stared up at him and nodded. 'So simple.' His face betrayed nothing.

So that was to be the new strategy, thought Forrester. They would abandon the advance through the Thames valley, instead thrusting deep into the south-east and punching London in her soft underbelly. 'I appreciate the information, Mister Killigrew, but—'

'But why would I deign to inform you in person?' Killigrew cut in. A great cheer erupted from the throng watching the wrestling match, and he waited a moment for the noise to die off. 'I have a task for you. Or, rather, Lord Hopton has a task for you. He recalls your service in Devonshire this last spring. Would employ you again.'

Forrester's heart quickened a touch. 'And what service would he have me perform this time?'

'You know of Basing House?'

Forrester nodded. He knew it all too well. It had been the place at which he and Stryker had rested on their way into enemy territory almost exactly a year ago. That mission – to catch a rebel double agent – had nearly made an end of them, and he was not inclined to dwell upon it. 'The seat of the Marquess of Winchester.'

'Once a very pretty seat, by all accounts. Though now turned to martial duty. It is made a fortress.'

'In a sea of Roundheads.'

'Quite so. The great house sits in disputed land, surrounded by enemies and a stone's throw from the rebel garrison at Farnham. But the marquess is loyal and ready to fight. We would alert him to Hopton's intentions. Warn him of our coming so that his resolve is strengthened. Urge him to sally out from his fortress, take the fight to the enemy.'

Forrester nodded. 'Divert the rebel eye from Hopton's advance. An advance now made all the more vital after the news from Westminster.'

'Shrewd indeed, Captain.'

Forrester shrugged. 'It is a logical tactic. You would have me take this message?'

'You know the place. You know the marquess personally, do you not?'

Forrester's mouth turned down at the corners. 'I met him once, briefly.'

'And your reputation has grown immeasurably since Crown and Parliament came to blows. The marquess has heard empty promises of aid before. We fear he will ignore them, unless they are conveyed by the right person.'

'Traipse across hostile territory,' Forrester said, 'to take a message to a man who will likely dismiss my platitudes out of hand.' The wound on his shoulder seemed to throb a little more at the thought. But then he glanced up at the swinging cadavers, their faces purple, eyeballs bulging, lips distended. He hated the insidious lethargy that camp life could engender, and overseeing executions for the next few weeks was not his idea of soldiering. Besides, Stryker had been let off the army's leash, so why not he? He blew out his cheeks and straightened his back. 'When do I leave?'

The ghost of a smile flickered across Killigrew's face. 'The morrow will be sufficient. You'll go alone, for secrecy's sake.'

'The morrow, then.'

'Take this,' Killigrew said, producing a folded square of vellum from within the depths of his cloak. It was held fast by a chunky seal of red wax. 'A letter from Hopton for the marquess. And make certain you take a good horse.' He stole a glance at Forrester's ample midriff as the captain took the paper. 'Your reputation is not the only thing to have grown immeasurably these past months.'

CHAPTER 2

Atlantic Ocean, 1 October 1643

It was the sand that woke Innocent Stryker. The gritty crunch reverberated around his skull as his teeth ground together. The tang of salt was on his tongue, and he felt suddenly cold and wet. He opened his eye. More sand. Richly yellow, darkly flecked and smooth, stretching away in a golden band towards an off-kilter horizon. He heard the mad caw of gulls somewhere above. It was a beach. But the world was wrong, spun about, turned on its head, the coast running at a strange tangent that seemed to take an age to become clear in his mind. Half of his face felt colder than the rest, and he realized, slowly, that the odd sensation was the tide-lapped sand pressing against the scar tissue where once his left eye-socket had been. His face was part of the beach, driven a good inch into the soft terrain like some washed-up spar. He pushed himself up on to all fours, hands and knees sinking with the movement, and failed to stifle a groan as a juddering violence rippled up from deep within him. He vomited. It was mostly sea water. The salt burned in his throat. He swore savagely, coughed, vomited again. The gulls seemed to jeer.

Coughing and hacking from somewhere at his flank made him look up, ignoring the hammering in his head. His vision was blurred, but he could see the figure of a man well enough. Red-coated, doubled over and evacuating the brackish water from his own innards. There were others with him. Half a dozen, he reckoned, some in their distinctive red, others down to shirts, all looking like scarecrows thrown up to frighten the gulls. Stryker forced himself to stand. His clothes felt inordinately heavy, and he realized he was soaked to the skin, shivering madly and swaying like a willow in a breeze. He stumbled towards the first coughing redcoat. The beach was littered with debris, black and brown smudges punctuating the wind-whipped shore, the detritus of the night's rage. The sky was a mix of grey and white, placid for now but full of threat. To his left, the sand sloped up to a high ridge of lichen-draped rocks, a natural palisade against the elements. He could not see what was beyond.

He pulled the gloves from his hands and dropped them at his feet. Planting a cold, bluish palm against his eye, he pressed, rubbing and grinding mercilessly until it hurt. He stared again, forcing himself to focus on this battered stretch of coast. Still things were blurry, but the mist was beginning to clear. He could discern more edges from the darker smudges and knew now that they were people. Or at least they were bodies, punctuating the shore at intervals for as far as he could see. Some were up, crouched or standing, bewildered and staring mutely at these harsh new surroundings. Others did not move. They lay crumpled and twisted, faces flat against the sand, ominous in sheer inertia.

It was chaos. Carnage. As though some great maritime battle had been fought off shore, the dead and wounded spewed up by the ocean with the spars and shrouds shredded by flaming cannon and whistling shot. Except war had not come to this cold place, nor had guns belched across the waves. But battle, it seemed to Stryker, had been joined nevertheless. Man had taken on nature, and he had been found wanting.

'Beelzebub's ballocks,' a deep, droning voice intoned behind him.

Stryker managed to turn and focus. The man he saw was tall and thin. He wore no coat, for the garment had seemingly been stripped off by the night's furious tides, and the shirt left behind was dishevelled and tattered. 'Sergeant Skellen,' he said. 'How fare you?'

'My noggin, sir,' Skellen said, lifting a hand to his bald head. 'Feels like I've been cudgelled by a bleedin' bear.' His sleeves were pushed up to his elbows, exposing forearms that were long, and, though thin, knotted with lean, taut muscle. The veins on his hands and wrists were raised, as if the skin was layered in an intricate web of whipcord, and his palms were like shovels. He was several inches taller than Stryker, with eyes set deep within darkly hooded sockets.

'You look hearty enough to me, Sergeant,' Stryker said.

Skellen ran a huge hand over his stubble-shadowed chin as he perceived his captain. 'You don't, sir.' Squinting down the length of the curving shoreline, he said, 'Think we've lost a few.'

Stryker used his tongue to corral a few errant grains of sand from along his gums, spitting them into the wind. 'More than a few.'

He followed Skellen's narrow gaze. Of the forty or so people he could make out amongst the wreckage of the *Kestrel*, only half of those were visibly moving. And in that moment he understood that Stryker's Company of Foot would never be the same again. He had lost them. Or, at the very least, a good portion. They had been swallowed by the sea, chewed in its vengeful maw and tossed on to this lonely beach. He stared out at the slate-grey water. How many were still out there, food for the monsters of the deep?

'Muster the men, Will. Let us see what we have left.'

Stryker stood on the rocky ridge and stared down at the men on the beach. He could hardly countenance what he saw. Debris was everywhere, lapping on the gentle tide or working its way on to the saffron-coloured sand. A single sail bobbed in the surf a little way out to sea, while a large amount of rigging wallowed in vast tangles that made the shallows appear to be infested by a colony of giant octopuses. Amid those hempen tentacles were black shapes, the detritus of life aboard a ship. Splintered timbers, square trenchers, sacks, barrels, clothing, blackjacks and a myriad of other items, all turned to flotsam by the great storm that had put an end to the doughty Dutch fluyt. There were bodies, too. Face down for the most part, drifting with the water out of reach, already becoming bloated and pale.

'That's the lot, sir,' Sergeant William Skellen announced morosely as he clambered up to his commanding officer's granite perch. He spat towards the sea in impotent defiance. 'Eleven lads left.'

Stryker nodded as he counted the ragged line of survivors for himself. They were arranged below the ridge, wan and exhausted, mere shadows of the hard men they had been. 'Eleven. Along with you and I.'

'And Jack-Sprat.'

'Must you?' Stryker admonished, though he did not begrudge Skellen his laconic mirth in so dire a place. He gave a wintry smile. 'And where is he?'

For answer, the tall sergeant pointed to their left, his long bony finger tracing the curved spine of rocks. Sure enough, perhaps a hundred paces away, the diminutive figure of Simeon Barkworth, formerly the Earl of Chesterfield's bodyguard and a member of the feared Scots Brigade before that, was gesticulating animatedly at a trio of men. All were taller than the bald fellow, who was no bigger than a dwarf, but each nodded with every gesture as though he were their natural superior. He might have been small, Stryker mused, but with eyes as yellow as a feline and a temper as explosive as black powder, he was as intimidating as a rabid ban-dog.

'Getting' the pit dug,' Skellen elaborated when Stryker did not speak. 'Plenty o' bodies to be rid of.'

Stryker stared at the Scot's three companions. 'Our sailors?'

'Aye. Them three's all that survived.'

'Jesu,' Stryker rasped on a sighing outbreath. So three of the ship's twenty-strong crew had made it to shore, in addition to eleven of Stryker's thirty musketeers. He shook his head with the sorrow of it. 'We lost nineteen men as well as Ensign Chase, Corporal Mookes and Drummer Lipscombe.'

'That we did, sir. A terrible day.'

Stryker nodded, though in truth it was a miracle that any had survived. He remembered nothing after the ship went down. It was cold and black and then he was in the angry sea. He understood in that moment, as chill salt water poured into his mouth and nose and ears, that he would die. The next thing Stryker knew, he was awake on a beach. At least, he reflected as he turned his back on the shore to study the terrain inland, he had only taken half the company. The rest of his officers and all twenty of his pikemen were safely back in Oxford. He supposed he ought to thank God for that small grace. His company had come through the smoke-wreathed hell of Newbury relatively unscathed. If the Almighty saw fit to temper Stryker's growing confidence by wiping out half his men in one fell swoop, then it was truly a cruel lesson to learn. He blinked and stared down at the island.

'Where are we, sir?' Skellen asked.

'I know not.' Suddenly craving his pipe, he put a hand to his shoulder, forgetting that he no longer had his snapsack. Indeed, he no longer had much at all. Unlike most, he still had his coat, saturated though it was, and his boots had been tight enough at his thighs and calves to repel the pull of the current, but his pistol was gone, as were his brace of dirks, his powder horn, water flask and snapsack. He planted his hand on the ornate hilt of his sword. It was a beautiful weapon, a gift from the queen herself, and he was glad that it fitted its scabbard so snugly and the baldric in which it hung had clung to him well. Most of his men had nothing but shirts and breeches to their names. *Christ*, he thought, but what had he brought them to? It was his arrogance that compelled them to climb so willingly aboard the ill-fated *Kestrel*. His promise to Cecily Cade – as she lay dying with an assassin's crossbow bolt lodged in her flesh – that he would make the journey to retrieve her family fortune for the Crown. Why had he made so rash a pledge? Was it to assuage the guilt he felt for the bolt that had taken its fatal course after he had knocked the bow? Or had he made his promise because Lisette Gaillard, the woman he loved, had sworn hers? He stared up at Skellen. Whatever the reason, the company had followed him without question, even after marching through the hail of lead that was Newbury Fight, and now they had been destroyed for their misplaced trust. 'Hubris.'

Skellen screwed up his leathery face. 'Sir?'

'I have brought us to this.'

'You give the orders, sir, and we see 'em through.' The tall sergeant shrugged. 'Not a man 'ere, nor on that ship, nor back 'ome what'd have it different.'

'We came through Newbury to wash up here.'

'We came through Newbury, sir, aye. And Gloucester before that. And Roundway, Lansdown and Stratton. Every day is a day I hadn't expected to see, sir.'

They fell silent as the miniature figure of Simeon Barkworth scurried along the granite barrier to reach them. 'Fuck me, sir, if those salty bastards ain't the worst gravediggers I ever saw!' His voice was a rasp, as though a ligature throttled the sound as he spoke. 'Don't know one end of a shovel from t'other.'

Skellen wrinkled his long nose. 'They ain't got shovels, Tom Thumb.'

Barkworth's yellow eyes sparkled as he glared up at the sergeant. 'Well spotted, you lanky goat's prick.'

The Scot was a reformado, a man who had enlisted with Stryker after the Battle of Hopton Heath, but who held no official rank. As such, he was, technically, not subordinate to Skellen, but that did not mean the sergeant would tolerate the insult. The tall man stepped forth, eliciting a mad cackle of a challenge from Barkworth, before abruptly stopping in his tracks. He stared down at the bar that had swung heavily across his path.

'Not now,' Stryker said, keeping his forearm solid against Skellen's sternum. 'Or I'll drown you both myself, understood?'

Skellen swallowed and nodded.

'Aye, sir,' Barkworth croaked, rubbing the livid band of scar tissue that swathed his neck, the mark of a failed hanging. He looked back along the line of the dune. 'Was a figure o' speech, sir. The shovels, I mean. The sailors are next to useless. Can rig a bastard-big boat, I'm quite sure, but they can'nae dig for shite.'

Stryker lowered his arm and followed the Scot's bright gaze. 'With their hands, Simeon?'

Barkworth shrugged. 'We've no tools, sir.'

'Send some of our men to assist.'

'Sir.'

The pair watched as Barkworth scrabbled his way down the treacherous escarpment to corral a squad of Stryker's men. At length, Skellen cleared his throat awkwardly. 'Thinking 'pon Miss Lisette, sir? Beggin' your pardon.'

In another place and time, Stryker would have scolded the sergeant for his impertinence. But he nodded as he watched the waves lap the shore. 'Aye.' He could not hide his worry. She had gone ahead of the main force, typically unwilling to wait for Stryker to be released from duty. Lisette was supposed to locate the house where Cecily Cade claimed her father's fortune had been stored, and await Stryker's arrival. Now, and not for the first time, he had let her down.

'She'll have found the gold already, like as not,' Skellen said hopefully. 'Frightened the living ballocks out of some poor local, got him to help her take it back. If she's in Oxford right now, sir, suppin' claret and cursin' all English heretics – 'cept the King, of course – I wouldn't be a bit surprised.'

Stryker could not help but laugh. Lisette was an agent of the Crown, more specifically of Queen Henrietta Maria, and she was not a woman to be underestimated. The men, including William Skellen, found her bewitching, for her beauty was matched by her talent for death and deception. 'You're probably in the right of it, Sergeant,' he said, though he was not so sure. He peered inland to hide his discomfort, and studied the terrain.

They were on an island, clearly, for he could see all the way to the far side, where another craggy coastline nestled against the dark of the sea. The water pressed in to the right and left as well, but further away, and he realized that the island must be long and narrow. As far as he could see, the beaches were yellow with sand, separated from the interior by crumbling cliffs that appeared almost white below the grey skies. Beyond the rocks, the interior was green but sparse, rising at either end to rocky hillocks. He could not see any buildings, nor even the tell-tale smoke trail that might betray a hidden hearth. He recalled a discussion with Captain Jones. 'The Scillies are made up of many islands. Most uninhabited. And we were near the eastern-most when . . . when it happened.'

'So we could have landed on our feet.'

'I would hardly say that,' Stryker countered. 'But the point is made, Will, aye. Seems it may not all be disaster.'

Skellen picked his nose, inspected the end of his finger, and cracked his neck loudly. 'So how in the name of Joseph's pretty coat do we find out where we are?'

At first, Stryker thought the sharp click was another one of Skellen's stiff joints, but when he caught the sergeant's eye in alarm, the pair of them spun round to see the huge fowling-piece pointed directly at them.

'Allow me to help, gentlemen,' the man wielding the gun said. He did not look like a soldier, but his demeanour seemed calm enough for Stryker to hesitate in his natural urge to attack.

Stryker raised his hands. 'Ho, sir, do not be hasty with that thing.'

The newcomer smiled behind the black muzzle, a gesture that did not reach his wide, brown eyes. 'As I said, I am here to help. You're on the isle of Great Ganilly.' He drew the firearm to full cock. 'And you're in a spot 'o bother, rebel.'

'The island's the better part of a thousand yards from north to south. And the terrain's a bitch at either end. Fortunately, there, in the very middle, she's not a hundred yards across, and barely above sea level.'

Their captor's name was Jethro Beck: a man of the Scillies, born on St Martin's, and a fisherman by trade. Now, as the boat slid out between the jagged rocks, he indicated the place to which he had forced them to march. The spot where the vessels had been waiting on Great Ganilly's western shore. 'Can get from one side o' the island to the other in a matter of a few minutes.'

'You are sentries?' Stryker said as he gripped the side of the bobbing vessel. They were in one of Beck's trio of single-sailed skiffs, along with Skellen, Barkworth and the three sailors. Beck had appeared on the ridge with six men, all armed, and one of those sat in the stern. The rest, along with Stryker's eleven wretched musketeers, were divided amongst the other boats, and together, forming a tiny fleet on the grey swell, they made their way south and west from Great Ganilly.

'Aye.'

'But you're fishermen?'

'Garrison now,' Beck grunted in a voice worn harsh by salt air. 'Since this war started, least wise. Men of fighting age called to serve.'

'Our war?'

Jethro Beck nodded. He sat with his hand cupping the priming pan of his fowling-piece in order to keep the powder dry. That piece never wavered from its mark, its black mouth gaping at Stryker's chest, swaying with the waves. 'We're peaceable folk, 'ere, cully. Loyal to our sovereign, devoted to our Lord. The blood shed on the mainland would be no concern of ours.' He spat over the side. 'Except you makes it our concern. You and your rebel knaves.'

Stryker gritted his teeth. 'I have told you before, sir, we are no rebels.'

Beck shrugged. 'Rebels, Roundheads, righteous bleedin' men o' justice. I could not give two bouncin' tits for the name you gives it!'

Barkworth, at Stryker's side on the foremost bench, seemed to twitch, and a constricted croak, like the whining of a rusty hinge, escaped from his throat. 'Christ, man, are you an ignoramus?' He shifted forwards a touch, amber eyes bright as they darted up at Stryker. 'Would ye like me to knock some sense into that thick fucking skull, sir?'

Jethro Beck snorted his derision, jerked the fowling-piece. 'Easy now, cully, or you'll get to feed the fish.'

Stryker placed a hand on the Scotsman's forearm. 'Do as he says, Simeon.' He stared Beck in the face as Barkworth slumped back. 'We are not for the Parliament, sir. That is the truth. We are Royalists. For King Charles. Sent here by His Majesty in person.'

'Papers?'

Stryker sighed. 'As I have told you, we have no credentials. They were destroyed in the wreck.' He splashed the surface of the water with his fingers. 'My damned papers float out here somewhere.'

'Shame for you then, cully,' Beck said. 'P'raps they'll bob past, eh?'

Stryker balled his fists in frustration, thinking of his sword that now sat between Beck's feet. 'Why do you not believe us?'

'Why should I believe you?'

The skiff dipped off the back of a wave and was hit by the crest of another as its bow began to lift. The men were jolted together like powder charges on a shaken bandoleer. Stryker gripped the sides and looked to Beck, hoping the man had been thrown off balance, but there he was, steady and alert. Stryker waited for the skiff to regain some semblance of calm on the choppy water. 'You say the islands declared for the King, and that no blood has been spilt here. We come to Scilly in the name of that same king. Why would you choose *not* to believe us? I do not understand.' A thought struck him, then. The face of a man with a wispy auburn beard and grey eyes, whose deeply lined cheeks had been spattered by Roundhead blood on a hill above a place called Stratton. A hill that had become a charnel house one summer afternoon. 'Bassett!'

'Eh?' Beck grunted.

'Sir Thomas Bassett. I fought with him. I *know* him, sir.' He looked down at Barkworth. 'Major-General of our Cornish army. Governor of the Isles of Scilly.'

'Lieutenant-Governor,' Beck corrected. 'Sir Francis Godolphin is our lord here.' He gave a harsh laugh. 'But both men are long gone. Sailed to the mainland when war was declared.' They rounded the pale granite cliffs of the southernmost island Beck had named as Little Arthur, and tacked more sharply to the south-west, where, perhaps a mile away, Stryker could see the craggy coast of yet another land–mass. Beck risked a swift glance over his shoulder. 'St Mary's. Our destination. The King's men await us at the Hugh.'

'The garrison?' Stryker asked.

Beck shook his head. 'From the mainland. Emissaries from Governor Godolphin himself.' He brayed at his captives' obvious bewilderment. 'You see? You claim to be from the King, but his men are already here!'

Stryker could not keep the puzzlement from his face. 'I do not—'

'And they have warned us of your approach,' Jethro Beck went on, his mirth slipping away on the whipping breeze. 'A company of soldiers led by a one-eyed devil, claiming to be for the King, but secretly a gaggle o' bastardly rebel gullions, intent on taking this fair place for Pym an' his hounds.'

Stryker's pulse raced. He stared at the headland of St Mary's, wondering what fate awaited them. '*Other* men have told you this? They are on St Mary's now?'

Beck nodded, eyes brimming with indignation at his pris-oner's perceived ruse. 'Aye, cully.'

'Is that where you take us? To these men?'

'To the castle at St Mary's. And aye, to these God-fearing, loyal men.'

Skellen, silent until now, craned forwards from the bench behind to whisper in Stryker's ear. 'He's mad, sir. Put the wrong bloody mushrooms in his pottage.'

But Stryker was not so sure. 'Who?' he pressed the fisherman. 'Who are they?'

Jethro Beck grinned, exposing little brown teeth and equally brown gums. 'You'll know soon enough, cully.'

CHAPTER 3

Romsey, Hampshire, 2 October 1643

Colonel Richard Norton eased his substantial bay gelding to a halt beneath the massive elm that marked the entrance to the abbey complex. From here a cinder path led pilgrims through the grounds to the vast edifice of grey stone blocks that climbed like a castle over the land hereabouts. The horse craned its head to inspect the foliage, the leaves fanning out in the warm gusts from its flaring nostrils, and he arched his back slowly, revelling in the gentle pain of stretching muscles. He looked down, pleased to see the grass was firm, evidence of a dry spell this far south. He took a moment to glance at his shadow, an oversized forbidding ghost of himself snaking across the green turf. He liked the image very much.

'Sir?'

Norton looked round to see one of his gentleman troopers approach at the head of the column. 'We'll rest here, MacLachlan.'

The trooper reined in close by, unstrapped his three-barred helm to reveal a thin face with cleanly shaven, hollow cheeks and small, deep-set eyes. He propped the pot between his thighs and watched as cavalrymen trotted past in pairs, breastplates gleaming, hooves crunching heavily on the path. He waved at some of the men, indicating that they should spread out on the grass. 'Will they feed us, do you think, sir?'

'They will have to,' Norton said with a shrug. He gazed about the open ground on to which his force filed from the road beyond. It was an area of tree-lined lawn, split by the cinder path and punctuated by a forest of wooden crosses and moss-clad stones. The grass had grown long so that it slanted to one side like a field flush with corn. He looked at MacLachlan. 'Even a house of God is left to moulder in these dark days.' He leaned forwards to pat his gelding's solid neck. The beast whickered and dropped its head to the long green blades. 'Still, at least there is plenty of fodder for the horses.'

MacLachlan raised a single thin brow. 'House of God, sir?'

Norton plucked his own helmet free, scratching at the red-raw patch of skin that blighted the side of his neck. 'Perhaps you're right, MacLachlan. It is an old nest of vipers, I suppose.'

MacLachlan smirked. 'Vipers wearing wimples, sir.'

Norton laughed. 'Aye.' He stretched again. 'Well, let us proceed. It may be a bastion of the old order, but no longer. And besides,' he added, looking round to see that, with the rest of his three hundred troopers, the rickety cart had made its way past the line of timber-framed houses and on to the cinder path that stretched out from the mouth of the abbey like a tar-stained tongue, 'it is where our dear Francis wished to be laid to rest. We shall give him that.'

Norton twisted in his saddle to look up at the ancient complex. And what an impressive thing it was, he conceded. Romsey Abbey utterly dominated this little market town. Once home to the Benedictine order, it was a monster of a building, climbing above the skyline and reminding the world that England had once, long ago, bent the knee to Rome. Norton was a Presbyterian, and the idea of life under a Catholic boot-heel was utterly repugnant to him, but he could appreciate the looming buttresses and ornate craftsmanship that made this place so impressive, and so compelling.

He slid nimbly off his bay, leaving the lobster-tailed helmet fastened to his saddle, and caught MacLachlan's inquisitive eye. 'See to the men, Major. And find somewhere,' he rubbed a gloved hand through his copper hair as he searched for the word, '*befitting* Captain St Barbe.'

MacLachlan nodded and turned to the men, but Norton did not wait to hear what was said. St Barbe had been a good officer, a close friend, and a staunch man for the Parliament, and he found the business of burying him difficult to dwell upon. Instead he scanned the grounds for signs of life, eventually spotting a hunched fellow skulking in a tangled copse some way to his right.

'Ho there!' Norton called. 'Come hither!'

The man had been clutching a mud-caked spade, which he promptly tossed away before trudging, glum-faced and nervous, towards the waiting horsemen. 'Did not hear you, zir,' he said when he had reached Norton.

'I've no time for lies, fellow,' Norton said with a dismissive wave. 'You are a gravedigger, I presume?'

'Aye, zir.'

'Then where might I find the priest? There is one, is there not?'

The gravedigger nodded. 'He'll be in chancel, zir.' He pointed a grimy finger towards a sweeping archway some twenty yards along the wall. 'North door'd be your quickest way.'

Norton turned his back on the frightened man and caught the eye of another officer, who dismounted and went to his side.

'Colonel?' the officer said. He was taller than Norton, with hair that was almost white and a beard that might have been the same colour, save the patches stained deep yellow by tobacco smoke. His face was badly pock-pitted, his nose huge, and his eyes pale and pitiless.

Norton plucked the glove from his right hand and unfastened the metal gauntlet from the other. 'I have business inside,' he said, picking at the red bristles of his beard. The inflamed skin beneath was burning again, and it took all his will to push it to the back of his mind. He indicated the arch with a curt nod. 'Accompany me. You may have an interest.'

The big man brandished a set of impressively white teeth as they made for the entrance the gravedigger had said was the north door. Sure enough, a thick timber doorway, studded and decorated with swirling iron patterns, was set deep into the arch. 'It will be a pleasure, sir.'

They were plunged into darkness as they pushed open the door, and it took a few moments for their eyes to adjust, but as Norton led his companion into the building, making straight for the wide nave, he began to see why the abbey was so revered by the High Church. It was huge, built in the Norman style of large, imposing windows, soaring pillars and rounded arches. The nave itself was laid with vast flagstones, scattered with clean rushes, and flanked by wooden seats that were clearly not the rough-hewn, functional offerings one might find in a Puritan chapel. They turned left, stalked up the nave and through the choir to the chancel, where the gravedigger had suggested they might find someone. Sure enough, a cluster of black-robed men had gathered at the far end of the vast chamber, near the high altar.

'My name is Colonel Norton,' Norton called loudly, his voice echoing like cannon fire high up in the chancel's curving trusses. He smartly brushed the dust from his buff-coat and the tawny scarf at his waist while he waited.

One of the robed bodies left the group and scuttled down to greet the two soldiers. He was small and crook-backed, moving almost sideways like a crab. 'I am Father Samuel,' he said, trying to smile, though his face was tight with apprehension. 'And I have heard of you, sir, of course.' He bowed obsequiously. 'Parliament's chief man in Hampshire.'

'I do not know about that,' Norton blustered, unwilling to display the rush of pride that threatened to colour his cheeks. 'But, aye, I have laboured for the just cause of Westminster, it is true. Indeed, I have come direct from one such trial.'

The clergyman's little head bobbed. 'We heard there was battle at Newbury.'

'A bloody day. Victory for the Earl of Essex, thank King Jesus.' Norton picked pointedly at his scarf with thumb and forefinger. 'We make for Southampton, but rest here, seeking a place for a brave confederate of ours, slain at Newbury Fight. One Captain St Barbe.'

Father Samuel nodded. 'I know the family, sir.' His face clouded suddenly. 'I knew Francis St Barbe when he was a boy. May God save his immortal soul.'

Norton looked back along the sweeping nave. 'We will bury him outside.'

Samuel nodded his agreement, though both knew it had not been a request. 'In the meantime, Colonel Norton, please be at your ease in our beautiful home.'

'Beautiful indeed,' Norton said, peering at the altar, the opulent-looking chambers behind it, at the big organ in one corner, and the tapestries and the ornately carved pulpit. 'But Romsey *Abbey*?'

'You refer, of course, to its suppression,' Samuel said.

Norton raised his red eyebrows. 'Or the lack thereof.'

The priest's face flushed. 'It was suppressed, Colonel, I assure you. Along with every other Popish monument in the land.'

'And yet your abbey survives,' the colonel persisted, noting his tall companion's grunt of amusement echoing at his back. 'Do the nuns lurk still?'

Samuel's hands had gone to his stomach, fingers worrying at the string of his robe. 'No, sir. It was suppressed, right enough, but escaped complete dissolution, for it was bought by the local parishioners.'

'Bought?'

'Aye, sir. They paid £100 to make it their church. A pretty sum.'

Norton looked up at the curving beams that seemed to lurch out from the tops of the thick pillars. 'A pretty parish church.' He turned to his companion. 'What say you, Wagner?'

The ice-blue eyes sparkled in the gloom. 'Stinks of Rome.'

Father Samuel stepped back a pace, startled. 'I assure you, sirs—'

'Altars, seats, baubles, music,' the trooper said, his broad Germanic accent becoming more pronounced with each word. 'And what is this?'

Samuel followed Wagner's gaze to the square patch of ceiling

39

that was painted in rich greens and reds. 'Jacobean, sir. Painted in the reign of the last king.'

Wagner screwed up his mouth. Norton laughed. The men in black robes, like a flock of jackdaws, dispersed suddenly in all directions, and he turned to his right, making for one of the small chambers behind the altar. 'Places to store your gold?'

'Simple chapels,' Father Samuel said, his voice higher than before, pleading. 'We have four back there. The one yonder is the St Anne Chapel.'

Norton continued to walk, though he heard his subordinate's footsteps as the white-haired officer closed upon the clergyman.

'No earthly whore is saint in the Lord's eyes, you foul Pope's turd.'

Norton looked back. 'What is this thing?'

Father Samuel skirted the white-haired officer like a frightened hare before a fox, and moved swiftly to Norton's side at the entrance to the chapel. He followed the colonel's gaze to look upon the carving that stood upon the small altar. 'It depicts Christ upon the cross, flanked by Mary and John. Two angels perch upon the arms of the cross, waiting to escort Jesus to heaven. It is one of our oldest possessions, sir. From the time before the Conquest.'

'Hear that, Captain Kovac?' Norton called back. 'From the time of Alfred, who, with God's divine assistance, did smite your heathen kinsmen.'

Wagner Kovac shrugged. 'He fought Danes. I am half Carniolan, half Croatian.'

Norton looked back down at Father Samuel. 'I do not like this place. It is rank with the mildew of the Papacy.'

'Colonel Norton, I—'

But Richard Norton was not listening. He waved the priest away with a derisive flap of the hand, and went to his grinning subordinate. 'Pull up the seats to begin with, and destroy the organ.'

Samuel was at his back immediately, wringing his hands. 'Please, sir—'

Norton spun round suddenly. 'Still that tongue, man, or it'll be the worse for you.' He felt heat at his cheeks. Knew the raw skin would be as red as a ripe strawberry. 'Observe, sir. We call Wagner Kovac our master gardener, so adept is he at tugging up the weeds of the old religion.'

With that, Captain Wagner Kovac went to work. The priest began to weep.

'Find the plate next,' the colonel ordered, 'books, any baubles you may discover. We'll take them for the cause.' He stood back and folded his arms as the sound of splintering wood echoed from pillar to beam to chancel to nave to choir. Soon he would turn upon all the strongholds of the enemy, and, with God's help, crush them once and for all.

Near Basing, Hampshire, 2 October 1643

Basing House was not the same place as that which Lancelot Forrester had visited the previous year. Even as Oberon clattered across the stone bridge over the River Loddon, that broad glistening band that barred the estate's northern flank, he sensed a tension in the air that had not been present before. The house was still there, walls and gatehouses and turrets looming over the landscape like a brick-built mountain range, but the very atmosphere was different. Basing was still principally a house, but when hostilities were declared, the marquess's Catholic faith had made him as staunch a Royalist as the king himself, and Basing's location, straddling the main route from London to the western counties, made it a pivotal stronghold. When Forrester and his comrades had last visited, there were already signs of intent, from the deepening of ditches that had formed the original motte and bailey, to frantic repairs made along the walls and the transformation of some of the older buildings into billets. But, in spite of this, it had still been a home. Now, Forrester reflected as armed men swarmed out from a spiked wicker screen that blocked the approach road, Basing House was nothing less than a fortress.

'Captain Lancelot Forrester,' he announced, reining Oberon to a halt as a dozen musketeers flocked like starlings around him. This level of vigilance was new, he thought, as was the barrier. The road, in truth little more than a bridleway, ran south until it reached the Lane, the main east–west thoroughfare through Basing Village. The vast Tudor edifice sprawled on the raised ground on the opposite side of the Lane, and even from this distance Forrester could see more armed men guarding that wider road. They were expecting trouble. 'For the King.'

The lead musketeer sidled over to take hold of Oberon's bridle. In his spare hand he clutched a vicious-looking halberd, the pale morning light sliding along the flat of the huge blade. 'I should hope so, sir. Regiment, if you please.'

'Mowbray's Foot, Sergeant,' Forrester replied, guessing at the man's rank by dint of the menacing weapon. 'And I'll thank you to get those grubby paws off my horse, lest I shove that halberd so far up your arse it'll pick your nose.'

With a grunt the sergeant released the bridle and indicated that the barrier should be cleared. 'Business, sir?'

'Here to see the marquess,' Forrester said sharply. 'I take it he is at home.'

The sergeant nodded. 'Would not leave, sir. Cannot. Roads ain't safe. You have papers, sir?'

'Aye, though you'll not see them. Where is the officer of the watch?'

The sergeant pointed to the junction a hundred paces beyond the barricade. 'There, sir. You'll find him there.' He winced a touch. 'Beg pardon, Captain, but we'll need to escort you.'

'Pleased to hear it,' Forrester said. 'The marquess will thank you for your vigilance, I'm sure.'

He let his gaze drift away as hogsheads, storm-poles and sections of latticed wattle were dragged from the barricade, and stared up at the house. The towers and rooftops of the circular Old House, built on the foundations of the ancient Norman castle, rose in a forbidding display of power, while further to the east the square lines of the New House spoke of the splendour

42

bestowed upon the Paulet dynasty in the time of the Tudors. But even from this distance he could see black smudges where loopholes had been cut in the beautiful brickwork, and the tiny figures of men paced along the high walls while gangs with shovels worked in the outermost ditches. Above everything soared the four crenellated towers of the Great Gatehouse, set like brick giants in the northern wall of the Old House. Sharpshooters carrying long fowling-pieces stood on each tower, ever watchful beneath the marquess's fluttering flags.

They made their way south towards The Lane and the house beyond. To the right the bridleway was hugged by bare marsh, but to the left a smooth brick wall climbed to eight or nine feet, enclosing a large complex of agricultural buildings. Forrester remembered the area as the Grange, the centre of food processing and storage for Basing House. From his saddle he could see over the perimeter, and he noted that much of the daily life of a major estate continued: cartloads of supplies still trundled in and out of the large barns, and small herds of sheep and cattle were driven between pens by farmhands and their yapping dogs. But even here things were subtly different. The men seemed more sullen and watchful, while the gate at the far end was guarded by grim sentries. At the epicentre was the Great Barn, a massive rectangular structure built in brick and where the majority of supplies would be kept.

'There,' the sergeant levelled his halberd, gesturing towards the junction with The Lane.

A group of horsemen were milling at the junction, all mounted on fine-looking beasts, all clad in back- and breastplates, each replete with a sword, a carbine, two pistols and a red ribbon on his sleeve. They were harquebusiers, light cavalry, and just as he saw them a couple broke away from the party, kicking their mounts on to the bridleway.

Lancelot Forrester screwed up his eyes as they approached to see their faces more clearly, and then he laughed. 'By Moses' long walk!'

'Sir?' the sergeant said in gruff alarm. 'Something vexes?'

'Not a bit of it,' Forrester said. He lifted his hat, sweeping down in an arc as he bowed behind Oberon's neck. 'Major! Major Lawrence!'

One of the two cavalrymen spurred ahead. 'Captain Forrester? I am right, am I not?'

Forrester laughed again, turning to the sergeant. 'Thank'ee, my surly fedary, but I shall fare quite well from here. Frederick Lawrence is an old friend of mine!'

'How long has it been, Captain?'

'Better part of a year, Major,' Forrester replied as the pair let their mounts walk casually along The Lane. They headed east, hemmed on the right by Basing's high curtain wall, and on the left the walls encircling the Grange. 'You are still of that rank, one presumes, sir?'

Major Frederick Lawrence grinned, his eyelids flickering in the frenetic way Forrester remembered. 'Alas, I am yet to make colonel. Though so many good officers drop dead these days, it would not surprise me.'

Forrester nodded. 'Were you at Newbury Fight?'

'I was not,' Lawrence mumbled, embarrassed. 'His lordship would not countenance my leaving here.'

Forrester was not surprised. When last he had been at Basing, the Marquess of Winchester was just beginning to transform his family estate into the fortress it had become. Lawrence, the commander of his modest force of cavalry, had been vigorous in his defence of the house and courageous in his activities.

'It was a hard fight,' Forrester replied. 'Too many good men fell.'

'There have been a great many bloodlettings since last you visited the castle.'

Forrester raised his brow. 'That is what you call it now?'

Lawrence half smiled and slowed his horse. 'The men call it castle, aye.' He looked up at the twin houses. The ancient mansion, defined by the circular ditch and bailey, was connected by a bridge to the vast structures of the New

House. As a single entity they formed one of the most sprawl-ing complexes in England. 'It is hard to think of it in any other capacity now.'

Forrester looked at the cavalryman. He was extremely tall, but stooped by shoulders so severely crooked that he was forced to have armour specially made for his bent frame. His eyes were intelligent, his hair worn long, his chin narrow and clean-shaven. And yet he had aged. There were new lines around his wide, thin mouth and flecks of silver in hair that had been black. 'You have been hard at work this last year.'

Lawrence urged his mount on as a group of soldiers filed past, their leader bowing deeply to him. 'We have positioned new ordnance, deepened the ditches, barred the roads.' He shrugged, eyes convulsing. 'We must assume we will be attacked any day, any night, such is our rather precarious location.'

'You are certainly surrounded by enemies,' Forrester agreed. 'Portsmouth and Southampton to the south. Farnham close by. All for the Parliament.'

'We are not so far from London itself,' Lawrence added.

'But you may be assured of the King's intent, sir. His forces work their way towards you. Liberty will soon be yours.'

Lawrence smiled sadly. 'We had rather hoped Newbury would achieve that particular goal.'

'It was not to be,' Forrester said. The failure of the army at Gloucester and Newbury was none of his doing, and yet, seeing the forlorn hope etched across Lawrence's thin face, he felt guilty. 'But we smashed Fiennes at Bristol,' he offered, 'Stamford at Stratton and Waller at Roundway. Essex was fortunate at Newbury, but he has not the wit to outfox us again. That is why I am here. I must speak with Lord Paulet, Major Lawrence. Hopton comes hither.'

'Hopton?' Lawrence said, his tone incredulous. 'I heard he had his face burned off at Lansdown.'

'Not far from the truth, sir, but he lives, believe me. He thrives.' Forrester looked up at the tall, crooked form of Major Lawrence. 'Besides, a singed face does not a dead man make.'

45

The tension ebbed from Lawrence's expression for a brief moment. 'And how is our fearsome friend? Alive yet, I trust.'

'Captain Stryker is well, sir, so far as I know. Away on Crown business.'

'Say no more, Captain,' Lawrence said with what might have been a wink, though his tick made it hard to tell. 'Hopton comes, then? With an army?'

'He does,' Forrester confirmed. They had reached a large gateway, set into Basing's outer wall and adorned with carvings and crests. Paulet's flag flew from the pinnacle. 'Newly raised, freshly armed and poised to invade Dorset. It will be Hampshire after that. The marquess's forces – *your* forces – must take the fight to the enemy. Keep him busy. Shake the hornet's nest, so to speak.'

'They are not my forces, Captain. Not any longer. Colonel Rawdon is military governor now. But he and the marquess have heard such overtures before, old friend. They will be reluctant to so much as prod the hornet's nest with a stick.'

'I must deliver my message, nevertheless. Perhaps you might add your voice to mine?'

Lawrence nodded. 'Gladly.' He signalled the pair of sentries. 'Here we are, Captain Forrester. Garrison Gate. Welcome to Loyalty House.'

CHAPTER 4

St Mary's, Isles of Scilly, 3 October 1643

The face peered suspiciously through the slat set into the door. All that could be seen were the eyes, and they were like black slits, darting left and right, searching the little chamber's stone walls for signs of danger. Evidently deciding all was safe, the face retreated into the shadows, and the metal shutter slid closed with a ringing slice and heavy clunk. A voice, muffled behind the door's thick timbers, called out. It was the voice of a man, and another man immediately responded, his footsteps becoming louder as they shuffled along the flagstones. The men inside the windowless room stared up at the doorway through the gloom, flinching involuntarily as the jangle of keys echoed on the far side. A series of clicks and the sliding of bolts followed, heralding the squeal of large, aged hinges.

A gaoler stepped into the room. His face was ruined by livid ulcers that glistened at their white-crested summits, and in the glow of the flame held behind by the second gaoler, he seemed to leer like Lucifer himself, mocking his dishevelled, blinking charges as he filled the doorway with his bulk.

'New pot, lads,' the gaoler said. He held up his hand from which an empty bucket dangled by a fraying rope. 'Give us the old one, if you please.'

The chamber was full. Seventeen men were crammed within its slippery walls, some of them terribly weak, all shivering from their collective ordeal as they huddled together in the centre in search of warmth. One of them rose and scrambled to a far corner where he hefted another bucket. He was tall, with a bald head and long arms, and he took the bucket's weight easily enough, despite recent privations. It was full with a dark liquid that slopped over the rim, eliciting a hissed oath.

The gaoler grinned maliciously. 'That'll hum some.'

The tall captive spat into the stinking liquid and handed it over. 'All the better, for I shall drown you in it.'

The fat man chortled, sharing the jest with a glance across his shoulder at he who held the flame. 'That's the spirit.' He cast his gaze over the rest of the men. 'Getting tired of changing your bloody pots. Try to cross your pox'n legs, eh . . .'

With that he turned back, holding the slop bucket at arm's length with a look of revulsion. His companion moved quickly aside, swinging the flame clear, and pulled the door shut, the lock clunking noisily. Their laughter carried in smothered pulses from the far side, but darkness had already descended within the cell.

'Do not antagonize them, Will,' Captain Innocent Stryker said from his place amongst the mass of bodies.

The tall man made a guttural grunt as he strode back to drop the empty pail in the corner. Immediately he unfastened the string at his breeches and the tinkling of flowing water echoed around the low chamber. 'They're bastards, sir. Craven bloody bastards. Their locks and keys give 'em courage.'

'I'd like to see them,' a croaking voice with the accent of Scotland chimed in, 'walk up Stratton hill into Chudleigh's guns. See how brave they feel then.'

'Aye,' Skellen muttered as he hitched up his breeches and rejoined the group.

'We are here, at their mercy,' Stryker said. 'That is all that matters.'

'Two days of this, sir,' Skellen said as he sat down, 'and I'm dreamin' o' when I'll get the chance to throttle these whoresons. Just two days. Don't know how I shall cope much longer.'

'That all it's been?' Barkworth said.

Skellen nodded. 'Aye, I'd say so.'

48

'A day and a night,' Stryker corrected. 'This is the second day.'

'If we had a chunk o' chalk,' another of the men said, 'I'd scratch it down for you, sir.'

'No need,' answered Stryker bitterly. 'We have been here a day and a night.' Of course, they all knew that he spoke with no more certainty than any other in their dank hole, for none could see the passing of sun or moon, but Stryker had campaigned for more years than even Sergeant Skellen, and he was a man to believe, especially when a situation turned sour. And this one most certainly had.

As Jethro Beck had told them, Great Ganilly, the island on which the ill-fated *Kestrel*'s survivors had washed ashore, was little more than a minor outcrop of granite and heathland on the eastern fringe of the Scilly archipelago. The real hub of this ocean-borne community were the four major islands, chief of which was St Mary's, and that was where Beck's tiny fleet of skiffs had taken them. The small flotilla had skated its way relatively comfortably beyond Crow Sound, the stretch of water to the west of Great Ganilly and the other Eastern Isles, and on into St Mary's Road, and as they had slid round the jagged headland of that largest piece of rising rock, Stryker could well understand the infamy with which the Isles of Scilly were often associated. This was a harsh land, one defined by storms and waves and barren granite-pocked earth. Crops would be poor and fishing would be hard, which meant the locals would be forced to turn their hands to alternative enterprises if they were to survive. The islanders were often maligned for their propensity for smuggling and piracy, and as he had squinted against the salty spray jetting up from the bow of Beck's skiff, Stryker decided he would have done the same.

It had been daylight by the time they reached the Hugh, a large headland located on the south-western corner of St Mary's. Out of the grim dark, between the starry sky and the tar-black swell, they had seen the walls. They rose out from the high ground some hundred paces back from the shoreline, and Stryker had known that they were looking at a fortress. It was quite small, to judge from the sweep of the walls, but formidable for all that, the roof of a central keep jutting heavenwards from behind a stone-faced earthen rampart. And that rampart was built in the shape of a star, providing artillery with coverage of all flanks, its points sharp against the black of the night. Stryker had looked from the high walls to Jethro Beck, and the fisherman had grinned broadly, spat over the side of the skiff, and nodded up at the fort. 'Welcome to Star Castle, cully.'

And it was into Star Castle's dingy bowels that the seventeen Royalists, suspected of being Parliamentarians, had been thrown. They had grown accustomed to the dark, and, other than the surly guards who cleared away their effluent and occasionally gave them tasteless pottage and ominously gritty water, they had not laid eyes on a single soul. 'So where the pissin' hell is Miss Lisette?' Skellen said suddenly, his deep voice reverberating about the stone walls.

This was the very question with which Stryker wrestled throughout each hour of their incarceration. While the army's focus was squarely on the Earl of Essex at Newbury, Lisette had come ahead of the main party to locate the Cade fortune and keep it safe for Stryker's impending arrival.

'Dead?' Simeon Barkworth suggested.

Skellen jabbed him with a fist to the shoulder. 'Shut yer prattle.'

Barkworth shoved him back. 'Och, it's possible.'

Stryker put up a hand for peace. 'Aye, it is.' His guts twisted. Lisette had become something of a talisman for Stryker's musketeers over the last year. Their captain's love, and a woman who could wield a blade as well as any man.

Barkworth's yellow eyes, strangely visible in the darkness, seemed to widen as his head shot round to look at the door. 'Someone comes.'

'Should we ask 'em of Miss Lisette?' Skellen said.

'No. Do not breathe a word, unless you wish to see me upset.' Stryker cast his gaze about the shadowy outlines of his men. 'We give nothing away until we know what we are dealing with. Understood?'

The lock clanked, a bolt rasped, and light streamed into the chamber as the door creaked inwards. Stryker squinted against the new brightness and waited for his single eye to adjust. It was not the rotund figure of the gaoler, nor his usual confederate. The newcomer, stepping casually into the room, hands planted squarely on narrow hips, had skin that was so dark, Stryker's first thought was that the castle had been occupied by pirates from the Barbary Coast. His hair was black and thick, though beginning to recede at the temples, his brown eyes gleamed almost as brightly as Barkworth's, while his nose was almost completely flat, as though a sword had cleaved it through the bridge. There were other scars too, white as chalk lines against the copper complexion, highlighted as it was in the light of a flame held at his back.

The newcomer took another pace into the cell, and Stryker noticed half a dozen others behind him. 'Captain Stryker?' the dark-skinned man said, casting his sharp eyes across the bunched prisoners.

Stryker heaved himself to his feet. 'Aye, sir,' he said, relieved. 'You have heard of me?'

'Absolutely, Captain. Your reputation precedes you.' The man turned back briefly to address the small party. 'This is he, gentlemen. Stryker. Blackguard, cut-throat and notorious rebel.'

Stryker advanced a pace, feeling the weakness in his legs as he moved, and the party shied immediately away like trout below a kingfisher's shadow. 'I told Mister Beck, I am no damned rebel!'

The dark-skinned man simply laughed and slunk back with his gawking group, the lion-keeper at the Tower menagerie. And then the door slammed shut.

Basing House, Hampshire, 3 October 1643

'Glass. So simple a thing, yet so precious when made by talented hands.' Sir John Paulet, Lord St John, Earl of Wiltshire and Fifth Marquess of Winchester, was standing at the window of one of the upper rooms in the Great Gatehouse, the most prominent of Basing's sprawling structures. He traced the outline of the diamond-shaped pane, stained crimson to colour the light, and sighed heavily. 'Now these high pieces are all that is left of my forebears' exquisite home. Most have gone, shattered by the passage of time or removed for the good of our sharpshooters.'

'A terrible shame, my lord,' Lancelot Forrester replied awkwardly, feeling as if his presence as a soldier made him somehow culpable.

'This whole place,' Paulet went on wistfully, 'once glimmered with such windows. When Queen Bess visited for the last time, my father had every pane removed, washed, repaired and replaced.' He gave a short burst of laughter. 'Such grandiosity. It is what the Paulets are known for, Captain. And our loyalty to the Crown, of course. Now look where it has brought us.'

Forrester had been summoned to this audience after a comfortable night in what must have once been a sumptuous bedchamber. He had climbed the spiral staircase into the upper level of the Great Gatehouse wondering just what kind of toll the conflict had taken upon this most ardent supporter of King Charles. But now, he saw a determination that had not been present the first time they had met. Paulet was thinner than before, his dark eyes sunken and saddled with shadowy bags, but there was steel in the gaze.

'You hold this great seat in full defiance of the Parliament, my lord,' Forrester said. 'Your loyalty will be rewarded in time, I am certain.'

Paulet gave a wintry smile. 'Much has come to pass since last our paths crossed, Captain, would you not say?'

'Aye, my lord, it has. Too much.'

'Over by Christ-tide, the news-sheets gleefully pronounced,' Paulet said, staring down into the busy courtyard below. 'The rebellion dead and buried. Look at us now. A year slipped by and nothing buried but English corpses, slain at English hands.'

He looked up to meet Forrester's gaze, and immediately coloured. 'Forgive me, Captain. You have seen enough of the war, I'd wager.'

Forrester went close to the glass, unable to meet Paulet's eye. Down below, the people looked tiny, scuttling about their lives as though no war had come to this place at all. He knew it to be artifice, of course, but the aloof perspective cheered him none-theless. 'More than a man should see, my lord.'

'In that, thank the Holy Mother, we have been spared, I am relieved to say. There was an attack in July, led by that dog Norton. Villainy in human form.' Paulet moved to a large chest near the big hearth at the side of the room. It was made of ebony, and was polished to such a gleam that it might have been made of blackened glass. Paulet opened one of the doors to reveal a decanter and three silver goblets. He filled one and took a sip. 'Norton has a particular antipathy towards me, by matter of faith.'

Forrester was not surprised. The marquess's unashamed Catholicism inspired much derision from the Puritan-driven Parliament. 'I thank God the attack failed, my lord.'

Paulet nodded. 'Since then we have whiled away the months in preparation. We are a stone's throw from Farnham, Westminster's bridgehead hereabouts. It is a matter of time. The rebels will come, and there will be blood.' He set his goblet down and filled another. 'But enough of that for the moment, eh? Come, Captain Forrester. Share some claret with me. It will prove to your liking.'

As Forrester lifted the vessel to his lips, he closed his eyes. The wine seared his throat in a manner that was more welcome than he could possibly have described. He was about to say as much when there was a knock at the door.

'Aha!' Paulet exclaimed, setting down his goblet. 'Come!'

The man who pushed past the ornately panelled wood was of average height and build, though his bearing was of one who knew his business. He wore a coat of black, slashed down the sleeves to contrast bright yellow silk beneath, and a wide hat, which he now snatched off to reveal long hair the colour of slate. A man of advanced years, his once handsome face was creased so deeply by time that it looked almost like a mask of leather, and his whiskers and eyebrows were overgrown and grey.

'Colonel Marmaduke Rawdon,' the Marquess of Winchester said. 'May I introduce to you, Captain Lancelot Forrester?'

Rawdon limped into the room and offered his hand. 'Well met, Captain. Mowbray's Foot, yes?'

Forrester shook the gloved hand, noting its iron grip, and looked into the baby-blue eyes. 'You have it, sir, aye. Third captain.'

Rawdon sucked his upper lip into his mouth so that he might gnaw the longer strands of his moustache. 'Were you at Newbury Fight?'

'I was, sir.'

'How was it?'

Forrester blushed; he could never hope to describe such an experience. Just as he could not articulate the sheer terror of Edgehill or the silent march of Hopton's powderless Cornish-men up that blood-slick slope at Stratton. Could a man convey the rattle of musket-balls through swaying forests of pike, or the rib-juddering pulse of belching ordnance? Could he truly describe the acrid stink of the smoke as it slewed in horizontal cloud banks to obscure whole brigades of Horse and Foot? He doubted he could make Rawdon understand the screams of a thousand wounded men, all calling for their mothers at once, or the ear-shredding noise of a giant musket volley, or the thunder of a cavalry charge that would turn a man's bowels to water in a heartbeat. In the end he shrugged. 'Hard.'

The bushy brows shot up. 'Hard?'

'Very hard.'

There followed a moment of silence as Forrester searched his boots. He was relieved to receive a thumping slap on the shoulder and looked up to find Rawdon grinning. 'My apologies, Captain. It was not my intention to pry. Such things are difficult to dwell upon.' He spread his hands. 'I was a militiaman before all this. Played at soldiers for so long. Now that war befalls us, I feel envious of those who have seen real battle.'

It is nothing to envy, thought Forrester. 'No matter, sir.'

Paulet clapped his hands suddenly. 'Now, Captain Forrester, I must tell you that things have changed somewhat since last you visited.' He moved to the ebony sideboard, taking up the final goblet and handing it to Rawdon. 'The Colonel, here, is now my military governor, to advise in matters of blade and shot.'

'And defence,' Rawdon continued, 'supplies, ordnance, and the like.'

Forrester thought back to the digging of ditches and repairing of walls. 'Impressive, Colonel Rawdon.'

Rawdon dipped his head a touch. 'I work hard for this great house.'

'And for your reputation, eh, Marmaduke?' Paulet added through a strangely tight mouth.

Rawdon pointedly ignored the marquess, smiling instead at Forrester. 'Major Lawrence informs me that you have come direct from Oxford. I trust it is with news of an encouraging nature?'

'It is, sir,' Forrester replied, forcing Paulet's acidic comment aside. 'Plans are afoot to raise a new army under Lord Hopton.'

'Oh?' Paulet said, his eyes narrowing. 'Our new baron is recovered from his wounds?'

'Apparently so, my lord. He will lead this army out of the south-west, with the purpose of clearing Dorset, Wiltshire and Hampshire, ultimately advancing upon London from the south-east.'

Paulet's gaunt face beamed. 'And part of that force will be sent here?'

'Alas, my lord.'

The excitement dissolved as quickly as it had come. 'Alas?'

Forrester opened his mouth, but it was Colonel Rawdon who spoke. 'Baron Hopton is not set to aid us, my lord. Rather, we are to aid him.' He turned from Paulet's shocked face to look at Forrester. 'He would have us sally out, would he not?'

'Indeed, sir,' Forrester confirmed, 'you are in the right of it. He asks that you take the war to the enemy. Keep him occupied.'

'Occupied?' Paulet blurted, fury putting fresh blood in his cheeks. 'We are occupied enough here, by God!'

Rawdon blew out his cheeks, his grey moustache quivering in the blast of air. 'We sit and wait, my lord,' he said, and Forrester was sure he could detect a hint of exasperation in the older man's tone. 'Daily, we build our defences, position our guns, sharpen our swords. Always waiting for the Roundheads to strike.'

'What are you saying?' Paulet cut in, suspicion clouding his face.

'Baron Hopton,' Rawdon answered, 'will soon march towards us, and any marching general would rather not have an opposing army shadowing him, harrying his men, cutting his supply lines, plundering his baggage, poisoning wells, scouring the land of food.' The colonel had counted those points on his fingers, and now he curled them into a fist. 'Essex's army, made bold by Gloucester and blooded at Newbury, is in London. If the Parliament hear of Hopton's advance, they will doubtless send His Excellency to intercept, so we must keep Parliament's eye fixed firmly elsewhere.'

Paulet's thin neck quivered as he swallowed. 'Here.'

Forrester slipped a hand into his coat, pulling free the folded square of parchment he had been given by Ezra Killigrew. 'This letter tells all, my lord,' he said, handing it to Paulet, 'but Colonel Rawdon has it precisely. You are not asked to abandon your position, simply to disrupt the enemy hereabouts.'

Paulet cast his gaze to the parchment in his hand as though it contained a warrant for his own death, then up at the captain and colonel in turn. His cheeks suddenly seemed hollow. 'The King would have us tempt Parliament's army? Bring them here to smash us so that Hopton can march free?'

Lancelot Forrester felt a surge of sympathy for the Earl of Wiltshire and Fifth Marquess of Winchester. Another proud man whose very existence was threatened by this strange war that had no real enemy. All he could do was drain his cup and nod.

Forrester followed Colonel Marmaduke Rawdon out into the heart of the Old House having accepted an offer to view the new fortifications by the military governor in the face of Paulet's spluttering fury. At the centre of the enclosure, dominating the rest of the buildings, was the Great Hall. Through its large twin doors, servants scurried like so many rats, carrying bushels of corn and sacks of dried meat, the provisions of a garrison digging in for winter, while some wheeled dog carts full of surplus furniture, candlesticks and clothing. This was a house alive with preparations for war.

'How many men do you have, sir?' Forrester asked as they moved past a large stone fountain.

Rawdon grimaced in half apology. 'Hard to tell. More come here each day, seeking refuge from Parliament's hounds.' He paused to accept the bows of some of his soldiers. 'My regiment is near three hundred strong, though the marquess has conveniently gathered a fair few under his own colours.'

'He has,' Forrester noted tentatively, 'stolen your men?'

Rawdon gave a short grunt that was more growl than laugh. 'Absorbed, aye. It is a point of contention.' He waved the issue away as if he were swatting an irritating fly. 'Now where was I? Let me see. Lieutenant-Colonel Peake brought a hundred musketeers earlier in the summer. There might be another hundred able to bear arms, retainers and exiles, loyal to the marquess. And their families are here too. Some of the women and older children might—' Rawdon tailed off, scrutinizing the middle-distance, and Forrester knew that the idea was more than the old man could bear. He was not one of the damned few who had blooded their blades on the Continent. There, in those walled citadels where siege warfare was cruel and quarter was neither asked nor given, any man, woman or child would wield a musket if they were strong enough to lift one. For to lose your fortress was to lose your life.

Rawdon's eyes regained focus and he stared hard at Forrester. 'What did you make of him?'

Forrester was surprised at the sudden question. He decided the truth would do no harm. 'A man determined to hold his property, but fearful he will be undermined by his own side.'

Rawdon moved on, picking up the pace, until they reached a section of the wall guarded by the stout square walls of a gatehouse. 'His world is changing, and he does not know how to make it stop.' He let a pair of sentries move swiftly apart and went through a low doorway. 'In that, at least, I consider his lordship a kindred spirit.'

'Oh?'

They were in the gloom of the gatehouse as Rawdon glanced back. 'I made my name as a merchant. A trifle dissimilar to our dear Marquess of Winchester, I'll admit, but, like him, I was a man who knew himself. I was comfortable with my worth, with my wealth, with my place in the world, and sure in the knowledge that mine was a prosperous life.' They reached more sentries and another door. 'Now? I have reached my sixty-second year and I find myself playing soldiers, exiled from my beloved London, from my family, my homes and businesses, asked to advise the marquess on matters of which I am not expert.' The door was opened for him and Rawdon went through, evidently noting Forrester's consternation as he went. 'Do not worry, Captain, I am not entirely devoid of experience.'

But still, thought Forrester, you have not waded into the baleful gaze of a thousand primed muskets.

'I have led men,' Rawdon said, 'and I was a member of the Society of the Artillery Garden back in London.'

'Ordnance is your interest, sir?'

'When I was an officer in the militia, I felt often that the plodders did not comprehend their orders, while the horse generally ignored theirs altogether. The artillery were more sensible.'

'Ha!' Forrester barked. 'I could not venture comment upon such a statement, sir.'

'Naturally,' Rawdon said with a grin. 'But there you have it. I know what I am about, and yet I am thrust into this position of authority, at a time when I should be resting at ease with my grandchildren. Another curmudgeon whose world spins uncontrollably!' He moved out of the gatehouse, into a sudden blast of sunlight. 'Still, if this is what is ordained, then this is what we must bear.'

Forrester stepped out to where the colonel stood, realizing with a swimming sensation that they were standing on a narrow bridge over the deep ditch. At the far end of the bridge there was another gate, set into the red-bricked fastness of more formidable walls. 'The New House?'

'Aye,' said Rawdon, nodding back the way they had come. 'This is the Postern Gate. The only route directly between the houses. Pray God the enemy never know of its existence, for it is the old castle's single weak point.'

Forrester glanced down as they crossed the bridge, noting the fresh chalk beneath where the defensive work had recently been deepened. The slopes on either bank were splashed white where spoil had been tossed, steepening the gradient considerably. 'The works here are admirable, sir.'

Rawdon nodded. 'Kind of you to say, Captain. It is not yet ready, but we make progress.' The door to the New House jolted open on their approach, the pair seen by invisible soldiers through the loopholes in the wall. 'However, I am keen to act upon the orders you bring.'

'You are, sir?'

Rawdon nodded as he led Forrester through the doorway. 'Lassitude is a canker. It grows on the minds of soldiers, makes them slow and witless. We must keep them active, and for that, we must leave the safety of the castle. Do you not think so?'

Forrester's assessment of the gruff colonel received a boost, despite his misgivings. 'I agree wholeheartedly, sir. But do you not already? For supplies and so forth?'

'On occasion, aye.' They were in the New House now. Forrester remembered it, and yet it was starkly different to the images his mind recalled. Unlike its circular counterpart, this was no fort-turned-house, but a purpose-built mansion. It had not evolved from austere, easily defensible beginnings, but had been constructed by the Paulets to display and project their wealth and status, and to provide a vast home for their descendants to live in comfort. And yet now, as 1643 rolled inexorably towards its wintry conclusion, the New House had become a castle. It remained the weaker of the two houses by Forrester's reckoning, for it sat on lower ground and its outer walls were essentially buildings that had been joined to form a continuous face. Thus, there were windows and rooftops instead of loopholes and crenellations. And yet a deep ditch had been excavated all the way around its perimeter, as Forrester had witnessed on his approach with Major Lawrence, and the towers at each corner of the huge rectangle had been mounted with artillery. Inside, all around the large courtyard, the comings and goings of a major house continued apace, but, as in the Old House, the amount of weaponry and supplies was remarkable. Starkest of all was the sheer number of soldiers. Most wore coats of yellow, and Rawdon explained that they were his men, but there was an array of colours in this place that seemed to attract Royalists from every corner of the south-east. There had been a small garrison here when Forrester had last visited, but now the place fairly bristled. In one corner the song of swords rang out, sending icy fingers along the nape of Forrester's neck as men practised their swordplay to the cheers and jeers of their compatriots. A pair of drummers rehearsed their calls, bringing precision to the rhythms that would give an army its orders on the field of battle, while a queue of musketeers stretched out from the doorway of one building that Forrester presumed was employed as the powder magazine.

Rawdon showed Forrester to the south-western corner of the courtyard, and led him into the wall tower that overlooked this part of the house. They climbed silently up the steps, emerging on to the roof. It had once been conical in shape, but the ceiling tiles had been stripped away to leave the bare skeleton of the timber frame, allowing the defenders a clear line of sight. Rawdon stared down at the earthworks that protected this side of the fortress. 'In truth,' the colonel said, now that they were out of earshot, 'the marquess is reluctant to risk the men.' He pulled a sour expression. 'Reluctant to risk the house while the men are gone.'

Forrester had to raise his voice above the whipping wind, gripping his hat lest it fly away. 'But he will do as he is asked?'

'He will do as he is *ordered*. But he'll gripe, have no doubt, for he will see conspiracy where there is none.'

'Forgive me, Colonel. You refer to yourself?'

Rawdon sucked at his grey moustache. 'Come now, Forrester, you did not notice the barbs he slings?'

'He made mention of your reputation, sir, which, I confess, puzzled me a touch.'

Rawdon paused, moving to the edge of the tower, through the rafters of which a small artillery piece stretched. It was a falconet, Forrester saw. Not ordnance that could hurt a stone wall, but, turned upon a massed group of infantrymen, perfectly capable of cleaving bloody holes in their ranks. It guarded the southern approaches, warning any attacking force that terror awaited them. Rawdon patted the cold barrel. 'I was with the Parliament at the outset of this horror.'

That surprised Forrester, and it was all he could do to keep his face impassive. 'I see.'

'After Kineton Fight, the King's men made play for the capital.'

'I was there. I fought at Brentford. But the rebels we faced that day were Brooke's and Holles's. Some of Hampden's green-coats. You would not have been—'

'I was Lieutenant-Colonel of the Red Regiment,' Rawdon cut in.

'The London Trained Bands?' Forrester said. He did not recall their presence at Brentford, and was about to say as much when he remembered the conclusion of the king's thrust upon the capital. It had all come to a head, and an end, on a large swathe of common ground near Chiswick, where the London militia, bolstered by the very people of the metropolis they were sworn to protect, marched out to block the road. It was a daring gambit in the face of the all-conquering Royalist army, and it might have resulted in the worst bloodbath England had ever known. 'Then you were at Turnham Green.'

Rawdon nodded. 'I was. I stood in that vast barricade of flesh and bone, staring down the barrels of so many Royalist muskets. I thought the world must end there and then.'

Forrester remembered staring back at the Parliamentarians, wondering whether he would be ordered to fire on so many of the king's subjects. In the end, they had abandoned the advance, fearing the damage such violence would have done to their cause. 'We had not the stomach for it.'

'I am not certain we did either. Now we shall never know. And I will be ever grateful for that. I am a Londoner. The carnage that day would not have been worth even the Crown, though I'll thank you not to repeat such treason.'

'When did you—'

'Turn my coat? Winter. I had hopes for peace but attempted to maintain friendships with both sides.' He grimaced, perhaps reading the incredulity in Forrester's eyes. 'It may seem feeble to you, but I am an old man, Captain. Peace matters more than your opinion.'

'But the peace talks foundered,' Forrester prompted, unwilling to be drawn into an argument.

'They did, and then Parliament implicated me in a plot to seize the Tower armoury.'

'The Crispe plot?' Forrester said. He almost laughed. For all the old man's talk of desiring peace, he had been dabbling in espionage the entire time.

'The same. I knew I was in danger if I remained astride our terrible fissure. I threw myself on the King's mercy.' He shrugged. 'His Majesty forgave me, I raised my own regiment, and here we are.'

'Here we are, indeed.' Forrester went to the other side of the gun carriage and stared down at the ditch. Immediately below them it ceased to run straight, but angled out, forming a triangular bastion, spiked storm-poles lining the base like teeth. There was another curving feature to the west, thrust out to protect the southern approach to the Old House in the shape of a half-moon. Again, he was impressed by the ambition – not to mention the level of engineering prowess – that was on display. 'But the marquess has not forgiven you.'

'He does not truly trust me,' Rawdon replied, his voice muffled by the wind. 'But it is more than that, Captain. The Paulets are one of the foremost exponents of the old religion in this country.'

Forrester could guess what was coming next. 'And you are ardently for the new.'

The colonel shot him a wan smile. 'Basing has become a refuge for Catholics all across the land. A beacon, lighting their way to safety in a nation that has become fraught with danger. I do not begrudge them that, Captain, but they perceive the marquess as their hero.'

'And their commander,' said Forrester, beginning to understand.

'Aye. He is lord here, but I am governor. How can I make plans for defence or attack if those under my command do not consider me their leader?'

Forrester saw now that things were not as straightforward as he had first thought. Matters of military expertise, religious difference and deep-set mistrust were compounded by rivalry over who really commanded Basing House. He wondered how the great fortress was to remain strong if the unity of its leaders could not, but decided to keep his own council. 'Will the rebels attack Basing?'

'Eventually, they must,' said Rawdon. 'The south-east has a great many Royalists, but they keep mouths and doors firmly shut. The active men in these shires are those for Parliament. Militarily at least, Westminster's arm reaches all the way to the coast. And yet still there stand enclaves for our cause. Winchester, Donnington Castle, Basing House.' He looked across at

Forrester, plucking off his hat and ruffling his hair. 'For the rebel lion to truly take this region, he must first pluck those thorns from his paw.'

'You will prove a deep-set thorn, sir,' Forrester said truthfully. He might have concerns over Basing's divisive leadership, but Rawdon was intelligent, and his preparations for the house were genuinely robust.

'Aye, that we will,' Rawdon said. He met Forrester's eyes. 'And we pray Baron Hopton will punch through to relieve us before any real blood is spilt.'

Forrester kept his gaze level. 'He marches soon.'

'Then perhaps all will be well,' Rawdon said, looking away to the distant hills. 'And in the meantime, I shall arrange for our own forays to become more penetrating. Let us keep the rebel busy, so that he does not notice his enemy approach.'

'Thank you, Colonel Rawdon. I shall take pleasure in delivering your reply to Oxford.'

Rawdon turned to face him, his tone almost apologetic. 'Unless you might stay a while.'

'Sir, I—'

'You are engaged in something pressing at our new capital?'

A voice in the back of Forrester's mind screamed at him to claim that he needed to return to Oxford immediately upon pain of death. And yet part of him could not help but be enticed by the offer. Rawdon seemed a good man, and the prospect of languishing in camp for only God knew how long made him yearn to stay out in the field. Not least because Stryker had managed to slip Oxford's shackles, and the fact irked him more than he cared confess. He shook his head. 'What did you have in mind, sir?'

'My men are green, Captain,' Rawdon said. 'Raised only in April, they have sallied out for supplies, and, to their credit, were active in repulsing Norton's attack in July. But these raids you ask for will take skill and courage. My men possess the latter in abundance.'

'You would have me fight for you, sir?' Forrester asked.

Marmaduke Rawdon sucked his moustache again, and gave a firm nod. '*With* me, Forrester, aye. Lead one of the sally parties. Show them how a proper warrior goes about his business.' He extended his hand for Forrester to shake. 'What say you?'

CHAPTER 5

St Mary's, Isles of Scilly, 5 October 1643

The sea was part of Scilly. It surrounded, shaped and harassed the myriad rocky outcrops that formed this far-flung English outpost. Yet it was more than this. It pervaded everything: the smell on the wind; the salt in the air; the sound all around as the Atlantic sucked and broke in frothing whirlpools at the foot of every cliff. Stryker heard it now, forcing open his eyes, and imagined the great waves as they crashed home in their perpetual battle with the land. A stabbing pang of longing jolted through him. To see those waves, to feel that frenzied wind on his face. It would be very heaven, he was certain.

The dark-skinned man had not visited the prisoners again, leaving them for more long hours to wonder at their fate and the bizarre accusation that had been levelled at them. And then soldiers had come. They were garrison men, Stryker guessed, shipped over from Cornwall at the outset of the war, and here they had stayed, waited, watched the tumultuous seas and prayed the rebels would never come. Now they believed they had arrived in the form of a one-eyed officer, a Scottish dwarf and a motley assortment of hard-looking rogues. No wonder they would not speak with him. The soldiers had hauled Stryker up by his armpits and dragged him along a dank passageway through the heart of Star Castle, dumping him unceremoniously in another cell, one with manacles hanging by chains from the stone wall, and with only rats for company. There was a window, and, tiny though it was, the pathetic chink of light that streamed through was more welcome to Stryker than a feather bed. He could now tell dawn from dusk, at the very least.

That had been almost two days ago, he reckoned, and nothing had been forthcoming since. Food, water, a fresh piss-pot, all brought by sullen guards who seemed to shy away from him as though he were a fierce dog.

Stryker went to the window. His legs felt weak, almost numb. He knew that Star Castle was built on rising ground a short distance back from the shore, and he could see the bleak, white-foaming grey of the waves through his window, a tiny vista of rock and ocean, framed in cold stone. Thus he realized his cell must be set into the outer wall, a chamber within one of the eight points of the great star for which the fortress had been named. Between the castle and the foreshore the terrain was a plain expanse of green heathland, interspersed by the occasional smudge of grey where rocks broke the surface. And yet as he stared out with a flourishing desperation to feel the grass between his toes, he noticed the dark patches that flanked one particular granite outcrop. At first he had assumed they were scorch marks from fires, perhaps set by members of the garrison on picket duty, but as his eye adjusted to the light, he realized that there was depth in the image. He stared hard, finally coming to understand that the dark smears were, in truth, pits: deep holes had been carved out of the headland on either side of the stones. They were too wide to be graves, but he could not imagine to what other use they might be put.

He was still peering out through the tiny hole when the door opened. He spun around quickly to see a slender man dressed in a suit of dark blue enter the room. He was perhaps an inch or two shorter than Stryker, with a tight-lipped expression that suggested the very notion of stepping on to the grimy rushes was anathema, and he squinted at the prisoner over the wire rim of thick spectacles that made his eyes appear far larger than they were.

Stryker thought the fellow looked more scholar than soldier, and he might have said so but for the trio of grim men who entered the cell in his wake. One face Stryker recognized as the man who had shown him off to the curious group of onlookers some days previously, for his intelligent eyes and copper-toned skin were difficult to forget. But the others were new. They were the kind of ruthless men Stryker had known all his life.

'You bring your rooks to give me a beating?' he said, backing nevertheless into the wall behind. 'I shall show them a beating.'

The dark man did not move, but both his compatriots made to challenge Stryker. All were halted by the fellow in blue. 'Wait, sirs. This is not the way.'

Stryker still stared at the two rougher figures. 'Who are they?'

The bespectacled man pulled an expression of distaste. 'Our guards.'

Stryker studied them. One was short and bearded, so pallid that he seemed almost choleric, with a dense thatch of auburn hair that had been sheared into a wedge above his collar bones. The other man was huge. Bigger still than Skellen, and power-fully built, his head was completely bald and framed by ears that were tiny and strangely thick. His eyes too were small, and so pale that Stryker had initially thought them entirely transparent. He kept his gaze flicking between the two. 'Why have I been moved?'

The elegant man, clearly an officer, adjusted the clip that kept his spectacles fastened to his nose. 'I would speak with you privately.'

Stryker finally looked directly at him. 'Who are you?'

The man offered a twitch of a bow. 'I am Captain William Balthazar.'

'You command here?'

'While Sir Thomas is away, aye.'

A stab of hope punctured Stryker's thoughts. 'Sir Thomas Bassett? Major-general with the Cornish army.'

Balthazar nodded. 'That is he, sir.'

'I am known to him!' Stryker took a pace towards the blue-coated man and received growled threats from the two guards. Halting, he added, 'Fought alongside him at Stratton Fight.'

To Stryker's surprise, Balthazar turned to his dark-skinned companion. He gave an almost imperceptible shake of the head.

Captain Balthazar looked back to Stryker. 'I doubt that.'

'You doubt that?' Stryker spluttered, astonished at the man's bluff stupidity. 'Why, Captain? What makes you doubt me? I am here on the orders of King Charles himself.' He glanced beyond Balthazar to the man at the door. 'He shakes his damned head and you dismiss me? Things will go badly for you when His Majesty discovers your treachery, sir.'

Balthazar took a step back, scandalized. 'My treachery? Have a care, sir, for it is you who will struggle to survive this.' He waved the broad hat at his prisoner as if it were a weapon. 'You are Stryker; infamous mercenary, veteran of the Low Countries, and rebel officer. You are my captive, and you will refrain from accusations of treachery, lest I whip some respect into your knavish hide!'

This time, the swarthy man with the scarred face and bright eyes came to stand at the captain's side. He stared hard at Stryker as he spoke, though his voice was incongruously calm. 'Here to take the garrison by surprise. Here to slaughter the inhabitants of these loyal isles. Here to claim Star Castle for King Pym and his Satan-inspired Parliament.'

'You,' Stryker said in sudden understanding. He pointed at the man. 'It is you who whisper this poison. You pull this puppet's strings,' he added, immediately rewarded by the casting of Balthazar's eyes to the floor. 'What have you against me, sir? What is the meaning of this?' He stretched out a hand to the garrison's senior officer. 'Captain Balthazar, I beseech you. I am a mercenary. To some I dare say I am indeed infamous. But I am a servant of my king. My sword, the very sword your men took from me when first I was brought here, was gifted me by the very hand of Queen Henrietta Maria. You must believe me.'

William Balthazar lifted his chin. He put a spindly hand to his spectacles and fiddled unnecessarily at the clip. At his flank the scarred man muttered something and a look of renewed resolve crossed his features. 'Where are your papers, sir? For what reason did you take ship here?'

'My papers were lost with our vessel,' Stryker replied.

Balthazar cleared his throat. 'I put it to you, Captain Stryker, that you are – you *were* – part of a storming party, sent here to assault our loyal outpost.'

A voice in Stryker's head screamed at him to tell the truth, but still he was reluctant. 'I was not.'

'Then what brings you here?'

'I cannot say.'

The mulatto folded his arms. 'You see, Captain Balthazar? A rebel mercenary, sent to wreak havoc and murder in this peaceful land.'

Before Stryker could repeat his protestations of innocence, Balthazar leaned in to whisper in his companion's ear. There followed a short exchange, conducted in hushed tones, before Balthazar went for the door. He turned back briefly. 'Castle business, Captain Stryker. Good day.'

'There,' spoke the voice that Stryker now understood carried the real power. It had the accent of London's ramshackle slums and wharf-side tenements, and yet was rounded enough to be educated, and marked by a cool confidence that made Stryker shiver. 'He has seen the beast. The notorious enemy of the Stuart dynasty.'

'What did you say to him?' Stryker asked, though he could guess the answer.

The man grinned, exposing only a few teeth in otherwise empty gums. 'I told him to fuck off.'

'You? The commander of the castle defers to you?'

The man nodded smugly, patting his breast. 'I have a note from the highest authority, giving me permission to act here as I will.' He winked. 'Besides, I believe our dear Billy Balthazar is a tad nervous of me.'

'I am not surprised,' Stryker said. 'The Scillies are peaceful in the main. The garrison unused to men such as you.'

'Oh?'

Stryker nodded. This man might have been a merchant or

shop-keep, had the tell-tale flash of yellow buff-hide not poked out from beneath the coat's woollen hem. Moreover, the white scars engraved across his chin and cheeks spoke of a man who had survived many a scrap. 'You are ravilliacs. Hired fighters. Throat-slitters. I know your kind.'

Even the giant and his choleric companion seemed to chuckle at that. Their leader pointed at Stryker. 'You *are* our kind, sir!'

'What have you done with my men?' Stryker asked, ignoring the intimation.

'They are well, Captain, have no fear.'

'It is you who should be fearful, sir, not I,' Stryker returned. 'For I take unkindly to any who would do my company harm.'

The dark-skinned man and his confederates brayed at this, their laughter rolling like thunder in the small chamber. 'Then truly we must quake, lads, for it is harm we intend.' He winked again, though now the mirth was gone. 'Oh yes, sir, it is harm we intend. But you first, Captain.' He looked back at the two men at the door. They stepped forwards. 'You first.'

Near Southampton, Hampshire, 5 October 1643

Colonel Richard Norton adjusted the high tops of his boots. They were unfolded to their full extent, the leather peeled back to protect his thighs, but still they chafed, the skin of his legs as raw and livid as the rest of him. It was only when the itch had been well and truly obliterated that he turned to look back at the bedraggled group who stumbled and slipped on foot. What a sight they made, the half-dozen beleaguered, mud-spattered wretches. He relished it. 'They look like lepers, do they not? We should give them a bell.'

Captain Kovac was at his flank. He was bare-headed for this ride, and he tidied his long, white hair with a gloved hand, his pock-pitted face contorting in an expression of disdain. 'We should have stretched their scrawny necks.'

'Prattling Royalist priests,' Norton said with an admonishing look. 'Loud-mouthed malignants who should have kept their opinions to themselves.' He glanced again at the prisoners. They had been discovered fishing in the river almost a mile west of Romsey Abbey. His scouts claimed they were overheard declaring their support for the king and condemning Parliament. Norton had decided a forced march to Southampton might be an apt cure for their ills. 'It is punishment enough to make them trudge through this cold mud, I think. A lesson will be learnt.'

Kovac's pale eyes glittered. 'In my country we'd have dunked them in the very river they fished.'

'In your country,' said Norton, 'it is good reformers such as yourself who are the persecuted faction, is it not? Therefore it is you who would take a dip in the river.'

Kovac shrugged. 'I survived. Killed plenty Papists with these two hands.'

'I'm certain you did, Captain. But then you fled.'

If Kovac noticed the barb, he chose to ignore it. 'Skinned one once. Strangled his son and ploughed his wife.'

'Very Christian of you, Wagner.'

The captain smoothed the tobacco-stained strands of his beard. 'My father hailed from the south-east of the empire.'

Norton nodded. 'Carniola, as you never tire of saying.'

'He was a reformer,' Kovac went on unabashed. 'My mother was a Croat. Papist.' He paused to suck something from a tooth, spitting it back towards the miserable priests who shied quickly away. 'For their love, they were garrotted and burned. I was ten.'

'How very delightful.'

'The war in Europe is crueller than you English can imagine, sir. No man forgives. No man forgets.'

Norton shuddered. He was searching for something to say when he noticed the horizon was clawed by a hundred dark talons, rising skywards from as many hearths. 'Here we are, then. Our billet for the time being.'

They entered Southampton through the East Gate. Norton felt like Alexander as he trotted into the sprawling port city

72

at the head of three hundred veterans, the scars of Newbury Fight still worn on their iron-hard arms and leathery faces. His cornet of horse carried his colour aloft proudly and Norton felt a swell of content as he eyed the fluttering taffeta square of blue and black, with its white sword pointing towards the sun, a pair of laurel branches at the hilt. Around the sword was the inscription *Omnis victoria a domino*. 'On, my boys!' he exhorted.

The city was bustling: shop fronts open, wares arrayed on counters and tables for the folk to browse, the bellows of the shopkeepers ringing out in competition with one another. Hawkers and peddlers hovered about the groups of finely dressed ladies and their attendants, a ranting preacher battled to have his voice heard above the din, and somewhere further off the distant bells of a church wafted on the breeze. Norton's troop moved slowly along the road. It did not, Norton believed, befit his status to be dictated to by common folk, and the traffic simply had to move out of the way if they did not wish to be trampled. Sure enough, the townsmen shifted to either side, many waving and bowing, others cheering. This was a Parliamentarian strong-hold, after all, one of Hampshire's most powerful cities, second only to Portsmouth. Both were under rebel control, but the latter had required conquest before it would bow to Westmin-ster. Not so Southampton, and Norton was proud to accept the welcome from her like-minded citizens.

'Be at your ease!' Norton called to his men as he coaxed his mount past a pair of dogs squabbling over a discarded scrap of offal. 'Rest up, water the horses, gather supplies. Southampton will be your new home.' As the troopers disbursed, he looked at Kovac. 'The taverns should bear up under our weight. Inform me if they do not.'

'The taverns will be fine, sir,' Kovac said, his eyes drifting beyond his colonel's shoulder. 'But the 'fficials?'

Norton was nonplussed. 'Fish-oils?'

'Aldermen?' Kovac said with a shrug. 'Elders?'

'O-fficials!' Norton exclaimed.

'That is what I said.' Kovac tugged his beard and grinned. 'I'll leave this one to you, sir.'

Norton followed the Croat's amused gaze, turning his mount hard round to see a party of grim-looking men advancing upon him. There were eight or nine of them, most dressed in the fine clothes of gentlemen, though a couple were clearly soldiers. 'Give me strength, Lord,' Norton whispered, for he sensed trouble. He slipped quickly from the saddle, removing his helmet as they approached, and forced a smile. 'Sirs!'

'Colonel Norton!' called the man who was evidently the group's spearhead.

'Ah, Peter Murford,' Norton said, extending his hand. 'Good to see you, Sergeant-Major. Fare you well?'

Murford, swathed in a fine suit of dark brown with a crisp white collar and tall black hat, was a short man with fleshy jowls and fair hair that was lank and greasy, falling across his eyes so that he was forced to push it aside. '*Governor* Murford since my men and I secured the town for the Parliament. You are here to bolster our defences?'

'Here to take our ease,' Norton said pointedly. 'But we are at your disposal where there is threat.'

'There is ever threat hereabouts, sir. The malignants busy themselves like bees at the hive. Their thought is bent on our destruction.' Murford looked up and down the road furtively, as though a hidden assassin might come from the shadows at any moment. 'I have recently had cause to round up a good many enemies of the Parliament, setting them aboard ship so as they might nevermore be thorns in our flesh.'

'Setting them aboard ship?'

Murford nodded vigorously. 'To New England, sir. The cause of the King is the cause of Lucifer. We must do all we can to destroy the Cavaliers, however harsh our measures may seem.'

Norton could not conceal his surprise. 'You have had them transported to the New World?' But even as he awaited the answer, he noticed the other officials casting their eyes to their boots, as if unwilling to be associated with the governor.

Moreover, he could not help but catch the stares from passers-by. These were not the contented citizens he had taken them for, but men and women cowed into obedience. They might be Parliamentarians, but that did not necessarily guarantee loyalty to a man who ruled as tyrant.

'Aye, Colonel,' Murford said firmly. 'And any who refuse the new oath will suffer the same fate.'

'Oath?'

'The Solemn League and Covenant,' Murford said with more than a hint of surprise.

Norton felt annoyed at having to explain his lack of awareness. 'I have been in the field, Governor.'

Murford smiled as if humouring a child. 'Of course, Colonel. It is the pledge we all must take. The act has not yet passed, but the news from London is that Parliament will require every grown man to adhere to it.'

Norton frowned. 'To what end?'

'To uphold the reformed religion in accordance with the Kirk.'

'The Scots?' The implication hit Norton like a blast from a culverin. 'In exchange for their army,' he said in barely a whisper.

Murford gave a sly smile. 'Aye.' His own voice dropped a touch. 'We take the oath, they give us their war machine, and the Royalists are crushed.'

Norton did not like the idea of any alliance with the Scots, much less adhering to their damnable Kirk and its dour clergy, and yet it seemed a small price to pay for the destruction of King Charles's formidable forces. 'It seems things move on apace. If the Scots march into England, we will provide a serious challenge to the malignants.'

'But first we must ensure England is prepared,' Murford said. 'The likes of you and I will sweep the Royalists from our good county, eh?'

Norton agreed, but even as he spoke, he wondered what damage Murford's harsh governance had caused this loyal city.

75

'You are too accustomed to trading on your name, sir.'

Stryker was standing before his trio of captors like a condemned felon. 'What do you know of it?'

The mulatto picked at something in his ear, inspecting his nail with casual interest. 'Trouble is, they do not know you in these parts. Out here in this wilderness.' He evidently read the sudden understanding on Stryker's face, for his lips turned slowly upwards at the corners. 'Oh, *we* know you, Mister Stryker. The man with one eye and one name. Famous and feared. Prince Rupert's ban-dog. Aye, we know all about you.'

Stryker struggled not to show his shock. 'If that is true, then you know I am not for the Parliament.'

'But yellow-belly Balthazar does not know, and that, my good captain, is all that matters.'

Stryker's head was spinning now, his mind wrestling with the shards of information in a vain attempt to sculpt something whole. 'What is the meaning of this? We sailed here at the King's order. Took ship from Bristol, a Dutch fluyt called the *Kestrel*. But she was lost in a storm.'

'And why did you sail here, Captain? Let me have a stab at it, eh? You're after the gold.'

Stryker felt as though he had been kicked squarely in the crotch. He swallowed hard. 'I do not—'

'You seek the personal fortune of Sir Alfred Cade,' the dark man went on, his tone laced with relish. 'Seek it for Cavalier coffers. Well you're out o' luck.'

'Cavalier coffers?' Stryker echoed the phrase, but before it had passed his lips, he understood. 'It is you who are the rebel.'

The man shrugged. 'If the Cropheads pay me more than the malignants, aye. And for this enterprise, certainly.'

'A mercenary.'

'Like you.'

'And you seek the treasure, too.'

One of the bright eyes winked. 'Now we understand one

another. And you see why it is expedient for me to have the earnest Captain Balthazar think you a dastardly Roundhead.'

'Who are you?' Stryker asked.

The man bowed, eliciting a low chortle from his guards. 'I am Sterne Fassett.' He spoke the name as if expecting Stryker to give a gasp of recognition. Evidently disgruntled when he did not, he indicated the two sentries. 'These stoic fellows answer to me. The big bugger is Locke Squires, the other Clay Cordell.'

Stryker stared at the three hard faces and the picture began to take form in his mind. They were neither garrison men nor conscripted locals, no more associated with the islands than he. 'And Balthazar?'

Fassett's cheek quivered briefly. 'He answers to my employer.'

'You do not command this business?' Stryker asked, then he gave a slow, deliberate smile. 'No. Of course not. You are a mere hireling. Who pays you?' The man remained tight-lipped, refusing to take the bait. He decided to push against a different flank. 'Why am I here? Why am I alive?' He turned his back on his gaolers, walking to the little window to look out at the excavations. The grass that ran all the way between castle and shore bent away from the wind, except where those brown smudges broke up the terrain. The edges of the pits were smeared with loose soil, freshly deposited. He looked back at Sterne Fassett. 'You do not know where the gold is, do you? That is what this is about. You know it is in the Scillies, but you do not know where.' Something else occurred to him as a new tension seemed to tug at his captors' faces. 'That is why you are left here with me, Mister Fassett, is it not? Your employer has not come to me because he is not here. He searches even now.'

Stryker knew that he had spoken true, but with a deep breath and gritted teeth, the rebel mercenary gathered his composure, folding his arms across his chest like a barrier against his prisoner's jibes. He nodded. 'Very good, Captain, he seeks the gold. That is why I am here. I need to know where it is.' With that, Fassett clicked his fingers and the guards moved. They came like a pair of statues given life by black magic, lurching forth with

77

strong arms, faces utterly implacable. 'And you, good sir, are going to tell me.'

Stryker picked the bigger of the two, raising his fists to defend himself, but he was far too weak to muster the speed he needed and the giant swatted him away with a derisive backhand. The second man hit him from behind and he fell, turned roughly on his back by hands that seemed like bear paws at his shoulders and ankles. They had him pinned, though he spat and cursed, and a swift fist to his guts smashed the wind out of him. Stryker would have screamed if he'd had the strength, for he was transported to a dark room in one of Gloucester's back streets where a Parliamentarian soldier with a grudge had beaten him to near death. He saw that leering face now, while his eye was smothered by the palm of one of the guards, and recalled the sting of the blows with gut-wrenching horror. But no punches came, nor kicks or slaps. To his puzzled fear it was more hands that invaded, groping at his face, pulling hard against his jaw so that his mouth was prized open. Now he cried out and lurched up, bucking against the rough wooden tube that now nestled hard against his tongue. The fingers slipped from his eye, and he found himself staring up at those impassive expressions. The smaller man still pinned his legs, but the bigger one wriggled up to kneel across his chest, forcing his writhing torso down against the filthy rushes and jamming the tube further into Stryker's mouth so that it pressed hard on the back of his tongue, making him gag. Stryker felt his resistance fade with every jerk and his assailant must have felt it too, for he eased back a touch, allowing him to release one of his hands, and he put it to his belt, producing a frighteningly thin poniard that he now lowered to hover just above his captive's eye.

Stryker knew he was beaten. He fell limp, letting his own arms drop, nails scrabbling at the reeds as his throat seared in private flame, the harsh sides of the tube grinding against the soft flesh of his lips and throat.

He stared wildly about the room, searching for Fassett. When he saw him, a feeling of cold dread pulsed up and down his body. The man stepped casually across to where he lay, and Stryker saw that he was cradling a large jug.

'Where is the treasure, Captain Stryker?' Fassett asked, as if he addressed a half-wit.

Stryker could not shake his head, but he grunted his defiance and gave his shoulders a cursory shake that did nothing to move the weight of the man kneeling above.

Fassett sighed deeply, and stooped over his captive. He poised the jug near the tube that Stryker now understood was to be used as a funnel, letting it remain there in unspoken threat. Stryker simply stared back at him, unwilling to show the fear that crashed against him like the tide beyond. Fassett shrugged, tipped the jug forwards, and Stryker saw the liquid cascade down the funnel. It splashed his face where it clipped the wooden rim, and then it was in his mouth. He felt his tongue buck against it instinctively, though it did no good, pinned as it was by the wooden implement, and the liquid filled his mouth and swelled out over his lips, causing him to gag and splutter as it threatened his windpipe. All he could do was swallow. He tasted salt, intense and burning as he gulped it down.

'That's right, Captain,' Fassett said as he eased back the jug, reclining on his haunches at Stryker's side. 'It is our most abundant resource.'

Suddenly the funnel was gone, the weight was lifted, and Stryker sat upright. He vomited, hard and long, gasping for air and scouring his gums with his tongue. 'Seawater!'

Fassett nodded. 'Simple enough. I'd be content enough to cut your stones off, but it will not do to be seen torturing. This stuff won't kill you in small doses, but, by God, it'll make your guts raw.' He looked at the stone-faced giant. 'Not least after Locke, here, took a nice long piss in it.'

Stryker bolted forwards on all fours, retching again, a long trail of vomit-flecked bile dangling from chin to ground. 'I'll drown you in it. Drown you in the sea, you bastard.'

Fassett seemed amused. 'Good. Courage is always admirable, however futile.' He lifted the jug, frowning as he wiped spots of water from it with his sleeve. 'Not some clever poison, I grant you, but we shan't run out. Now tell me. Where is the fucking gold?'

'No,' was all Stryker managed to say.

'No?' Fassett mimicked. 'That is no kind of answer, Captain.' He tutted softly. 'Naughty boy.' He nodded at Squires and Cordell. Stryker tried to struggle, but they clamped him with iron hands and flipped him on to his back so that his head bounced hard on the stone floor.

Stryker found his voice and bellowed like a caged beast, the sound echoing about the gloomy cell, but the funnel was there again, hovering, looming, and it was jammed down, clattering his teeth and probing his throat. He gagged, the giant slapped him hard, and then the salty water was rushing into him again, a thick stream of bubbling, brackish torment. He thought he would drown, then he knew he would vomit, and all the while Sterne Fassett leered above him, grinning, muttering, pouring.

They released him. He rolled away, smacking lips together like a landed carp and desperate to find an escape. The guards laughed. Fassett handed his jug to the choleric-looking Cordell and advanced on Stryker, cocking his head inquisitively in the way a child might study the contents of a rock pool. 'This can continue for as long as you like. Though eventually, of course, you will die.'

'I—' Stryker gasped.

Fassett bent lower, turning his ear to the feeble voice. 'What say you?'

'I will kill you.'

Sterne Fassett laughed. It was a cruel sound, too loud in this confined space, and Stryker shuddered involuntarily. 'Pity.'

'Bastard,' was all Stryker managed to blurt.

Fassett had his lackeys haul the prisoner upright, the seat of his breeches becoming wet as he sat in the pool of seawater and bile. 'Let us try again,' he said when Stryker had been allowed a few moments to gain control of his breathing. 'You were sent here to recover the personal fortune of Sir Alfred Cade. Where, exactly, is it?'

80

'Up your arse.'

Fassett ignored him. 'Where is the Cade treasure, Captain?'

Stryker stared up at him. 'You were sent here too,' he rasped, throat ablaze. 'Who by?'

'That is no concern of yours.'

'And if they knew it was in the Scillies, why did they not know exactly where?'

With a jerk of Fassett's chin, Squires and Cordell descended upon Stryker and the funnel was there again, clattering teeth, scraping gums, pinioning his tongue. The jug loomed in judgement for a second, tilted rapidly, and a thick stream of water gushed over the rim and into Stryker's gullet. It burned again, he gagged and choked, and growled and twisted, and they jumped back to avoid the splashing fountain that pulsed hot and fast from the depths of his wracked body. Stryker went on to hands and knees, coughing and spluttering and staring at the rushes as he dribbled the last of the liquid between his flattened palms. He tried to stand, but found no strength in his limbs, so he keeled on to his side, utterly beaten.

'Now then, sir,' Sterne Fassett said. 'You take your time. Have a think. Ponder your future, such as it is. I'll be back in time. See what's what.'

Stryker closed his eye. He heard the door creak open and slam shut. He spat a lump of something acrid from his mouth. A soft keening echoed around the dank walls. After a while, he realized it came from him.

CHAPTER 6

Near Holybourne, Hampshire, 7 October 1643

It was not yet dawn, but already the misty shroud draped over the thick forest gave the darkness an ethereal glow. The sky was cloudless and black and glittered with a million pricks of starlight, while droplets of dew, clinging on the jagged tops of beech and ash that punctured the mist, winked back at the bright moon like a countless hoard of jewels. Below the canopy, on a narrow bridleway that was soft and made treacherous by invisible roots, a long line of men trudged in the gloom. They were armed with muskets, swords and daggers. Bandoliers hung across their chests, wooden flasks dangling heavy with black powder, for they knew that this day would begin with blood. The soldiers were silent, save the muffled oath grunted when a man tripped, clattering into the body in front. All were watchful as foxes in a field full of hounds, scrutinizing the darkness for that tell-tale glint of blade or helm that would give away a concealed foe. This was dangerous, hotly disputed territory. Every lane, bridleway and crossroads was splashed with blood from one skirmish or another. And the further south they travelled, the further they were from the safety of Basing.

Captain Lancelot Forrester was out in front. He stared up at the stars, whispered a silent prayer, and let his gaze drop to the treetops to gauge whether a breeze shifted the mist. Nothing. All was still. He ignored the pounding in his chest and listened to the crunch of his boots over the twig-strewn bridleway. The first he saw of the village was the spire of the ancient church. It

82

rose above the trees that cloaked the northern fringe of the settlement, serving as a marker for this night's enterprise. They were a hundred paces off now, and the bridleway began to taper sharply so that the thick branches of the trees crowded on both sides, starving the moonlight. The earth here retained some of the night's damp, and Forrester was forced to slow the pace lest they slip in the cloying mud.

They reached the limit of the trees. Beyond was the church-yard. It was a small patch of land surrounding the chapel, marked by pale stones punctuating long grass. Forrester peered between the branches masking their approach, searching the dark near-distance. There they were; pastel smudges dotted here and there, irregular shapes strewn on the grass between the angles and lines of the tombstones. He felt his palms slicken, and wiped them instinctively on the dark wool of his coat. He turned back to his sergeant, a man with a nose so narrow and hooked that he put Forrester in mind of a gigantic bird, and nodded mutely. The sergeant spun on his heels and whispered orders down the wait-ing line.

Out of the darkness came dozens of bright orange lights. The risk of an errant spark alerting the enemy had been too great for Forrester to entertain, especially given the inexperience of his new charges, and he had ordered that only two of his musket-eers carry lighted matches on the march out of Basing. Now that they were safely here, the glowing tips were brought to life and passed back along the line. He had thirty raiders, drawn mostly from Rawdon's yellowcoats, and it was a matter of moments before all thirty men had the means to ignite the charges already set inside their weapons.

Forrester pushed out through the branches. Colonel Rawdon's spies had reported that the half-company billeted at Holy-bourne's church were only setting pickets to the south of the village, presumably expecting trouble to come from the estab-lished highway. Forrester thanked God, for he saw that the information had been correct, and only silence greeted his advance. At his back he could hear the rustling of branches as his men inched on to the long grass, skirting the first crooked stones, edging ever closer to their sleeping prize. He glanced over his shoulder, waving frantically for them to fan out in a wide arc.

A shout went up. He knew instantly that it had not come from one of his men. He drew his sword, the ringing of steel sounding unnaturally loud in the blackness. More shouts came from among the stones. The shapes were shifting, melding blotches of grey like so many wraiths. The enemy was awake. Forrester drew breath into his lungs. His mouth was saltpetre-dry.

'*Fire!*'

Flame roared out from the thirty muskets, sparking pans turned to tongues of fire in the jet darkness. A dense volley of shots rippled along the yellow-coated line to spawn a vast, roiling cloud of white smoke that billowed immediately at their front, scudding out and up, obscuring the cemetery as though a thick fog had descended. But they heard the screams. Shrill and blood-freezing, splitting the darkness as though the very gates of hell had been flung open in this quiet little village.

'*Forward!*' Forrester bellowed. 'On! On! On!' The momentum was with his men, and he would not let it slip. He advanced through the powder smoke, revelling in the familiar stink of rotten eggs, feeling exhilaration bring strength to his limbs and sharpness to his senses. The enemy would be reeling, he knew, stumbling backwards, bleary-eyed and stunned, still hoping against hope that this was all some horrific nightmare. He swung his sword in a high arc. 'Reverse your muskets, damn your hides! Give 'em a battering, by God!'

The sergeant was with him, his own sword naked and gleaming, and then Forrester saw the rest as they stepped through the smoke. They snarled and crowed, teeth bared like wild dogs scenting the kill, muskets turned about to present wooden stocks that would club a man like the heaviest cudgel imaginable.

The enemy were close. Half a dozen bodies threw twisted shapes on the ground to Forrester's front, but most had survived that first volley, and they were beginning to gather their bearings and regroup near the doorway of the church. Some frantically scrabbled at muskets, but it was difficult to load the weapons in the dark, and near impossible with a howling band of killers closing in, and most turned the long-arms about to meet the threat, while others tossed them away in favour of steel. There were probably forty, Forrester reckoned. Enough to bloody his party's noses if allowed to gain some semblance of order, and he pressed in quickly, breaking into a run and yearning to hear the steps of his men at his back.

He hit the first man hard. The fellow was taller, wielding a wicked-looking partisan that glinted in the moonlight, and Forrester realized that he must be one of the officers. He ducked under a wild swing, kicking the man between the legs, and brought the heavy pommel of his sword down at the exposed temple. The officer crumpled with a grunt, not even managing to put his arms out to break his fall. Another man darted from the pack near the doorway, brandishing a reversed musket that he jabbed out at Forrester's head. The move was slow, easily read, and Forrester side-stepped calmly, thrusting the point of his blade at his opponent's throat. He did not stay to see what damage had been caused, jerking back the steel and moving on while the man slumped, gargling, to his knees.

The men of Marmaduke Rawdon's Regiment of Foot surged on, leaping the black patches of long-cooled fires, swarming about their leader for this night's killing, screaming banshee cries at the moon. Forrester could just make out his own party, thankful for the yellow coats that gave them a wan glow in the night. His blood rushed, his senses razor-keen. He told himself he hated battle. It was moments like this that made him realize such sentiments were false, however well meant. Another man lurched out from the shadows by the church wall, emerging in Forrester's face as if from nowhere, and it was all he could do to parry the sword that flickered at his throat. He hit the man, noticing his coat of light green as he drove his free fist squarely at the exposed chin, but it was just a glance, merely forcing his opponent to take a step back. But that step met with the body of a prone Parliamentarian, blood still jetting from a tear in the side of his neck, and Forrester's challenger lost his footing. Forrester seized his chance without consideration, leaping at the floundering rebel before he could find his balance, barrelling into his unarmoured chest. The pair fell, careening over the bleeding body and landing in a tangle of limbs on the rough ground.

Neither man kept hold of his sword, and it became a battle of hands, each clawing at the throat of the other, scrambling for purchase, searching for soft flesh, desperate to lock tight and squeeze. Forrester was on top. He was the heavier of the two, and he used his whole weight to pin the Roundhead, grinding him into the grass and crushing the wind from him. The man's mouth flapped open, gasping for air, and Forrester was assailed by a blast of fetid breath. He slammed his forehead down, butting the greencoat squarely on the bridge of his nose. He was rewarded by a splintering crunch. The man slumped back and Forrester rolled away, scrambling quickly to his feet. When he gathered his senses, he saw the greencoat rise to his knees, but then his own sergeant was there, the hooked nose prominent in the gloom, stepping smartly across the wheezing greencoat and bringing his halberd up in a crashing blow that scraped across the exposed chest. The coat flapped open, slashed from naval to sternum, and the emerald wool was suddenly dark, the shadow growing with every beat of the rebel's failing heart. He fell back, eyes staring sightlessly at the night sky.

Forrester nodded his thanks to the sergeant, stooped to retrieve his blade, and looked to the next opponent. But none came from the dark.

'It is over, lads!' he called. 'They'll not be back this night! You've done well!' He paused for a desultory cheer to ripple through the ranks. 'Now let us be rid of the bodies, and we'll get some rest.' He looked at the sergeant. 'Set pickets. Make sure I am not proved a fool, eh?'

The sergeant nodded. 'Very good, sir.'

Lancelot Forrester watched the young men of Rawdon's

regiment. They chattered excitedly as they stripped and searched the corpses for valuables. They had proved themselves, and he did not begrudge them their joy. In the morning they would realize the peril to which they had been exposed, but for now, awash with exhilaration and relief, they deserved happiness. He sheathed his sword and went to light a fire.

They stirred just as dawn cracked across the horizon. No one had slept, too excited were they by their overwhelming victory, but Forrester had insisted they rest about the fires. The long march home would come with first light, and he was unwilling to risk lingering in the area.

'How many, Dewhurst?' Forrester asked as the sergeant walked over to him from the direction of the rebel bodies.

John Dewhurst, known as the Hawk by his yellow-coated charges, drove the butt end of his halberd into the dew-softened turf and leaned against it. 'Baker's dozen, sir.'

Forrester glanced towards the flint wall of the church, where the thirteen naked bodies had been arranged in a line. 'All theirs?'

Dewhurst's head nodded in short, staccato movements. 'Aye, sir. Ours are all accounted for. Few scratches, but nowt that'll snuff a man out, unless it turns bad.'

'Good,' Forrester said, turning away so that he was not caught smiling at the Hawk's pecking. He scanned the makeshift encampment; the wisps from dowsed fires dancing with tobacco smoke, the rasp of steel being sharpened, the chatter of men as they broke their fast with rock-hard bread and skins of weak ale. He looked back at Dewhurst. 'You have my thanks, Sergeant.'

'Sir?'

'Chopping that man,' Forrester said.

Dewhurst wiped the red tip of his nose with a grubby sleeve. 'You were doing well enough, sir. Know how to fight, an' no mistake.' He ventured a wry smile. 'But squashing the bugger's a new one on me, beggin' your pardon, sir.'

'I'll thank you to mind your manners, Sergeant,' Forrester

replied sharply, before breaking into an amused snort as he patted the taut coat stretched over his midriff. 'Though I confess it is not often that my size plays to my advantage.' He watched the men as they made ready to march. 'Fought like lions, Sergeant, did they not? Colonel Rawdon will be pleased.'

Dewhurst pecked the air. 'Proud of 'em, sir. Still, experienced officers are hard to come by for new regiments. They learnt a few things.'

Forrester acknowledged the compliment with a dismissive wave of his hand. 'Then we are each content with our night's work.'

'Long walk home then, sir?' said Dewhurst as he jerked the halberd from the soil, using it like a shepherd's crook as he walked away.

'As soon as we might,' Forrester returned. 'The better part of valour is discretion.' He sighed when Dewhurst turned to cast him a blank expression. '*Henry the Fourth, Part I.*' He shook his head in exasperation. 'Let us be on the move.'

Southampton, Hampshire, 7 October 1643

The shouts were deafening. Norton had been summoned from his quarters in the tavern near the West Gate by a messenger saying only that Southampton's disgruntled aldermen wished to meet with him. He had at once ridden out, but somehow the ordinary folk had got wind of the meeting and in moments a crowd had gathered. And they were baying for blood, clamouring to reach him as he dismounted at the steps of the Bar Gate. Near fifty of his troopers had escorted him, and they moved their mounts into a half-moon around the foot of the steps, hedging him as he met the party of dour city elders, who trundled down from the grand building. One of the aldermen held out a hand for Norton to shake and said something, but the din was overwhelming. Norton pulled an expression of apology and turned to face the crowd. 'Hold, good people, please! Be at your peace!'

Captain Kovac was one of the protective horsemen, and he brought his bay round a fraction so that he could see Norton. 'They will not shut their mouths, sir.'

'I can see that, Wagner.'

Kovac sniffed the chill air into his bulbous nose. 'You want me fix?'

Norton nodded. 'Aye.'

Kovac drew a pistol from his saddle holster, primed and cocked it, and fired into the air. The pack collectively gasped and juddered back, people at the very rear stumbling under the sheer weight of retreating bodies. A small pall of white smoke slewed out over their heads. All fell silent.

Norton strode to a place just to the rear of his bristling cordon. 'Now let me speak to your elders in a civilized manner,' he called. He turned to the alderman who had extended his hand. 'You summoned me here. What manner of grievance do you harbour that it must be laid at the feet of a soldier? You have a governor. What place is this where he is not given leave to govern?'

The alderman had seen at least seventy winters, Norton guessed, for his beardless face was wrinkled and lined. 'It is just such governance that brings them hither, Colonel,' he replied in a frail voice. 'They rail against Murford's hard ways.'

Norton shrugged. 'These are hard times.'

'And this is a Parliamentarian city,' the alderman retorted, thin wisps of vapour curling from his mouth as he spoke. 'It has been so from the start. Murford rules in the manner of an occupying enemy.'

'He is a tyrant!' a woman's voice shrieked from the crowd. Immediately a chorus of similar cries went up, echoing against the houses and shops of the street, causing a hundred birds to flee into the grey clouds at once.

'Aye!' the alderman agreed, his aged voice becoming stronger now that he had the overt assent of the mob. 'It is a tyrant I have sent my sons and grandsons to overthrow. We shall not have one here while they are gone.'

The mob cheered and jeered, and it surged, pulsing from back to front so that the foremost of its number collided with the chests of the horses. Those beasts whinnied and reared, a couple kicked, and the pulse waned, folding back on itself like a wave hitting rocks.

Norton turned back to look at the delegation. His regiment had been in Southampton for just two days, and he had busied himself with arranging supplies, writing notes to Westminster and plotting his designs upon the rest of the county. Yet mutterings had reached his ears of disgruntled citizens unhappy with Murford's rough tactics. He had dismissed them, but perhaps, he reflected as the noise reached a deafening crescendo, the resentment was a more deep-rooted problem than he had assumed. He planted his hands on his hips. 'Well?'

The alderman set his jaw. 'Murford's excesses destroy this fine place as sure as any of the Cavaliers who might threaten us. He taxes us to the hilt to fund his revelry.'

'Revelry?'

'A banquet, for his own pleasure! He took the coin from our purses with menaces. Threats of plunder and violence.'

Another city elder came forwards, moving to his colleague's side now that the die had been cast. 'The villain pulled down the picture of Queen Bess from above Bar Gate!' he decried with shaking fists. 'He claimed this tribulation was Her Majesty's own fault. For if her reformation had been prosecuted with true faith and vigour, our current strife would be avoided.' The veins were visible on the man's temples as he spoke. 'I may be a Parliament man, sir, but I would never speak ill of so venerable a sovereign. No, Colonel, the scoundrel is rotten to his core.'

It was the coldest morning of the autumn so far, and the biting air made the skin itch about Norton's cheeks and neck. It was all he could do not to fling away his gloves and tear at himself with fingernails. 'And what would you have me do?'

'Do, Colonel Norton?' a new voice bellowed from atop the gate. 'You'll do nothing if you wish to remain within my walls.'

Norton looked up to see a short, heavy-jowled man. 'Governor Murford, I was merely—'

'Your men have spread out like the French Welcome,' Peter Murford interrupted, 'in homes and shops and taverns. There are horses stabled in our churches.'

'And I thank you for it,' Norton replied.

Murford's fleshy cheeks trembled as he cleared his throat noisily. 'You thank me by inciting revolt amongst my people?'

'I do no such thing, sir!' Norton retorted. 'I came to speak with the aldermen, to take their words and messages back to London. *Your* people descended upon me like the locusts of Exodus.'

'*Pah*!' Murford exclaimed, waving a chubby fist in the air. 'They are perfectly contented, sir.'

Norton gritted his teeth. 'They seem perfectly discontented, sir.'

Murford's little eyes raked across the angry faces ranged before them. 'I do not believe such slander.'

'Look for yourself, sir,' Norton replied mercilessly. He cupped a hand to his ear. 'Listen. A tide appears to rise against you, does it not?'

Murford had turned deathly pale and looked as though he might vomit over the Bar Gate's rampart. 'You are a rogue and a blackguard, sir. Your presence ignites the flames of dissent.' He uncurled a fist, extending his forefinger to point accusingly at the red-haired colonel of horse. 'No longer are your disreputable men welcome in this city, Norton. No longer, I say! I want you gone. The whole regiment. Out of here this very moment!'

It was then that Richard Norton had an epiphany. Hampshire was a lawless place. Godly towns like Southampton and Poole were counterbalanced by malignant hives like Winchester or Basing. The countryside in between was a dangerous frontier infested by brigands and deserters, patrolled only by smaller units such as his own, fighting petty wars for every crossroad, bridge and ford, every village, every road, hillock and copse. It pained Norton because he was a Hampshire man. His estates were at Southwick, his kin spread from the coast to the Downs, and he had long yearned to bring it under Parliament's heel, for the good of the people. But how? He was free of Essex's field army for the time being, able to impose his veteran horsemen upon the land, and yet he could never hope to build something permanent without a real base. A bridgehead from which to launch his private campaigns. But here, now, the opportunity had presented itself; it was as a lightning bolt to his mind, delivered by the hand of God Himself. He showed Murford his back, pacing the few yards to where his horse waited in the midst of the twitchy cavalry cordon. With the governor's incensed oaths ringing in his ears, he took the reins from a gentleman trooper and clambered up into the saddle, wheeling the beast about to face the mob.

'Would you have me go, good people?' Norton bellowed. As he expected, the crowd screamed their opposition. He wrenched on the reins again, this time coaxing the horse from the protective line and back to the foot of the stone stairs. The aldermen scattered like starlings in the face of a cat, and Norton stared up at Murford, still standing upon the rampart. 'They do not feel safe without me, it seems. Though is it the Cavaliers they fear, or their own governor?'

'How dare you, sir—' Murford blustered. 'How dare you! *Men*!' He looked left and right, seeking the assistance of his garrison. Half a dozen musketeers had come down from the Bar Gate and, though they responded smartly enough to the cry, the presence of so many of Norton's cavalrymen kept their pieces firmly shouldered.

'Sensible fellows,' Norton observed.

Murford's jowls shook violently. 'To it, men!' he persisted, pointing at Norton. 'Take him!'

'Try,' another voice rose above the clamouring crowd. Norton looked to his right to see Wagner Kovac's white-bearded face. The Croat's icy gaze was locked upon the governor's nervous men. 'For love of God, try, I beg you.'

Norton grinned. 'Captain Kovac yearns for a scuffle, as you

can see. It has been a great many days since he killed a man.' The musketeers seemed to baulk at the threat, some freezing where they stood, a couple edging back up the steps.

Murford raged on, crimson-faced. The elderly alderman took to the bottom step, positioning himself between Norton and Murford, his milk-white palms raised in supplication. 'Colonel Norton. We would have you as our governor.'

'By what right?' Murford spluttered, thrusting his lank hair to the side of his forehead.

The alderman threw him a look of pity. 'He is the power here, Murford. We need his strength.'

'This—this is—Insurrection!'

'He is the only man able to guarantee our safety,' the alderman replied. He turned to Norton. 'Will you answer our plea, sir?'

Richard Norton had forgotten the dreadful itch that so often made his life a misery. Instead his heart swelled and his mind soared. He thanked God, and offered a solemn nod. 'I will.'

St Mary's, Isles of Scilly, 7 October 1643

'You are a mulatto?' Stryker murmured, trying to think of something to divert his interrogators from their infernal questions. He lay on his side. The air carried the tang of vomit, though he had become almost inured to it now. It astonished him how much damage mere seawater could do. Fassett had intimated that his hirelings had urinated – or worse – in the brackish, filthy concoction, which might have exacerbated the effect, but ultimately it was the salt that burned his innards and turned his guts to a mess of twisted anguish.

Sterne Fassett had brought a low stool into the room this time, and he perched on its edge, cradling the jug in his lap. 'The man who stuck his pizzle in my bitch of a mother was a blackamoor. A sailor. I knew him not. And I hated her.' His face split in amusement. 'Perhaps that is why I am such a bastard.'

Stryker did not know how long it had been. He thought he

had counted two days and nights, but he was too confused, too weakened, too agonized to know for sure.

Sterne Fassett had returned as promised. His obedient creatures, Squires and Cordell, had pinned Stryker again, though with increasing ease, and more of the foul liquid had been sent into Stryker's stomach, searing him, purging him. More questions had come. He had railed at them in return, threatened their lives, to which the echoes of laughter had broken through his spasms like distant thunder. And then nothing. They had gone once more, leaving him crumpled and retching, passing hours with only the sound of his gargling chest and the crashing ocean for company. It was only now, after so many lonely hours, that they had paid him this most recent visit, and he had wanted to weep as the lock had clunked in the door.

He was as weak and brittle as dry leaves, unable to eat the food that was offered, and never able to quench his torturous thirst with the paltry amount of fresh water they had allowed. He knew the pattern, of course. They did not want him dead, not quickly, and seawater would kill a man in days if he did not dilute it with the fresh equivalent. So they offered him tiny amounts, enough to keep his body from shutting down altogether, yet never enough to slake the gnawing need that would slowly drive him mad. They were dragging the torment along, spinning it out like a mile-long thread, weakening their prisoner, crushing his spirit, until he would say anything to cut that thread and make the horror end. But he would not speak. They already knew why he had sailed to Scilly, but they did not know to which island he had been bound, and that thought sustained him in the cold and dark of his cell.

He tilted his head up to look at Fassett. 'What happened to your nose?'

'Whore-runner in St Giles.'

'You refused to pay?'

'*Ha*!' Fassett barked. He shook his head. 'I never pay. I was working a job for one of the fat bugger's rivals. Visited him to . . . *suggest* . . . he move his operation elsewhere. In truth my

94

employer fancied the look of some of the blubber-belly's Winchester Geese.' He licked his lips slowly. 'Some juicier cunnies you'd be hard pressed to find, I'll give him that.'

'The fellow took exception?' Stryker mumbled.

'Of course!' Fassett flicked the stubby nose, severed so unnaturally flat half-way down its length. 'Came at me with a bleedin' cleaver.'

'And he now lies at the bottom of the Thames . . .'

Fassett fiddled with one of his few remaining teeth. 'Along with a great many more.' He slid off the stool so suddenly that Stryker flinched, causing him to smile. 'Worry not, Captain. I do not intend to share my special claret with you today.'

A shiver of hope ran up Stryker's spine. It was only when he looked up at the grinning Fassett that he knew the truth, and his pathetic gullibility made him sicker than any amount of the foul potion. 'You damned liar.'

He screwed shut his eyes, twisting away with all his might as the dark shapes of Squires and Cordell advanced upon him.

CHAPTER 7

Basing House, Hampshire, 9 October 1643

'I understand your reticence, Captain. The territory is danger-ous.'

Sir John Paulet, Fifth Marquess of Winchester, paced slowly through the bustling agricultural enclosure known as the Grange.

Captain Lancelot Forrester kept pace at Paulet's side. 'It has nothing to do with danger, my lord, I assure you. I was sent here to deliver my message to you, and that is what I did.' He stared at a large bird of prey as it wheeled silently above the distant trees. 'But you have kept me here, my lord.'

Paulet slowed down, lacing his fingers behind his back. 'You make it sound as though you are my prisoner, Captain Forrester.'

'I am certain that was not his intention,' Colonel Marmaduke Rawdon said. He walked on Paulet's other flank, leaning back slightly to shoot Forrester a caustic look as he spoke.

Forrester cleared his throat awkwardly. 'Not at all, not at all. Indeed, I have been happy to assist in the blooding of Colonel Rawdon's troops, my lord, for I believe our mutual masters at Oxford would have me employed in such worthwhile service while the army remains inactive.'

Paulet seemed happy with that, his pace increasing again. 'Then what is your new concern, sir?'

'May I?' Rawdon cut in, perhaps reading Forrester's appre-hension. 'Captain Forrester is too respectful to say, my lord, but he is a soldier. The command of a sortie against the enemy is his meat and drink. What you now propose is something more clandestine. He is not comfortable with such a plan.'

Paulet's brow climbed up his thin head as he turned to the captain. 'What say you, sir?'

'I am a soldier, my lord,' Forrester said, having to bite his tongue to bring some moisture into his mouth, 'not a spy.'

Paulet stopped. They were beside the Great Barn, the vast brick storehouse that would soon be crammed to its soaring rafters ready for winter. 'My house is full of soldiers, Captain Forrester. Men ready to fight for their king. But the soldiers are green as cabbage, the commanders are elderly, and the rest are peaceful fellows. Poets, artists and the like. Driven here by men of the new religion. A religion that covets brutality and strength over beauty and contemplation.' He began to walk again, either missing Rawdon's reddening complexion or choosing to ignore it. 'Tell me, Captain. Which of those would you send with my warrant?'

Paulet had backed him into a corner and, when all was said and done, Forrester had no recourse but to agree. Paulet, after all, had a point. He was the best man to perform the task, however much he disliked the notion. 'I will go with a happy heart, my lord.'

Paulet beamed. 'And you will have my eternal thanks.' He snapped his fingers, summoning a servant, who sprang from beyond the soldiers to produce a folded rectangle of pale parchment. Paulet handed it to Forrester. 'Take this warrant to our agents in the county. It must be proclaimed wherever possible. Alton tonight, Petersfield the morrow, and as far south as Rowlands Castle. It beseeches all right-minded subjects of our faithful sovereign to dig deep in their coffers. We must raise money for the defence of the realm and the destruction of our great enemy.'

'I understand, my lord,' Forrester said dutifully, half expecting the marquess to ask him to break into Portsmouth itself. He looked down at the warrant. It was a small thing, nondescript. A piece of folded, sealed vellum within which, he could imagine, some words had been scrawled in the educated hand of the Marquess of Winchester. But those words, Forrester knew, contained an incendiary power. The marquess had taken the decision to raise the stakes in Hampshire's regional war. Forrester did not know whether it was in response to Killigrew's order to make a nuisance of himself, or whether he somehow felt that, in spite of the order, Basing could become a major force in the longer term; a genuine fortress in the south-east, rather than the persistent itch that Killigrew was keen to encourage. For now he presumed it mattered not. It was a warrant for the gathering of funds to help the Royalist cause, and he would be the one to deliver it. And that meant, once again, Forrester's life would be in danger.

St Mary's, Isles of Scilly, 9 October 1643

The first thing Stryker noticed was a metallic jangle. He could not place the sound. Too many days had been wasted in this private hell with only the sea and the wind and the grinding of his own teeth for company. His ears were playing tricks on him. When the door at last had opened, he had been sure that Simeon Barkworth was in the dark with him, speaking with that constricted, croaking voice. It had been the creak of the hinges, of course. Barkworth was gone. Held elsewhere with the rest of the captives or long dead, for all he knew. The door had swung open only to reveal the glowering visages of his tormentors. When they had left him, grown bored and frustrated with his stubborn responses, he had been certain that the door had been left ajar, the opportunity of escape gloriously afforded to him. It was only when he had rolled through his own filth to reach the studded timber that he had seen the truth. It had all been an illusion.

And yet this day, above a whipping wind that was angrier than before, the jangling continued unabated. Stryker lay there, blinking hard, his eye stinging viciously. He forced himself to sit up, gasping as his mind swam so that his empty guts cramped. He stared through the gloom at the door. It was open. He blinked again and again. Nothing changed. Then the noise once more. So rhythmic and purposeful. A figure resolved below the lintel as his eye began to adjust to the light coming from out in the passage beyond.

'Spurs,' Stryker whispered to himself. He shuffled back, recalling that Sterne Fassett did not wear them, and stared hard at the newcomer. 'Who is it?'

The man performed a half-turn and swept an arm towards the open door. 'Come.'

They walked through the poorly lit passage. Stryker moved slowly, in the lead, almost shuffling, for his innards screamed and his legs seemed empty of strength. The man behind did not hurry him. He was cloaked and hooded, the jangling of his steps his only sound. Fassett and his men were nowhere to be seen, but Stryker could not allow himself to consider anything but the worst explanation. He decided, while he loped painfully between the dank walls with their flickering braziers, that, wherever they were headed, a noose would be waiting.

They came out into daylight. It was a courtyard – the area between the large central keep and the star-shaped outer wall. The ground was muddy but quite firm, though the clouds threatened violence as they scudded upon the whistling wind. Stryker swayed a little and adjusted his stance to compensate for the lack of balance. He looked up at the high walls. There were gun batteries at intervals all around the sharp projections of the eight-pointed ring, providing covering fire in every direction. The fort would be a formidable opponent for any ship attempting to threaten Hugh Town, the island's capital, which lay a short way to the east.

'Impressive in its own way, do you not think?' the hooded man said.

Stryker turned, revelling in the freshness of the building gale against his face, but was quickly stunned by what he saw. The cowl hid most of the man's head, but it billowed outwards, flapping in the wind, and he could glimpse skin that was heavily pitted, entirely hairless and white as milk, save the lips, that were thin and deeply purple. 'Impressive?'

'Star Castle. Built by the Tudors, it protects the Hugh well. A kind of stoic beauty.' He lifted an arm, heavy with the voluminous grey sleeve, and traced the course of the rampart. 'But it is the encircling defences that truly impress. The outer face forms an eight-pointed star in plan. A covered entrance passage passes through the rampart on the north-east. Simple and effective to my mind.'

'You are a soldier?' Stryker stared at this strange man.

'I do hope that Mister Fassett,' the hooded man said, ignoring the question, 'has not been unkind to you in my absence.'

So this was the employer his torturers had alluded to. Stryker hawked a wad of viscous spittle into his dry mouth and spat it into the void between them. 'You jest, sir.'

The man laughed, It was a hoarse, strained sound. 'Indeed I do! Fassett has a nasty streak, I am afraid.'

Stryker coughed, forcing him to double forwards. 'So do the others,' he said when he had straightened. 'The half-wit and the corpse.'

'Very good, Captain! Though not entirely right. Locke Squires . . . the half-wit, as you put it . . . is not the fool you take him for. He betrayed Fassett, many years ago, and lost his tongue for what, you must agree, was a terribly poor decision. Clay Cordell was struck with the plague as a stripling. He survived it, but, as you've evidently noticed, it left him rather pallid.'

Stryker took a tentative pace to the side so that he might get a better look at the eerie face. He forced a malicious smile. 'And what is your excuse?'

The hood turned so that the face within peered out squarely at Stryker. It was like something from a nightmare, taut like a drum-skin, though not clear and smooth, but blemished and patchy, almost as though it had been ravaged by disease. Except

Stryker knew that it was no disease, for his own face had suffered something akin to this horror. It was a burn, a suspicion only confirmed by the lack of brow or lash about his eyes. It put Stryker in mind of a dead man, a walking, talking, breathing cadaver, risen from the tomb by some satanic spell. Only the eyes themselves had life. They were blue, impossibly bright, like flaming sapphires. 'What a pair we make,' he said quietly, before staring directly into Stryker's lone grey eye. 'How many did you lose?'

For a moment Stryker forgot the pain. 'How many?'

'When your ship foundered.'

Stryker braced himself at the memory of the cold, choking, burning, tumbling abyss. 'Too many.'

'But you had many to begin with. I envy you.'

'Envy me?'

The pale head nodded. 'Your masters are keen to recover the Cade fortune. I do not blame them. I would have brought an entire company too.' His narrow mouth turned down at the corners. 'But where to find such numbers when we are losing the war? Besides, my predecessor's feeble efforts have left Whitehall with a sour taste for the whole affair. Thus, I am left with my paltry team. Four of us to win this infernal prize.' He turned, leading the way to a small door set into the wall of the central house. A group of soldiers milled at its entrance. They shied away like scolded children at his approach. He gave an amused grunt. 'Fortunately the garrison have the sense to fear we four.'

'They are not soldierly men.'

'No, they are not.' He opened the door, showing Stryker in to what appeared to be a storage room. Light streamed in through two large windows, though it was plain and sparse, save the dozen hogsheads stacked against one wall. A door was positioned near one corner, apparently leading into the inner sanctum of the building, which, to all intents and purposes, was Star Castle's keep. The blue eyes swivelled around. 'Captain Stryker. When I learnt it was you who sailed for the Scillies . . . well—' He flashed a smile full of teeth so white that they seemed out of kilter in a face so ravaged. 'When last I saw you, you were locked in the house of Sir Richard Wynn at Brentford. Of course I was a might different then. I was an ambitious young thing. Handsome, if I might say so myself. A good officer in my own way.'

Stryker simply stared. Sir Richard Wynn's house, to the west of Brentford, had been the place where the first blood had been shed in the Cavaliers' great play for the capital. But the fine house would forever be etched on Stryker's memory, for, while Prince Rupert's cavalry had clashed all around it with the red-coated foot regiments of Denzil Holles, he and his men had been engaged in their own fight for survival in Wynn's deep cellar. Stryker had escaped to join the battle, and a man named Malachi Bain, one of the villains who had taken his left eye so many years before, had met his death. Yet it was another who had condemned Stryker to that God-forsaken hole. A young officer of horse. A tall, golden-haired and black-armoured Parliamentarian who perished, Stryker had been led to believe, later that same day.

'Brentford Fight,' Stryker said. 'Tainton, isn't it?' He searched the pallid face, finding a hint of something he recognized in those twinkling eyes. He strove to hold his stunned revulsion in check, and yet, even as he spoke, he felt bile rise in his throat. The man he thought deceased had risen from the grave, turned by death into something monstrous. 'Yes. Captain Tainton. I remember you.'

The man swept back the hood. His pate was bald, the skin a patchwork of white and pink. 'Now plain Roger Tainton. No commission for me.'

'I heard what happened,' Stryker said. After all, he had had the incident recounted to him by the very person who had sent Tainton to his fate.

Tainton's white skin seemed to darken as though layered with a film of ash. 'Headlong into a vat of pitch. Left to drown like your comrades.' He touched thin fingertips to a cheek. 'Singed me quite well, I'm sure you'll agree. Took a while to heal.'

'And now?'

'Now I am as staunchly for the cause of King Jesus as ever I was. More so, in fact, for it was His hand that healed my broken form. All I do is for Him. For His glory. But I do not see as well as I did, and I cannot ride so effortlessly. Even my armour is a chore to don.'

Stryker looked down. 'Why the spurs?'

Tainton managed a tight smile. 'A reminder of what once was, Captain. Now I work outside of the field armies. Much like yourself. I have gained something of a reputation, if I may be so proud. A reward of faith after my—tribulation.' He closed his eyes, his voice dropping to barely a whisper. 'If we confess our sins, he is faithful and just to forgive us sins, and to cleanse us from all unrighteousness.' The eyelids sprung up to reveal a gaze that was suddenly serene. 'One John, chapter one, verse nine.'

Stryker thought back to the young officer who had been his foe at Brentford. That man had thrived upon war, relished his self-importance and his gleaming black armour, his fine troop of horse and the destiny that seemed both lofty and preordained. He might have invoked God in justification for his acts, but he was no zealot. But suffering, he knew all too well, could change a man. 'How do you know about the gold?'

'That is of no consequence.'

'Balthazar believes you are Royalists,' Stryker pressed, because for him, the matter was of vast consequence. Stryker had been sent after Newbury Fight with his half-company to locate and retrieve the Cade treasure, a mission known only to the Royalist high command. The Roundheads knew of its existence. Indeed, they had held Cecily Cade, Sir Alfred's daughter, hostage for much of the summer in an attempt to break her resolve, but she had guarded the location of the gold with a stubborn courage that had protected the prize and, ultimately, ensured that she would sacrifice her own life for it. She had whispered the location of her inheritance to Stryker as she lay dying, a crossbow bolt intended for the king lodged in her breast. There was no suggestion in Stryker's mind that she might have given up her secret to another living soul. And yet here, on a remote island of Scilly, was Roger Tainton, risen from the grave and seeking that same fortune.

'Captain Balthazar is a fool,' Tainton said. ' He and his garrison believe I am here on secret Crown business. Moreover, they know that you, Mister Stryker, are the commander of a Parliamentarian assault party, foiled by the sea and incarcerated by the brave islanders. Balthazar is a meek sort. Fear grips him when he looks into my eyes.'

'You knew I was coming,' Stryker said. 'Probably with many men.'

'I was not lying in wait for you, Captain,' Tainton replied, shaking his head. 'I had prayed God would reveal the gold to me before your arrival. We were supposed to be away from here days ago.' He went to the far door.

'Where are you taking me?'

Tainton gripped the door's iron ring. 'I must find the gold, Captain. I have spent the better part of a week searching Hugh Town and the interior of St Mary's, but to no avail. I cannot waste any more time with speculative digs.' With his free hand he pointed at Stryker. 'But you must know where it is. The Royalist grandees would not send their best man . . . and resourced so well . . . without some idea of where the Cade hoard is hidden.' He pursed his thin, purple lips. 'Mister Fassett tells me you have not been helpful, despite your privations.'

'Who is he?'

'Fassett?' Tainton shrugged. 'My creature. A Godless thing, but a hard man, tough fighter and loyal to a fault if paid well enough. I use him on occasion. He wanted to put out your eye, you know.'

'That is what I'd have done, were I him,' Stryker said.

Tainton nodded. 'Seems logical enough, but I do not think it would make you talk. And, as you have said, our success here turns upon what William Balthazar chooses to believe. The mutilation of prisoners may just be enough to compel him to grow some stones and ask some questions. I would rather he left me to my work. But no matter. I have other means.'

That sent a stab of worry through Stryker. 'My men?' he asked, a little too hastily, immediately chiding himself for the show of weakness.

'Goodness, no!' said Tainton. 'If I know you at all, Captain Stryker, then you won't have disclosed the information to your compatriots, for just such a reason as this. Besides, I cannot be seen slicing up captured Parliamentarians without arousing our hosts' suspicions. Your men are safe. Balthazar can hand them over for trial, if he wishes.' His taut face contorted in what Stryker guessed was a grin. '*Ha*! He will get a rude awakening when they're identified as king's men! By which time, of course, you will be long dead and I'll be long gone.'

'You'll kill me?'

'Most certainly,' said Tainton. 'I can explain away one or two deaths, and yours would give me tremendous pleasure. After all, it was your association that led to my sad demise.'

'Then why would I tell you the location of the gold? What could possibly compel me?'

That strange expression again, a twisted concoction of delight and malice. He turned the iron loop and pushed open the door. 'I'm so glad you ask, Captain.'

The woman on the other side of the door was short, blonde and angry. She was dressed like a man in shirt, breeches and riding boots, her long hair cascading in tousled golden strands across shoulders that were pinned between the spindly frame of Clay Cordell and the meaty stature of Locke Squires. She struggled with them, twisted and thrashed in their grip, spat and cursed and pledged their demise. Behind her, a glinting dirk in his fist, Sterne Fassett was positioned, his face strained, like a man struggling to tame a wild beast.

To Stryker's eye it was as though they had snared an angel, and his body, so depleted of strength, so raw at its core, was invigorated in that moment. He did not know whether to laugh or cry. In the event, the contrasting emotions each held the other in check, so that he stood, dumbfounded. He had dreamt of seeing her again, had been terrified that she was dead – lost at sea or murdered by Tainton – but he had been too afraid to mention her presence, lest she remain at large on this wave-lashed archipelago. Now that she was here, even captive as she was, a great, bubbling torrent of relief coursed through him. And Fassett's expression, his stern poise, as though he dealt with a furious lioness, gave him cause for much pleasure. 'I hope you have not given them trouble, Lisette.'

Lisette Gaillard, favourite agent of Queen Henrietta Maria, let her glowering features shift into the hint of a smile. 'I have been sweetness itself, *mon amour.*'

The huge man, Squires, seemed to shy away even as she spoke, and Fassett lifted his blade to the space between Lisette's shoulders. 'A she-devil! A witching whore! Let us cut her up and be done with it.'

Roger Tainton shook his head, the skin wrinkling and pulling with the motion. 'All in good time, Mister Fassett.'

They ushered Lisette into the room, pushing her hard so that she barrelled into Stryker. He caught her, though he nearly toppled, so weak was he, but he swept his arms about her, clinging to her as though she were the spar that had saved him after the *Kestrel* had gone to the raging abyss. She looked into his face and he wondered whether she might cry, such was the anguish that came into her eyes.

'What have they done to you?' she said, her accent more pronounced than usual as the strain took hold. Her hands were bound, but she raised them both, scraping his new beard with light fingertips. 'I will kill them.'

'What have they done to *you*?' Stryker replied hotly, his mind reeling with horrific possibilities.

'Be calm, sir,' Tainton cut in. 'I am a man of God. I do not torture women. We stumbled upon her, in truth. She came to greet us in port, would you believe?'

'No,' Stryker said, 'I would not.'

Tainton chuckled softly. 'Can you imagine my surprise upon laying these poor eyes on her? Naturally we kept her in our company, though I confess she has been of no help.'

'Should have flayed her alive,' Sterne Fassett growled, turning his blade so that the light slid up the length of the wicked steel. 'If her skin peels, she'll squeal, that's what I always say.'

'Very poetic,' Tainton said. 'But, as I have told you before, she and I have crossed paths, and swords, before. She would never talk.'

Fassett sniffed derisively. 'You fought her?'

Tainton's blue eyes seemed to blaze as he stared at the diminutive Frenchwoman. 'At Brentford.'

'Where we smashed the Roundhead barricades,' Stryker cut in to deflect Tainton's building ire.

The bald head did not flinch. 'That is, I was present at Brentford Fight. For my part, I was engaged in a rather more personal duel. One that ended in—' he traced a circle in the air before his face. 'This.'

Fassett indicated Stryker with the point of his dirk. 'He did that to you?'

'I did it, you pig-nosed bastard,' Lisette blurted, stunning Fassett to silence. She shot Tainton a look of pure relish. 'Gave him a bath in steaming pitch.'

Roger Tainton clamped shut his eyes. 'She is quite the firebrand,' he muttered when finally his bare eyelids snapped open, 'as you seem to have deduced for yourselves.'

Fassett nodded. 'Fights like this one,' he said, meaning Stryker. 'I did not know whether to swive her or slay her.'

'Neither, for the moment,' Tainton replied. 'And have a care with your language.' He looked to Stryker. 'Had you not wondered what became of your dear Gallic lady?'

'What do you want with her?' Stryker said.

'You know what I want, Stryker. She is in Scilly because you are in Scilly. She was waiting for you.'

Lisette stepped out from Stryker's embrace and spat at Tainton's feet. 'I was not.'

Tainton hit her hard across the cheek. 'Yes, my dear, you were. That is why you sought us out. You thought my ship carried Mister Stryker, not Mister Tainton. And you would not have come ahead of the main force without knowing where the treasure was hidden. It makes not a jot of sense. But I know you will not talk.' He flashed his incongruously white teeth at Stryker. 'I shall see you die. Both of you. I despise you, Stryker. Everything you stand for. And your whore?' He ran the tips of his fingers over his face. 'I have waited a long time for my revenge. Every moment since they hauled me from that cauldron, spluttering and wailing, praying for death as my skin melted from my bones.' He moved to where Lisette stood, his shadow slipping over her. 'Every moment, Mademoiselle Gaillard, my thought has been bent towards you. Towards the day when I could look you in the eye and tell you what the Book of Revelation told me.'

Lisette pulled a sour expression. 'And what did it tell you, you prattling bloody ranter?'

'It whispered to me at first. Quietly, in the darkest, most silent hours of the night.' Tainton closed his eyes as he intoned the scripture. '"He hath judged the great whore, which did corrupt the earth with her fornication, and hath avenged the blood of his servants at her hand."' The eyes snapped open as a serene smile tugged at the corners of the purple lips. 'But as the words went round and round and round in my mind, they gathered strength until they were shouting at me. Screaming about my skull. Deafening me with their truth. He hath judged the great whore, which did corrupt the earth with her fornication, and hath avenged the blood of his servants at her hand.'

Stryker reached out to Tainton. 'You are a Godly man, sir. Does Jesus not tell us to turn the other cheek?'

'I have no cheek to turn, Captain Stryker,' Tainton rasped angrily. 'Because of your whore! But He hath avenged my blood, shed at *her* hand,' he said, jabbing a finger at the Frenchwoman. 'I knew the Lord would deliver you to me, Mademoiselle Gaillard. He is truly a faithful God.'

She spat again. 'Kill me, then, pizzle-rotten heretic.'

'Lisette—' Stryker warned, but he was cut off by the hulking form of Locke Squires, who stepped into his path and swatted him down with the flat of his pawlike hand.

Roger Tainton grasped Lisette by the shoulders. She twisted and writhed to no avail, and he hooked a leg behind hers, sweeping back at her ankles so that she toppled in a heap. Then he was above her. Outside, the wind howled like a hungry pack of wolves. It looked as though she might kick out at him, but his henchmen were quickly at his sides, and she lay back, staring up at them in wild-eyed fury.

'A great storm brews on the king's horizon,' Tainton said. 'It builds and rolls and sweeps down from the north.'

'*Vous êtes malade!*' Lisette hissed.

Tainton shook his head. 'The Scots are coming.'

'I do not believe you,' Stryker said, slowly regaining his feet.

'Believe what you will, Captain, for it matters nothing. The Scots have agreed to enter the war for the Parliament. Their army is large, and it is experienced; it will sweep through the north like wild flame.'

Something in the cool blue of Tainton's gaze made Stryker pause. 'Why would they—?' he began, but immediately tailed off. 'Money. The Parliament is paying for the privilege. That's why you're here.'

'Very good,' said Tainton. 'Westminster has made a great many concessions of a religious ilk, but they will not adhere to those once the war is done.'

'Stryker?' Lisette said, utterly confused.

He looked down at her. 'They've promised the world, and in return the Scots will march into England. We will be trapped between Parliament's armies and their new allies. In the long term they will wriggle free of whatever promises they've made. But the Scots will not march without money. And that is why Mister Tainton is here.'

'Where,' Tainton asked, 'is the gold?'

Stryker tasted the metallic tang of blood at the corner of his

mouth, and he wiped it with his sleeve. 'I did not tell your creature, and I will not tell you.'

Tainton let out a theatrical sigh. 'I swore to kill you both.
And I will. But first, Stryker, you may have my parting gift.' His
hands went to the fastenings at his breeches. 'I am going to
plough your French whore, Stryker. One never knows, she will
likely enjoy it.' He glanced at Sterne Fassett's grinning face. 'But
she will not enjoy Mister Fassett's charms, for he is . . . rather
rough with his lovers.'

'Me?' Fassett planted a palm on his chest to protest his innocence. 'I'm tender as a virgin.' He licked his lips slowly. 'She'll
want more, I shouldn't wonder. Can't say the same for the
others, mind. Squires and Cordell won't leave much of her to
execute, truth told.'

Lisette slid backwards sharply, pushing with her heels. 'Do
not tell him, Stryker!' The hulking form of Locke Squires took
two paces to reach her, and he took a shin in either hand and
dragged her back. 'God damn it, Stryker, do not tell him!'

'Where is the gold?' Tainton said calmly.

'You said you would not torture women!' Stryker snarled, his
skin crawling, heart pounding in his ears.

'And I won't. This is not torture, but copulation. Besides, it
is not her who must tell me what I wish to know. She will never
talk, I know that. You, on the other hand—?'

Stryker launched himself at Tainton, stopping short as Fassett's
dirk appeared before his face. He gritted his teeth, knowing that
there was nothing he could do. He looked down at Lisette.
Locke Squires was kneeling over her now, pawing clumsily at
her shirt as she spat malice. 'I—' Stryker began.

'I'll kill you myself!' he heard Lisette shriek. 'I swear it,
Stryker, I'll—'

'Tresco,' Stryker said. Now he could not look at Lisette, not
because of Squires's drooling ministrations, but because he knew
she would never forgive him.

'Truly?' Tainton answered, his tone slightly higher than
before, as if he had not expected to break his opponent.

Stryker nodded sullenly. 'It is on Tresco. There is a house owned by the Cades.'

'You lie.'

Stryker thrust his finger at the Roundhead agent. 'I speak true, damn your serpent skin! That is all I know. A house on Tresco, overlooking the sea. Sir Alfred kept a retainer there.'

'Where precisely?'

'I do not know!'

'Desist, Mister Squires,' Tainton snapped. He turned to Fassett as he fastened his breeches. 'Well?'

Fassett still held the knife poised in Stryker's face, and he did not look round as he spoke. 'We ain't looked on Tresco.' He shrugged. 'Might yet be there.'

Tainton licked those purple lips. He nodded at Fassett. 'To Tresco with us.'

'Weather's too bad,' Fassett said.

Tainton went to one of the large windows and stared out at the raging sea. Eventually he turned back. 'Then as soon as the wind dies.' The corners of his mouth peeled back in something like a smile. 'Thank you, Captain Stryker. That was not so diffi-cult, was it? Praise be to King Jesus for lifting the scales from your eye. But remember one thing: as sure as there is a heaven and a hell, the punishment will be severe if you are lying to me. Her virtue, such as it is, will be the least of it.' He went to the door, pausing only to address Fassett. 'Put them back in the nest with the other rats.'

CHAPTER 8

'Winter comes, sir. I pray the rivers do not freeze.'
The man in the workshop looked up from the stout oaken frame of his lathe. He was sweating profusely from the work, though the air sweeping in through the open double doors was chill, and he set down the sharp tool with which he had been hollowing out a piece of wood, snatching up a cloth in its stead. 'And I pray the hearths are warm.'

'Master Webb?' asked Captain Lancelot Forrester, stepping under the wide lintel. The workshop was bright, so the craftsman could see the detail of his work.

The man mopped his brow with the cloth, smoothing back his shock of black and silver hair with a gnarled hand. 'That is I, sir. George Webb. Wood-turner and' – his cleanly shaven face, tanned and deeply lined, became suddenly furtive – 'friend of the King.'

Forrester blew out his cheeks with relief, stepping further into the open-fronted building. The floor was thick with wood shavings, and he noticed a young lad busy sweeping in the shadows to the rear. 'Then I have my fellow.'

'You are from Basing Castle?'

Forrester gave a short bow. 'Captain Forrester, at your service.'

George Webb extricated himself from the frame and extended a hand for Forrester to take. 'Well met, Captain.'

'A magnificent contraption, Master Webb.'

Webb glanced back at the machine, his face splitting in a

broad grin of large, yellow teeth separated by wide gaps. 'A great wheel-lathe. My pride and joy! The wood-turner's livelihood.'

Forrester gazed about the workshop. It lay, as he had been told by Rawdon, on the northern outskirts of the modest market town, and he had had little difficulty in its finding. He noticed an array of finely crafted items as his eyes adjusted, but his interest was immediately taken by a bandolier that was hanging from a high beam. He made straight for it, running his hand down the looped belt, its full complement of powder boxes clattering together at his touch. A warrior's wind-chime. 'A fine collar o' charges, sir,' he said as he inspected the dozen boxes that would eventually each carry enough black powder for a single musket shot. There was a small pouch too, limp at the moment but destined to carry a goodly supply of bullets, while a flask for gun oil hung at its side. 'By your hand?'

Webb nodded. 'My wife cuts the leather and I fashion the boxes.'

'Exquisite work,' Forrester said, genuinely impressed. He was no expert in the highly prized art of wood-turning, but he knew a good powder box when he saw one.

Webb moved past the soldier, pushing closed the pair of large doors so that the light was suddenly cut out. He turned back to Forrester, his face tightening. 'What do you have for me, Captain?'

Forrester stole a look at the young boy who still swept energetically at the back. 'I may speak freely?'

'Aye, he is trustworthy, I assure you,' Webb said. 'His father has paid a great deal for this position. He would not jeopardize it for idle gossip.'

'But he is not kin?' Forrester asked, unable to rest easy.

Webb shook his head. 'Apprenticed to me for seven years. At the end of which, I intend to marry him to one of my three daughters.' The corners of his brown eyes crinkled with mischief. 'So he shall be kin in the fullness of time.'

Forrester still felt wary, as though his nerves were lengths of thread, their frayed ends tugged by this place that was at the very forefront of the war. A place where a man could never truly know who was friend and who was foe. But the task at hand was all that mattered, and he decided to press on. 'I carry a warrant for the raising of money for the King's cause. It is too dangerous to read out publicly, but the Marquess of Winchester prays like-minded men will see that its message is passed through the county.'

Webb rubbed his face with a calloused hand. 'He would take the fight to the Roundheads.'

'He would.'

'The Puritans,' Webb said, his voice rasping and sour. 'They call us Popish. Can you countenance such a thing? I am simply for tradition, Captain.'

'A supporter of Archbishop Laud, Master Webb?' Forrester asked, still taken aback by the wood-turner's sudden anger.

'Like most humble folk,' Webb said.

Forrester could not argue with that. The Puritan faction had become the most vocal in recent years, and the focus for their increasingly hostile ire was the remnant of the old Catholic faith that lingered still in parts of England. But he supposed the majority of ordinary people would have been content enough to follow the Anglican way espoused by William Laud. He offered a sympathetic smile. 'But the Laudian Church, Master Webb, is too similar in its ways. The reformers cannot simply leave it be.'

'Similar to the church in Rome?' Webb said. 'Of course it is, sir. Archbishop Laud wished to create compromise where there was discord. He carved each side into pieces, like a master woodworker. Took slices of the Puritan way and joined them with those of the Papacy, brought elements of each to his High Church at Canterbury. A grand compromise that might be accepted by both sides. An admirable thing for which to strive.'

A foolish thing, Forrester thought. The result of Laud's machinations had not been a seamless sculpture, but a cobbled, disjointed monster. 'In the end he pleased neither side. Only those, like yourself, who wished to keep to the middle ground. Papist eyes still look to Rome, while Puritan eyes look to revolution.'

Webb's eyes narrowed. 'And where do you look?'

'To my colonel and my king.'

Webb sniffed derisively. 'I pray your conscience will be at ease when finally this horror finds its end. For me, I fight for the old ways. Since the ranting preachers and their ilk began to plague our towns, decent folk have lived in fear. My goodwife is barracked as she walks down the street if one strand of hair breaks loose of the coif. They would make an end of our feast days, squeeze the pleasure out of life.'

'In that I am with you, Master Webb,' Forrester agreed. 'My particular interest lies in thespian realms.'

Webb's brow rose. 'A man of the playhouse? They would put an end to such frivolity too, sir, mark me well.'

'They have done so already in the cities,' Forrester said glumly, imagining his old stage at Candlewick Street, layered thick with cobwebs and dust, or torn up for kindling.

'The modest towns such as ours will be next,' the wood-turner returned gravely, sadness ghosting across his face. 'Petersfield was a pleasant enough place in the old days.'

A half-memory of conversation struck Forrester, and he asked: 'Did you ever know a man named Stryker?'

Webb considered the question for a second. 'Aye, I believe I remember him vaguely. A wool merchant. Lived out to the east, just past the River Rother. Long dead, God rest his soul.' He frowned suddenly. 'You seem a little young to have known him, Captain.'

Forrester smiled. 'A business acquaintance of my father.'

'Shall I tell you the moment I decided to fight?' said Webb. He nodded towards the door. 'I took a stroll down High Street, thither, and Richard Axon, one of the reformers hereabouts, passed by. He is known to me, an acquaintance of many years. I wished him good-day.'

'And?'

'And he berated me, sir,' Webb exclaimed, as though the

incident shocked him still. 'Bellowed and brayed like a damned mule. All thrusting finger and scarlet face, rebuking my words in the most boorish manner.'

'Because you cannot wish a man well for his day,' Forrester said, having encountered similar folk himself, 'when the day's fortunes spin on the word of God alone.'

Webb clicked his fingers. 'You have it, sir!' He laughed, the sound mirthless and bitter. 'A man is no longer permitted to bid another good-day. What times are these? I will not sit idly by, sir. Not for a moment. But, alas, I am too old for the pike block. Yet it occurred to me that my position here, a man of some influence you understand, might work for the good of the King in other ways.' He went to his lathe. Webb saw Forrester's interest, and slid his hand across the block that was to be fashioned. 'Look here, the timber that will be turned for our good fighting men. I have a requisition for a thousand powder boxes. Bound, when ready, for our forces now in Winchester.'

Forrester was certainly impressed. Wood-turning was a skilled craft, and Webb was clearly dedicating his rare knowledge to the cause of the Crown. 'And what if Parliament troops come to Petersfield?'

'They do, often. At which time I show them this.' Webb stooped to a leather bag at his feet, from which he fished a folded parchment. 'The same requisition, but for our dear Parliament.'

Forrester eyed it warily. 'A forgery?'

'A good forgery.'

'And a big risk.'

'A worthy risk,' Webb chided. He put the paper away. 'Besides, my position sees me afforded a deal of safety not offered to other men.'

Forrester could not argue against that point, for wood-turners were near priceless in a time such as this. He supposed Webb would be shown leniency even if he were caught. 'Oak?' he said, looking at the timber that would soon become a powder box for a bandolier. 'It is plentiful hereabouts.'

'*Ha!*' Webb cackled, as though he had been treated to some great jest. 'No, sir. Oak is too hard for such fine workmanship. Ash is better, but it maintains great strength all along its length, so we must keep it aside for our pikes and halberds.' There was a pile of timber near one of the walls, which he indicated with a wave of his hand. 'The wood I use for the boxes is a mix of beech and birch. Much easier to work, turned on this very lathe, and thrice laid in sallet oil until nicely sealed.'

'Then I commend you on your business, Master Webb. Our armies are in your debt. But it is not simply your skill with wood that is your gift to good King Charles.'

The corner of Webb's mouth twitched. 'The road betwixt London and Portsmouth runs through our little town, Captain. We see many troops, many pilgrims, many lords and ladies, of divers allegiance.' Now he let his voice fall to a more clandestine note. Evidently the apprentice was not privy to all Webb's secrets. 'It is a good place for a man to watch and listen. From here I may glean information.' He winked. 'Or pass it on.'

'That is what the Marquess instructed. At Petersfield, find George Webb. He will see the warrant's message spread far and wide.'

'He flatters me, Captain, but aye, that is something I can see done. Where next for you?'

'Rowlands Castle.'

Webb winced. 'Wait another day, sir. The Roundheads are abroad.'

'Are they not always?'

'They patrol, of course, and they skirmish with our side every other day. But I hear tell of a large troop of horse coming up from Southampton. They are not to be trifled with, so reports suggest. Perhaps you will accept my hospitality this night? I will have further news by sun-up, and you will know which road to take.'

There had been little discussion in the hours following the return of Stryker and Lisette to the main holding cell. The place reeked worse than Stryker remembered it, for days had slipped by, and the unwashed bodies of his sixteen fellow captives were becoming pungent in the extreme. Now there were eighteen with the Frenchwoman, who sat hard into the walls at one of the corners, broiling with animosity and frustration. Stryker had been tight-lipped, evading questions from Barkworth and Skellen as to his interrogation, and ultimately they had left him to his own counsel. He curled into a foetal position against one of the slick walls, too ashamed to even look at them. He had betrayed these good men, betrayed the men lost to the seas, and betrayed the memory of Cecily Cade. This journey upon which they had so willingly embarked had turned sour, and that was to be regretted, but the moment he had blurted a single word to Roger Tainton, he had rendered their efforts and sacrifices worthless. Tresco. That was all it took.

Thus the bedraggled group had spent the following hours huddled in twos and threes around the single wax taper afforded them by a more kindly member of Balthazar's garrison. Hard, mould-furred bread had been brought at a point that they supposed must have been dawn – though they saw no sign of Tainton, Fassett or the others – along with some gritty water and a new piss-pot.

It was only then that Stryker stirred, for the sound of the slopping water had been like a siren's call to his thirst-tortured mind. He crawled on all fours to the pail, snatching it up and pouring it straight down his parched throat. The sensation was divine and he heard himself groan as though in a lover's embrace, caring nothing for what the others must have thought. When the water bubbled up over his lips, cascading in a torrent over his tattered shirt, he set the pail down for the next man and rocked back on his haunches. The water was brackish, dirty and flecked with pieces of what looked to be seaweed, but it gave him his first real surge of strength since before the shipwreck. His eye seemed to clear along with his head, and he breathed deeply, arching his back to a chorus of deep, satisfying cracks. When he looked out into the dingy chamber he saw the men were smiling at him tentatively. Then he saw Lisette, her eyes blazing despite the darkness. He clambered unsteadily to his feet and went to her, stretching out a hand.

'Lisette, I—'

If she had possessed a blade at that moment, there was no doubt Stryker would be several fingers short. 'Do not touch me, coward!' She spat the last word. 'Do not bloody look at me.'

'It—it was for you, Lisette,' Stryker protested weakly, hating the words even as they left him.

She stared up at him, her smile malicious. 'For me? I plead for you not to tell those bastards, and you tell. You fucking tell. If I had my dagger, Stryker, I would pin you to the floor by your stones, God help me! I had it. Had the gold. Found where it was, and still I did not tell them.'

'Jesu . . .' Stryker retreated a step, searching for something, anything, to say. 'They were going to rape you.'

Lisette slapped a palm across her lips in an exaggerated gasp. 'Mother of God, no! And what of it? You think it would be the first time I've spread my legs to protect your stammering bloody king? Tainton hates me. He was going to kill me. So he rapes me first. What will I care when I'm dead?'

'I would care.'

'*Exactement*!' Lisette hissed. '*You* would care. The great Stryker does not like his woman touched by other men. It does not matter if the whole bloody world depends upon it!'

Stryker wanted her to see what he saw, to feel the dread that he had felt. But in the end he knew that the facts spoke for themselves. She was right. 'I was prepared to tell them about the gold for you,' he said softly. 'To protect you.'

She spat at his feet. 'Then you are a bloody foolish bastard, Stryker. A bloody foolish, jealous bastard. You do not own me! All you had to do was keep your damned mouth shut! But you could not do it because you could not see other men have their way with me. It is pathetic, Stryker. And now they will have the gold. All our work. Cecily's death. All for nothing.' She sat back against the wall. 'You could not keep your silence before. Well keep it now and leave me be.'

'Good to see you back, sir,' William Skellen said as Stryker went to slump against the wall he had made his own. 'And I see Miss Lisette's in fine fettle.'

Stryker glared caustically. 'Have a care, Skellen.'

Skellen swallowed hard. 'I will, sir.' He went to sit nearer his captain. 'I will.'

Barkworth's yellow gaze glowed like a pair of lighted match-cords in the murk. 'You're no in fine fettle, sir.'

Skellen pulled an admonishing expression, but Stryker held up a hand. 'They poured seawater down my throat every few hours.'

'Bugger me backwards . . .' The diminutive Scot's voice was little more than a croak at the best of times, but here, despite the silence of the rest of the men, seemed barely audible at all.

'After a while it felt like my innards were coming out with the vomit.'

'They wanted you to tell 'em where the gold was?' Barkworth said.

'Aye.'

'And now they know.'

'They always knew it was in the Scillies,' Stryker said. 'But not which island it was on.'

'How did they know?' Skellen spoke now.

Stryker spread his palms to show that he was as puzzled as they. 'Remember Collings? The major-general who sought the gold? He is in disgrace for his failure, as far as I can ascertain. These new vipers work in his stead.'

Barkworth cleared his throat gingerly, glancing back at Lisette. 'Take it you told 'em, sir, beggin' your pardon.'

Stryker wanted to follow his gaze, but fought the instinct. 'Aye, I told them.'

'Shite,' the Scot muttered.

'Indeed.' He looked at Skellen. 'It's more than that.'

The sergeant frowned, his bald head creasing above deep-set eyes. 'Sir?'

'Our gaoler is Roger Tainton.'

'Tainton?' Skellen echoed, cocking his head to the side like a hound listening for its quarry. Then his mouth lolled. '*Captain* Tainton?'

Stryker nodded. 'As was.'

'The stripling with the blackened armour?' When Stryker nodded again, Skellen looked at Barkworth. 'Gilt rivets and everything. Very nice.'

'Very rich, I'll wager,' Barkworth replied.

'Pappy funded the regiment,' said Skellen. 'Tainton was good, though. Proper horseman. We saw his lads smash one of our troops to bits.' His head swivelled back to his captain. 'But he— he drowned.'

'It appears he was saved,' Stryker said. 'But he was badly burned. You would not recognize him now.'

'I bet he remembers Miss Lisette.' The sergeant turned to stare at the sullen Frenchwoman. 'That's what happened, sir, ain't it? He recalled his *meeting* with her.'

'Beg pardon, sir,' Barkworth interrupted upon seeing Stryker's face, 'but you'll nae find privacy in here.'

Stryker sat back. How could they help but eavesdrop? 'That is what happened, aye. Tainton threatened to—'

He tailed off, but Skellen simply set his jaw. 'Understood, sir.'

'And I told him the treasure was on the island of Tresco,' Stryker went on.

'Every man has his weak spot, sir,' said Skellen. 'His Archimedes elbow, as Cap'n Forrester would say.'

Barkworth thumped the tall man's shoulder. 'His Achilles heel, you willow-armed bloody bufflehead.'

Skellen shot him a grin that was black-gummed and amber-mottled. 'If you say so, Tom Thumb.'

'That is all beside the point,' Stryker said. 'She will die either way. Tainton wants his revenge.' The pains gripped his guts again and he pressed a balled fist into his midriff. 'All I have done is stop her rape.'

Skellen shrugged. 'Well, I do not blame you, sir.'

Stryker let his shoulder-blades hit the cold stone behind. He wished Lisette saw it that way.

Petersfield, Hampshire, 10 October 1643

Forrester shared a cup of passable claret with George Webb before turning in for the night to a room at the rear of Webb's workshop.

Unfastening his baldric, he collapsed fully clothed on the dense pallet, happy to rest his body despite the tumbling of his mind. He had taken a map from his saddlebag and now unfurled the scroll above his face, plotting his route south to the village of Rowlands Castle, where he would meet his final contact. He could not travel on the major thoroughfares, but there were plenty of alternative tracks that, albeit more circuitous, would have to suffice. Where were those Parliamentarians Webb had mentioned? The roads were full of soldiers, footpads and highwaymen, and he was well accustomed to dealing with such dangers, but Webb's reputation was not something to be dismissed. If he made mention of a particular force at large, then that was a force to be reckoned with.

Forrester set down the map. He needed to get back to Basing and then north to Oxford. He felt sorry for the folk of Petersfield, but it was no place to linger. For once he would be pleased to rejoin the wintering regiment.

It was the smell he noticed first. He sat bolt upright, scrambling for his sword without consideration, because the odour was a mix of things he knew well: tobacco smoke, sweat, leather and horse flesh. Soldiers.

There was no time to collect his belongings, and he was thankful he had kept the Marquess of Winchester's warrant stitched firmly into the lining of his coat. He could still get himself out of this, so long as the soldiers had approached the rear of the premises first. If he was lucky, they had not reached the front. He eased the latch and moved into the workshop. He could make out the shapes of tools hanging from nails on the walls all around, straps of leather dangling from the beams and the huge black shadows of the lathe and its great wheel. He went quickly to the entrance that fronted on to the street, surprised that the doors were not barred. Something moved to his left, catching his eye. He froze, turned slowly, blade levelled and ready. Beyond the long spokes of the great wheel a figure lurked. Forrester took a step back as it slid out from its hiding place.

Forrester let a huge breath gush from him. 'Jesu, boy,' he said to the apprentice, 'I almost ran you through.'

Webb's apprentice was, now that Forrester saw him up close, probably about fourteen years of age, with a bowl-shaped thatch of black hair and a pinched, shrewish face. 'S—sorry, sir.'

Forrester moved past, making for the double doors. 'Wake your master, lad. He has visitors, I fear.'

'Nay, sir.'

Forrester spun round. 'What?' He need not have asked the question, for his answer was etched all over the apprentice's furtive expression. It was why the bar had been removed from the door. 'You treacherous little bastard!'

The double doors swung violently inwards at that moment, starlight beyond obscured by soldiers. They came quickly, filling the workshop. Four flaming torches were in the room, carried in gauntleted fists, and Forrester was forced to shield his eyes. 'What is the meaning of this?' he blustered.

'Mouth shut, sow-swiver,' one of the men commanded, 'or it'll be the worse for you.' There were nearly twenty soldiers packed into the workshop now, all with a blade or pistol brandished, the metal glinting in the glow of the flames like the winking eyes of some hellish beast. The man who had spoken stepped forth. He held a pistol, twitching it towards Forrester's poised weapon. 'Drop your hanger, fellow, or I'll blast this dag right in your belly.'

Forrester dropped his sword. They were cavalrymen, by the look of their clothing and weapons. The leader jerked his chin at Forrester and two men stalked out from the crowd to grasp him roughly by his arms.

'I say!' Forrester yelped, twisting away. 'Get your damned grubby claws off me!'

'Proper gent, this one,' the commanding trooper declared to a chorus of laughter. 'Out we go, your lordship.'

They dragged Forrester out into the night. More cavalrymen were streaming back from the rear of the building. A hundred yards down the road, near the timber-framed edifice of a large tavern, waited the rest of the troop. They watched his approach with grim interest, some clapping sarcastically, others spitting streams of brown tobacco juice in his direction.

Forrester quickly scanned the group. There were perhaps threescore men, all similarly dressed in the ubiquitous buff hide and metal of a well-equipped troop of horse. It was not a large troop, but he guessed this was the sum of the unit, for the cornet was present, clutching his pole from which, hanging limp but unfurled, was the colour. It was a square of black and blue material. Forrester did not recognize it as overtly Parliamentarian, and a jolt of hope punched through him. Perhaps this was not the feared rebel unit Webb had warned against, but a Royalist patrol, passing through the town by chance.

He saw the scarf then, almost glowing in the light of the moon, wrapped about the waist of a man who immediately slid down from his horse and removed his helmet. The garment was tawny, the colour of the Earl of Essex and, therefore, the device chosen by many sections of the various Roundhead armies, especially those who had been with His Excellency at Edgehill, Gloucester or Newbury. Forrester's heart sank.

'Good-evening, fellow!' the man in the scarf called, his accent strange to Forrester's ear. He strode quickly towards his new captive. 'And what have you been up to?'

Forrester shook himself free of the grasping fingers. He straightened, squaring his shoulders. 'I am Captain Lancelot Forrester, of Sir Edmund Mowbray's Regiment of Foot.'

The cavalryman had a huge nose and a thick, white beard, and he rubbed the bristles with a gloved hand. 'Cavalier.'

'Oxford Army.' There was nothing to be gained by lying. He was well armed, in possession of a good horse and clothed like a soldier. Honesty, about this aspect at least, would keep him alive. 'I would offer you my sword, sir, but you already have it.'

A growing group of onlookers was gathering on the roadside now, disturbed from their beds by the commotion, and the tawny-scarfed man offered a curt bow, playing to the crowd. 'I am Captain Wagner Kovac. Richard Norton's Regiment of Horse.'

Now that the man was close, Forrester could see that his skin was badly marked by the pox. His eyes were very pale, almost like clear glass. They showed no sign of friendliness, despite the spoken pleasantries. 'You are abroad late, Captain.'

'We hunt,' Kovac said bluntly. He looked back at his men with a wry smile, exposing the ostentatiously large knot of his scarf, which bloomed like rose petals at the small of his back.

'Then good hunting,' Forrester said, fighting to keep his fear in check.

Kovac was taller than Forrester by an inch or two, and he seemed to raise himself to his full height as he spoke. 'Tell me, Captain Forster.'

'Forrester.'

'Forrester,' Kovac corrected himself. His left cheek twitched. 'Tell me, what are you doing here?'

'I was captured at Newbury Fight,' Forrester lied. 'I escaped, stole a horse, rode as far away from London as I could.'

Kovac stared at him, gaze pitiless and implacable. 'You come direct from Oxford.'

'I was at Newbury,' Forrester protested hotly.

'You might have been at Newbury, Captain,' Kovac cut him off, 'but you were not captured. I say you carry a warrant from Pope-lover Paulet.'

'I do not know what on earth—' Forrester blustered, but rough hands immediately took him. They tore the coat from his back and tossed it to Kovac, who held it up high, patting it with a palm until he rested upon a particular spot.

'Truss him up,' Kovac ordered. He turned, still carrying the coat, and went to his mount, climbing up with the agility of an expert horseman. He lay the coat across his thighs and crammed the helmet on to his head, tucking strands of white hair behind his ears as he tugged the three-barred visor over his face. 'In my country,' he called to Forrester, 'you would be dead already. You are lucky, Cavalier spy, for it is not I who will decide your fate.'

'I am no spy!' Forrester shouted as he was dragged to his own horse and thrown like a roll of sacking over its back. In the doorway of the workshop, George Webb stood, ashen-faced, with his goodwife. Forrester twisted his head away. 'You cannot execute me!'

'You are not a proper soldier, either,' Wagner Kovac replied. 'Caught by God-fearing, honest folk while you creep about the land like some witch's puckrel.' He looked down at the side of the road and tossed a coin into the night air.

Forrester watched the silver piece glimmer as it spun. It was caught by the wood-turner's apprentice. The lad bit the coin, glanced over his shoulder to check that his master had left the scene, and grinned, offering Forrester a small shrug.

CHAPTER 9

The Governor of Southampton was not what Forrester had expected. Here was no crusty clerk, buried in a drift of paper and ink, nor some flamboyant power-broker with daggers hidden behind a warm smile. He was a soldier, Forrester knew instantly. One without armour or weapons, save his sword, but a fellow marked by simple manners and gruff courtesy. It was dawn, and the governor, one Richard Norton, sat behind a near empty desk, his booted legs stretched out to the side, one crossed over the other. 'You are a Royalist officer?'

'I do not deny it,' Forrester replied. He was tired, exhausted, for the ride had taken all night, thundering south and west to this most Parliamentarian of cities, but still he kept his nerves in check, his gaze firmly fixed upon a smudge blighting the wall slightly above Norton's left shoulder.

Norton was eating a yellow pear dappled with brown and green blotches, and he sliced a thick chunk with a small knife. He slipped it into the side of his mouth so that it bulged as he spoke. 'You are a spy.'

'Now I deny *that* with every fibre of my being.'

'How very verbose of you, Captain,' Norton said. He tilted the knife up to scratch at his red beard. Even from this distance Forrester could see that below the bristles the skin was nearly as livid as its coarse covering, ravaged by some disease. Norton took the knife away, inspected the tip for a moment, and set it to cutting the pear once more. 'You might have made a name for yourself on the stage, had not the play-houses been closed.'

'True is it,' Forrester said, 'that we have seen better days.'

The governor smiled. '*As You Like It.*'

Forrester was impressed. 'You have an interest in theatre?'

Norton gave a derisive sniff. 'I was forced to study such friv-olous drivel in my youth, but that does not mean I approve. Parliament have done the Godly thing in putting an end to it.' He set down the knife beside the fruit's stripped core. 'Let us be about our business, eh? I have recently been made governor of this place, and I see it my sacred duty to prosecute the cause of Parliament throughout Southampton's environs.'

'Keep this side of the Hamble, then.'

Norton laughed, sitting up straight and leaning into the table a touch. 'The river is no border, Captain. The county is key. As governor, it is left to me to ensure Southampton is safe. She cannot truly be so until Hampshire itself is right-minded and loyal to Westminster.' He glanced at the door where the white-haired Captain Kovac stood like a grim sentinel. 'I am a colonel of horse. Wagner, there, patrols on my behalf, his task to weed out traitors and enemies from whichever hole they may crawl into. We are well aware of Master Webb's allegiance. I have watched him since long before my tenure here.' He paused, studying Forrester's face. 'You are shocked? Do not be. His skill is invaluable. We let him think he is clever, let him fulfil his commissions for the King, then swoop in like kites upon a dead lamb. His thousand powder boxes will not reach Royalist hands, I assure you.'

'And Webb?' Forrester asked, concerned for the man who had shown him such hospitality.

'He will never know. The shipment will leave his custody bound for his friends at Oxford. We will intercept it on the road, and he will believe it went to its intended home. When later he discovers it went missing, as surely he must, he will think it an accident of war and begin another commission.'

'Which you will steal.'

'Which we will commandeer.'

'Why do you not simply stop him?'

'Stretch his neck?' Norton said, his expression darkening for a fraction of a moment. 'Because men of his ilk are few, and their necessity to this war increases daily. He is more useful alive.'

'Then order him to make them for you,' Forrester offered.

Norton shook his head, scratching in turn at his face and a scalp that was layered in greasy russet hair. 'He is a king's man. Boxes he makes for the malignants will be crafted with care. The very best quality. That is what I would have my men use. Let him believe he shifts for the Cavaliers, and let him supply the Roundheads.' He grinned, sharing a look with Kovac so that they might dwell upon their own cleverness. 'And the entire scheme turns upon his young apprentice, who, you will be amused to learn, is my kinsman!' He leaned back in the chair, folding his arms heavily across his stomach like a man who has just enjoyed a satisfying repast. 'It is exquisite, do you not think?'

Forrester could indeed see the near perfection in Norton's ruse. Except that it was not perfect, for Webb was not simply a Royalist wood-turner. 'It is abhorrent,' he said, deciding outrage would hide the fact that he was glad Webb would be left in situ.

Norton sighed deeply. 'If you are not a spy, Captain Forrester, then what are you?'

'A soldier.'

'One caught creeping around Parliament territory at night.'

'I was sleeping, Colonel,' Forrester retorted, 'not creeping.'

'In the home of a notorious malignant.'

'And Hampshire,' Forrester persisted, 'is not Parliament territory. Not all of it.'

'You refer, of course, to Basing House. From whence you came, it seems.'

'I admit, I was taking Sir John Paulet's warrant into the county.'

Behind him, Captain Kovac let forth a guttural growl. 'And you were spying.'

Forrester rounded on him. 'I was not, you beef-brained bloody

German! I know your game, sir, do not think me a fool. You may not hang a soldier, but you may hang a spy.'

'I am not German,' Kovac said. 'I am Croatian.'

'We shan't hang you,' Colonel Norton interjected, 'and I'm certain, Wagner, that the good captain is not interested in your heritage.' He picked up a quill that was on the table and turned the blackened nib between thumb and forefinger. 'But you shall be imprisoned, Mister Forrester. There is not a great deal of room in Southampton's gaols, I confess,' he added with a look that was wolfish and full of relish, 'but you will be well looked after.'

'You scrofulous rogue!' The prisons would be overcrowded, Forrester knew. Full of men turned to skeletons and driven mad by hunger and filth.

'Mind your tongue, Captain,' Norton commanded, 'or I shall let Captain Kovac off his leash to teach you the ways of his countrymen.' He squared his shoulders, looking past the big Croat to the doorway. 'MacLachlan!'

The door swung inwards immediately and a thin-faced man stepped smartly into the room. 'Governor?'

Norton set the quill down having written something on a piece of parchment that he now folded and sealed with red wax. When it was done, he lifted the sheet, blowing gently on the seal, and held it out to MacLachlan. 'Here is Paulet's treacherous warrant. Take it to London.'

'Sir,' MacLachlan said, stepping forwards and tucking it carefully into a snapsack hanging from his shoulder. 'Right away, sir.'

'Hand it to John Pym himself,' Richard Norton ordered. 'Let them see what menace we face hereabouts.'

Off St Mary's, Isles of Scilly, 11 October 1643

Roger Tainton's ship was a square-rigged pinnace called the *Silver Swan*, and it battled out of the wharf at Hugh Town and into the bay. The inclement weather had delayed their departure through the night and much of the morning, but now, though the noon gusts remained strong, Tainton's expert crew had advised an attempt to cross the treacherous stretch of water known as St Mary's Road was no longer suicidal. Thus, the sailors had set about earning their coin manfully, scuttling about the deck of the small, three-masted galleon, tugging on the ropes and setting the shrouds and bawling at one another in terms that Tainton and his trio of hired killers could never hope to understand.

He looked to the south, back at the largest settlement in the islands, the houses of stone like pale warts on the green and grey mound of land, smoke trails belching out of chimneys and immediately swept by the wind into a dark mass above, like an ominous storm cloud. But there was no storm on the horizon, and Tainton was confident that he would reach his destination without difficulty. And what a destination. The place where he would make his name as a hero of the rebellion. He took a last glance at St Mary's, to the jutting peninsula from which the brutish form of Star Castle rose like a hoary boil. He prayed Stryker and his Popish poll-cat were wallowing in their defeat, feeling the pain and humiliation with keenness that was white-hot.

He turned back to face northwards, pushing up against the prow of the pinnace as the sea sprayed a salty mist into his face. There, the better part of two miles away, was the dark mass of Tresco. It was smaller than St Mary's but still one of the more significant islands in the remote archipelago, and it loomed above the isle of Samson, which lay off its south-west tip. Tainton revelled in the chill wind, wishing he could feel more of its bite than his thickened, dulled skin would allow. He was a better man than he had been before the fateful day in that battle-ravaged village to the west of London. And yet it was ever difficult to remind himself of the fact. The torment of his wounds haunted him still.

The Royalist soldiers who had found him at Brentford had assumed him dead. They must have received quite the shock when he had shown signs of life. A sudden gasp or a jerking limb, perhaps. He would never know, for he had no recollection of that day beyond the moment he had tumbled into the steaming cauldron, the leering face of Stryker's whore the last thing his old self would see, but the thought of those frightened soldiers had ever amused him.

He had woken towards winter's end, staring up at a fat chirurgeon by the name of Ptolemy Banks and the armed guard he had summoned. The wounds Tainton received in his duel with the French witch had been tended expertly, largely healed, but his skin, left so long to cook beneath its layer of sticky tar, had never recovered. His doctors were also his captors, and he had affected an air of confused vulnerability during his rehabilitation on an old farmstead just outside Oxford. A man so horribly, irreversibly shattered by war that he could barely recall his own name, let alone his allegiance. In the end they had let him go, as much out of pity as any other reason, and he had headed back to London. But the city that had been his home was no longer welcoming to a man with a face that sent children screaming to their mothers, and he had spent just one miserable week in the capital. It was, he now understood, a providential week, for there, at a chapel in Southwark, he had met a man who had talked of a new military force being raised on the flat plains of East Anglia. One that cared little for a man's appearance or heritage, but only for the strength of his faith. Tainton had touched his father for funds and purchased a good horse, and then he had left the throng of the capital behind. He had gone north and east, to his new promised land, and found the welcome for which his heart had been searching. It was there that he had rediscovered his passion for the cause, and his passion for Christ Jesus.

'They cared for me,' he said, voice muffled by the wind.

Sterne Fassett had come to stand beside him, and he picked at his empty gums as he spoke. 'Who did?'

Tainton did not look round. He was transfixed upon the dark hump that was Tresco. 'The congregation of a little chapel outside Cambridge.'

'Saint Big Tits, or something?'

Tainton turned, looking down at his employee with disdain. 'Have a care, Fassett, I have warned you before.' He breathed deeply, the air hurting his chest as ever. 'The Chapel of Jesus the Redeemer.'

Fassett's upper lip twisted. 'Puritan.'

Tainton shrugged. 'If you wish to term it so, but that name is derisive, mocking. We are merely those God-fearing folk who seek self-discipline in the ways of the spirit, on the path set out by pure, reformed doctrine.'

'None of the bells an' baubles of the Romish sort.'

That made Tainton smile. 'Indeed. And of the Anglicans. Canterbury is, after all, simply a dilution of Rome.' He craned his head over the side. The ocean seemed like an infinitely large cauldron, its potion a melee of grey and blue and green and black. 'The folk of that simple congregation helped me recover my health and my wits. Through them, God healed me. Through them, I was able to see the truth in life, in creation, in all things. See that their way was God's way.'

'Their way?'

'Independent,' said Tainton. 'Protestantism has many creeds and colours. Many shades, Mister Fassett. The true way is the Independent way. Where a life might be built upon the Word of God, and only on His Word, rather than on the chatter and lies of mankind; of hierarchies placed upon congregations to shackle and oppress God-fearing folk.'

'If Presbyterianism is so bad,' Fassett said, surprising Tainton with his understanding, 'Then why have we signed up to that bleedin' covenant?'

'Because the Scots are Presbyterians, and we need their army. I told you before, we will throw off the yoke of the covenant as soon as our mutual enemy has been destroyed. The Scots can go back to their own country, and we will follow the true path in England. My master and his friends will see it done, have no fear.'

Fassett spat over the edge. 'That fellow from St Margaret's?'

'Margaret's, if you please,' Tainton corrected, 'I do not hold with saints.' He thought back to the day when he and Fassett had watched members of Parliament accept the Solemn League and Covenant. 'You speak of Sir Henry Vane. A Godly man, 'tis true, but not my worldly master. Vane is powerful, but he is no visionary. My master is on his way to the very highest echelon of our new order, the breath of the Holy Spirit at his back, lifting him like the seabirds above us. He has given me purpose. I have eschewed the trappings of my commission. No longer will I wear armour and ride for glory beneath an earthly banner. The only glory worth winning is that reflected by King Jesus.'

Gulls mewed madly, soaring and dipping and climbing, carried and buffeted on the wind. Black silhouettes of shags and cormorants interspersed their flock, tracing vast arcs against the pewter clouds. Sterne Fassett watched the birds with disinterest. 'Did she really best you?'

Tainton had felt himself drift into something of a trance, but now the reverie was shattered. He swallowed hard, blinking away the glassy film that had descended over his eyes. The gulls and the sea and the land came sharply into focus. 'Aye, she did. She is skilful with blade in hand.'

'Bet she's skilful with other things in hand.'

Tainton shot Fassett a withering look. 'I was a good soldier. I have shed my pride, Mister Fassett, and can tell you with no hint of bluster or boastfulness that I was one of the best leaders of horse the Parliament had. In the saddle, with pistol, with sword, I did not believe I could be beaten.' He gripped the damp rail. 'And pride was my undoing. The French harlot was sent as a test.'

'And you failed.'

'Or perhaps I passed, Fassett. I would not have found salvation without her.'

'And yet,' Fassett said, not bothering to conceal the amusement in his tone, 'you would still spill that girl's guts on the floor.'

'God will allow me to punish the wicked. There is always an

134

allowance for war, if one strives to attain peace. Remember what the psalmist tells us.' He glanced at the wind-driven sky for inspiration. 'Let the high acts of God be in their mouth, and a two-edged sword in their hand.' He pushed away, stepping back from the edge, the gulls that ventured close to the deck in search of scraps veering away at the tune of his spurs. 'Still, we have business on Tresco, you and I. When we return, we will put an end to the wretched woman.'

'Balthazar's wet as piss. He won't like you killing the bitch.'

'I'll deal with Balthazar. She will die a secret, painful death.'

'And Stryker?'

'He will swing. I've told the garrison to construct gallows outside the castle.'

'Should've snuffed 'em out already,' Fassett muttered darkly.

'And what if he lied? We may need them yet.'

'You think he lied to you?'

Tainton shook his head. 'No, but nor will I take the risk. We will find this promised prize before we bury our captives. Then, and only then, shall we head for home. My master will be pleased. There will be reward in it for you, Fassett, for I know you covet such worldly trappings.'

Fassett followed him along the deck. 'I do, Mister Tainton, I do. And look forward to the next assignment, should your master see fit to keep me in his employ. May I ask—?'

Tainton stopped, and turned on his heels. 'Speak.'

'If your master,' Fassett said, 'ain't Sir Henry Vane, then who is he?'

Southampton, Hampshire, 11 October 1643

The late afternoon was cold and dark. Flickering iron braziers lit the way for Captain Lancelot Forrester and his guards as they crossed the courtyard. The yard was a wide rectangle, hemmed on all sides by mouldering, tumbledown buildings that had once formed a large slaughterhouse. Now the units were prisons, their crumbling walls, rotting timbers and holed roofs barely strong enough to keep a mule inside, let alone scores of angry soldiers and dissidents. Their poor state necessitated the number of sentries, who swarmed the complex, grim threat etched on their faces, halberds, hangers and muskets brandished in plain sight as the starkest deterrent imaginable.

'In there.'

Forrester, stripped of his sword, his snapsack and his spurs, drew to a halt before the dilapidated doorway of what looked to be an ancient storehouse. One of the large hinges had come away and the door hung slightly lopsided, and several chunks of whitewashed daub had come away from the outer wall, ragged patches of wattle left exposed like wounds to the elements. He wrinkled his nose, glancing back at the half-dozen musketeers. 'Positively palatial. On what do we dine this evening? Roast lamb and some rich claret, perhaps?'

The guard who had spoken spat a stream of dark tobacco juice through the gap between his front teeth. 'Turnip-tops, your lordship. Or you are at liberty to snare a rat.' He checked that his long-arm's pan cover was safely shut and handed it to a comrade, the glowing tip of his slow-burning match kept tight between middle and ringfinger. It danced at his side as he rifled with his free hand in the snapsack hanging from his shoulder, tracing fiery shapes that lingered in Forrester's sight. He shook the keys. 'Knew I had 'em somewhere.'

Even as the lead musketeer moved to the door, things shifted behind it. Forrester watched, disconcerted, as flashes of something solid ghosted past the holes, grey wraiths slithering silently behind the wattle trellises, indistinct glimpses of the unnatural. The particular key was selected, and, before it had turned, the five remaining muskets were trained upon the doorway.

The key turned in the lock and the musketeer dragged back its iron loop, the door juddering as it scraped the hardening mud. He had no time to think as they shoved him inside, barely keeping his footing as the door was slammed shut in his wake. The key turned.

Forrester saw the eyes first. They glinted in the dark like the gaze of so many cats, lit by orange light that penetrated the holes in the walls. It took time to adjust, and he blinked rapidly, forcing himself to be patient amid the rising tide of panic. In seconds the eyes were framed by faces. They were lacklustre, devoid of detail, but he could discern the outlines of the men who stood at the far side of the makeshift prison. He reckoned there were twenty of them, perhaps twenty-five, and they shifted towards him in the gloom, a flock of ghouls drawn to new blood.

Forrester extended an arm, holding up a flattened palm. 'Stay where you are!'

'Who might you be?' one of the ghouls murmured.

'Captain Lancelot Forrester, Mowbray's Foot,' he replied with bluster he did not feel, 'and I'll batter the next man to take a step closer.'

'Sir?'

Out of the murk came one of the prisoners. A skinny man with a long, severely hooked nose and eyes that were like pebbles of jet. 'Dewhurst, sir. John Dewhurst. The Hawk, the lads call me.'

Forrester drew closer, feet sinking a fraction in ground carpeted with bird droppings. He saw that the man's head bobbed as he spoke, a motion akin to pecking. 'The Hawk,' he repeated. He saw that the man wore a yellow coat, and his memory was all at once in a place called Holybourne. 'Sergeant?'

'That's me, sir, aye,' the man said. 'Rawdon's Foot. Good to see you again, Captain.'

East of Tresco, Isles of Scilly, 11 October 1643

The *Silver Swan* came into Old Grimsby harbour as dusk darkened the sea. Roger Tainton, former Roundhead cavalry officer, lately Parliamentarian agent, felt utterly invigorated as the crew of his hired pinnace set to work guiding the big ship into the calmer waters protected by the curve of the high cliffs. He stood at the rail, the spot from which he had barely moved during the rough journey, and scanned the shore, the creak of sail and constant roar of water familiar friends to him now. Old Grimsby, its thatches and stone hugging the high ground above three sweeping beaches of sand and shingle, looked much like Hugh Town, only smaller. A warren of humanity fighting the elements, cut off from civilization, and utterly reliant upon the sea. He wondered why on earth any sane person would choose to grind out an existence in a place such as this.

'It is fit only for goats,' he said when Sterne Fassett came to stand with him.

'Like the rest of these bloody islands.'

'Aye.'

'I'll be glad to get back to London.' Fassett was rubbing at his jaw again, probing and prodding the lump that had faded from livid red to a collage of browns and yellows along the curve of the bone, and he winced a little when he spoke. 'Where do we start?'

'Ask for properties owned by the late Sir Alfred Cade. Beginning with Old Grimsby.' Tainton's eyes were never the same after Brentford, and he was forced to squint to make out the individual buildings. 'If they do not know, then we move to the west coast.'

'New Grimsby,' Fassett said scornfully. 'Imaginative lot, aren't they?'

Tainton ignored him. 'Then there are houses elsewhere. Lonely homesteads. My guess is it will be one of those, but we must start here and move on.'

'How long will that take?'

Tainton pulled a face to show he did not much care. 'Tresco is two miles long, from north to south, and perhaps a mile wide at its broadest point. We should cover it swiftly enough.'

'Stryker said Cade's house was overlooking the sea.'

'Everywhere,' Tainton growled, 'overlooks the sea, you dullard.'

Fassett's scarred face seemed to tense, his lips pressing into a rigid line, but he thought better of whatever retort had first sprung to mind. 'He said Cade had a retainer there, looking after the place.'

One of the seamen trundled past, doffing his wax-encrusted cap to the men. Tainton waited until he was out of earshot. 'We must find him.' He fell silent for a short time as both men noticed the stone blockhouse that perched upon the high cliff to their left, the southern point of the harbour. Like the rest of Scilly's fortifications, it was plain and functional, but it was afforded a clear view of the approaches to the harbour, and its batteries would be easily trained upon any vessel making an aggressive play for Old Grimsby. 'The Lord has provided,' he said, ignoring Fassett's contemptuous expression, 'for we know the gold is on Tresco. We are not spread so thin in our enquiries as before.'

'Only so many places left to look on St Mary's,' Fassett said.

Tainton set his jaw, finally feeling as though the mission was moving forwards. 'Let us sniff out this treasure once and for all,' he said, feeling the breath of the Holy Spirit invigorate his broken body. Because now — wondrously, miraculously — he even knew where to look.

Fassett blinked hard as he looked away from the high battery, perhaps imagining the same scene of destruction in his mind's eye. 'Then back to Star Castle?'

'Aye. It is still too treacherous to risk the open sea. Consider the fate of Stryker's ship.' Out in the harbour a small, single-masted boat was fighting against the waves, thrown high and low and side to side on the angry swells as its crew of four wrestled to keep control. Tainton waved, realizing that the boat was intended to collect him and his three men, for the harbour was much too shallow and confined for the *Silver Swan* to negotiate. 'Besides,' he said, still waving, 'we must see the one-eyed black-guard and his doxy pay for their crimes against God. Balthazar can do what he likes with the rest of them, but Stryker and the woman are mine.'

CHAPTER 10

Southampton, Hampshire, 12 October 1643

It was an hour before dawn. Only two fires were left in the courtyard of the gaol, their flames bathing the old slaughter-house in a diluted, tremulous light. This was the quiet time between the regular night-watch and those allocated to patrol the new day; when tired sentries began to think of their beds, red eyes becoming heavy after a night of wandering the silent complex, secure in the knowledge that their cowed charges would all be snoring soundly into their filthy rags.

Five musketeers converged around one of the braziers. One hung back, watchful despite his yawns, while the rest set down their muskets and bandoliers a half-dozen paces from the flaming iron cage. The leather collars held a dozen stoppered boxes apiece, each containing enough powder for one musket shot. Bandoliers and open fires were a potentially lethal combination, and none of the men wished to have their face blown off while they warmed their bones.

One of the sentries stamped his feet as he pushed his palms as close to the flames as he could bear. The mud crunched like dry twigs beneath his shoes. 'Soon be winter . . .'

Another man was packing a blackened clay pipe. He brought it close to his face to gently blow specks of tobacco from the rim. 'Drink the smoke,' he muttered. 'Keeps you warm.'

'I told you,' the first man replied testily, his breath leaving a wispy trail of vapour, 'it makes me cough like I got the consumption.'

'Suit yourself.'

'Just get these other fires lit, eh? The next watch'll whine like speared hogs if we leave 'em cold.'

'*Guards!*' a voice called in sudden, shrill panic. '*Guards!*'

The musketeers at the fire looked at each other. The man with the pipe sighed heavily. 'Jesu, I'm in no mood for this. See what he wants, Gregor.'

The sentry who still had his musket nodded. 'Yes, Corporal.' He was a youngster, in his mid teens, with a pimply, sallow complexion. He nodded sullenly, adjusting his Montero so that the flaps covered his ears, and walked gingerly towards the building whence the cry had come. He stayed well away from the rickety door, levelling his musket. 'What is it?'

A wracking cough rang out from within, followed by a lingering groan. 'Plague!'

'Wh—what?' Gregor stammered, edging back a step. He blew on his match, keeping it fresh and hot. 'What did you say?'

'Plague, sir!' the voice repeated its warning. 'King Death! Help us, I beg you!' A face appeared from the darkness within the makeshift gaol, pressing up against a palm-sized patch of exposed wattle in the wall beside the doorway.

Gregor's mouth fell slack. 'Pl—plague?'

The men at the fire had all heard the exchange. The corporal pulled a sour face, spitting into the flickering flames and thrusting his pipe into his belt. He marched angrily over to the tumbledown shed. 'Tell 'em to keep it down.'

'But they got the pestis, Corp,' Gregor bleated querulously.

'Nonsense! You ever seen someone wi' plague before, dunderchops?' The corporal waited for his young protégé to shake his head. 'Then who's to say what sickness he's got? Stupid bugger swived the wrong filthy slattern, like as not.' He thumped on the door with a fist, causing it to shudder noisily. 'Show yourself, man, damn your hide!'

The face that had so shaken Gregor now appeared again in the gap between door and frame. The corporal leaned in squinting, but he could not get a good enough view, and he quickly unhooked the iron ring at his belt. Finding the right key, he unlocked the door, waiting for Gregor to flip open the priming pan of his musket before he opened it.

What they saw made them step backwards involuntarily. The man within looked as though he was a half-rotten corpse. He was stooped and sobbing, dry, juddering coughs rolling through him like never-ending thunder. But that was the least of his problems. The skin of his face was utterly ruined. A swollen, undulating mass of sores and bulges had spread over his cheeks and neck. The wrinkles at the corners of his eyes were lumpy and flaking, the corners of his mouth pitted and moist. The disease had not simply afflicted the wretched fellow, it had utterly, ruthlessly consumed him.

The sentries still revelling in the brazier's heat were beginning to twitch now, unwilling to relinquish their comforts, but unable to ignore what was happening at the dilapidated cell block. One of them called: 'What is it, Corp?'

'I know not,' the corporal responded, though his eyes remained locked on the prisoner.

'He has been coughing blood through the night!' a man shouted from the gloom. He appeared behind the afflicted fellow to address the soldiers. He was tall, with a large nose, and his head nodded exaggeratedly with each syllable he uttered. 'Splutters his guts and shits his britches all at once. Look at him!'

'Jesu,' the corporal whispered. He stepped back. 'Out here, you corny-faced bastard. Out where I can see you properly.'

'Out?' the boy, Gregor, yelped. His musket trembled in his grip. 'Jesu, Corp, what if he gives it us?'

'On second thoughts, stay there,' the corporal growled. 'Stay there, I say!' He turned to the men, who had finally edged away from the heat. They seemed transfixed in the face of this horror. He clapped his hands vigorously. 'Fetch the captain, lads, and be swift about it. Fetch the fackin' captain!'

The three guards disappeared between two of the crumbling buildings. The corporal watched them go, but before he had turned back, Gregor fired his musket.

★   ★   ★

Lancelot Forrester's face felt like it was coated in dried wax for all the movement the caked bird shit would allow, and he was glad to feel clumps of the stinking excreta break off as he launched himself at the musketeer. Gregor was not watching properly. His musket was loaded and primed, pan exposed to the glowing coal, but its owner was more interested in watching his corporal than watching his mark. So Forrester, face smothered in a poisonous poultice of mud and sand, splinters and saliva, bird droppings and mucus, took his opportunity. Gregor saw him coming, pulled the trigger, but it took time for serpent to snap, match to fall, charge to ignite, and when the bullet had flown, Gregor's muzzle was pointed at the cloudless sky.

The young soldier hit the ground hard, wind punched from his body as Forrester's heavier frame smashed into his chest. He cried out, but no sound would come, and Forrester, wreathed in the white smoke still pouring from the musket, jammed his fist into Gregor's face, obliterating his nose in a shower of blood.

The corporal drew his sword, but he had no musket, for he and his exhausted colleagues had dumped their weapons to approach the fire. He held the blade out, beckoning Forrester to him, but the rest of the prisoners were streaming out of the tumbledown shed like rats from a flaming granary, whooping and bellowing and pledging revenge, and the corporal knew he was beaten. He retreated immediately, tripping on his comrades' muskets in his flight, desperate to be out of the courtyard before he was overwhelmed.

'Go!' Forrester screamed, yanking savagely on the length of match coiled about the hapless Gregor's forearm. He threw it about his neck, pausing to scratch at his face so that some of the vile paste came away in sweet relief, and snatched up two muskets, a snapsack and a bandolier. Tossing one of the weapons to Sergeant Dewhurst, he called: 'I go to Basing. Are you with me?'

The Hawk pecked the air as he caught the musket, pointing the barrel towards the courtyard's southern arch. 'The horses are stabled through there!'

A bell tolled, deep and repetitive. Forrester looked back

towards the officer's billet. 'They've raised the alarm. The whole garrison will be out here in no time.'

'What about the others?' Dewhurst asked, casting his gaze about the chaos as fellow prisoners ransacked the buildings, smashed open doors to free their friends, or scattered in search of escape.

Forrester was already running. 'Each to his own. We got 'em out, the rest is up to them.'

Dewhurst followed. They passed under the archway and made straight for the stable doors, found them unlocked, and hauled them open. A man in soldier's clothes stood within, rubbing bleary eyes having evidently been disturbed by the ringing of the bell. He stared in stunned surprise, then darted to his right where, from a hook on a low beam, his scabbard dangled. Forrester was on him before he could draw the hanger, sweeping the butt end of the musket in a low arc that scythed through the man's shins. A crack echoed about the building, and the man was on the floor, scrabbling at the filthy hay as he pawed at his legs.

'There,' Dewhurst said.

Seven or eight horses were tethered in pens at the far end of the rectangular building. Forrester saw his own mount, fixed to a rail by reins and a cheap-looking head collar. 'Oberon! Good Lord, I'm glad you're here! Come, Sergeant, choose a horse and let's be gone from this damnable place.' Dewhurst hesitated. 'What, man? What is it?'

'I cannot ride, sir.'

'Then it is with us you must throw in your lot,' Forrester ordered. He handed his musket and snapsack to Dewhurst, put the bandolier around his shoulders, and untied Oberon's reins from the side-rail of the pen. He jumped up, clinging to the black gelding for dear life as he swung a leg across. There was no time to saddle the beast, and he had to clench his thighs tight to avoid sliding straight off. He took the muskets, laying them across his lap, and held out a hand. 'Get your arse up here, Sergeant. They'll be at our heels any moment.'

Dewhurst did as he was told, scrambling indelicately up on to Oberon's muscular back. He took the muskets from Forrester, jammed them across his legs, keeping the stocks tight in the crook of an arm, and gripped the captain's waist like a drowning man. Forrester kicked hard, bellowing encouragement into Oberon's pricked ear, and the beast wheeled about, breaking into a canter before he was even out in the open. A blast of cold air hit them as they left the stable, and they could see men running through the archway now, blades and pistols, muskets and halberds brandished as the sun began to lighten the dawn.

Forrester gave the soldiers a wave, wrenched at the gelding's reins, and they were away.

St Mary's, Isles of Scilly, 12 October 1643

The man stepping on to the wharf had a face that fitted well with the Scillies. Like the storm-beaten cliffs, it was hard and craggy, the nose crooked, a scar bisecting the narrow, cleanly shaven chin along its width. It was a face weathered almost to a sheen by seas and gales, scorched to the colour of honey by the sun and framed by long, thick hair that was a battleground of dark brown and silver. It was a face that belonged to a man used to hard living, a man accustomed to violence. The kind of man Captain William Balthazar dreaded welcoming to Hugh Town.

'The storms have waned, thank God,' Balthazar said, forcing the trepidation from his voice. He was standing on the end of the timber platform that extended like a huge tongue licking the shallows, hands clasped firmly behind his back. The wind was strong, forcing him to lean into it for stability, the sea glistening below the morning's fresh sunlight.

The tall, wiry newcomer snatched off his wide, feathered hat and bowed low, like a royal courtier, the cliff-edge face splitting in a smile that was at once predatory and handsome. 'Gave us a battering out at Lundy, I can tell you.' Before the captain of Star Castle could respond, the man clicked his tongue. From down beyond the jetty's edge there came a lingering howl and a short, sharp bark and a pair of dogs appeared. One was a scrawny mongrel, with a shaggy coat of black and white and one milky eye, while the other was a brindle mastiff, a hulking figure of slobber and muscle. They pressed about their master's legs and he replaced his hat so that he might use both hands to ruffle the fur of each in turn. 'Good boys.'

The skiff from which the newcomer and his hounds had climbed rocked wildly as its two-man crew shoved off with dripping oars, grunting against the capricious currents as they headed back out to deeper water. Balthazar let his eyes flicker to the anchorage at St Mary's Pool. He adjusted his wire-rimmed spectacles so that he could better see the warship that had arrived just two hours earlier. 'But your ship looks to be hale and hearty, Captain Gibbons.'

Titus Gibbons was master of the *Stag*, an English-built sloop of light ordnance and sleek lines, designed for speed and ambush. She was smaller than the frigates with which she frequently tussled, but much faster, and her crew, veterans of the never-ending fight against the Barbary pirates, invariably outclassed anything they came up against. But Gibbons, Balthazar thought bitterly, was, after all, not a great deal more than a pirate himself. It was common knowledge that the captain of the *Stag*, a native of Penzance, had been a smuggler in his time, only keeping his neck from the noose by his invaluable effectiveness against the feared corsairs who cruised out of North Africa to plague Europe's Christian coasts, stealing their gold and enslaving their women and children. Now, of course, his attentions had turned to the Parliamentarian navy. As an experienced privateer and proud Cornishman, Gibbons had been licensed by the king to roam the seas, harassing Roundhead shipping, plundering their merchantmen and snapping at the heels of their ponderous, if formidable, men-o'-war.

Gibbons opened his mouth in a wide yawn, smiling in satisfaction as his strong jaw cracked loudly. 'We would replenish supplies, if we may, and take the opportunity to repair a mast and a gun.'

Balthazar frowned. 'You had trouble?'

Gibbons pulled down the hem of his green and silver doublet as if to flatten out any creases. 'Rebel frigate off Port Isaac. Bastardly gullion slung a brace o' chain-shot 'cross our deck.'

Balthazar looked again at the lazily bobbing sloop. 'Toll?'

'Three dead men, a cracked murderer and a damaged mast,' Gibbons replied. 'The bodies have long since been committed to the depths, but the repairs are not so swiftly dealt with.'

'The mast you may see to, Captain,' Balthazar said. 'But the murderer,' he added, thinking of the gunwale-mounted swivelling hand-cannon used to rake a ship's decks, 'may not be so straightforward. We have but one forge in Hugh Town, and its time and resource is stretched to breaking already.'

Gibbons shrugged. 'So be it.' He stooped to pat the mastiff's wide pate, eliciting a barely perceptible whine for his trouble. 'This bluff cove is Sir Francis.'

Balthazar bobbed his knees in something like a curtsy, immediately regretting the gesture. 'I'm sure he is an obedient companion.'

Titus Gibbons laughed loudly, the sound vibrating in Balthazar's ribcage. 'That he is, Captain Balthazar! And well put! This other fearsome beast,' he said, stroking the bristles of the smaller mongrel, 'is Sir Walter. He is not an obedient companion, I do not mind telling you, but I would never be without him.'

Balthazar forced another smile. 'You are welcome as ever, Captain Gibbons, naturally,' he lied cheerfully. For all his affected style and grace, Gibbons was an uncivilized wretch as far as William Balthazar was concerned. Much, he reflected, like Roger Tainton and his motley gaggle of bullies. But as Scilly's senior officer and de facto governor, Balthazar was hamstrung by the war. He must make every concession to these ruthless men, for they fought under the colours of King Charles, and that made them his allies, whether he liked it or not. He realized he was fiddling furiously with the pearl earring at his left lobe, and he snapped his arm down, stuffing it behind his back.

Titus Gibbons beamed, at once charming and terrifying. 'Always a pleasure, Captain Balthazar. My crew will stay aboard the *Stag* for the most part, so there'll be no trouble in town.'

'I would appreciate that.'

'But I'll be grateful if you might allow them ashore in small numbers. They have been at sea a long time. They require a moment of . . . *comfort* . . . if you understand my meaning.'

Balthazar knew exactly what the privateer meant, and the notion repulsed him. 'In twos and threes.'

'Twos and threes?' Gibbons echoed. 'One per man will do well enough, sir! Well, perhaps a brace for me, eh?' he added with a wink.

'The men,' Balthazar snapped, irritation beginning to puncture his calm exterior, 'are permitted into Hugh Town in their twos and threes.'

'Understood,' Gibbons said, holding up placating hands. 'Clear as the chime at dog-watch.'

Balthazar tugged at the sharp end of his waxed beard. 'You'll stay at the castle?'

'An honour, Captain. Have you heard from Godolphin or Bassett?'

Balthazar moved aside to show the privateer along the walkway. 'Not in weeks. They fight on the mainland with Hopton, as far as I'm aware.'

Gibbons walked at Balthazar's side, the dogs winding in and out of their legs, padding softly on the damp timbers. 'They made him a baron, did you hear?'

'I did not. News takes its time to reach us here, truth to tell.'

'He is Lord Hopton of Stratton now.'

Balthazar glanced up at the tall sailor. 'He is recovered, then? We heard tell he was wounded in battle.'

'So they say. Burned badly, but mended in the main.'

'And what of the sea?' Balthazar asked. 'The Parliament ships harry you?'

Gibbons nodded. 'They rule the waves, except in the south-west. We may put in at Bristol and the Welsh ports, and here, of course. East of Plymouth becomes a tad more challenging, I'll confess.' He blew out his cheeks. 'In truth, we are outshipped, outgunned and outmanned. Those vessels remaining loyal to the Crown may only inconvenience the enemy. The war must be won on land.'

'Pray God our forces prevail, for all our sakes.'

'Indeed,' Gibbons said. He looked over at the castle, adjusting his hat to shield his gaze from the rising sun. 'Ah, my old friend. The ugliest star I ever saw, and yet the most welcome to mine eyes.'

'The hearths are ablaze, Captain Gibbons. Come and take your ease.'

Southampton, Hampshire, 12 October 1643

The breath of the guards wreathed their shouldered muskets as though the pieces had been recently discharged. The ground was solid and uneven underfoot, mud churned by boots and frozen by a bitter night. The new sun had brought with it a touch of warmth to thaw feet and hands, melt the veil of frost that whitened the iron hinges and bolts of the cell doors, but still the surface of the well was glazed and the roof tiles glistened. The courtyard's braziers raged red and orange, belching out heat for the guards to enjoy, yet none dared draw close to the iron cages. None had the nerve to snatch comfort in this grey dawn, for shame required penance.

Richard Norton, Parliamentarian colonel of horse and newly made Governor of Southampton, felt the skin at his cheeks and neck burn and knew it was as much borne of fury as of the cold air. 'Speak, man, and be quick about it.'

'F—forgive me, Governor—' the sentry intoned through a roiling vapour cloud.

'I do not want apologies, Corporal,' Norton snapped, 'I want answers!'

'Sir, may I—' another man began tentatively.

Norton rounded on him. 'No, Captain Miller, you may not. You may command this pigsty of a prison, but you were not present when our piglets were let loose, were you?'

The captain, a fastidious little man with immaculate uniform and permanently pursed mouth, shook his head, his gloved hands worrying at the brim of his hat. 'I was not, sir.'

Norton shifted his attention back to the sentry. 'Well?'

The musketeer who had commanded the pre-dawn watch stared apple-eyed around the abandoned slaughter-yard as though the answer might come to him from one of the decrepit sheds that had been crammed full of enemy prisoners. When his gaze fell upon the only one of the low, rectangular buildings that was open, he took a deep, lingering breath. 'They fooled us.'

The empty unit was behind Norton, and he turned to stare at it. 'That much is obvious.' He looked back at the corporal. 'How did this humiliation transpire, pray?'

'They—that is to say—we—'

'Spit it out, man, or you will find yourself the next guest of this establishment.'

As ever, Wagner Kovac was at Norton's side. 'You want me make him talk?'

'His face was covered in muck, sir,' the corporal blurted, transfixed on the huge man with the bushy beard, ice-blue eyes and strange accent.

'Muck?'

The corporal nodded vigorously, deciding speed of confession would stave off the governor's Teutonic henchman. 'Bird—*doings*. And whatever else they could mix with it.'

'And he put this on his face?'

'Aye, sir. Smeared all over. Like a diseased man. A leper, like, or some terrible pox. They cried plague.'

'Then you should have put an extra lock on the door, Corporal, not opened it.'

'I realize that now, sir. I thought to take a look, is all. See if they was lying.'

Norton gritted his teeth. 'Well you certainly found out.' He scanned the courtyard. 'We have a score of escaped malignants.'

'Aye, sir,' the corporal said sheepishly. 'I am sorry, sir.' He straightened suddenly, setting his jaw and casting his eyes towards the gathered musketeers who looked on in contrite silence. 'I'll find 'em, 'pon my word. Me and the lads, we'll—'

'No, Corporal,' Norton cut him off with a dismissive wave. 'You've done enough, I think.' Footsteps crunched behind. He twisted to see a party of men advance from the direction of the brick house that served as the captain's quarters.

'Norton!' the man at the forefront of the group called. 'Norton! Why was I not summoned?'

Norton smiled wolfishly. 'Sergeant-Major Murford. How nice it is to see you this crisp morn. Though I must insist that you employ my correct title when addressing me.'

Murford halted a few paces from Norton. 'Governor,' he rasped through gritted teeth. 'Why was I not summoned? These are my men.'

'Not a claim I would be quick to make, if I were you,' Norton replied. 'You were not summoned because you were not required. But be assured, Sergeant-Major, that, in time, I shall see these pathetic minions of yours fill a pike block on some God-forsaken field. They might learn their trade properly, or die in the trying. For now, they may keep the remainder of our charges secure. My men will see our fugitives rounded up. Captain Kovac?'

The Croat stepped forwards, deliberately moving between old governor and new. 'Governor Norton, sir.'

'We have twenty missing Cavaliers. Take your troop and hunt them down.'

Kovac dipped his head solemnly. 'A pleasure, sir.'

'It will not be too taxing, for they are all on foot.'

'Sir, I—' the corporal blurted, his bottom lip trembling now.

All eyes went to him. 'What is it?' Norton asked, sensing trouble.

The corporal's head looked as if it might shrink into his shoulders as he spoke. 'They're not all on foot.'

Sir William Waller was high up on the great castle's eastern rampart, body tensed against the icy wind. His elbows were planted firmly on the crenellated stone, perspective glass pressed against one eye, the other eye clamped shut. He trained the instrument on the convoy that had trundled into town. It seemed to have no end, stretching back along the road that coiled about the high walls, wagon after wagon piled with provisions, eventually vanishing as the muddy thoroughfare curved through Windsor's gates and out into the countryside. The long train slithered like a great serpent into the dense woodland that smothered the land between here and Staines. It had rained during the night, enough to make the ground – churned by shoe and hoof and wheel – into a sticky morass that clung to feet and sucked at each vehicle. The going, there-fore, was infuriatingly poor, drivers forced to leap out of their wagons to beat and berate their lowing oxen. Every few yards there was another blockage, another cart tipped to the side, two wheels sliding in the grime, their opposites hoisted impo-tently in the air.

Waller moved the glass from one vehicle to the next. Between the struggling wagons and their plaintive beasts of burden were the soldiers. They were arrayed in marching order, fixed in dense units so that it was difficult for them to negotiate the trees that hugged close to the road's flanks. They were stuck, there-fore, behind and between the vehicles that carried the provisions destined for their bellies and the ammunition bound for their muskets. Officers raged, sergeants bawled and the men stood in their files, sung songs, chattered and complained. Some pissed at the roadside, their urine mixing with the dung of the animals to make the mud all the more viscous and vile. The officers had long since abandoned their efforts to prevent them from adding to the mess, for too much time had passed to order a man to cross his legs.

'If the Cavaliers were to attack now,' Waller muttered, 'all would be lost, by God. They could smash and loot our carts with impunity.'

'You have a whole army here, General,' an aide, one of three men standing just to Waller's rear, responded smartly.

Waller trained the glass on the town. Its thatches spread out from the foot of the royal fortress like mushrooms at the base of an ancient elm. 'Really?'

The aide moved to the rampart and looked down. 'Perhaps we should send some dragooners out to hurry them along.'

The town was a mass of roads and alleys separating cottages from shops, and warehouses from civic buildings. From where he stood, it looked to Waller like a vast nest. But what was most striking was the sheer number of people. His new army was here, spread out in taverns and homes, within the town and without, all the way across the smaller hamlets and into Staines-upon-Thames to the south, and Slough to the north. Waller had begun raising the force a month earlier in the wake of his devastating defeat at Roundway Down, rebuilding from the nucleus of his Western Association that had been so completely obliterated on those bloody slopes. Yet just as the new army had looked promising, momentum had stalled. His commission had been retracted after a long-running dispute with the Lord General, the Earl of Essex, and only now, after being forced to grovel in the glow of Essex's new-found glory, had Waller been returned to some level of authority. Essex was the leading light after his heroics at Gloucester and Newbury, but Waller was finally in possession of the commission he needed to complete his own force.

The general nodded. 'There is a good portion of an army down there, I grant you. But which of them is ready to march, let alone fight? It is only a month since we moved them here, and yet they act as though their war is done. Chasing the local girls and wallowing in the taphouses and stews. If our convoy were attacked, they'd not drag their britches up in time, let alone find their muskets. Get some dragoons out on the road, as you suggest. Let us have our supplies inside the castle before any brave Cavalier thinks to snaffle them.'

'Aye, sir,' the aide replied, taking his leave.

Sir William Waller lowered the glass, stood back from the wall and stretched, covering his mouth as he yawned. 'We shall have a commendable force when we are done, Colonel Vandruske.'

One of Waller's remaining two companions was a tall man with fair hair cropped close to the scalp, a large scar running jaggedly across his left cheek, and dark blue eyes. He wore civilian, if expensively cut, clothes beneath a breastplate, and a huge broadsword hung at his waist. 'I do not know about that, General.'

Waller was short and portly, with an oval face, light brown hair and a long, hooked nose above an auburn moustache. He raised a hand to tug at the strands of his beard, which was trimmed into a triangular wedge at the point of his chin. 'Speak plain, Jonas.'

Vandruske frowned as he evidently calculated something in his head. 'We have good numbers,' he said in a thick Dutch accent. 'Your regiment of horse, General, plus your five hundred dragooners, and your own foot regiment.'

Waller nodded. 'And Heselrige's horse, do not forget, along with the regiment commanded by Colonel Turner.'

'And this is good,' Vandruske answered. 'Then Colonel Burghill's foot, which I am pleased to lead.'

'For which you have my thanks,' Waller added, suddenly uncomfortable at the reference to one of the men who had taken retirement after the catastrophe at Roundway. 'You must not forget Potley's,' he said hastily, wishing to steer the subject to the present.

Vandruske counted the units on his fingers. 'And infantry under colonels Popham, Carr, Cooke and Harley.' He stared up at the great circular edifice of Windsor's round tower. 'But it is an army founded upon failure, sir. We took terrible blows at Roundway. Just terrible. How can these men recover to fight? And now they say Lord Hopton will strike east.'

'Do not forget,' Waller returned, beginning to feel irritated at the Dutchman's lack of faith, 'we have been assigned three new regiments from the London militia.'

Vandruske grimaced.

Waller sighed. He knew the colonel was simply reflecting the doubts of many. Waller's ambition had almost seen his entire army destroyed once before, and now that the star of his old enemy, the Earl of Essex, was on the rise, could Waller be trusted not to sacrifice sanity amid the temptation to compete? 'It is true that the Trained Bands have not seen active service thus far, but their counterparts who marched with my lord Essex acquitted themselves admirably at Newbury Fight. And the largest of our imminent contingent, the Westminster Liberty Regiment, brings near two thousand men.'

'The Red Regiment, aye,' Vandruske said, using the term commonly used for the regiment that marched behind a red banner spangled with silver stars.

'But the Greens and Yellows, I hear,' the third man spoke now, 'bring only that number between them.' He was tall, willow-wand thin, with a clean-shaven face that was extraordinarily long. He had long, black hair and huge, pointed ears, an effect that had always reminded Waller of a donkey. 'Which is not spectacular.'

'You would pour water 'pon my powder too, Colonel Adair?' Waller said in exasperation. 'Very well, I cannot deny it, but they are still good numbers. The Trained Bands will be with us in a matter of days, whatever you might think of them, and we will have a force to be reckoned with, upon my honour we will. Did you hear tell of Winceby?'

Vandruske shook his head. 'It is man or place?'

'A place,' Colonel Adair replied.

Waller nodded. 'The Earl of Manchester joined forces with Cromwell and the Fairfaxes. They defeated the Lincolnshire Royalists in battle.'

'At this Vinceby,' Vandruske said.

'Just so.' Waller set his jaw, unwilling to be dispirited by the council of his officers. 'Since Gloucester, the tide has turned in our favour, gentlemen. We are winning battles where hitherto we were not. Myself and the Lord General are reconciled, so that we might now each lead a grand army, and of course, we have made the Solemn League and Covenant.'

'I have read the news-books,' Vandruske said. 'King Charles denounced it.'

'Of course he denounced it!' Waller laughed. 'He called it traitorous and seditious, as I recall. Presumes his subjects will not take the vow. But they will, and we will be saved, pray God.'

'By the Scotch, sir? I like them not.'

'On the contrary,' Waller replied. 'They are good fighters, professional and soldierly, but bolstered with just the right dash of zeal for our Lord.'

'For my part,' the Dutchman said, 'I confess I find them awkward, braggartly and ever inciting quarrels.'

'That is your opinion, and I shan't attempt to change it.' Waller wagged a finger at Vandruske. 'But mark me, Jonas, I see good things to come. They will win us this war.'

Colonel Adair screwed up his equine face. 'And force upon us their damnable Kirk.'

'Would that be so terrible?' Waller mused.

'It is a yoke about our necks, General. Synods and assemblies commanding our churches, controlling them.'

'Oh, Colonel Adair,' Sir William Waller said with a heavy sigh, 'I do tire of your belly-aching. We may debate this further, I am sure, but for now I would see our burgeoning army make ready for its first great task. Hopton will soon march into the south-east. We will meet him, and we will crush him. Gather my most senior officers, and tell them we are soon to leave this place.'

Adair looked as though he might argue his case further, but in the end he simply said, 'Where do we go, General?'

'Farnham. We will muster there, and look to the west.'

Adair nodded crisply, bowing to the little general, offering a curt nod to Colonel Vandruske, and spinning on his heels.

'He worries too much,' the Dutch officer said as they watched Adair go.

'Indeed,' Waller lied, for in his heart he sensed a storm brewing on the rebellion's horizon; one that threatened to split the Parliamentarian cause apart. He forced it to the back of his mind. The time for reckoning would come, he knew. But that time was not yet upon them. Now it was time to win a war. That was all that mattered.

Tresco, Isles of Scilly, 12 October 1643

Old Grimsby had proven a waste of time. Tainton, Fassett and Cordell had spent the previous evening and much of the morning asking questions in the village. There was a tavern of sorts, taking up the front half of a boat-builder's house, and a small, whitewashed chapel on the rising ground to the south. But in the main it was a fishing village, and the modest dwellings of families scratching a living from the treacherous sea were Tresco's real hub. The tongueless Squires had lurked in the street, guarding the small wagon they had purchased, his very presence an encouragement for questions to be frankly and swiftly answered. But no one could tell them of a house owned by Sir Alfred Cade. At least on St Mary's they recognized the dead lawyer's name. Here, it was as though he had never existed.

Now, as the skies darkened for the approach of dusk, Tainton and Fassett were in New Grimsby, the older settlement's sister-village, which hugged the opposite coast. Like Old Grimsby, it was sheltered by a harbour that sat between twin cliffs curving out into the waves like two pincers, turning the coast into a crescent moon and the waters within a little calmer. What differentiated the two hamlets were their defences, for where Old Grimsby had the blockhouse, New Grimsby was overlooked by a much larger artillery fort perched upon the higher ground to the north.

'King Charles Castle,' Tainton muttered as the pair strode down one of New Grimsby's outlying streets, the former cavalryman's spurs calling out the rhythm of their boots.

Fassett stared up at the rocky bluff to the north–east. 'Looks too old to carry the bugger's name.'

'It is. They have recently renamed it in honour of him, so Balthazar tells me.'

'Dear Billy. A font o' knowledge. Not much of a castle, though, is it?'

Tainton shook his head. 'It apparently has deep earthworks, so it is not so feeble as you might presume.' He pointed to a building about fifty paces further along the road. A broom was nailed to the wall beside its low doorway. 'Taphouse. We'll begin there. One hopes your apes will discharge their duties diligently.'

Squires and Cordell had been dispatched to the west side of the settlement to make inquiries amongst the fishermen. Fassett shrugged. 'Locke will loom, Clay will do the talking, and folk'll squeal, have no doubt.'

'I truly pray so.'

'As do I. We ain't had a lot o' luck so far.'

'Luck has nothing to do with it,' Tainton said, shaking an admonishing finger at his employee. 'God's hand is in every-thing. *Everything*. He will deliver the gold to us when the time is right. We must but strive.'

'But they do not know of Cade hereabouts,' Fassett said, frus-tration straining his words. 'I think Stryker lied. The gold's back on St Mary's.'

'You saw how shamed he was. He did not lie. Who's to say the locals would know of Cade's house?'

'Of course they'd know,' Fassett persisted. 'Grand lawyer like Cade? They'd know exactly what properties he'd have owned.'

Tainton could not argue against Fassett's logic. A powerful man like Sir Alfred Cade would be conspicuous in an insular place like Scilly, and a veritable beacon on so tiny an island as Tresco. But still he believed Stryker had spoken true, for the humiliation and regret had been etched deeply on the soldier's face. Too deeply to be false.

Inside the tavern the room was dingy but warm, a fug of tobacco and wood smoke roiling about the dark roof beams. A counter had been installed at one wall, behind which a fat fellow stood with folded arms, grimly guarding his ale barrels.

'Christ,' Fassett said under his breath as he shut the door and stepped in, 'you'd think he had liquid gems in them casks.'

'Out here good ale is worth its weight in gold,' Tainton answered. 'And do not blaspheme.' There were three other men in the room, all hunched over their pots, but they did not look up, and he decided it would be more expedient to make directly for the tapster. He leaned against the counter, suppressing his revulsion at its stickiness. 'Have you heard the name Sir Alfred Cade, good sirrah?'

The fat man moved his head slowly from side to side. 'Can't say I have, sir.' His face gleamed beneath a sheen of sweat and he ran a thick forearm across his brow. 'Feel free to ask 'em.'

Tainton turned, raising his voice. 'Sir Alfred Cade,' he announced. 'Do any of you know the name?'

Silence. Sterne Fassett cleared his throat. 'Half a hog to the man who might tell us if Cade owned property on this goat's turd of a rock.'

The insult, at least, raised two of the faces. They stared up at Fassett through bleary, red-rimmed eyes but neither spoke. The third man's head snapped up, and Tainton's hopes were raised, only to be dashed when the old soak drained his pot, belched loudly, and slid to the floor, a thin stream of vomit leaking from the side of his mouth.

Tainton steeled himself against the wretched stench and looked at the other two men. From a concealed pocket in his coat he produced a gold coin, turning it deliberately slowly in the candlelight. 'A full angel for the man who might help us.'

One of the drunks stood, swaying slightly. 'Does the reward stand,' he said, pausing for a wet-sounding hiccough, 'if'n I tells you a guess?'

'What kind of guess?' Tainton said, slipping the coin back into the folds of his coat.

The swaying patron blinked rapidly, rubbed an eye with one hand and scratching his backside with the other. 'There's a house down at Carn Near.'

'Carn Near?'

'The southern tip of the island,' the tapster said.

'Tha's it,' the drunk said with a half-witted smile. 'Carn Near, like I said. Big house. Blast me if I knows who owns it.'

'Who lives there, you copper-nosed bastard?' Fassett pressed impatiently.

'Local looks after the place. Never says who 'is master is.'

This sounded promising. Tainton stepped forward a pace, the angel in his palm once again. 'Take us to this fellow, sir,' he said as calmly as he could. 'This warden.'

'Already have,' the drunk said. He belched loudly, and pointed to the man lying in a pool of his own vomit. 'Meet Toby Ball.'

CHAPTER 11

The Duchy of Carniola was a tiny state at the south-eastern extremity of the Holy Roman Empire. Trapped between Venice, Hungary and Carinthia, it was never under threat from the Protestant states of the north, nor the thrusting efforts of the Swedes under Adolphus. But it was painfully close to the Ottoman Empire, and that proximity alone made its Catholic majority suspicious and intolerant of those viewed as working against the Papacy, regardless of whether they were heathen or Christian. And that was why, when Wagner Kovac was just eleven, he had watched his mother and father strangled to death. On that cold December day, when the crowds had gathered in the marketplace, Wagner Kovac had discovered that life was cruel and hard. He had taken the first steps on his new path, a path that would take him across Europe, from the Hungarian peaks to the rugged French coast, fighting, killing and plundering. Now England's rebels wanted his services, and what was more, they encouraged him to dismantle the houses of God, plank by righteous plank. He rather liked the place.

'We've come too far, sir,' one of Kovac's troopers said, his tone hesitant.

'No,' Kovac replied bluntly. They were deep in an expanse of dense woodland, having tracked their prey along winding bridleways and rough paths for a day and a night. 'You English are all the same. Pious on surface, bloody pagans underneath.'

The trooper looked up at the trees, the deep creases on his

brow giving away the truth of the captain's words. He swallowed hard, evidently wrestling with an innate fear of the forest. 'Aye, sir.'

'They're still here,' Kovac went on undaunted. 'We follow this track.' Following Norton's commandment, Kovac had divided his troop into squads, each taking a different road or track out of the prison complex in order to round up their lost Cavaliers. Most, he knew, would be easy enough to corral, for they were enfeebled by captivity and travelling on foot. But two of their pale-faced birds had flown the cage with purpose, stealing weapons and a horse and riding north. Kovac had taken a trio of his best cavalrymen and had pursued those ambitious fugitives. He would bring the malignants to heel, truss them up, and drag them all the way back, because his reputation rested upon it.

'What if they've doubled back again?' one of the other men asked.

'They haven't,' Kovac answered disdainfully, pointing to the ground. 'The mud is wet enough to leave tracks. See there? Hooves.'

'Could be a different horse.'

Kovac shook his head. He had learned to track while fighting for the Protestants against the emperor's forces and he was as competent as any man. 'Keep your eyes sharp. They're here. I can feel it.'

Tresco, Isles of Scilly, 13 October 1643

'Ho there, friend!'

The water was so cold it hurt. It crashed over the man's face, invaded his nostrils and soaked his hair and chest. Toby Ball jolted upright, spluttering and gasping, clawing at his eyes and spitting saliva flecked with vomit. He tried to stand, but his legs felt like molasses, and he immediately collapsed on to his rump. There he stayed, gasping. A vague memory of stale smoke and strong drink ghosted into his head. 'I was in the taphouse.'

The man standing over him grunted. 'You were in your cups.' He was cloaked from head to foot, so that only a glimpse of pallid skin and blue eyes could be seen. 'We saw you home safe.'

Toby Ball looked round. Sure enough, the substantial stone edifice of Whinchat Place loomed at his back. He was at the front of the building, just outside the arched doorway, the wind gusting in violent swirls all around. But then it was always windy on Carn Near. He had lived here almost twenty years, and he prayed he would die here. Another word struck him then. 'We?' he rasped amid his struggle for breath. Water dripped off his chin, creeping inside his collar to race down his neck and chest in chill beads that made him shiver. He wrenched his gaze away from the cloaked man and realized there were others. One, a huge fellow with tiny, thick ears and a neck like an oak bough, was clutching a wooden pail in bear-paw hands. Flanking him were two other men, neither as impressive in stature as the first, but both hard-faced and impassive. They stood beside a high-sided wagon drawn by two bony oxen. 'What do you want?'

'To talk,' the cloaked figure said, his voice soft and rasping, carefully controlled. 'We are friends.'

Ball patted his wet clothes. 'Friends? Do friends drench a man from his slumber?' He glanced quickly at the others. One of the smaller pair looked to be a mulatto. What was striking were the scars unnaturally highlighted against his skin, like hairs from a white cat scattered across a brown cloth. They told a story about their bearer that made Ball's stomach lurch. 'Who are you?'

The cloaked man held a hand to his hood as it flapped madly in the wind. 'My name is Tainton. I am a commissioner for the King.'

'King Pym?'

The hood moved from side to side. 'King Charles Stuart. Be assured that we mean you no harm.'

Ball was not assured. 'Then why am I here?'

'We have come to collect Sir Alfred Cade's gold.'

'Never heard of him,' Ball lied. He had been warned that men would soon converge upon Tresco. He had even been told that the men would be hard and determined, the kind who looked more like brigands than soldiers. The Frenchwoman had appeared one morning with a note from Queen Henrietta Maria herself, and knowledge of the Cades that few could possibly have possessed, and Ball had believed her story. He had told her where the gold was hidden, listened intently as she had prepared him for the arrival of a band of Cavaliers that would see the prize safely back to the king's coffers. But something was not right.

'Do not dissemble, Mister Ball,' the cloaked man said. He handed the dishevelled islander a square of parchment. 'I have been sent all this way to retrieve Cade's fortune for the Crown, in order to prosecute the war to its fullest. It is what Sir Alfred would have wanted.'

Ball glanced at the parchment. He had guarded the secret for so long that it had become part of him, but the knowledge ached. It was a burden, for the Cades were a powerful dynasty in the years before the war, and the house was their bolt-hole, where they might secrete themselves if the capricious political tide ever changed. Ball almost laughed at the irony. The tide had not only changed, it had sucked Sir Alfred down with it, long before he could make use of this far-flung hiding place that had been two decades in the making. It was such a waste. Perhaps now was the time to finally shed the lies, to lift the burden. And yet, as Toby Ball stared from face to face, he felt the uneasiness build. And then he remembered. The Frenchwoman had said that the man in command of the mission had one grey eye. Ball tightened his resolve. 'It is not mine to give.'

'Then you do understand me?'

Ball gave back the commission. 'Aye, sir, I do. But the gold is not here. It is hidden away. Known only to Sir Alfred's daughter.' She had been a joy to know, her laughter drifting over Carn Near like the song of the birds for which the house was named. 'Where is Cecily? Why did they not send her with you?'

'You have not heard, of course,' the cloaked man replied. 'Cecily Cade was killed. Murdered by a rebel at Gloucester.'

'Oh, good Christ,' Ball whispered. He felt sick to his stomach. 'That poor girl. Jesu, help her.'

The wind was picking up, ravaging the hood so that its wearer was forced to pin it to his skull with both hands. 'Where is the gold, Mister Ball?'

'I cannot—' Ball began, trailing off when he saw the blue eyes narrow to slits. A voice within screamed for him to speak plain, for the Cades were gone. And yet he knew that to give up his secret would be to betray the family he had served for so long. It was not simply that the man in the cloak was not the one-eyed soldier of whom he had been warned. There was something so deeply unsettling in the eyes that now fixed upon him, Toby Ball was frightened to the depths of his very soul. 'That is to say,' he stammered eventually, 'it is not mine to give. I am merely warden here. A simple retainer for Sir Alfred, God rest his soul.'

The cloaked man stepped close. The skies behind were quickly turning black. 'You are compelled, by order of King Charles, to relinquish the Cade fortune.'

'Only four of you,' Ball said suddenly.

The man shook his head. 'What say you, sir?'

'The King personally sends a delegation,' Ball answered, clarity finally beginning to puncture his ale-fuddled wits. 'If I were him, I'd send a goodly number of men for such a task.' Indeed, the Frenchwoman had said as much.

The blue eyes seemed to twitch. 'He has not the men to spare.'

'He is winning the war, is he not?' said Ball. There was something amiss here, he was certain. 'It is the Parliament who have not the men, by my reckoning.'

The mulatto launched forth without warning, stooping to grasp a fistful of Ball's collar, lifting him a fraction so that the hapless warden dangled like a hooked fish. 'Just fuckin' tell us, you old soak,' he growled, flinging spittle over Ball's face, 'less'n you want me to yank every one o' those teeth out your skull.'

'Roundhead,' Ball said, suddenly sure. He slid his gaze from the mulatto to the hooded man. 'You're Roundheads, damn your treasonous bones!'

Lightning cracked out over the sea. A furious gust buffeted them so that they had to brace themselves against its ire. The hood came free and Toby Ball wondered if he did not deal with men at all, but a band of demons. The man in the cloak had been burned clean of his features, as though his face had slid away like molten wax.

'My name is Roger Tainton,' the apparition said as more lightning rent the sky, 'and I have come here for Sir Alfred Cade's gold. Tell me where it is, Mister Ball, or, as King Jesus is my witness, you will never see another sunrise.'

Near Chilbolton, Hampshire, 13 October 1643

Forrester eased back the curtain of branches and squinted through the dense foliage. It might have been a bitterly cold autumn morning, but much of the forest's canopy had not yet fallen, and it was as though the whole area had been smothered by a near impenetrable cloak of reds and browns. This was the reason why he and Dewhurst had opted to stay within the trees rather than risk the northbound road, but now, as he strained to identify from whence the soft whickering had come, part of him cursed the heavy-laden boughs. Behind him, in the small grove, Oberon snaffled something noisily from a bramble thicket. Forrester glanced back. Dewhurst shrugged, blowing gently on the tip of the match they kept lit at all times. Oberon chewed happily, and Forrester went back to keeping watch.

He steadied his breathing so that it was deliberately shallow, and settled down to wait. They had seen their pursuers on the horizon within an hour of their escape, and had resolved upon going to ground as soon as the terrain allowed. During that first evening, after doubling back twice and laying trail after trail of false clues, they had reached the woodland. A deep cleft in the forest floor had provided a little shelter, and, though food was scarce, they had managed to gather mushrooms and berries, and that, along with the rock-hard hunk of bread that had been at the bottom of their stolen snapsack, had kept the hunger to a dull gnaw for the night. As sunrise returned their sight, they had attempted to leave for Basing, but a rapid reconnaissance revealed the four troopers still patrolling the area, and Forrester had decided to find a new place in which to hide. Thus they had come to this grove, a bucolic chapel of wizened elms as old as the earth itself, and had dared wonder if it might be the kind of secret hideaway in which fugitives could lay low for days or even weeks. But now they heard what sounded like horses. They must wait and watch.

Everything seemed eerily silent as he scanned the edges of the low bridleway and the place where pilgrims would be forced to climb up to ground level. The birdsong was gone, the whipping wind muffled by heavy branches. He was conscious suddenly of how exhausted he felt, the pounding of his heart now present in his ears, blood rushing noisily as if to remind him of the need to rest.

There it was again; the soft, almost tuneful outbreath of a horse. Someone was coming, albeit slowly, along the bridleway. Forrester reached behind, flapping a hand at the sergeant who ran as softly as he could across the leaf mulch of the forest floor. The grove was concealed enough to keep even the tall Dewhurst hidden, but still he hunched low, as if his head would be blown from his shoulders at any second. He handed Forrester the red-tipped match, lit his own against it, and handed over their only loaded musket. He slunk back immediately, match pinched carefully between thumb and forefinger as he set about making the other musket ready.

'Is it them?' Dewhurst asked as he levered the stopper from one of the powder boxes.

'Wait,' Forrester replied quietly. He fixed his own match in the serpentine, so that it loomed over the closed priming pan, and eased forward, bracing his chest against a particularly sturdy bough. He settled into position and levelled the long-arm, adjusting the wooden stock by fractions until it was comfortable against his shoulder, testing the trigger twice to ensure that the gently smoking embers would touch the pan when the time came.

The first thing he saw was the horse's muzzle. It was white, dappled with grey touches, and Forrester instantly tensed. The rest of the beast came into view, rising from the ancient track in a flurry of hooves and snorts, and on its back was a soldier. He wore the helmet of regular cavalry, comprised of sheets of steel riveted at the back in a protective tail and a visor with three thin vertical bars enclosing the face. He was coated in buff leather, one hand gloved, the other gauntleted, and a long sword hung at his side. Two more riders came next, both atop large black horses but dressed in exactly the same way. 'Yes, it is them,' he whispered.

Dewhurst swore. 'You're certain? Per chance they are Royalists?'

A fourth horseman emerged on to the higher ground. He straddled a muscular bay that had white fetlocks matted and mud-spattered from hard riding. He too wore a helmet, but Forrester could see the thick white beard that cascaded from his face and the tawny scarf tied about his waist. 'They are not Royalists. It is that bloody Croatian fellow.'

'Kovac.'

'The same.'

'He'll kill us, Captain,' Dewhurst hissed. 'He's a villain, that one.'

Forrester nodded, flicking back the pan cover so that match would meet naked powder if the trigger was pulled. For a moment he considered keeping silent, letting the cavalrymen pass by, but they had tailed him in the manner of consummate professionals and he knew that any respite in this chase would be fleeting. They were not going to shed their pursuers without a fight. He drew breath into his lungs. 'Turn about, gentlemen, or you'll be breaking your fast on lead!'

The Parliamentarians looked towards him, squinting into the tangled foliage. One of them drew his sword, but Kovac spoke quickly and the blade was immediately returned. There was evidently to be no crazed charge. The big Croat kicked his bay, urging it closer by ten yards or so. 'There are four of us, Captain Forrester!'

'He knows it is us, then,' Dewhurst muttered at Forrester's back as he hurriedly loaded his musket.

'The four horsemen!' Forrester shouted. 'How very apocalyptic, Captain!'

Kovac laughed. 'It will be your Armageddon if you do not show yourselves this instant!'

'You are four, and I have four pieces!' Forrester responded defiantly. 'One ball for each of you!'

Kovac laughed again. 'You have two! Do not waste your breath with bluffs, Forrester, it demeans us both!'

Forrester was grudgingly impressed that Kovac had checked how many weapons had been taken during the pair's escape. He eyed the mercenary along the length of the black barrel, fixing his sights upon Kovac's chest. He knew the range was too great for any kind of accuracy, but the horsemen were bunched, making the likelihood of hitting one of them much more realistic. 'But that means two of you will die this day! Is it truly a wager you are willing to make?'

Kovac snapped rapid orders and the three troopers surged out, two to his left, the other to his right. Forrester cursed viciously. 'Where's that musket?' he hissed at Dewhurst.

The Hawk scrambled to his side. In his talon-like fingers he clutched the weapon, and he settled down beside Forrester, training the barrel on one of the cantering targets. 'Ready, sir.'

'Check your coals, Sergeant.'

Dewhurst pulled the trigger. The match fell slightly long, overreaching the pan by a fraction that might render the musket impotent. He immediately coloured, smothering his embarrassment by busying himself with the match's readjustment. 'Thank you, sir.'

'Wisely and slow, Sergeant,' Forrester said. 'So says the Bard. They stumble that run fast.' There was no profit to be made in berating the man. Dewhurst, Forrester reckoned, was entitled to be nervous.

The horsemen had fanned out, dividing a single, static target into four that were fast-moving and obscured by trees. Kovac went left, whooping at his snorting bay so that great clods of soil flew up in its wake. The beast whinnied in its exhilaration, weaving at speed through the trees at right angles with the grove. He was daring Forrester to discharge his guns, waste the two paltry shots he had. And yet Forrester knew there was nothing else to be done. He had no sword, nothing with which to stand and fight, and the cavalrymen would be on them in moments.

'What now?' Dewhurst hissed.

'Pick one and pull the trigger,' Forrester returned. 'And try not to miss, there's a good chap.' He moved the musket sideways, keeping the muzzle fixed upon Kovac. 'The leader's mine. If that card falls, the rest of the pack just might collapse as well.'

Two of the horsemen came directly at them, screaming, teeth bared, drawing their swords as they stood in their stirrups.

'Hold,' Forrester warned. 'Let them come close.' But even as the words left his mouth, he realized Kovac had not turned his mount in to face them. He kept going, galloping to the fugitives' right, and Forrester understood that the Croat meant to outflank them. The fourth Roundhead would be following suit, he guessed, heading about their left side to attack the rear. There was no time. Even if they got their shots off, what good would it do? He pushed back off the low bough, breaking the trance between muzzle and target. 'Forget it, Sergeant!'

Dewhurst twisted back to stare in horror. 'Sir?'

'Now, man!' he barked, pausing only to grasp the bandolier, slinging it over his neck in one motion. 'Back to Oberon before we're surrounded!'

Dewhurst did as he was told, scrambling out from the tangle of branches to run after Forrester. The captain reached the jet gelding and handed Dewhurst his musket. He clambered up on to the horse's bare back, reaching down to take the long-arm again, and wheeled the mount about. 'We make our stand here, then ride like the devil. Ready?'

The sergeant's beaklike face pecked the air. 'Ready, sir.'

The first two cavalrymen crashed through the brush. One from the direction of the initial charge, the other from the rear. They were each twenty paces away, and Dewhurst raised his musket and fired, immediately vanishing in a cloud of his own powder smoke. Oberon juddered, hooves thudding as he tried to bolt, but Forrester held him still, hauling at the reins with every ounce of strength and hoping the rough-stitched halter would bare the strain. He saw that the second horseman was Kovac. The air was smoke-misted and grey, but he took aim nonetheless. Kovac snarled, sword high and glittering, and Forrester fired. The smoke billowed about his head so that he could see nothing. He did not wait for the remaining two attackers, instead slamming the musket across his lap and grasping Dewhurst's outstretched arm. He hauled the sergeant up just as the next rider burst into the grove, and raked Oberon's flanks with his boots, cursing his gaolers for confiscating his spurs. Oberon lurched forwards, rearing slightly so that his two passengers were forced to cling to his mane and to each other.

Another shot rang out, cracking across the grove in the sharp report of a pistol. The other riders would be upon them, Forrester knew, but he did not look back. Oberon reached a gallop, thrashing across the leaves with a raging whinny that rose above the shouts of the men. Out of the corner of his eye he caught a glimpse of Wagner Kovac through the smoke, the implacable hunter had been punched clean from his saddle and lay flat on the forest floor. Forrester crowed to the trees, for they had escaped, and as they pushed through the ring of elms and out into the open wood, he could feel Oberon picking up speed, as if angels had lent the redoubtable gelding their wings.

'*Ha!*' Forrester cried. 'They won't follow now their damned leader's down! No, sir, they will not! To Basing with us, Sergeant Dewhurst!'

He twisted back when his companion did not reply. It was only then that he understood why Oberon could gallop at such pace. Dewhurst was gone.

St Mary's, Isles of Scilly, 13 October 1643

Titus Gibbons hated the rebellion. His Cornish roots and penchant for rich living lent him a natural antipathy for the new kind of Englishman who would turn the country on its head. But it was more than that. A deeper feeling, one that stirred his very heart's blood. Those men who seemed intent on shattering the long-held traditions and principles upon which his own character was moulded did not understand the world beyond Land's End or Dover, Carlisle or Berwick. They knew nothing of the savages found in the New World, or the pizzle-slicing Turks plaguing the Mediterranean. They had never seen whole cities of blackamoors, nor the slant-eyed multitudes that came from the most easterly reaches of civilization. But Titus Gibbons had seen them all, traded with them in European, African and Asian ports. And they had taught him one thing; England, for all its divers faults, was to be cherished.

'As far as I'm concerned,' he said as he sipped wine from his goblet and leaned closer to the fire, 'any man meaning to change my country must go through me first.' He supped again, listening to the roar of the storm outside. The tempest had renewed its anger in the last few hours, and he was pleased to have docked after weeks at sea. The *Stag* was at anchor out in St Mary's Pool, but it was safe enough in the shelter of the harbour. Even so, he took another sip in private salute to those of his crew left aboard her stomach-churning decks.

'Will we win this war?' Captain William Balthazar's gentle voice reached him above the crackle of the hearth.

Gibbons closed his eyes, revelling in the heat of the flames on his face, imagining the film of sea salt being scorched away from his skin. 'Losing faith, Captain?'

Balthazar was standing further back, staring out of a large window at the dim dusk. They were in the governor's suite of rooms on the upper level of the castle's central house. 'It is difficult to gauge matters from so distant a range. You visit all the ports, you see the manner of things with your own eyes.'

Gibbons drained his cup, set it on a little table at his side and bent to pet his dogs. The animals were curled about his chair, snoring loudly. 'I suppose you are rather isolated out here.' He smiled as the mastiff, Sir Francis, rolled over to allow Gibbons access to his belly. 'Yes, we'll win. We have to win. God is on our side.'

'You believe that?' Balthazar said distantly. He set his own goblet on a sideboard that was set along the wall adjacent to the window.

'I believe enough people believe it.'

'I hope you are right.'

Gibbons straightened, twisting in his seat to look over at the man left in charge of the Isles of Scilly. He liked Balthazar. The bespectacled officer was soft as a new-born pup, but he was also a kindly fellow, and such men were few in days of war. 'As do I. Things are not easy. The Parliament has the navy, they have most of the ports. They have London's wealth and the forges of the Weald.'

Balthazar turned and removed his spectacles to rub the bridge of his nose. 'But our armies are in the ascendancy.'

'They are,' the privateer conceded, sensing his earnest host was engaged in an exercise to overcome his own secret doubts. 'But some brave fool named Massie held Gloucester against the King himself.'

'Gloucester is of no great import.'

'But it was so unlikely a thing that it did unfathomable good to the rebels' spirits,' Gibbons said. 'It was victory there that made Essex's success at Newbury possible.'

'He did not win,' Balthazar said, his tone querulous.

'He did not lose,' said Gibbons bluntly. He rose from his seat, making the hounds twitch and grumble, and strode to the sideboard. Set on its ornate walnut and mother-of-pearl surface was a thin-necked wine decanter, the kind he had often seen used in French ports. He took it up and replenished his goblet. 'And that has served as a spur. The bastards in the north have begun to turn things about, our supporters under Newcastle are on the back foot. And now there is talk of an alliance with the Scots.'

'A Royal alliance?' William Balthazar bleated hopefully. When Gibbons ignored him, moving instead to stare out of the window, his face flushed. 'Oh, Christ.'

Gibbons gave a rueful smile. 'It was rumour only when I heard. Let us hope it has come to nothing.' He took a lingering draught of the crimson wine. 'You are fortunate to be out of it.'

Balthazar looked at him, his gaze angry. 'We are hardly out of it,' he blustered. 'Why, only two weeks ago a Roundhead assault party was foiled in its attempt to take our fair islands.'

'Curious,' Gibbons said, leaning into the pane of glass so that he might counteract the glare from the flames to peer out at the windswept eve. 'Why would they bother with the Scillies? With the utmost respect, of course.'

'Of course,' Balthazar echoed irritably. It was his turn at condescension. 'We are a strategic gem, Captain Gibbons, you must know that. Consider how important we have been to the King's ships.'

'I do not question that, sir, but the rebellion in the south-west is in its death-throes.' Gibbons stared at the empty courtyard below. Sentries would be up on the walls, huddled in the corners of each of the star's eight points, counting the hours until their turn on duty was at an end. Beyond the sturdy stone, a little way down the grassy slope on which the castle perched, a gallows stood like a lone giant against the wind. It was dark and tall, forbidding against the grey of the ocean horizon. The noose moved with the wind, never still, pointing the direction of each gust as though invisible bodies already swung from its thick loop. 'But one must ask oneself: why would they spare men in the taking of Star Castle when they ought to be pouring everything into wresting back Devon and Cornwall? Not to mention Bristol. I mean no disrespect when I say that these islands are small beer by comparison.'

'I cannot answer the question of Westminster strategy, Captain Gibbons.' Balthazar left the window and went to refresh his own cup, leaving his spectacles on the sideboard in its stead. 'All I know is that a fluyt by the name of *Kestrel* was lost off our waters, and it was found to be carrying Parliament men, bound for St Mary's.'

'Found to be carrying them?' Gibbons asked. 'How, if it was lost? You took prisoners?'

The captain of Star Castle nodded. He was a meek man, but a hint of steel came into his tone as he spoke. 'We did, aye. They languish in our dungeons even now, awaiting transport back to England, save their leader. A murderous cabal of ruffians if ever there was one. I dread to think what horrors might have been inflicted upon our good folk had they been able to land.'

'They sound positively hell spawned, Captain Balthazar. I congratulate you on their capture.'

Balthazar dipped his head in acknowledgement. 'They were led by a rogue who looked like the devil himself. All scars and malice.'

Gibbons remembered the gallows. 'The chates are for him?'

Balthazar glanced out of the window and nodded. 'Never a better fate was prescribed.' He placed a hand across his left cheek and eye socket. 'The knave has but one evil eye and half his face is missing, like so. It is a vile thing to behold, 'pon my honour, it is.'

Titus Gibbons stared at Balthazar, who still held a hand against his face. 'One eye? Tell me, Captain, what is his name?'

CHAPTER 12

St Mary's, Isles of Scilly, 13 October 1643

'I'm just sayin' you can'nae fail to be impressed,' the croaking Scots accent echoed in the darkness.

'Don't you ever shut that trap o' yours?' a man with a voice hewn by the rough taverns of Gosport retorted harshly.

Captain Innocent Stryker listened to his men snipe in the gloom, punctuated only by the damp-sounding coughs of the other prisoners and the harrying wind. Only Barkworth and Skellen, he reflected, could pick a fight in a windowless cell when there was practically nothing to talk about. The thought made him smile, something for which he was grateful. He was sitting on the cold floor to one side of the cramped chamber, knees drawn up to his chest, while the rest of the captives were strewn about like so many rag-dolls, some huddled for warmth in the centre, others seeking solace in the darkest corners. No one had come to them in the days since he had given Tainton the location of the treasure, save the stony-faced garrison men.

'You're tellin' me you weren't impressed?' Barkworth went on unabated. 'She bested a bloody harquebusier captain . . . in full armour, mind . . . and tipped him into a vat o' tar! It's astonishing!'

Skellen sighed. 'Don't know how many times I have to tell you this bleedin' story, really I don't.'

'There's nowt else to do, you steamin' yard o' dog piss,' Barkworth snapped irritably.

'Mind your—'

'He was bested by his armour,' a woman's voice interrupted Skellen's doubtless stinging retort.

Skellen peered through the darkness at her. 'Miss Lisette?' She had kept almost completely silent since returning with Stryker to the cell.

'The armour,' she said again. She was sitting against the wall on the far side from Stryker. 'It was blackened, I remember. Beautiful work. But it weighed him down, made him slow. I had no armour.'

'Why was he tryin' to kill you, lass?' Barkworth asked.

'Because I was trying to kill him,' she said simply. 'He stole something precious from me. I wanted it back.'

'And?'

'And I got it back.'

Barkworth chuckled his appreciation. 'And you did'nae know he'd survived his swim?'

'I was wounded at Brentford Fight,' Stryker said by way of explanation, inwardly hoping the memory would stir something within Lisette. 'She stayed with me, nursed me.'

'This water tastes like horse shit,' Lisette said, paying him no attention as she lowered a wooden pail from her mouth. 'It will probably poison us.'

'Be thankful they've brought it at all,' Stryker answered. After his ordeal with the seawater, the dubious liquid Balthazar's men had provided was like a glacial lake. His guts still griped when he ate anything, and his limbs were only regaining their strength at a snail's pace.

Lisette set the pail down hard, the sound clattering about the chamber. 'Do not tell me when to be thankful.'

'Just open the damned door, you thick-skulled dolt!'

The man's voice, spoken from the far side of the door, punctured the sullen atmosphere like a culverin blast. Stryker, Lisette and the sixteen others looked up, eyes straining to pierce the murky air. 'I said open it!' the man bellowed again. 'Now, you slovenly half-wit, or must I take the back of my hand to you?'

In a blaze of light, the door flew back on its hinges. Three soldiers burst in, holding flaming torches that cast long shadows throughout the cell, and between them strode the captain of Star Castle, William Balthazar. He glanced quickly about the room, then twisted back to address the man following in his wake. 'I—I do not understand the—'

'Christ, man, have I not explained myself enough?' the second fellow snarled again. 'You said his name was Stryker, yes?'

Balthazar nodded quickly. 'I did, I did.'

The angry man pushed past his confused host and planted his hands of his hips as he scanned the room. Finally he set his gaze upon the man he so furiously sought. 'Bless my soul. It *is* you.'

Stryker struggled to his feet. Despite the numbness in his limbs and the pains that still lanced mercilessly at his guts, he managed to smile. 'Good-morrow, Titus . . .'

Tresco, Isles of Scilly, 13 October 1643

Roger Tainton was becoming increasingly frustrated. The obtuse Toby Ball had suffered the beating with a serenity that had antagonized the former cavalryman to a point of high vexation, and that was not the way in which he had envisaged this meeting playing out. They were in a substantial chamber near the front of Whinchat Place. As soon as he stepped inside, Tainton knew that Ball had not lied. At least not about the house. This was a place constructed for a wealthy family, but inhabited by a lone, simple man. A man who kept watch over Whinchat Place, waiting for the day on which his master would return.

'Sir Alfred is not coming back,' Tainton said. 'You know it to be true.'

'I do,' Toby Ball mumbled. He was slumped in a high-backed chair at the centre of the room, wrists tied behind, swollen face lolling. Though the last vestiges of daylight clung on outside, the gathering storm had darkened the late afternoon, and

Tainton had ordered the chamber lit using a trio of fat beeswax candles they found in a cupboard. Now they were set upon a shallow shelf behind Ball, held by sturdy brass candlesticks that Clay Cordell had discovered in an upstairs room, their glow flickering and ominous.

'His daughter and heir,' Tainton went on, his shadow snaking over the walls as he paced, 'is gone as well.'

Ball managed to lift his head. The eyes were puffed to black slits, the nostrils dark with congealed blood. 'So you claim.'

'There are no Cades left upon God's earth,' Tainton continued undaunted. 'No man, woman or child to give your life purpose.'

'Purpose?' Ball echoed. He spat a gobbet of saliva on to the boards between his feet. It was thick and crimson.

Tainton nodded. 'Your purpose, Mister Ball, is to guard Cade's wealth.'

'My job was to guard his house.'

'And his money,' Tainton said, 'which is here.' He turned away, staring about the hall's high ceilings as if golden baubles would hang in the beams. 'Secreted within these walls.'

Ball managed a coarse, stuttering cackle. 'You're mad, sir.'

Tainton glanced at Locke Squires. The giant had been waiting patiently in the wings, but moved without a blink to line himself up with the hapless warden. He twisted his shoulders a touch, winding them like a muscle-bound spring, and unleashed a punch that sent Ball's head snapping back. The chair rocked on its rear legs, teetering for a brief moment with the front pair in the air, before crashing back down again, the scrape of wood on wood echoing unnaturally loudly in the room. Toby Ball's mangled face was concealed as his head hung limp, bobbing slightly with the juddering of the rest of his body, a thick trickle of blood trailing from his chin to stain his lap.

'Too hard!' Tainton snarled. There was a large rectangular tapestry hanging on the wall behind, and he could see that it was spattered in bloody droplets. The work depicted the moment Jesus miraculously turned water into wine, but now his face, and those of the awed onlookers, was violated by a trail of scarlet dots. Tainton did not approve of such frivolous furnishings, nor did he condone the imbibing of strong drink, but the damage irked him all the same. 'Fetch the water, Squires, and be quick about it! I am tired of your stupidity, you lumbering oaf!'

Locke Squires went to the corner of the room, stooping to collect a bucket of water and proceeding to dash it across Toby Ball's head. The warden woke immediately, screaming as if the pain had been hiding like a beast poised for the moment to pounce. Now it leapt at him, took hold, made him rock back and cry out in terrible, shrill anguish.

Behind them, a door swung abruptly open. Sterne Fassett strode in, the choleric-looking Clay Cordell in his wake.

'Well?' Tainton demanded.

Fassett spread his palms. 'Not so much as a groat.'

'You've looked thoroughly?' Tainton asked, cool dread seeping into his chest.

Fassett nodded. 'We've searched every nook and cranny. The cellars, the rafters, the outbuildings, the kitchens, even the fucking cheese cratch. Place is empty as a nun's cunny. It ain't here.'

'It is here,' Tainton insisted.

Ball spat a vile stream of blood and water as he looked up. A small noise rumbled from his throat. 'It is not.'

'Enough with your lies, Ball,' Tainton seethed. 'You know where the gold is hidden. You *must* know.'

'Sir Alfred placed me here to watch his house.'

'Because his fortune is within!'

Toby Ball let his head loll. 'No.'

The denial was enough for Tainton, whose mind raced with increasing desperation. 'Mister Squires, if you please.'

Locke Squires dropped his bucket and went to the fettered warden. Without breaking stride, he hit him with a thunderous upper-cut that knocked both man and chair on to the blood-slickened floor. Beyond a quick, sickening crunch, Ball did not make a sound.

Tainton glared at Squires. 'What did I tell you, you dundering simpleton? Slap him, shake him, hurt the man, but keep him with us! Set him right this instant! Mister Fassett? You may take a turn.'

Before the words had completed their passage across Tainton's lips, Fassett was grinning. 'Wake him up, Locke,' he said, producing his nasty little blade. 'We'll see how he likes his fingers with no nails.'

Locke Squires lumbered over to the stricken Ball and stooped to haul the chair upright. He leaned close, touching thick fingers to the back of Ball's dangling head before turning back to mumble something unintelligible to Fassett. The mulatto's dark face seemed to take on a veil of grey as he discerned the giant's stifled mutterings, and in turn he indicated that Clay Cordell should take a look.

Cordell pushed his fingers into the same spot his comrade had inspected. When he looked back, he held them up. They were bloody all the way to the knuckles. 'He's gone, Sterne,' he said in a thin, reedy voice.

'Gone?'

Cordell held up the gore-drenched hand. 'Dead, Sterne. He's snuffed it. Smashed a bastard-great cavern in his bonce.'

Fassett looked to Tainton, and Roger Tainton stared at the body of Toby Ball in disbelief. He gritted his teeth until his jaw ached and drew his own knife, a curved length of serrated steel that appeared to glow blue in the feeble light. Outside, the storm raged, howling its violent song like Lucifer's own choir. Tainton went to the newly made corpse, taking a thicket of Ball's matted hair in his fist, and wrenched the limp head upright. He drove the knife upwards into one of the warden's nostrils, twisting so that its jagged edge cut the thin flap of flesh easily enough, stopping only when it met with the bone of the bridge. He jerked it savagely free. Toby Ball was unflinching. There was nothing.

Tainton thrust his thumb between the swollen lids of Ball's grotesquely puffy eyes, prizing the swollen flesh apart. The eye beyond was dull, sightless, canted off to the side so that only some of the iris could be seen. He really was dead, and with that understanding came a sudden, white-hot pulse of rage that caught Tainton by surprise. He brayed like a gelded bullock, heard his own scream echo about the polished panels of Whinchat Place, but could do nothing to stem it. He might have killed Locke Squires in that moment. He wanted to spin about and plunge the knife deep into the heavy-handed ox's guts, but knew he might yet need him. So Tainton stabbed Toby Ball instead. He shoved the knife into the eye that was still pinned open by his thumb. The steel slipped in without resistance, blood gouting either side, squirting Tainton's cloak and boots. He pulled it free and stabbed again, this time to the other eye, and then at the throat and stomach, again and again, venting his rage the only way he knew how, blood oozing out, streaking his hands and clothes, and in his rage he revelled in it. When there was nowhere left to destroy, Ball's torso a ragged mass of torn flesh and shredded cloth, he let loose another wretched scream and spun away, pushing past Fassett as though he was not even there. Roger Tainton had failed. Right at this very last fence his horse had faltered, the golden deer had given him the slip, foiled his hunt, crushed his reputation, and, infinitely more importantly, diminished his faith.

'How can this be?' he roared at the floor and the walls and the ceiling. He kicked the body so that it flung rearwards to crash down on to the slick timbers again. He screwed shut his scarred eyes. 'How can this be, Lord? I can do all things through Christ which strengtheneth me! *All things*, Lord!' His hands were aloft now, and his feet were shuffling so that he turned circles where he stood, the beams above spinning madly as though he stared at the spokes of a racing coach, the world an utter blur. He sensed the other men with him, gaping at the savaged cadaver and at him, but he needed answers. God had led him this far. 'Show me, King Jesus! Show me what I must do!'

'We need to go,' Sterne Fassett's coarse accent rang out.

'Can't be found here like this. Looks like a shambles on market day.'

Tainton ignored advice and kept spinning, praying, begging for just the briefest word to guide him. 'The fear of the Lord is the beginning of wisdom!' he intoned. 'So says the Word of our Creator! I fear You, Lord. Lead me to wisdom now, I beseech thee in the name of Jesus!'

It was then that Tainton stepped in a pool of Toby Ball's blood. He might have trodden upon a frozen pond for all the traction it afforded, and he lost his footing violently, sliding sideways as he spun, groping for balance and careening into Locke Squires, who in turn shoved him hard away. Tainton collided with the panelled wall, clattering into a high shelf, the wind knocked out of him, and there he stood. His head swam. He gasped for breath. He felt as though he might weep.

Sterne Fassett muttered a filthy oath and Tainton regained his senses. He stared at Fassett, but the hired killer had not been addressing him. Still clutching his wicked knife with knuckles gripped to milky whiteness, Fassett was staring wide-eyed at the tapestry. Tainton followed his gaze, immediately realizing that flames licked at the bottom of the material. 'Oh, Lord,' he whispered, for he saw that he had knocked the candlesticks from their perch. Two had been snuffed out when they hit the floorboards, but a third persisted, and it had rolled a few paces, coming to rest below the tapestry and quickly finding the dry textile. 'Oh, Lord,' he said again, because the fire had already caught hold, racing up the cloth's length, spreading like a stain on a sheet, its orange and red and yellow colours blooming uncontrollably. 'Lord help us.' Suddenly he was sharp-witted, his fury and desperation devoured by the flames. '*Out! Everyone out!*'

But they were already on their way to the door and the stormy cliffs beyond, Squires and Fassett bolting first, Cordell close behind. Even as Tainton reached the threshold and looked back, he could see that the fire was spreading quickly, leaping from tapestry to panelling, climbing the walls and lapping at the ceiling like the shore of the lake of fire he had studied in the Book of Revelation. The blaze had taken hold, and there was no stopping it.

St Mary's, Isles of Scilly, 13 October 1643

The jaws of the garrison men dropped open in disbelief as the procession made its way out into the open space between the thick outer walls and the large central keep, heads dipping immediately as rain greeted them in thin but relentless diagonal sheets. The Captain of Star Castle was up ahead, babbling in urgent tones to the men at his flanks. A line of bedraggled men and one woman filed in their wake, each as pale-skinned and grubby as the next, while two dogs yapped happily as they wound their way in and out of the striding legs, content to be outside and oblivious to the evidently terse conversation conducted at the front of the line.

The men on either side of William Balthazar were his very antithesis. They were tall, as he was tall, but their faces were hard and grim, their frames strong and lean, and their gaits confident. These were creatures of a different world. One of violence and blood and cruelty. The Captain of Star Castle seemed to shrink in their presence.

'Blithering fool,' Titus Gibbons snarled as they strode rapidly over the muddy yard. The winds were vicious, buffeting them so that he was forced to clamp a hand to his hat as he walked. 'They are shipwrecked. Instead of aiding them, you sling them in gaol like common footpads!'

'How dare you, sir—' William Balthazar spluttered, peering above the rim of his spectacles, for the lenses were speckled with raindrops. 'I am Captain of Star Castle, and—'

Gibbons halted, pointing at the tattered man who walked with them. 'And this is Captain Stryker of Mowbray's Foot! Killing Cavalier, ban-dog of Prince Rupert himself, and a particular friend of mine.'

'Jesu—' Balthazar whispered as the others gathered around them. 'I—I do not understand. They said you were a rebel.'

Stryker's innards griped, stabbing and twisting. He spat at Balthazar's feet. 'I told you who I was.'

Balthazar adjusted his spectacles unnecessarily. 'You had no credentials.'

'*Pah!*' Gibbons roared. 'If this man is a rebel, then I'm the bloody Pope!'

Stryker hoped the sailor could not see the colour rise in his cheeks. His allegiance had never been iron-bound, and his time with Gloucester's rebels had muddied the waters further. He cleared his throat quickly. 'You have my deepest thanks, Titus.'

Gibbons grinned, rubbing his freshly shaven chin and flicking water from the end of his nose. 'What a place to find men so fond of land, eh? And Will Skellen! Bless my blackguardly soul, sir, but you were never a friend of the high seas!'

''Pon my honour, Cap'n Gib,' Skellen's rough-hewn voice replied, his head rising above the rest of the ragged assembly, 'I verily despise it now.'

Gibbons laughed, looking back to Stryker. 'And what brings you to this God-forsaken rock?'

'Crown business, of course.'

'Of course.' Gibbons looked pointedly at the cowed Balthazar. 'And imprisoned by that same Crown, it seems.'

Balthazar swallowed awkwardly, as if his mouth were full of nettles. 'A misunderstanding, Captain Gibbons. Captain Stryker, I—I was mistook.'

Skellen stepped forwards, his deep-set eyes more shadow-darkened than ever. Stryker held up a staying palm. The tall sergeant's anger would get him killed if he raised a hand to so senior an officer with half Star Castle's garrison looking on. 'Misled,' Stryker said quickly. 'No matter. Where is Tainton?'

Balthazar swallowed again. 'I do not know. He took ship two days ago, but would not disclose his destination.'

'Hold,' Titus Gibbons interrupted, clearly baffled by the man's ignorance. 'Are you not in command of these islands? De facto governor? How does this Tainton fellow travel without your permission?'

'He had papers,' Balthazar said, his voice rising to a bleat. 'A royal commission.'

'It is over, then,' Stryker said. He glanced up at the bilious clouds blooming like inky toadstools overhead, then at the pale faces gathered like white pearls in the closing dusk. 'We need food and water. My men are in dire health.'

Captain Balthazar nodded. 'Y—Yes, right away.' He clicked his fingers to summon an loitering officer. 'Lieutenant Lowe, see to vittles for these men.'

'Do not expect a decent meal, Stryker,' Gibbons said as they watched the garrison men scuttle off in search of provisions. 'Balthazar could not empty his boot of water if the instructions were etched into the sole.'

Balthazar visibly bristled at that. 'I have apologized, sir,' he said through lips set in a tight line. 'Tainton's papers were—wait.' He looked at Stryker. 'Who is he?'

'Tainton?' said Stryker. 'He is an agent of the Parliament.'

'But his papers—'

'Were falsified,' Lisette Gaillard interrupted, pushing her way through the beleaguered crowd, 'you stupid bastard.'

Titus Gibbons had evidently not noticed her up until now, for he stepped towards her, snatching off his hat – the feather sodden and drooping – and finishing the motion in a sweeping bow. '*Enchanté*,' he said as he straightened, stealing her hand, filthy as it was, to kiss her knuckles lightly. 'Titus Gibbons, master of the good ship *Stag*, placed upon this earth to see to your every whim.'

She ignored him, glaring instead at Stryker. 'We must go to Tresco.'

'He'll be long gone, Lisette.'

Her blue eyes blazed in the gathering gloom. 'And you wish to tell our masters how we lost the gold? Without so much as trying to get it back?'

Stryker considered her words. At best their mission would be considered a failure. If she decided to tell Killigrew exactly how events had come to pass, he might be in deadly trouble. He looked at Gibbons. 'We must go to Tresco.'

'My ship is yours, Stryker.' He winked, replacing his hat.

'I am in your debt.'

Gibbons blew out his cheeks in mock relief. 'It is a welcome feeling to be finally out of yours, old friend. To where do we sail? New Grimsby or Old? The weather turns against us, and I would not risk a landing outside their protected harbours.'

Lisette reached out, touching fingertips to Gibbons's elbow. She might have stabbed him such was the immediacy of his attention. 'As far south as you may go, Captain,' she said sweetly, sweeping a matted strand of soaking hair from before her eyes. 'We are bound for Carn Near.'

Gibbons gnawed his lower lip, raking her with a salacious stare he did not bother to conceal. 'The southernmost tip?'

'That is right.'

Gibbons thought for a moment, keeping his eyes on hers. 'Dangerous waters in winds such as these.'

She licked her lips slowly. 'For me, *monsieur*?'

A small sound rumbled from the sailor's throat and he sighed. 'There is a place I know. We'll put you ashore on our skiffs.'

'*Merci, monsieur.*'

Stryker bit down on his annoyance. 'Titus   ' he cut in, pointing at the seamen who had survived the *Kestrel*'s descent beneath the waves. 'These three were part of our first ship's crew.'

Gibbons tore his eyes from Lisette and touched the brim of his hat to the sailors. 'You'll join my crew?' They said that they would. 'Then welcome, my lads. Now what,' he said to Lisette, 'is at Carn Near?'

'A house,' the Frenchwoman answered, glancing at Stryker. 'It is there, at Carn Near. Cecily told me about the house, and I found it.'

Stryker nodded. 'She told us there was a retainer in place.'

'*Oui.* A good man.' Her expression darkened. 'Now Tainton will have him.'

'Will he talk?'

She shook her head. 'I do not think so. That is why there is no time to waste.' She looked at Gibbons again. 'Is it possible to sail in this storm, Captain?'

'You do not yearn for a bath and some rest? A few hours' sleep, perhaps?'

'I do not,' Lisette said. She looked up at the angry sky. 'Is it possible?'

Gibbons screwed up his craggy face, a gesture that suggested the notion was risky at best. 'I enjoy a challenge, mademoiselle. Get some food in your bellies and we'll be off.'

'And weapons?' Stryker said to Balthazar.

The Captain of Star Castle nodded rapidly. 'Yes, yes, I will see to it immediately.'

Stryker kept his single eye fixed firmly upon Balthazar. It glittered quicksilver in the rain-lashed dusk. 'You have my sword, sir.'

The storm battered and harried their crossing. The *Stag* was a redoubtable little sloop with as much compact strength as she had speed, but the winds were vicious and the waves lapped all the way up the hull to send stinging spray over the deck. The sky was not black, but a blue of the deepest hue, lit by a bright moon when the blanket of clouds scudded from out of its way.

Stryker gripped the hilt of his sword with one hand and clung on to one of the taut ropes with the other. The rope was as thick as a man's upper arm, a fact offering a modicum of reassurance, but in spite of that he found himself praying for the first time in what seemed an age. He chided himself for his timidity, yet the sinking of the *Kestrel* had left so indelible a mark that he feared he would never truly recover. The salt and the wind and the burning, choking, relentless water, sucking him down, tossing and tumbling him like a child's toy, dragging him to the bone-chilling deep. As the *Stag* leapt like its namesake, rising on the crest of a swell that threatened never to end, he gripped the rope tighter and prayed to God that they would stay afloat.

They had departed St Mary's as the storm turned evening to night. Balthazar had been true to his word, filling their bellies with food and providing clean water, muskets, blades, coats, bandoliers and good-quality black powder. He had returned Stryker's sword with a look of utter relief, perhaps, as Skellen later suggested, imagining the consequence had he not been able to produce it, and then they had left him to wallow in his wretched confusion, standing on the sharply angled rampart of Star Castle, hunched and forlorn against the rushing gale.

Gibbons had cast off as soon as his crew were ready, his bluff confidence fooling nobody in the face of the tempest, and Stryker, guts in constant spasm after the rich food, was thankful that the men did not entertain thoughts of mutiny. Ordinarily he would have threatened and bullied them, but after the *Kestrel*'s sad demise, he could hardly have blamed them. In the event, they seemed as keen to reach Tresco and wreak revenge upon their captors as he, while he suspected Lisette's determination was as intoxicating for them as it was for him. No man would want her to think less of him.

Now, as the black rise of Tresco's southern coast loomed out of the sea like Jonah's whale, Stryker looked over at her with a lancing pang of longing. Gripping the rail some ten or twelve paces along the deck, she was staring out to sea, dressed in the green soldier's coat Balthazar had issued from his stores, her hair ragged and tangled, tossed and twisted by the wind. Stryker yearned to reach out to her; craved her.

'We shall not land!' Titus Gibbons bellowed at his side.

Stryker turned to see the Royalist privateer, cassock buttoned tight over his chest, hat consigned to his cabin so that his hair flowed freely. 'So you said!'

Gibbons shook his head. 'No, you do not understand, Stryker! The skiffs will be taken if we lower them, splintered and swallowed. There is nothing for it!'

'We will take the risk!' Stryker called back, stealing a glance at Lisette.

'No, you won't!' Gibbons persisted. 'I owe you my life, old

friend! Remember Antwerp? I will never forget. The Diegos had my ship pinned under their guns. Then one battery turned upon the other. It was a miracle!'

'A simple enough thing! They were looking out to sea, paying no attention to the landward!'

'Even so,' Gibbons pressed, 'your intervention saved us, and I will be eternally grateful. But this—' He paused as a jet of salty spray dowsed them. 'This is too much. You will not survive it.'

'If we find the gold, you will have a cut!' argued Stryker.

'*Ha*! Take a look for yourself, old friend!' He let his eyes drift to where Lisette stood. 'And take your blinkers off!'

Stryker craned his neck over the rail. The waves were huge, white-crested, fizzing and frothing as though giant sharks thrashed just beneath the surface. He imagined small skiffs bobbing amongst those heaving swells, and knew there was nothing to be gained by forcing the issue.

'We must remain aboard the *Stag*,' Gibbons said. 'Wait the tempest out. Pray we have more patience than she.'

Stryker chewed the inside of his mouth, already imagining Lisette's anger, but there was nothing to be done. And then he saw the light. It was orange and red, tremulous, huge flames dancing on the edge of Tresco's cliffs, defying the storms. He looked at Gibbons with raised brow.

The privateer nodded. 'Carn Near.'

Tresco, Isles of Scilly, 13–14 October 1643

Roger Tainton had staggered from Whinchat Place in a daze, unable to countenance the sight of those licking flames as they leapt and crackled their way up through the panels and beams and furnishings of Sir Alfred Cade's mansion. But despite his prayers, it had taken only moments for the building to become engulfed in flames, the rain making no difference to the conflagration, the winds only feeding the fire's insatiable hunger.

Sterne Fassett had tugged at his sleeve in those first moments. They must take ship before too many questions were asked. Before the garrison up at the fort in the north of the island came sniffing around. But Tainton had resisted. The garrison would not venture out of their warm guardhouses until the storm had broken, he said, but in truth, Roger Tainton simply wanted to watch. All the sacrifices he had made, all the pain he had endured and the long hours of healing, the hours at prayer and at study with his new master. And now it was over. A failed escapade that had cost much suffering and repaid little. He needed to watch the place burn, because he knew he would never believe he had failed unless he saw it with his own eyes.

Tainton and the others stood on the rising ground to the landward side of the house until the night was deep and black. They were drenched, the rain not heavy but blanketing, the droplets fine but steady. The orange flames bathed this rocky finger of coast in a warm glow, so that each of the roof's blackening timbers was highlighted as it shrivelled and collapsed inwards on the floors below. The stone walls were dowsed in a thick layer of soot, and though they were not devoured, they were weakened sufficiently for large sections to fall away, leaving stacks that resembled ancient monoliths. In a matter of a few hours the house was a ragged black ruin, only the largest structures managing to survive. It put Tainton in mind of a burning corpse, ribs pushing out of the peeling, bubbling flesh to claw like black talons at the sky.

The *Stag* reared and bucked on the waves below Carn Near, but it did not falter. Titus Gibbons might have refused to lower his skiffs into the savage swell, but he was confident that his sleek sloop would ride out the storm, and, as night began to give way to day, he was proven correct.

The privateer crew had come on deck to join Stryker's contingent, and there they had braved the wind and rain to stare up at the flames. They were helpless, utterly impotent out in the sea, but still they watched as the pale mass of the house Lisette

had identified as Whinchat Place had been gutted and disman-
tled by the blaze.

Lisette was up at the prow, alone in her rage, her face deathly
pale. Stryker, further back along the rail, found himself wondering if it was truly the rain that dampened her cheeks. He wanted
to go to her, but knew he could not.

'Well?' Captain Gibbons said smartly as a grey band of light
thickened out to the east.

Stryker looked at him sourly, no longer willing to suffer his
ebullience. 'What is it, Titus? Spit it out man, or hold your
peace.'

Gibbons shrugged. 'Have it your way, Stryker. I shall retire to
my cabin. But do let me know as and when you wish to cast off.'

Stryker reached out, grasping Gibbons's shoulder and spinning him back as he made to turn. 'Cast off?'

Gibbons's narrow face peeled back in a wolfish grin. 'Dawn
approaches, the rain is enfeebled, and the winds are weakening.
I am willing to put you ashore. That is, if you should like to go?'

'We're done,' Sterne Fassett said as at last the blaze began to
wilt and gutter. The winds had died away too, no longer
fanning the flames, and the rain, more desultory now, gradually won its duel with the heat. The sun was rising to their
left, spilling light over the sea and over what was left of Whinchat Place. 'Nothing more for us here. You've seen it, Mister
Tainton. May we go?'

Tainton had witnessed an entire house swallowed by fire and
with it his ambitions had been turned to ash. He nodded. 'Aye,
Mister Fassett, we may.'

'Fortuitous,' Clay Cordell's reedy voice ventured from somewhere behind, 'to have that body gone.'

Fassett said that he agreed. 'Go and find the warden. Ensure
there's nothing left. If there's a body, bring it out. We'll drag it
over to the cliff edge in the wagon.'

Cordell motioned to Squires and the pair strode down the
slope to the house.

'Ship's still at New Grimsby,' Fassett said while he and Tainton watched their compatriots plunge into the smouldering ruin beneath the carved stone archway, which was still intact, albeit dyed a shade of coke. 'Could meet soldiers marching down to see what's what, now the gale's died.'

'I still have my papers,' Tainton said, barely able to consider such worldly concerns. 'They will be fooled as ever.'

He watched as Clay Cordell sifted the first tranche of debris, checking for the warden's body in the path cleared by Squires. The huge man was out in front, hefting steaming spars in his shovel-like hands, seemingly impervious to the latent heat and happy to kick through piles of rubble without concern for himself. They moved gradually through the seething ruin, from the main entrance into the space that had once been the open and high-ceilinged entrance hall, and finally vanished into the house's inner sanctum.

Fassett was again fiddling with his jaw, and Tainton found it suddenly irritating. 'Will you stop that, damn you!'

The dark brow twitched in amused interest. 'Have a care, Mister Tainton, I took you for a Godly man.'

Tainton gritted his teeth, refusing to take the bait. But he was angry nevertheless. His faith, he sensed, was slipping. He had clung to it in his darkest days like a falling man clinging to a ledge, but now he felt his grip loosen by the moment. He breathed deeply, desperately fighting to keep his feelings in check. 'What is wrong with your tooth, Mister Fassett?' he asked with forced calmness.

Fassett thrust his grubby fingers back into his mouth. 'Rotten,' he rasped awkwardly. 'Hurts like buggery. What the bloody hell's that?'

Cordell was back at the arch, waving excitedly. Tainton expected to be presented with some grim token of their search, such as one of Toby Ball's charred limbs. He drew breath to admonish them, and instead found himself praying. He had not wept since the days following his grievous injuries at Brentford, and had believed himself dry of tears, but now they came, filling his eyes and blurring the world. He swept back his hood and felt the cold breeze on his scar-webbed pate, and called in exultation to the Lord Almighty.

Because Cordell and Squires were waving. And in their hands was gold.

CHAPTER 13

Carn Near, Tresco, 14 October 1643

The landing party was fifteen strong. It comprised Stryker and his remaining musketeers, and was led from the front by the steely and vengeful Lisette. In better times Stryker might have at least made a show of ordering her not to come. This morning was different, and he opted to keep his counsel to himself. They rowed ashore in two skiffs, skirting the tip of the peninsula and its band of splintering rocks, and sliding up on to the sandy stretch of beach to the west. Gibbons and his crew, their complement swollen by the three new recruits, waited out at the anchorage. Stryker suspected Gibbons was too intrigued to abandon matters now. Curiosity alone would keep him in Scilly.

The party swarmed quickly off the skiffs, shoes and boots sinking in the fine, tide-soaked sand, and funnelled on to the track that wound its way up to the gorse and heather plateau from which the charred carcass of Whinchat Place rose. They looked up as they went, craning necks to get a look at the blackened giant that still smoked – a recently spent pyre, vast and forlorn.

Lisette was first off the path and on to the plateau, the men hefting Balthazar's muskets taking longer to cover the ground. But instead of making directly for the house, she froze, raising her hands. Stryker saw her gesture and signalled to his men, who, still below the lip of land, blew on their matches and prepared for action. They had half-expected Tainton and his band of mercenaries to still be at the house, for Lisette had told of a treasure that was well hidden, and a firefight was anticipated.

Stryker crept to the edge. The rest of the men were fanning out left and right, Skellen gesticulating to ensure they were each ready. Stryker opened the pan cover and swung out over the edge, bracing the long-arm against his shoulder and curling his forefinger round the trigger. But Tainton was not there and immediately he knew that disaster was close. He bellowed for the men to hold their fire as they each followed his movement, swinging out to form the volley with which they planned to eviscerate their former captors.

'*No!*' Lisette was shouting too. '*Hold! Hold!*'

She did not look back, and still her hands were aloft, but the shrill desperation in her tone was stark and clear. Stryker's men did not fire. A line of fourteen dark muzzles lay along the crest of the ridge, pointing inwards toward Carn Near, each with a glowing match that was poised in its serpentine, ready to be plunged into gunpowder. And opposing them, arrayed in a line the other side of Lisette Gaillard, were a score of almost identical firearms, equally primed and aimed, a return volley to sweep the landing party back into the ocean.

'Ground your arms!' a man clutching a halberd snarled from the leftmost end of the line. He was short, squat and bearded, wearing buff gloves and a green coat, beady eyes peering suspiciously from beneath the rim of a morion helmet. 'I said ground your arms or we'll shoot yer skulls off!'

'Do it,' Stryker ordered. The men lingered, unwilling to relinquish their weapons after so long a period without them, but Stryker glared at Skellen, who repeated the command. They grudgingly did as they were told, Stryker taking a mental note of the most stubborn amongst them, and he cupped his hands around his mouth. 'We've done as you ask! May we come up?'

'Aye,' the man with the halberd replied, 'but if you lie you'll be dead afore you can blink!'

'Understood!'

Stryker and his thirteen musketeers snuffed out their matches and laid down their arms. They rose from the ground and climbed out on to the plateau to face the men whose own guns were still poised to shoot.

'Sergeant,' Stryker said to the bearded leader. 'It is sergeant, is it not?'

The man nodded. 'Upton. And who are you?'

'Stryker. Captain, Mowbray's Foot.'

'Never heard of 'em,' Upton said dismissively. 'Rebels?'

Stryker shook his head slowly. 'Royalists, Sergeant Upton.'

'Don't believe you, sir.'

'I have a note of free passage from Captain Balthazar,' Stryker said, 'If you'll allow me leave to reach into my coat. My coat,' he added, 'that is the same shade as yours.'

That caught Upton's attention, and his brown whiskers shifted as he pursed his lips. 'Issued?'

'Issued by Balthazar himself at Star Castle, from whence we have come.' Stryker twisted back to point out to sea. 'There is our ship, you see it? We have sailed from Hugh Town directly.'

Upton indicated that Stryker should retrieve the note. 'You did not burn the house, then?'

Stryker let his gaze flick beyond Upton's stocky shoulder to the shell of Whinchat Place. 'We are here to apprehend those responsible. Am I to assume you have not encountered anyone else?'

Upton sent one of his greencoats out of the line to fetch the folded paper from Stryker. He shook his head as he scrutinized the inky scrawl. 'None at all, sir.' He flapped a hand at the bristling line. 'Lower your weapons, lads. They're ours.'

The tension evaporated as glinting barrels were dropped and priming pans made safe. The two lines, dressed almost identically, converged, Sergeant Upton removing his helm in salute to the officer he had threatened to kill. 'Forgive me, Captain Stryker,' he muttered, attempting to inject gruffness into a voice made thick by embarrassment. 'These are dangerous times.'

Stryker nodded. 'Indeed they are. You do your duty, Sergeant, and that is commendable.' He looked beyond Upton. 'The house. There is no one there at all?'

'Not a soul, sir. We came out from the fort as soon as the storm allowed. The house was destroyed, as you can see.'

'Was there not a man in residence? A retainer for the owner of the place?'

'Aye, sir, but he is nowhere to be seen.' The tiny eyes narrowed as a thought struck him. 'You were sent by Captain Balthazar? May I ask why he would not leave this to us, sir?'

'No, Sergeant, I regret it is a matter I am not permitted to discuss at this time.'

Upton's stocky frame twitched in a resigned shrug and he looked back along the gentle slope to the smoke-wreathed pile. 'As you wish, sir. Shall I show you up?'

Stryker realized Lisette was gone and he looked past the group to see that she was running towards the ruin. 'I think you'd better.'

Whinchat Place was a soot-stained shell. The greencoats formed a loose cordon around the smouldering plot, Sergeant Upton determined to find useful employment for his sally party, while Stryker led his men into the ruin. Approaching from the west, they entered through the rear of the house, where a breach had opened in the walls after the collapse of a section of stone. Lisette was already inside, and they followed her lead, picking their way over the crackling debris like kites at a carcass, tearing at shards that were still warm, tossing them aside when nothing but more charred rubble lay beneath.

While he sought Lisette, Stryker ordered his party to spread out in search of casualties, a small hope that Tainton might have been trapped tugging at the back of his mind. He balanced upon a black slab that he supposed had once been a large table, though now it was precariously poised upon a mass of other furniture, evidently having crashed down from above. He was forced to brace himself, stance wide, so as not to topple the precarious perch, but it afforded him a valuable view over the scene. The

198

ground–floor ceiling was completely gone, and he could see right across the tumbledown grid of walls that now contained the contents of the upper floors as well as the lower, like so many lidless boxes. He could see Lisette at the far corner of the house, in a chamber close to the main arched entrance.

Skellen was close at his side, hauling at the debris in a deep hearth, the brick stack of which was still standing, alone and incongruous where the walls on either side had fallen away. The tall sergeant cursed softly as he snagged a finger, sucking it like an infant. 'None survived this, sir.'

'But who died?'

'You think Tainton?'

Stryker shook his head. 'We would not be so fortunate. But keep looking. I'll go to Lisette.'

Skellen pulled a face, but Stryker leapt down regardless, boots crunching as he landed in the carpet of ash. He picked his way from room to room, shell to shell, until he reached her.

Lisette was half sitting, half slumped against one of the decrepit walls. She was filthy, more so than the others, her hands and knees and face smothered in soot. He realized that she had been grovelling on all fours, digging at the layer of grime with her nails, and he noticed, too, that the debris in this chamber had already been thrust to the edges, leaving the centre of the floor clear. And in that space, a deeper patch of black amongst the shrivelled floorboards, he saw a hole. It vanished into the bedrock beneath the house, a gaping maw that looked as though it had come from purgatory to swallow souls. He looked back to the Frenchwoman. 'The gold.'

'Is gone,' she said.

'It was down there?'

She nodded, not looking up. 'I thought it was so safe. That we might catch Tainton still searching, or that he might have given up.'

'The warden talked.'

That made the blue eyes dart up, fixing him with a venomous glare. 'Not every man is so easily coerced as you, Stryker.'

Stryker felt as though he were a cooking pot, a mixture of guilt and anger bubbling up so that the concoction might overwhelm him. He swallowed hard. 'Then where is he, Lisette?'

'They killed him,' Lisette said, 'fired the house, and the boards burned away.'

Stryker looked at the hole in the floor. 'It is empty?'

'Of course it is bloody empty, you half-witted English dullard! It is over! Wait, where are you going?'

Stryker bit back another surge of anger and spun on his heels. 'Let us be on the move.'

Old Grimsby, Tresco, 14 October 1643

The cart creaked and groaned under the weight of its clanging bounty. The ox, underfed for such a burden, bellowed to the grey skies and snorted its discontent, but still it trudged on, the big wheels trundling inexorably in its wake. Tainton, Fassett, Cordell and Squires walked at the sides, too heavy to sit in the wagon, though the latter kept the reins looped tight about his powerful wrist lest the beast think twice about its work. They followed the track north through the island because it gave them the best chance of avoiding any curious soldiers coming from King Charles Castle, and so far they had been fortunate. Down in the bay, Tainton could already see their means of leaving Tresco. The *Silver Swan* was a large blot against the waves, its dark hull and white shrouds huge amongst the scores of fishing vessels that bobbed all around, so many horseflies harrying a magnificent mare.

The vehicle was full. Tainton did not know what exactly he had imagined. Jewels, he supposed, more colourful than a hundred rainbows and glittering like a lake in an August dawn. The reality was somewhat different, of course, but nonetheless impressive. The secret pit below Whinchat Place had revealed riches of a less ostentatious nature. The treasure took the form of plate, in the main. Gold and silver salvers, ceremonial dishes adorned with exquisite friezes of the ancients; Greek, Roman and Byzantine myths, false idols and scenes of debauched paganism. Tainton despised such trinkets, the baubles of a bygone age, prized by the likes of Sir Alfred Cade but soon to be ushered out of Britain by the new wave of enlightened and Godly men. There were almost two-score of the objects, and he had Fassett's lackeys stack them on their edges, pressed together in rows, so that they fitted neatly in the wagon, leaving ample room for the rest of the hoard. There were three finely worked jugs, made in gold and decorated with rubies and emeralds, a thick golden cross that weighed more than a musket, a small garnet twinkling at its base, and a dozen rings of various size and worth. What remained was coin. Hundreds and hundreds of pieces, dozens of denominations, all piled high within seven stout chests. There were groats and farthings and shillings, silver sixpences and golden crowns, even solid, glittering angels worth eleven shillings a piece. It was a true trove, a cache of delicious, gorgeous metal the like of which Tainton and his comrades had never seen. In short, a fortune.

They drove the plaintive ox northwards with renewed purpose, now that the ship was in sight. When the terrain became difficult, Locke Squires lumbered out in front, taking the harness in hand and lending his great strength to the beast, dragging animal and vehicle together as one. They no longer needed to rest, for the final act in their great enterprise would soon come to pass. They would return to St Mary's, put an end to Stryker and the French harlot, and then make for England. The Parliament was calling to them.

Tainton prayed constantly. As they descended the final slope that would take them down to the bay, he could only thank God for His providence. Just as their failure to extract information from Toby Ball had rocked the foundations of his faith, so the exposure of the hoard by divine fire had reaffirmed it a thousand-fold.

He glanced from the harbour to the wagon. His three hirelings had removed their coats, using the garments to cover the precious bounty as best they could. He had refused to donate his own, for he needed the voluminous cloak to conceal his hideous appearance, but he was satisfied that the treasure would reach the ship unhindered. His main concern was the confederates themselves. Fassett, Squires and Cordell were evil men; thieves and murderers; the kind of men with which he would not usually consort over matters of vast wealth. But there were no alternatives in this case, and he was forced to trust them. Even so, the cloak concealed more than scarred flesh, and he rubbed his hand across the solid hilt of one of his two hidden pistols as he paced.

They reached the beach in less than an hour. Tainton tossed a tupenny coin to the lad guarding their boat, and added another when he had located a second vessel, and they began unloading the hoard, wading out to the boats that now bobbed in the shallows. Cordell and Fassett did the majority of the work, supervised by Tainton, whose hand never left his side, while Squires positioned himself a little way up the sand, standing with folded arms and a grim expression between the boats and any curious fishermen. They divided the treasure in half to spread the weight, then clambered aboard, Tainton with Cordell, Fassett with Squires. And then they were away, another penny thrown to the boy so that he would push them off. Tainton twisted to wave at the men aboard the *Silver Swan* while Clay Cordell worked the oars. When he turned back, he caught a flicker of movement up on the rising land above the coast. His eyes were not as good as they once were, but still he could make out the shapes of more than a dozen men on the grassy hill. They stood in a line, very deliberately gazing down at the bay, at Tainton's boats. He could not see their faces, nor the detail of their clothes, but one of them, smaller than the rest, was tiny, the size of a child, and another seemed to have long hair that was as golden as the ornate salvers piled at Tainton's feet.

'Is it?' Clay Cordell said as he heaved against the waves. He too gaped at the figures. 'The froggy bitch?'

Tainton shielded his eyes with his hands 'I believe it is, Mister Cordell. Somehow they have escaped.'

'Fuck,' Cordell said, splashing them both with water.

Tainton's heart thundered like the drums at Brentford Fight. His revenge would not come, and it made him want to weep and vomit both at once. All this time, all these months, he had thought of the moment when he would give Lisette Gaillard a lingering death of exquisite, horrific agony. And now somehow, inexplicably, she was free.

'Balthazar must have lost his nerve,' he said eventually. It was the only explanation.

'Just as well we've got ourselves away, then.'

And Roger Tainton's pulse began to slow, because the choleric-looking mercenary was right. How and why Stryker's band of Cavaliers had managed to extricate themselves from Star Castle, he could not fathom. And the escape of Lisette Gaillard was particu-larly vexing. But, he realized with the most perfect, uplifting rush of relief, it mattered not a jot. He had the gold. He had defeated Stryker, defeated the French whore, and would be a hero of the rebellion. He wept now, but out of joy instead of sorrow, and he thanked King Jesus at the top of his lungs, waved up at his enemies, and began to laugh.

Near Overton, Hampshire, 14 October 1643

Forrester's initial elation at his escape had been cruelly punc-tured by the knowledge that Dewhurst had been plucked clean away by a pistol ball. But that sorrow was compounded further when, around noon the previous day, he had looked back to see three horsemen on the horizon. They had closed the gap, gradually but inexorably, and Forrester had known that he would not make it to Basing House before nightfall. As even-ing descended, he had veered off the most direct course to Basing, plunging into the enclosed fields and coppiced forests to the north. The trio of hunters had followed, and, before the light faded completely, he had been able to make out the white hair and beard of Wagner Kovac, and he had understood that his shot had simply unhorsed the Croatian. Kovac was no longer riding his big bay, but the grey of another of his troopers, and Forrester had realized that Dewhurst's shot had been the killer. Kovac, unharmed, had merely lost his mount to Forrester's bullet.

Now, while this second day wore old, somewhere in this forest of silver birch, Wagner Kovac and his two remaining troopers were prowling; silent, watchful and hungry for blood. After hours of slinking from one tangled thicket to the next, Forrester had decided to go to ground. He would make a stand, once and for all.

He had scanned the terrain and picked a place where the soil had been ruined by a coney warren and where men had once asserted their ancient grazing rights by digging shallow ditches that were now furred with moss and capsized by tree roots. And now he waited.

Forrester blew on his cord of slow-burning hemp. His mouth felt terribly parched. He ran his tongue around his gums, biting the inside of his cheek gently to force some saliva to come. He had supped from the last stream he had crossed, but already the heady mixture of exhilaration and weariness was beginning to take its toll, and his sticky lips scraped on his teeth. He rubbed his eyes with his free hand, yawned and stretched, keeping to his feet but leaning back on a thin, peeling trunk. When he opened them he saw the horseman, a charcoal silhouette some sixty paces into the watery mist, made unmistakable by the outline of lobster pot, sword and mount. This was it, Forrester knew.

'Come then, sirs, for I grow weary of this game!' he bellowed, his voice echoing amongst the trees. As if responding directly to his challenge, two more figures resolved from the gentle miasma. Forrester offered a deep bow as their collective attention fixed upon him, fishing in the side of his boot for a couple of musket-balls as he did so. 'Then we shall have our reckoning at last!'

He popped the leaden spheres into his mouth and blew on

his coals again, sidling backwards to where his musket rested, muzzle up, against a gnarled stem. The spot he had chosen was a small half-moon of a clearing carpeted in the yellow of fallen leaves. The curved side was thick with silver trunks around whicch clustered thorny brambles and decaying bracken, while the straight front was open, the trees more sparse. It was from this side that the horsemen came now, breaking into a gallop that sounded more like an entire cavalry charge in the eerie stillness.

Forrester shouldered the musket. It was primed, and at this distance he did not bother to fix the match in place. He exposed the pan, dipped the burning tip into the powder, and the world exploded. He fell back immediately as much to clear his own field of vision as to remove himself from danger, and was horri-fied to see three troopers racing towards him. He had missed. He dropped back further to where his snapsack and bandolier rested, and flicked the stopper off one of the powder boxes. He already had the next bullet wedged against his lower gum, and he spat it down the muzzle after the charge had been decanted. They were close now, too close, at the very edge of the clearing, leaves and mud flinging up in clods to blur their fetlocks, and he knew they would be upon him before he could prime the shot.

The horse screamed. It brayed and snorted and tried to rear but was unable to find its footing, and instead it juddered forwards on to its fore-knees, its long head ploughing a deep furrow in the forest floor, its rider flung violently out of the saddle. Kovac and the other trooper stayed mounted, but they slewed about to view the commotion made by their comrade and his injured horse. Forrester did not look up. He frantically reloaded the musket, thanking God over and over for inspiring the conies to infest this part of the forest.

Kovac was snarling, furious at having been gulled into charg-ing across a warren. His orders finally rose above the agonized calls of the felled trooper and the pathetic thrashings of his horse. The white-whiskered Croat wrenched his sword free, circled it above his head so that the sound of slicing air carried all the way to his cornered quarry, and set off again, slower this time, the remaining trooper in his wake. They made it across the pocked earth without further trouble, but Forrester had retreated to the very rear of the open ground, tossing the bandolier and snapsack ahead of him, over a stretch of slightly raised terrain that scarred the leafy turf and into the first trees of the clearing's curved edge. Oberon was beyond those trees, waiting for his master's return. The horsemen were near, but not near enough to stop him shooting, and he took aim, fixing the match in the serpent this time. He picked the nearest, easing back the trigger and vanishing in his own smoke once again.

This time Forrester heard the scream and the crash as ball met man and man met earth. He squinted through the smoke to witness a riderless horse turning frightened circles in its attempt to flee, and knew the shot had flown true. He could not hope to reload the weapon before the third hunter reached his position, and he gritted his teeth, waiting for the vengeful killer to burst through the acrid cloud. But more screams came, more cacophonous grinding of metal and flesh, more savage oaths, this time mingled with the whip-cracks of splintering branches.

The third rider had not recognized the stretch of raised earth for the ditch it was, and had galloped straight across it. It was only shallow, no more than three feet at its deepest point, but a heavily laden horse dashing pell-mell over its branch-latticed and leaf-concealed surface would find itself in immediate difficulty. Now Forrester could reload, and he took a knee, blowing gently on the match, taking another powder charge from the collar and fishing primer from the sack. The smoke was lifting into the higher branches, and he began to see the horse. It was Kovac's, and it writhed and twitched, legs splayed out and upwards from the ditch, front half wedged into the lip of earth on Forrester's side. The fall had demolished its front limbs so that it collapsed forwards and flung its master clear. Then Forrester saw Kovac. The mercenary seemed dazed as he pushed himself to his feet. His helmet had been dislodged in the fall, and he staggered a touch as he tried to reach Forrester's position, ice-blue eyes blinking rapidly, before spinning on his heels and making for the horse.

Forrester took the priming flask and braced it between his knees, blew again on the match, then slid the scouring stick from its place on the underside of the barrel and jammed it down the muzzle, scraping it up and down the smoking tube half a dozen times. It was a delay he could not afford, but a musket was like a chimney; it clogged with soot every time it was fired. Two shots had been loosed already, and the third would be compromised unless he cleared its path. He scoured the barrel quickly, tossing the stick away rather than replacing it in its slot, and upended the next charge, but a quick glance at the pan told him the touch-hole was also soot-caked. The shot would be nothing more than a flash in the pan. He swore viciously, stooped to fish the sharp pricker from his snapsack, and used it to dig out the debris from the touch-hole. He blew the blackened flakes free, but the ball in his mouth skittered past his dry lips to roll amongst the leaves.

'Damn it all to hell!' he hissed, snatching the flask from between his knees and pouring a measure into the pan before tossing the vessel away. He hurriedly scanned the leaf mulch for the missing ball.

'You're mine now, Cavalier!'

Forrester stopped dead in his tracks. He looked up to see Wagner Kovac, pistol raised in the Croat's grip. 'I say,' he called back, knowing he could not find the bullet in time, 'I don't suppose we can discuss this?' He saw Kovac grin maliciously. 'No, I didn't think so.'

'I admire your trick,' Kovac said, jerking his head back at the carnage of the shallow ditch.

'Glad you appreciate my hard work,' Forrester replied. He was holding the musket horizontally at waist height, and eased his free hand along the warm barrel so that it was beside the muzzle. 'Took me a good hour to collect all those leaves.'

'You have killed two of my men, Captain Forrester.'

'Sergeant Dewhurst must take half the credit, in truth.'

'And he is dead.'

'So we're even.'

Kovac laughed. It was a dry, mirthless sound. 'No, we are not. You owe me a death.' He cocked the pistol. 'You have given me much trouble, Captain Forrester. Too much.'

Forrester dived forwards, tilting the musket up so that the pricker slipped from his fingers and slid all the way down the barrel. He fired without looking, and heard the sharper report of Kovac's pistol compete with his own shot. Wherever the pistol ball went, it did not find Forrester, but Kovac's deep bellow echoed about the birch phalanxes like the howl of a wolf. Forrester stood quickly, turning to plunge through the trees. He glanced back briefly to see Kovac staggering lopsidedly, face a deep crimson hue, a stream of foreign oaths spewing from his mouth. His hands were clamped over his thigh, the pricker glinting as it jutted from his flesh like a metal thorn.

Lancelot Forrester took a long, lingering breath and bowed deeply. 'I will raise a glass to your health at Basing, Captain Kovac!' He went to find Oberon.

Off Carn Near, Tresco, 14 October 1643

Titus Gibbons, master of the *Stag*, stood on the gun-deck of his small warship with hands firmly on hips. He peered along his crooked nose at the newly boarding passengers who scrambled up the hull on rope ladders that dangled into the skiffs below. 'And did fortune favour your mad dash?'

Captain Stryker, first on to the lower deck, craned his head to look up at the figure above. 'It did not,' he answered breathlessly. 'They were gone.'

Gibbons frowned in thought. 'The gold?'

'They have it.'

'S'blood!'

Stryker stooped to help the others up, though when it was Lisette's turn she refused his hand. He looked quickly back at

Gibbons. 'We followed their wheel tracks all the way to their vessel, but they were casting off.'

'Where?' Gibbons asked. His two dogs, Sir Francis and Sir Walter, bounded past him and down to the lower deck, weaving in and out of the new bodies, sniffing each green-coated figure and yapping to one another enthusiastically.

'Old Grimsby,' Stryker said, patting the head of the brindle mastiff. 'They have a ship in the bay.'

Gibbons tugged sharply at the hem of his green and silver doublet, the weak light sliding along the sparkling thread. 'Then we shall give chase.'

Everyone was on deck by now, milling at Stryker's back. There was an air of relief about the party, and yet the mood was sombre too. Everyone had known Cecily Cade, protected her on the bleak and bloody plains of Dartmoor, and they shared a collective duty to retrieve the fortune she had so desperately wished to donate to the king's cause. Now Cecily was dead, her inheritance bound for Parliamentarian coffers, and Stryker's company had been obliterated in the process. Stryker spoke for them, feeling the catastrophe more profoundly than any. 'Did you not hear, Titus? They were casting off some hours ago. They will be well away.'

Titus Gibbons looked out at the darkening horizon. Brooding clouds were gathering above the waves. 'The weather will soon be inclement, Stryker. Difficult to handle,' he glanced at Lisette and winked at Stryker, 'like the very best mistresses. And I am pleased to say that a small wound received by one of my beloved ship's masts has been neatly rectified, thanks to Captain Balthazar's assistance.'

Stryker shook his head in exasperation. He had the sudden urge to sleep. 'He'll have a hired crew.'

'Aye,' Gibbons allowed, 'but I have the very best. Besides, the *Stag* is built for speed. What does he have?'

'A big thing. Bigger than this. Three sails, rigged squarely.'

'A pinnace, I should imagine,' said Gibbons. He spun about, bellowing orders at his startled crew. Immediately they sprang into action, scuttling into the shrouds and hauling up the anchor.

'Titus?' Stryker called after him.

Gibbons looked back only once, his face taut and enthused. 'We can catch him, Stryker,' he said, slapping his thigh excitedly. The cliff-edge face opened into a grin of predatory delight. 'Upon my honour, we can catch the bastard!'

CHAPTER 14

The English Channel, 15 October 1643

The small hours of the morning were anxious ones for Roger Tainton. Satan's minions would, he knew for certain, be shifting against him, desperate for God's plans to be foiled. He lifted his cup, slumping back in the chair that had been placed in the little cabin, and drank deeply of the small beer that the ship's captain had provided. It was not particularly refreshing, but he had tasted worse. The others – Fassett, Cordell and Squires – were drinking vinegary wine, cross-legged on the floor in the cabin's corner, tossing dice and growling as they won and lost the few little coins for which they played.

Tainton swallowed hard as the ship pitched sharply to one side. The Devil was working. The winds were capricious out in the darkness, changing direction without warning, whipping with a vengefulness that had the *Silver Swan*'s masts creaking and groaning against the snapping shrouds. He prayed they would be safe, that the pinnace would make it through the squall, that the crew knew what they were about.

'A toast!'

Tainton looked down at the speaker. 'I do not imbibe strong drink, Mister Fassett, as well you know.'

Sterne Fassett smirked. 'We'll drink, you pray.' He raised his wooden cup, the dark liquid sloshing at the rim as the ship swung to centre again. 'To our success.'

Tainton pulled a sour expression. 'Success?'

'Still simmering over that one-eyed bugger?' Fassett asked, tilting back his head to swig heartily at the wine.

'I had planned to kill them,' Tainton said softly.

'But we have what they came to find, haven't we?' Fassett countered. 'You've won!'

'And we shall receive our remuneration,' Clay Cordell offered.

Tainton glanced at Cordell now. 'I am intrigued. You are an educated fellow, are you not?'

A tiny suggestion of colour came into the pallid man's cheeks. 'I was a clerk, sir.'

'Then you have fallen far,' Tainton said. 'Now you have nothing to live for but gold. Is reward all you desire?'

Cordell's shoulders bunched involuntarily like the hackles of a dog, but at a narrow-eyed stare from Fassett he licked thin lips and took a drink. 'As desires go,' he said, wiping his mouth with his sleeve, 'it's a snout-fair one, I'd say.'

'Do you not want your slice, Mister Tainton?' Sterne Fassett said.

'I will have expenses recompensed.'

'That's it?' Fassett's surprise was evident.

'It is all I require. My reward is the glory of God's coming kingdom. We will build it when the crown is knocked from Charles Stuart's head. This treasure will see that great day come to pass.' He looked at each of them in turn. 'You are all part of a pivotal moment in the history of England. Is it not enough to revel in that?'

Fassett gave his hard, cruel laugh. 'No, Mister Tainton, it is not.'

Tainton sighed. 'You will receive what is due when the gold is safely in London.'

Cordell set down his cup, gathering up the dice for his throw. 'Would not we be better putting ashore at Plymouth, sir? It is the nearest safe port.'

'And it is surrounded on the landward by the malignant horde. We would be trapped for weeks, even months, and the gold would be of no use.' Tainton placed his beer on the table, absently moving his fingers to his temples, pressing them in circular motions into the flesh. 'It must go to hands that will put it to work.' And that meant taking it directly to London. It was a long and dangerous journey, and part of him most certainly craved the rebel haven of Plymouth, but, beyond its proximity, the town offered no benefit to men transporting treasure to Westminster.

'Sir!' a man's voice barked from beyond the cabin door. Before anyone could respond, the man had pushed inside. He was young, fair-haired and skinny, with a face like a raptor and skin that had the burnished hue of a career sailor.

Tainton hurriedly covered his ruined scalp with the hood and got to his feet, spurs applauding loudly in the confined space. 'What is it?'

'Sail, sir.'

'Well?'

'Frigates. Men-o'-war, sir. Four of 'em, to the larboard beam.'

Tainton heard Fassett curse softly. He ground his teeth till it hurt. 'Ours or theirs?'

The lad's face twisted in a way that was answer enough. 'Cap'n says they're out o' Plymouth Sound.'

The ships were hunting in a pack. They had sailed out from their prowling grounds at the edge of the harbour at Plymouth and immediately given chase, and that had told the *Silver Swan*'s captain all he needed to know. The Royalists were in the ascendancy in the waters of the south-west, and, though they had not the strength to blockade rebel Plymouth, they endeavoured to harry enemy shipping as much as was possible. They were pirates, as far as the Parliament was concerned, for the bulk of the English navy had taken up the cause of the rebellion at the outset of the conflict. But some vessels had remained loyal to the Crown, and those, branded outlaws by Westminster, based themselves in the ports and harbours of the West Country and Wales. These four were part of the Cavalier pirate fleet, the captain judged; big ships of the line, each carrying at least forty cannon.

Roger Tainton was on the fore-deck with the *Silver Swan's* increasingly twitchy master, a man named William Trouting. 'Can we fight?'

Trouting was an elderly, irascible man. He muttered breathlessly to himself as he peered back at the four distant lights, the lanterns swaying on the decks of the men-o'-war so that they looked like fallen stars. Dawn was beginning to break to the east, but they stared westward, where the shadows yet reigned. A grunt rumbled from his throat as he adjusted his perspective glass. 'The leader's a full-fledged first-rater, Mister Tainton.'

'Meaning?'

'Meaning she'll be boastin' near three hundred souls and more than sixty big pieces.'

'In short,' Tainton said, 'they will annihilate us, given the chance.'

Trouting lowered his glass. 'We have a complement of fourteen modest pieces. If we fight, they will turn us to kindling.'

'And you're certain they're malignants?'

The old man nodded, scratching at the salt-hardened bristles of his chin. 'This far west, aye. They note our course, mark our merchantman colours, and call us fair prize.'

'Do you possess Royalist colours to deceive?'

'I do not, Mister Tainton. We could wait for 'em, let their lads board, and convince them we're for the Crown. They'll not fire till they're certain we are not king's shipping.'

Tainton shook his head firmly. He could not allow the Royalist crews aboard for fear of them discovering the hoard stowed below deck. 'Can we outrun them?'

'To Poole, aye. It is the next friendly port.'

'Poole?' Tainton spluttered. 'It is no better than Plymouth. The garrison is hidden there like beetles under a rock. It is no good to me.'

'Southampton, then, if we are lucky.'

'No,' Tainton said indignantly, thumping a fist against the rail. 'Luck has nought to do with it. I go to London, Captain, for that is the Lord's command. My cargo is too precious to take across land, especially this far west.'

Trouting gave a dry, grinding cackle. 'They will catch us long before London, Mister Tainton.'

'God will provide!' Tainton pressed, beginning to shout amid his desperation. 'Push as far east as you can! They will lose their nerve!'

A grey cloud suddenly billowed on the gloomy horizon, blooming like the petals of an ugly rose to snuff out one of the ship's lights. The captain swore harshly. Then the thunder-clap rumbled across the sea, up into the deck and through their ribcages. They did not see the iron ball until it hit the water some two hundred yards off the stern, the sea frothing white with sudden vehemence. Tainton began to pray, even as the trio of smaller warships coughed their fury towards the *Silver Swan*, the sea pocked with white marks where the balls splashed home. All the shots fell well short, but the danger was clear enough.

'What are they about?' Tainton yelped. 'We might be for the King for all they know!'

'Warning shots! The next'll be proper if we do not run down our sail!'

'Strike east, I say! The Parliament will reward you . . .' Tainton could see the consternation on the old sea-dog's face, and he grasped the man by his waxy collar. '*I* will reward you!'

Trouting scraped urgently at his scaly chin again. 'They will be snapping at our heels before we round the Isle o' Wight!'

'Then fire back!'

'We will all die in the attempt!'

'Worthy deaths, Captain!'

William Trouting blew out his cheeks theatrically and shook off Tainton's grip, striding away down the deck, screaming orders at his crew. They responded in turn, scuttling to various positions about the heaving vessel, manning guns and clambering up into the shrouds. Tainton found himself alone, left to remonstrate with the chill breeze and wonder at the baffling ways of divine providence.

★ ★ ★

The pinnace struggled stoically into the rising sun for the next three hours, circled by gulls and escorted by dolphins, and pursued by enemies. The first-rater was in the van, the spearhead of the hunting party, as they carved white-tipped lesions in the grey-blue waves. The morning developed into a day of stinging cold and whipping wind, and Tainton, remaining obstinately on deck, found that his face became numb and his eyes perpetually watered. His fingers were in excruciating pain where he gripped his hood so hard to his head, nails drawing blood where they burrowed into flesh. And all the while the Royalists' ships kept coming, vengeful gusts filling their sails as they skidded over the depths.

'They're close,' Sterne Fassett said as he joined Tainton and Cordell at the bow during the late morning. Squires was somewhere in the cavernous warren below decks, spewing the contents of his guts into a bucket.

Tainton stared at the four dark shapes, so large at this proximity. He imagined the wings of demons lifting them over the water, the angels of his own vessel glancing over their shimmering shoulders at the enemy host. 'We will fight them off, Jesus willing.'

Fassett pulled a sour expression. 'And if that does not work?'

'They will give up.'

'Give up?' Fassett echoed indignantly.

Tainton nodded. 'The east is held by our forces.'

'Your forces,' Fassett corrected.

'The malignants will not venture much further than Portsmouth,' Tainton said, 'for fear of running into rebel shipping. We must keep them at bay until they realize how far they have striven.' There was at that instant a booming report from the chasing pack. A pall of smoke jetted out from one of the frigates. Fassett stepped back instinctively, though Tainton threw him a derisive glance. 'They've not a chance of finding their mark.'

The sea fizzed and seethed less than fifty yards out, a huge halo of water droplets growing above the surface where the ball had hit home. Tainton felt his jaw drop. Fassett hissed a filthy curse.

The *Silver Swan* did not have many guns, but Trouting had had the sense to sacrifice his broadside complement by placing a single piece fore and aft, and his voice carried across the decks as he snarled for the bow chaser to be deployed. It coughed bitter smoke, its recoil juddering up through the ship's timbers to vibrate at Tainton's feet as its small iron shot flew westward to pick at the men-o'-war. It fell well short, but the men in the shrouds cheered all the same, and Tainton returned to his prayers as the gun-crew swabbed, reloaded and adjusted the cannon.

The biggest Royalist ship tacked about as the *Silver Swan*'s lone bow chaser barked again. It seemed unaware of the meagre threat, like a Shire horse menaced by a fly, and presented its full broadside, the guns belching their fury. A plume of smoke spewed out, smothering the ship. The huge blast reached Tainton's ears, heralding the whistling iron spheres and all their viciousness. He found himself ducking, shrinking into the damp rail as if it might protect him from the frigate's wrath. At this range even the most wide-mouthed of the pieces would have scant effect on the *Silver Swan*'s structure, but the whining shots would cleave savage rents in her sails and bloody swathes across her decks, so he prayed aloud, beseeching God to smite these behemoths before it was too late.

Miraculously the broadside missed Tainton's plucky pinnace, but it had been too close to call. William Trouting was still screaming orders somewhere back along the deck, the men in the highest rigging were bellowing information down from their heady posts, and the gun-crews flitted about their precious weapons like wasps at a sugar plum. Tainton realized that they were preparing to offer more than a single shot to their implacable foes, and, just as he said as much to Fassett and Cordell, the *Silver Swan* luffed about, lurching on a frothing peak. They gripped the rail, bracing themselves for the noise. Finally she opened fire with the guns along her port side, the six pieces roaring like angry lions towards the approaching frigates.

Nothing seemed to happen, for their small cannon could do little against the monstrous frigates, but their defiance seemed to serve as a poultice for their fears, and the crew cheered again, turning the *Silver Swan* back to the eastward course and safety.

Now another of the Royalists fired. Just one cannon belched its fury from a porthole in the stern, but the noise of the large piece seemed deafening. The ball tore mercilessly across the waves and Tainton felt himself shy involuntarily away, but the *Silver Swan* dipped violently into the hind part of a swell and the shot went high, ripping through the shrouds, splitting a rigging line with an almighty crack that sounded like a giant's whip. One man fell from up high, his scream cut abruptly short as he hit the deck with a dull thud. Trouting was braying more orders, the *Silver Swan* reared and pulled away, an opportune gust thumping into her sails and kicking her on, salty spray showering the decks.

The gulls and the dolphins had all vanished now. The air was strangely warm and the sky hazed yellow with a smoke that smelled bitter and sulphurous. The chase went on.

Basing House, Hampshire, 15 October 1643

Lancelot Forrester felt like singing as the exquisitely sweet gooseberry fool made its way to his stomach. He had reached the seat of Sir John Paulet, the Marquess of Winchester, during the night and been immediately conveyed to the infirmary, where he was given water, some fresh bread and oysters, even some heady beer from the stores stacked to the rafters of the Great Barn. He had slept for several hours, waking with bleary eyes and a sense of unreality in the cold morn. Now the next repast was served, a thick and herb-flecked pease pottage followed by the sugary gooseberry concoction, and he found himself contemplating whether this was all some dream. Perhaps Kovac had actually won their duel, and this was heaven.

Between courses, one of Colonel Rawdon's officers had

debriefed him, running through the events of the past few days and ascertaining how far and wide the marquess's warrant had been spread before its capture, but he had quickly been left to recuperate, the chirurgeon clucking like a hen as he made sure Forrester had no significant injuries.

Forrester scraped the bowl clean and set it down on the wood panelling of the floor. He was perched on the end of a firm palliasse, the compacted straw positively luxurious compared with recent privations.

'And you are hale and hearty, sir, truly?' the chirurgeon asked as he came to stand before his patient.

Forrester looked up at him. 'Aye, sir, I am.' He pushed up on to his feet. 'And ready to take my leave of this place.'

The chirurgeon tutted gently. 'Rest, Captain Forrester. A few days to recover your strength, eh? Have you so great a need to be back with the Oxford Army?'

It was a point well made. In the main, a soldier's life was one of waiting. An existence that revolved around marching, making camp, digging in, and wasting time. That, in truth, was precisely what the king's army were doing at Oxford. Waiting.

'A few more days shan't hurt, I dare say,' Forrester acquiesced. 'Food is what I shall require, sir! Give me good, solid meals, and my muscles will be like iron, I promise you. I hear you have fresh fish here.'

The chirurgeon nodded. 'We have carp in the ponds. But do not eat it, Captain, I implore you. There is a drain running thither directly from the stables. The fish feed on the horse dung.'

'In my experience, that ensures big, juicy fish!'

'In my experience that ensures big, juicy worms making their homes within the bellies of those who eat said fish.'

Forrester felt his jaw drop. 'Good lord.' He pressed a palm to his midriff protectively. 'Then I shall stick to the gooseberry fool, sir.'

The chirurgeon's mouth twitched at the corners. 'I had wondered how a man used to campaigning managed to maintain such a healthy physique!'

'It is a cross I must bear, my friend. Now pass me the bowl.'

Just then the door to the infirmary swung open. Stooping below the lintel was a very tall man who was so severely hunched that his entire frame curved like an archer's bow. His clean-shaven face, dominated by a hugely oversized nose, twitched incessantly. 'Taking your ease, sir!' he declared happily.

Forrester grinned. 'Major Lawrence. Well met, sir.'

'We thought you long lost, Captain,' Frederick Lawrence said as he strode into the room. 'Feeding the worms, as it were.'

Forrester grimaced. 'Do not speak to me of worms, sir, please.'

The cavalry officer looked a tad confused. 'As you like, Lancelot.' He waved towards the door. 'Care to take the air? I would show you how busy we have been.'

The garrison of Basing House, under Rawdon's military governorship and with Paulet's money, had indeed been busy in the week Forrester had been gone. He and Lawrence strolled to the western periphery of the fortress, where new earthworks had sprung up and existing ones extended. The ditches had been deepened, the walls buttressed with earth and the ramparts carved into the land like raw wounds. Forrester clambered to the summit of one such rampart and looked along its length. There were new fieldpieces set upon bastions of piled soil. Sakers or minion drakes, by the look of them. Light, compared with big siege cannon, not worth pointing at a wall, but devastating against massed ranks of flesh. They were protected by bunched cannon-baskets that, though made simply of wicker, were packed to the brim with spoil from the palisade, making them dense and almost impervious to small-arms fire. This part of the defences fairly bristled with ordnance and staked ramparts, and Forrester could not help but be impressed.

Lawrence leaned on a cannon-basket and looked out upon the wild terrain. 'I hear the conditions in Norton's prison are not good.'

'I've experienced worse, I can assure you,' Forrester said. 'My only regret is losing the warrant.'

Lawrence nodded. 'The rebels will make merry with it, I fear.'

'Aye.' It was just a piece of parchment, and yet the warrant would, he knew, be used to condemn the marquess in the eyes of Parliament. They already considered him an enemy, for his religion marked him as a Royalist without the raising of arms, but now it could be proved that he posed a real threat to the rebellion in the south, he would doubtless become an active target.

'Still,' Lawrence said, his eyes narrowing in a look of ruefulness, 'that is what the powers in Oxford wanted.'

'They did not wish to lose Basing, Major.'

Lawrence shrugged his crooked shoulders as he absently watched two labourers hauling a dog-cart laden with earth clods along the base of one of the outer ditches. 'Shake the hornet's nest, you said.'

'I assure you, sir,' Forrester protested, 'that shake is what I intended. I never wished to pull the whole damnable nest from the tree.'

'All the same, your purpose in coming here was to capture Westminster's attention, and that is what you have achieved.'

Forrester felt heat come into his cheeks. 'You do not think I lost the warrant intentionally, Major?'

Lawrence shook his head. 'Never, Captain. Simply that we will not be required to sacrifice any more men by sallying out needlessly. Parliament will soon know that the marquess is raising the county against them. We, in turn, should look to our defences.' He slapped Forrester's shoulder. 'And we must rejoice, for you have returned to us. God is to be thanked for that.'

'God and Sergeant Dewhurst.'

Lawrence's temple twitched violently as he nodded. 'May he rest in peace.'

Forrester thought again of the warrant, how gleeful Norton had been to have it in his possession. 'If Parliament had no design upon Basing before, they will surely come now. The marquess cannot be left to rouse the local Royalists.'

'I am ready for the fight,' Lawrence declared, rubbing his hands at the prospect.

'Good luck to you, Major,' Forrester said.

'You think the Roundheads will come?'

Forrester nodded, again reflecting upon the fire that he had seen blaze in Richard Norton's eyes. 'I'm certain of it.'

CHAPTER 15

The English Channel, 15 October 1643

The rugged shore climbed out to port, a grey crescent above the evening sea like the spine of an unfathomably vast whale. It was the Sussex coast, the cliffs of the Isle of Wight having been left behind them. Hope swelled like a tide in Roger Tainton's breast as he dipped his shoulder into the northerly wind. He knew they could not reach London if matters went on unchecked, but Sussex was, at least, a Parliamentarian county, its towns and ports generally declared for the rebellion, and the prospect of overreaching themselves must, he felt certain, soon become a genuine concern for the bold Cavalier crews. They were not a real navy, he told himself, but a rag-tag fleet of privateers. He prayed they would abandon the chase. Either way, the crew of the *Silver Swan* had performed admirably, plying their trade amid the thunder of cannon fire, adjusting canvas fraction by fraction as the wind changed direction and strength. The chase had worn them to red-eyed ghouls as the afternoon dragged, the need for rest overtaking their innate instinct for survival, but still they would battle on. God would compel them.

Tainton watched the undulating coastline, the dark mass pocked white where villages hugged the cliffs. More explosions made him flinch, and he was thankful his cowl concealed his timidity.

'It is over, Mister Tainton, sir,' the ship's captain, Trouting, called above a rumbling volley from one of the frigates. Expert seamanship had dragged out some distance between predators and prey, and they were just out of range, but the shots were still too close for comfort as they smashed the surface of the sea. 'We must put in.'

Tainton felt as though he had been hit by one of the whistling iron shots. He stepped back to brace himself. 'We agreed—'

'You agreed.'

'I asked you to have more courage!'

Trouting shook his narrow head. 'You commanded me to run east, and I have done so, but the men have had enough. They are worked to the bone! You claimed the enemy would disengage, but they have not!'

Tainton drew breath to launch a stinging tirade, but the captain's watery eyes were full of determination. 'Where?'

Trouting scratched roughly at his salt-stiffened bristles. 'Selsey Haven.'

'Selsey?' Tainton blurted. 'Might we not choose Chichester? Is it not for the Parliament?' In truth, he was already forming a strategy in his mind, a tactic for dealing with the local authorities wherever they landed. Chichester's Roman walls would offer the best protection for his precious hoard, and protection was what was needed, regardless of the political leaning of a town. So much gold could capture a man's heart, twist his allegiance and disintegrate his scruples, and Tainton needed to be sure that he could get the treasure behind the thickest walls he could find.

The captain shrugged. 'I could not give a goat's ballock, Mister Tainton. Who's to say it ain't gone back to Cavalier hands?'

'It has not,' Tainton rasped through gritted teeth. 'I am sure.'

'Not sure enough. Towns change colours from one moon to the next, and I ain't of a mind to brave the harbour guns if they've turned their coats.'

Tainton could see that he was beaten. He pulled his cloak tighter about his chest and stared out at the rugged coastline. 'Selsey Haven.'

'Pagham, to be more exact. The harbour offers good shelter.'

'Will not the men-o'-war follow us?'

Trouting licked cracked lips. 'Too treacherous for them what don't knows the tides, sir. Specially for those big bastards. Besides, we're far enough east for 'em to think twice afore they risk trappin' theyselves in harbour.'

Tainton rubbed cold fingers over the dull skin of his jaw. His mind whirled with the difficulties of removing the treasure from the ship and having it stranded in a little provincial town miles from any rebel stronghold. Mercifully, a thought struck him. 'Can we not wait, then? Sit in harbour for the malignants to lose interest, turn back?'

Trouting nodded. 'You may wait, sir, aye, but you'll be waiting a goodly while.' He glanced up at the tattered topsail and the dangling strands of rigging. 'We've repairs to make.'

Tainton could not believe his ears. He felt the fury bubble up inside his throat. 'How do you know you are safe in Pagham? What about *their* guns? Or their men, for that matter?'

'I've kin there, sir,' Trouting replied brightly. 'The *Silver Swan* is welcome in its waters, whichever way the tide of war might turn. I should like to stay a while.'

'What am I to do?' Tainton spluttered, aghast. He thought of the gold stored below decks. 'I cannot very well remain aboard ship. Eventually someone will discover our cargo, and things will go awry.'

The grizzled seaman pushed thick fingertips into the dense thicket of an eyebrow, pulling at errant hairs, just as the *Silver Swan* began to tack about, making for land. 'Do what you will, sir.'

Tainton wanted to choke the stubborn old man with his bare hands. 'You'll see no payment, you mutton-headed palliard.'

William Trouting cackled and spit at Tainton's feet. 'You have three men wi'you, sir. I have thirty. You'll cough up some golden nuggets or I shall tell the crew what really sits in our hold.' He pointed back at the tailing warships. 'Then you'll wish those sons of whores had caught us after all.'

Roger Tainton chewed on the inside of his mouth, seeing his avenues of opportunity blocked suddenly with high walls. 'Very well.' He jabbed the captain's chest with his forefinger. 'God will judge you, sir.'

Trouting beamed and spun away with an agility that belied his advancing years. 'Sounds good and well to me, Mister Tainton!'

The waters off Sussex were inky as the light dimmed. They made for a choppy fastness that made Stryker's insides dance as he stared out of the boat. The oarsmen hauled on their paddles, water droplets leaping up to spatter his face, but he cared nothing for the cold spray, his mind in turmoil. The *Stag* had followed the four frigates as soon as they had sighted them off Plymouth. They had watched as the men-o'-war belched bitter fury from their bristling flanks, topmen shouting down from the most precarious sections of rigging, calling the action as they saw it. But the fight was spread across the eastern horizon, rendering it difficult to discern until the sun had pushed further overhead on its perpetual arc, and by then the focus of the warships' ire was well hidden by smoke, by the coast of the Isle of Wight and the hulking bodies of its pursuers.

In due course the floating fortresses had tacked about, a quartet of ocean-borne monsters falling silent as abruptly as they had opened fire. The *Stag*'s range was such that it was impossible to tell precisely what had transpired. Gibbons had blankly refused to come too close to the frigates while their collective blood was up, lest their rows of black-mouthed killers be turned upon the privateer, so they had been forced to amble in the rear, wagering on the chance that the Royalists' ships were tailing Tainton's vessel.

'Worry not, Stryker!' Titus Gibbons had exclaimed happily as they cut through the writhing waves. 'The men-o'-war will make short shrift of their quarry and we, like a ravenous red kite, will swoop down and pick at the pieces.'

But even Gibbons's seemingly indefatigable ebullience had

withered as the frigates struggled to keep up with their prize, all the while coughing broadsides into the sea with no obvious joy. No flotsam bobbed past the *Stag*, no bodies drifted on the roiling water, tossed and battered in the angry meeting place of Solent and Channel. Instead, and to everyone's surprise, the day's end was signalled by the abrupt cessation of fire and the slow turn of the masted behemoths. Gibbons had quickly run up every Royalist colour he could lay his hands upon and, with Stryker's hopes fading with the light, ordered one of the *Stag*'s boats made ready.

An hour later, accompanied by one of Gibbons's officers, captain on sea and captain on land were skidding over the darkening depths, the vast shape of a first-rate warship looming like a storm cloud above them.

They hove to, coming close to the ship's hull but careful to keep an oar's length away until strictly necessary. The coarse bellows of seamen rang out above, a ladder of thick ropes dropped, unfurling along the barnacle-speckled keel, and they let the boat slide in, bumping worryingly off the huge hull. Then they were up, scuttling over the side of the frigate, more harsh voices sounding above their heads in gruff encouragement. Stryker had wondered at first whether he would manage the climb, but the fresh air and sense of renewed hope had invigorated him more than he dared expect, and he felt some of his old strength as his fingers curled around each rung of twisted hemp.

Big, calloused hands manhandled them over the rail. They stood and waited like a trio of lambs in a slaughterhouse, utterly at the mercy of the crew of the warship, who stared at them unabashed. Calls sounded further along the walkway, and all heads turned to see a man in a crusty coat emerge from below deck. He looked like an old fisherman to Stryker's eye, for he was grizzled by the wind and sun, with one blue eye peering brightly over a wedge of ash-coloured beard, the other eye milky and sightless. His nose was bulbous and pulpy, his gait marked by a severe limp, and his teeth dark brown and strangely

227

out of kilter with his mouth, as though his lips did not quite stretch round them. He offered a brief bow, a motion that made the cloak flap open a touch to reveal an elegant green doublet and breeches beneath. 'Captain Nehemiah Walsh; *Eagle*.'

Stryker's companion returned the gesture. 'Captain Titus Gibbons; *Stag*.'

'Well met, sir, and I have the pleasure of introducing Lieutenant Rowland.' Walsh nodded to the lieutenant, a young man barely out of his teens, with wide, terrified eyes and a thin moustache of fluff. He moved to the rail, dragging his left foot behind, and studied the *Stag* as it rose and fell with the restless swells some quarter of a mile to the west.

'A fine little bitch, my man,' he said, his words slurred so that at first Stryker thought him in his cups. 'Apologies, my man,' the sailor added, evidently noting Stryker's expression. With a wink, he opened his mouth and slid out what seemed to be his entire upper jaw. Stryker realized the teeth were false. Walsh sucked them back in wetly. 'Made o' wood, and too damned big!'

Gibbons tapped a heel on the deck. 'Much like your ship, sir.'

Walsh seemed taken aback for a moment, then he slapped his thigh and brayed like a donkey. 'Good, my man, good, good! I like you already!' His lone eye slid over to Stryker. 'A kindred spirit.'

'Sir,' Stryker mumbled, uncomfortable, acutely aware of his disfigurement.

'This is Stryker, sir,' Gibbons said. 'Captain of Foot.'

'A plodder?' Walsh said in surprise. 'Lost your breakfast yet?'

'Almost, sir,' Stryker answered.

'Must have iron guts,' Walsh said. 'This ain't no millpond.'

Stryker merely smiled, considering the damage Sterne Fassett's seawater brew had done to his insides. Perhaps they were worn leathery by the salty concoction.

Walsh looked back to Gibbons. 'Now, my man, may I ask you your business this far east?' He gave an apologetic shrug. 'Compelled to pry, you understand.'

'We hunt a prize, Captain Walsh,' Gibbons said. 'A merchant-man. Square-rigger, out of Tresco. We heard your cannon fire and—'

'And thought we might have done you a favour, eh?'

Gibbons nodded. 'About the size of it, sir.'

'We ran into him,' Walsh confirmed. 'Sent a warning shot or three, and the cove bolted. We gave chase, naturally.'

'Where is he now, sir?' asked Gibbons.

Walsh looked suddenly awkward. He dislodged his teeth, taking them clean out of his mouth, a long tendril of saliva hanging off his beard, and rubbed them on his sleeve. Eventually he replaced them, the noise sounding like raw meat slapping on a butcher's block. 'Lost him.'

Stryker could not defer to Gibbons any longer. He spoke earnestly now. 'Lost him?'

'To my shame, my man, aye,' Walsh said. 'The wind changed its mind more often than my wife, and was twice as cunning as my mistress! We could not command the weather gage.' He stared up at the figures in the shrouds, draped amongst the rigging like a troop of monkeys in a forest. 'Moreover, the hands are raw recruits in the main. Wind, weather, tide and current,' he announced, counting each point on a rough-skinned finger. 'The four temptresses of my profession and, I am sorry to say, ones whose ways are yet mysterious to a great many of my crew. The experienced seamen went over to the Parliament, d'you see?'

'I do.' Titus Gibbons looked at Stryker. 'Seasoned crews are like raven's teeth, old friend.'

'Oh, our side have the Cornish, that I do not deny,' Walsh went on, 'but they are not aboard my ship, more's the pity. I am left with what I am given.'

'We must be after him, then,' Stryker said, unwilling to give up after coming so far.

Gibbons shook his head. 'The *Stag* is fast, Stryker, but if Tainton's ship could shake off these frigates, then she is good indeed. I fear they pass into rebel waters with every hour.'

'But—' Stryker began. His protest was cut short by the privateer's raised palm.

'No argument, old friend. We'll not catch her till Dover, and I shan't chase her that far, not even for you. The Downs contains half the rebel fleet.'

'Well, that will not be necessary!' Nehemiah Walsh barked in amusement. He offered a conspiratorial smirk. 'I said we lost her, not that she outran us.'

'Sir?' Gibbons prompted.

Walsh pointed north, to the black rise of the coast. 'Pagham, my man. I will not risk the harbour waters, for my charts do not illuminate it to my satisfaction. And, in all honesty, the place lies all too close to Chichester, which was in Roundhead hands, last I heard. That little merchantman was not worth the trouble. But that is where you'll find her, gentlemen. She went to Pagham.'

North of Selsey Haven, Sussex, 15th October 1643

'The lookout spied sail,' Clay Cordell muttered as they hauled the stolen cart up the wet sandbank. It had been the possession of a local fisherman, left on shore with its underfed nag while its owner had gone to sea. Tainton had commandeered it, ordered the men to discard the piled netting, and set about loading the treasure. He had not trusted the crew of the *Silver Swan* to help, for the glittering cargo was more than poor men could bear to ignore, but he had donated a handful of coin to the captain for distribution on the proviso that his gruff seamen found themselves elsewhere for the evening. For his part, William Trouting had obliged readily enough, dispatching his men to Pagham's taverns and pocketing a goodly number of heavy coins for his trouble. Now, as the day grew old, Tainton's party were making their way inland, weaving though the expanse of dunes that fringed the harbour in search of somewhere to rest for the night.

'There were more sails out there than gulls,' Sterne Fassett responded from the back of the vehicle, lending his lithe strength to the effort of reaching the higher ground above the salty dunes.

'But the men-o'-war did not give chase,' Cordell persisted, glancing back, though a large hillock of sand blocked his view of the darkening sea. 'They pissed off back to Cornwall or wherever the whoresons have their nest.'

'Your point?' Fassett asked.

'There was one sail,' Cordell said, his sickly face more pallid than ever. 'He saw one, lone ship, separate from them frigates, heading right for us.'

Fassett laughed scornfully. 'You think it was Stryker?'

'Crossed my mind.'

'On what ship?' Roger Tainton cut in.

'The one that took him to Tresco.'

Tainton scoffed. 'Some paltry fishing vessel? I doubt that would be enough to get him all the way to England.'

Cordell grimaced. 'A seaworthy ship, then.'

'He cannot simply have conjured one from thin air. His vessel was wrecked. It lies on the seabed even now. God has seen us prevail, Mister Cordell, have no fear.'

'You're letting your mind run you dizzy, Clay,' Fassett chided. 'We have the gold yet. Stryker's on Scilly, the malignants are all out west.'

They reached the summit of the bank and looked north. The land flattened out into a patchwork of arable enclosures and patches of woodland. In truth, Tainton was not a happy man. They were stuck on shore miles from London. But Sussex was not nearly as hotly contested as Hampshire, and he felt confident that God would lead them to safety with the rising sun. Chichester was to the west and Arundel Castle was to the east, both held by rebel forces for the whole of the year, and neither was blockaded to the landward by malignants. Danger lurked like noon-time shadows after men carrying such a quantity of riches, but the plan was simple. They would head north at first light, making direct for the capital.

Locke Squires left his position at the rear of the cart and

pointed to a little copse about a mile to the north-west that was bisected by a deep gully along which flowed a glistening stream. At the edge of the copse was a little hut. It looked uninhabited, for, even from this distance, they could see that the area around was overgrown and no smoke trail streaked the sky above.

Tainton nodded. 'Aye, that will suffice.'

'Should we not make immediately inland?' Fassett said. 'The captain said there is a road to the east of here, near a village.'

'Sidlesham,' said Tainton.

Fassett shrugged. 'Find Sidlesham, find the road.'

'You would stroll into the darkness with a wagon full of gold?'

Fassett said that he would not. 'But is Chichester not worth seeking out? For the night, leastwise.'

'Trouting reckoned it was six, perhaps seven miles from here. We would be walking half the night before we found it. I would rather take my chances in that pathetic shack than risk the roads.'

The shack was a simple, single-room structure of worm-eaten timber frames and wattle walls. There were two small squares cut out of the gable ends to serve as windows, a mass of gossamer cobwebs cloaking the internal beams, and a simple chalk floor that, thankfully, seemed dry. The roof was thatched, albeit shot through with mould and infested with birds' nests, and the centre of the room was blackened from fires. They collected the driest kindling they could find, piling it on the ash stain, and coaxed a new fire to life.

They had positioned the cart at the rear so that it was concealed between the building and the woods, having long since unloaded their rich cargo and arranged it neatly at one end of the room. Tainton had insisted upon carefully stacking each plate and lining up everything else in precise rows, so that it was easily audited at a moment's notice. 'I'll take next watch,' he said, moving to stare out of one of the windows. Sterne Fassett was first on duty, and Tainton could just make out a lone figure moving alongside the little stream about forty paces away, on the south side of the shack. He turned away, making for the warmth of the flames, and held out his palms to absorb the warmth. 'You have something to say, Mister Squires?' he said nastily when he caught sight of his two companions muttering in the corner of the room.

The mute giant drew an almost imperceptible grumble from deep within his broad chest, and for a moment Tainton wondered if the brute might launch at him, but Cordell stepped between them. 'What happens when we reach London?'

Tainton met Cordell's gaze. 'We go to Whitehall. My master will see the gold safely to the Parliament's treasury. Its destiny is preordained.'

Cordell and Squires exchanged a glance. 'And our payment?'

'Will be arranged.'

'I should very much like,' Cordell said softly, pleasantly, 'to renegotiate our terms.'

Clay Cordell was, to Tainton's mind, a weakling. A killer, for certain, but without the cruelty of Fassett or the sheer strength of Squires. Yet now, he privately conceded that he had under-estimated the man. Now he saw a glint of steel in the man's eyes and he began to see that what he lacked in outward presence, he made up for with ambition.

Tainton felt his pulse quicken. 'Well?'

Cordell looked back at Squires, then to Tainton.

'Cough it up, Cordell, for Christ's sake,' Sterne Fassett's voice came from the doorway. He was leaning on the frame, casually enough, scratching the abnormally flattened tip of his nose with a grubby finger.

Cordell stepped back a fraction. He swallowed hard. 'I've a mind to take my cut now. Locke agrees.'

Fassett sucked in his top lip pensively. 'What makes you think you'll do that?'

The sinews at Cordell's neck flexed. 'Sterne, there's three of us and one o' him. Cut his gizzard, leave him out in the forest for the beasts. We take the gold.'

Roger Tainton looked from man to man, desperately trying to gauge where each of them stood. He had two pistols, one of which he kept hidden deep in the folds of his cloak, and he yearned to reach for it, but it was unloaded and useless. 'You are a greedy sinner,' he accused Cordell.

The sallow mercenary rounded on him. 'And you are a sancti-monious bastard,' he hissed. 'You shouldn't even be abroad with a face like that. Should be living in a cave somewhere, not toss-ing orders about like a fuckin' general.'

Tainton noticed Fassett's stance relax, and he knew the man had made some kind of decision. If the mulatto had taken against him, then he was finished, so he took a chance to needle Cordell. 'Greed will be the end of you, Mister Cordell.'

'Greed?' Cordell rasped, almost spitting the word as though it had singed his tongue on its way past. 'I lost my apprentice-ship to the greed of others, sir. High-born buggers like you. They looked to save themselves a few groats and I was cut loose, discarded like piss poured down a gutter.' A blade had appeared in his hand from somewhere. His knuckles, already pale, were white as driven snow where he gripped the bone handle tightly. He advanced upon Tainton, a small knot of bubbling foam building at the corner of his mouth as he spoke. 'I knew then that I would have to find my own fortune to survive. Carve it from the grasp of men like you.' He looked to the figure in the doorway. 'Come now, Sterne, let us be done with this foul creature.'

For a moment Roger Tainton feared his guts would broil right up through his chest and into his mouth. Cordell was right, there was nothing he could do to stop them on his own. Fassett was his only hope, and he stared into the mulatto's dark eyes as if it were possible to manipulate the man's mind by gaze alone. 'Think, Mister Fassett, just think,' he whispered. 'Consider the possibilities. Gold now or limitless wealth later.'

It all happened so quickly after that. Sterne Fassett was out the doorway and over the fire before Tainton had realized what he was doing. It was a fascinating and terrible thing to behold, a man so rapier-fast, so agile and so merciless, produ-cing a blade in one instant and bringing it to bear the next.

Cordell was down without raising his hands. He had been caught flat-footed and gaping as Fassett leapt at him like a hungry leopard, almost silent in his movements but irresistible in his strength. He flattened the pasty-skinned Cordell, straddled his chest, knees grinding on the crushed chalk, and the blade was a blur as it went to work. Tainton could only watch, dumbstruck, as blood pumped in steaming jets from Cordell's thin neck. It was a mess, torn and ruined, as though a rope of rubies had been hung about the man's throat to glimmer in the guttering light. The fire hissed as the crimson lake reached it, Cordell's blood bubbling manically where it touched the edge of the white-hot kindling.

Fassett sat back, panting gently. He patted Cordell's still chest as though they shared a jest, and smiled sweetly at Squires. 'Tell me, Locke, as best you can. Did you truly agree with Clay's notion?'

Locke Squires, so huge in the dim hut, his head almost scraping the beams, his shoulders impossibly broad in so small a place, looked as though he might weep. He made a murmur from deep in his core, desperate to force words past the ruined stump of his tongue.

Fassett wiped his knife on Cordell's sleeve and stood up slowly, cracking his elbows and knuckles. 'Have a care, good man. A nod of the head will do.'

Locke Squires shook his head so hard it made Tainton feel dizzy to watch.

Fassett smiled again. 'That's what I thought.' He looked at Roger Tainton. 'The possibilities seem worthy of consideration.'

By the docks, Pagham, Sussex, 15 October 1643

Although the night was deep black, an ethereal halo settled above the harbour, birthed by the lights of taverns and houses that hugged the water's edge, Pagham on its eastern bank, Selsey to the west. In the town, beneath the halo, where the streets were tightly packed, the sounds of revellers whipped on the wind as it whittled walls and frayed thatch. The gentle lilt of a fiddle, a tuneful skeleton given muscle by men at song, was scythed intermittently by the bark of a dog or the scream of a woman. Shouts would ring out in bunches, coarse and earnest, louder suddenly as men were tossed on the salt and sand of the road to settle differences with knuckle and blade.

Down by the quay, where two large ships were silently docked, the only sound William Trouting could hear was his own heartbeat. He was on his back, arms pinioned to the deck of his ship by knees that were like twin anvils. The man straddling his chest was tall and bald. He was thin but seemed to possess an iron strength, and his eyes were unnaturally deep-set within their cavernous sockets. The hand at his mouth was huge, like a shovel, and it pressed back, grinding his lips into his teeth. He tasted the metallic tang of blood. His pulse clamoured over everything, thundering in his ears so that he wondered if he would expire there and then.

'Where is Roger Tainton?' a voice sounded to his right, hard, keen, like napped flint.

Trouting managed to force his stinging eyes far enough to catch the blurry image of a man in a green coat. He saw that the man had long, black hair, and that a sword with an ornate hilt dangled at his side, though he could not discern the face at all. The clamped palm lifted away. 'Sure 'an I don't know what the blazes you're talking about, sir,' Trouting babbled as the figure came closer, standing over the bald fellow's left shoulder.

Another figure came into view. 'You had passengers.'

It was difficult to make out the newcomer's features in the gloom, but a glimmer of silver thread shone in the glow of a deck lantern and he too wore a fine sword. 'Seems you know more than I, friend. Where did you—?' He thought of the sleek ship that had been sighted after the frigates disengaged. It had slipped into the harbour without fuss and moored a little way down the quay. 'You're from that sloop, aren't you?'

The broken-nosed man clicked his tongue. Trouting became

suddenly aware of the rapid padding of paws. Panting followed, disconcertingly close, and he caught sight of two dogs. They came up to him, licking his face; one a bulky beast, the kind he had seen fight bears at the Southwark stalls; the other a wiry thing, all matted tufts and stinking breath. He cringed as they snaked down his torso, past the man who had sprung out of the shadows to bundle him to the deck, and sniffed at his crotch.

'Jesu,' Trouting bleated, 'get 'em off! Get 'em off!'

The man clicked again, and the hounds went to heel, tongues lolling, breath pulsing in white clouds. 'You had passengers,' he repeated, his accent tinged with a Cornish drawl.

The figure with the long, black hair stepped forwards a fraction. 'A hooded man, badly scarred.'

'You'd know, sir,' Trouting retorted, seeing the mess of melted tissue that had once been the speaker's left eye.

The bald man slapped Trouting hard. 'Mind your mouth, you old goat.'

'A dark fellow,' the scarred speaker went on unabated, 'by the name of Sterne Fassett.' He made a chopping motion with his hand, sliding it over his face. 'Nose sliced like this. And two others. A pale, sickly fellow and a mute giant.'

These men had ambushed and immobilized him, and their faces told of a determination that he did not wish to cross. But it was also a determination that could, he sensed, be exploited. He forced a smile. 'My mind, as it is oft said, is a blank. A rusted wheel. Perhaps a couple o' coins would grease the old axle, eh?'

The man straddling him raised a fist. 'Perhaps you'd like to dine on your own teeth, arsehole?'

Trouting shied back against the timbers, the hard surface hurting his shoulder-blades. 'I have thirty good men, sir. Have a care.'

'Then where are they?' the scarred man asked calmly. He placed a hand on the hilt of his sword, glancing briefly in the direction of Pagham town. 'In the taphouses, I'd guess.'

'I have some aboard yet,' Trouting argued. 'They'll cut you to—'

'Do not be hasty, Captain. They are trussed up and locked safe.'

'The rest will return soon.'

'And I have thirteen soldiers with me. Veterans of the war in the west. I would wager your thirty would not stand, but you may try, of course.'

Ghosts came to Trouting then. Materializing from the dark at the sides of his vision, grouping behind his interrogators like ghouls risen from the depths of the harbour. He stared from man to man, face to face, each as grim and implacable as the last. There was nothing spiritual about them. One figure, smaller than most, with hair that shone like spun gold in the glow of the lantern, pushed to the front of the group. It was a woman, pale of face, with bright blue eyes and a small scar crossing her chin. She regarded him dispassionately. 'And he has me.'

'You?'

'She is good with a blade,' the mutilated soldier said. 'Fiend-ishly good.'

'If you wish to use your privy member again,' the woman spoke softly, her voice betraying the accent of France, 'you will speak plain and true.'

William Trouting would risk much for a full purse, but the woman's cool threat unsettled him deeply. He cleared his suddenly dry throat. 'I carried them, aye. But they're gone. Took a wagon from the quayside and went north.'

'They're not in the town?' the woman asked.

'The very fact that you're here,' Trouting said, 'tells me you have knowledge of what they possess. Would you stay in a busy town if you were they?'

'North, you say?' the man with the crooked nose and expensive garments asked.

Trouting nodded. 'Can't be travelling fast, with all that burden.'

'Where is the nearest garrison?'

'Chichester,' Trouting said, 'but it'd take 'em hours to reach it on foot.'

'They would not travel at night,' the Frenchwoman said. 'Too many footpads.'

The scarred man nodded at his companions. 'They'll have gone to ground.'

'That'd be my guess,' Trouting said, eager to please.

The scarred man turned to address the fellow with the canted nose. 'We will take our leave, Titus. We go inland, and I imagine you will not dally in port.'

The man called Titus responded with an ostentatiously low bow. 'A Sussex port is a deadly port for those loyal to the Crown. It has been a wondrous adventure, Stryker. Godspeed.'

William Trouting sat up as the steel-limbed man finally clambered off his torso. He made great play of breathing deeply and rubbing his smarting cheek, though, beyond the slap, they had not hurt him. He peered up at them as they chatted. They were certainly soldiers, he could see now, for they were armed and each, even the woman, wore the same green coat. Only the man named Titus was dressed differently, and Trouting felt a dread chill rise up through his bowels and into his chest. Because he knew of a Titus. Not personally, but by reputation.

'How can I thank you?' the fellow named Stryker was saying as he stretched out a hand.

'Consider my debt paid,' Titus said, shaking the proffered palm vigorously. He looked down at Trouting as a hungry cat would regard a mouse. 'Besides, I have remuneration enough.'

'Remu—?' William Trouting began, but the word died on his lips. 'You are Captain Gibbons, the privateer, are you not?'

Titus Gibbons's narrow face split in a broad grin. 'Indeed and I am, sir! Captain of the good ship *Stag*, and her new sister ship, *Silver Swan*.'

CHAPTER 16

North of Selsey Haven, Sussex, 16 October 1643

Roger Tainton woke exhausted from a fitful night. He had taken his turn on watch, paced out slowly along the hedgerows of the farmland that ran between the coastal flats and the foothills of the South Downs. Never straying out of sight of the hovel, he squinted into the inky near-distance, examining shrubs and stones and trees for signs that they might conceal some pistol-toting brigand. But all was silent, save the infrequent call of an owl and the constant trickle of the stream, and he had let Squires take over the patrol an hour or two after midnight. No real sleep had come as he lay his head on the hard ground, hood drawn up to provide a modicum of comfort. Instead he thought of the journey ahead. Part of him wanted to go straight to Chichester at dawn. Pick up a guard detail, perhaps cavalry, and complete the march with a proper escort, but in truth he simply did not trust his own side. Clay Cordell had been a wicked man, Tainton knew. And yet none in this war-ravaged nation save a chosen few were truly God-fearing. That, after all, was why the Lord had turned His back on England in the first place. Every man, woman and child would thrust a dagger in their neighbour's back if gold was the reward, and he would not risk the success of his mission by entrusting the wagon to anyone other than himself.

It was still dark outside, though the hut itself was illuminated by the last, crackling embers of the fire. Locke Squires was slumped the other side of the flames, his huge chest rising and falling with each growling snore. Fassett must be outside, Tainton surmised. He stood, moving by instinct to the small window, and pushing his head through the hole. There was the wagon, tucked between the building and the tree-line of the dense little copse, safe and snug and ready for first light. He went to the door, spurs rattling like sacks full of coin in the silence, and rested his shoulder against the frame as he peered out across the overgrown fields to the south. The stream gurgled out to his right, running from the miniature forest behind, meandering towards the coast at the foot of a creek that was probably the greater part of six feet deep. It lanced all the way through the arable patchwork and down into the flatter land that hemmed the harbour, a huge gash in the terrain. He imagined the *Silver Swan* at rest where the stream emptied into the sea, silent and peaceful in the glassy water at quayside, her crew sleeping off a night of sin in various hovels around Pagham town. Tainton considered himself a sanguine man, one who, notwithstanding Lisette Gaillard, would not bear a grudge towards his fellow humanity. And yet as he reflected upon the avaricious William Trouting, he found himself hoping the man had not enjoyed a pleasant night.

Something flickered out to Tainton's left, two bright glints, like floating gemstones, tracing the low hedge-line that split the fallow field in two. Tainton felt his muscles stiffen. There it was again. Eyes, catching the moonlight. He blew a long gush of cold air out through his nostrils. A verse from the Book of Corinthians fell into his mind. 'Be on your guard,' he intoned to the night sky, 'stand firm in your faith, be men of courage. Be strong.'

'Nerves fraying, Captain Tainton?'

Tainton's head snapped to the right. 'Do not address me thus.'

Sterne Fassett strode out of the gloom. 'Do you never yearn for those days? The days of galloping to battle on a big destrier? Beats all this sneaking around.'

'My destiny lies elsewhere,' Tainton said. 'Where have you been?'

Fassett jabbed a thumb over his shoulder. 'Walked the brook.'

'And?'

'Nothing to see. Quiet as a bawdy-house in the Vatican.'

Tainton scoffed. 'I do not imagine such a place would be quiet.'

Fassett laughed. 'Aye. Papist priests love a buttock banquet same as the next man. They just don't admit it.'

'The Catholic Church is rife with corruption and vice,' Tainton began, 'and that is why—'

But Sterne Fassett had already moved away to stare south along the course of the creek, eyes narrowed to black slits. He screwed up his mouth. 'I heard something.'

'Something?'

'A voice.' Fassett chewed his lip. 'Might've been a fox, I s'pose.'

Tainton's throat felt lined with fur as he swallowed. 'A fox?' he echoed dubiously.

'Or not,' Fassett said. He drew his pistol, made sure that it was loaded, and crouched, staring along the length of the ambling watercourse again. 'Best rouse our sleeping giant, Mister Tainton.'

Captain Innocent Stryker slipped through the shallow water, careful of the treacherously smooth stones under foot. They had followed the tracks of a cart northwards, cut deep and stark in the sandy flats that served as a buffer for the bay. It was a good enough lead, for Trouting had told them about the vehicle and its direction, while the roads out of the town either went east, towards Bognor Regis, or due west, to Selsey, and neither route seemed likely for a group of men dragging a wagon-load of gold. The northbound tracks ceased in the fields just beyond a lip of tufty grass and dune, where sand gave way to chalky soil, and Stryker's party had spent some hours moving gradually up through the arable expanse, eyes straining into the darkness and thankful of a bright moon. And then they had discovered the smoke. They could not see it against the night sky, but the rich scent of burning wood was unmistakable. They had pushed on, moving quickly so as to locate the source before the wind picked up and whisked it away, and perched on a hump of rising ground, one of the scouts had seen the building. It was a hut, probably used by shepherds or drovers, constructed flush against the periphery of a tightly packed stand of bare-branched trees. The land around was open in the main, a grid of overgrown fields broken up by hawthorn hedgerows, and, though the hedges would allow Stryker to approach, they would not take him all the way up to the building unseen. But there was a stream, set deep enough below ground level that a man could stand straight with his head concealed. It ran to the side of the hut and vanished into the copse, and it was along that gully that he had decided to make his move.

The line of thirteen men and one woman travelled at a steady pace. They could not see the hut from down in the water-cleaved channel, but Stryker had gauged roughly how many paces it would take to reach it. Moreover, he had sent a man ahead, slinking over the long grass to call out if trouble appeared. All Stryker's charges were armed, the soldiers with glowing matches and primed muskets, while he, Skellen and Barkworth carried swords. Lisette was somewhere at the rear, unwilling, it seemed, to breathe the same air as Stryker, but he knew she would have at least one blade secreted about her person. They were a war party, the kind of group he had led in half the states of Europe, cloaked in darkness and fuelled by the prospect of danger and blood. He knew it was not the kind of work to be enjoyed, and yet it was a delight to him. The risk and the fear could be tasted on his tongue, and after days locked in a cell, beaten, half-starved and stuffed full of grimy, piss-stewed seawater, to steal through the shadows to an uncertain fate was nothing short of bliss.

Stryker saw the body at the same time as the nearest men, and the entire column halted as one. It lay face down in the tangle of weeds and brambles at the foot of the bank, just above the trickling water, and even in the darkness the smear of blood could be seen at the side of its neck. Stryker clambered up to it, kicking a path through the undergrowth, and turned the corpse with the end of his boot. The face was beginning to bloat, the features exaggerated with the strain of skin stretched to bursting, but he identified it all the same. He looked down at Skellen. 'Clay Cordell.'

Skellen frowned as the rest of the green-coated party gathered around. 'How'd he go?'

Stryker let the body roll back on to its front. 'Throat's ripped up.'

'Slit?' asked Simeon Barkworth, the most strangely dressed of the group, given his oversized new coat.

'Ripped,' Stryker repeated the word, unable to think of another that told the tale so well. 'Like Gibbons's mastiff took a bite out of him.'

'Least we know they're here,' Skellen said.

Lisette Gaillard stepped through the crowd to stare levelly at the mutilated cadaver. 'And we know there are fewer of them.'

Stryker waved them back into line and stooped to check Cordell's pockets as the greencoats moved off, rejoining near the back when he was satisfied there was nothing of value to be had. The moon was white, lending a silver edge to the clouds as they scudded over its ghostly face. The occasional gust of wind whistled along the surface of the water as it murmured its homely sound that, pace by pace, was shattered by thrashing boots. The Royalists did not know if their enemy was in the hut, but they would soon find out. It was cold, the air stinging their lungs, but these were men who had suffered imprisonment and shipwreck, whose friends had drowned for the sake of a treasure that they suspected was just yards away. They fingered triggers and blew on matches, licked lips parched dry by salty breeze and rattling nerves, and stole along the stream to the fight. And then the firing began.

Sterne Fassett emptied the first of his pistols into the face of the leading greencoat. He had been close, lying on the top of the bank, and he knew without looking that the man was dead. The stink of powder smoke filled his nostrils as he rolled away, snatching up the pistol he had taken from Cordell's lifeless body. He cocked it, the click of the hammer lost in the screams from down in the brook, and crawled to the edge. Locke Squires resolved to his right and advanced a little way up the bank, a pistol in each of his bear-paw fists. They had agreed to stay on the eastern side of the stream to protect the hut and keep the creek from dividing them. They had four firearms between them, Tainton having relinquished his, and now the pair would do their best to stall the attackers while the former cavalryman got the gold into the woods. Things were desperate. Fassett had counted ten of the enemy before firing the first shot, and he suspected there were more further back. He had not known who these men were at first, but they were armed with muskets and dressed in green coats, which meant they were soldiers, and that was enough to make preparations for either flight or fight. Tainton had gone to the wagon, Fassett and Squires would be ready to meet fire with fire if necessary, and then they had waited. But out of the gloom came a woman. She too wore the green uniform, but her golden hair gave her away for the enemy that she was. Fassett knew in that instant that if the French slut was here, then so was Stryker. And if the one-eyed captain was on the mainland, so was death. It was a simple choice of kill or be killed. There would be no discussion.

Squires fired his short-arm, vanishing amongst the white tongues that licked the air behind a bright flash of red and orange. Someone bellowed down in the creek. The water raged as though a pod of whales had been thrown up from the sea, but the thrashing was caused by the feet of those ambushed below, uncertain as to the whereabouts of their attackers or even how many there might be. Fassett nodded quick approval to Squires and discharged his second pistol, moving immediately back as a desultory crackle of musketry began to sound in response. He took a knee, screaming at Squires to fire as he hurriedly reloaded. Squires emptied his second barrel into the writhing mass of greencoats, bellowing like a whipped bullock as he stumbled back over the long grass.

Fassett was up now, and he swatted the giant's bulky forearm to catch his attention. 'Fall back!' he growled, noting the crazed look in Squires's eyes. 'With me, Locke! Nothing stupid!'

Stryker was pressed into the chaotic bank, brambles digging into his shoulders and head, powerless with just his blade. The greencoats, his musketeers, were in utter disarray. The scout had vanished along with the advantage of surprise and now they were trapped like rats in a barrel.

'Get to the sides!' he snarled. 'Spread out!'

The riverbed was already filling with the smoke of roaring muskets. It smothered the Royalists as sure as if a thick fog had descended, but it also obscured their view of what was up at ground level. They reloaded their weapons, but darkness and fear made them fumble, and it felt as if an age ticked by between shots.

Skellen splashed along the brook to Stryker's position. 'Three down,' he said, panting. Even in the dark, the blood spatters were visible on his face.

'Jesu,' Stryker hissed, instinctively looking down the chaotic line.

'Not her, sir.'

Stryker nodded. 'Thank you.'

'Mad, though,' Skellen said. 'Angry as a sackful o' wasps.'

'I'm going up there,' Stryker said.

The sergeant stole a glance at the top of the bank. 'Don't know what we're facing, sir.'

'If it is Tainton, then he has just two other men.'

'Might have recruited some locals,' argued Skellen, but he drew his sword anyway. 'He can afford it.'

'He might have,' Stryker said, 'but I am not staying here all night.'

Skellen propped the long blade against his shoulder. 'Let us take a stroll, then, sir.'

The two men turned on to their fronts and sprang up. Barkworth was somewhere nearby, for Stryker could hear the shrill Gaelic war-cry of the Scots Brigader, and he knew Lisette would follow too. To his relief, the rest poured on to the open ground at his heels, a green swarm, scrambling up the bank and over the edge of the ditch, some charging straight over the rough grass, others pausing to fire, some stumbling pell-mell in the anarchic assault. High-pitched pistol shots came in reply, the small bullets whining their way past to vanish in the darkness. Stryker saw the men who had ambushed them, and for the first time he was certain that they had found their quarry, for he could see the large frame of Locke Squires lumbering at the edge of the modest building. Another man was with him, either Fassett or Tainton, he could not tell.

'*On!*' he screamed. The battle-rage had overtaken him, intoxicated him. All the frustration and regret of recent weeks, the sorrow and the fear, pent up like a stoppered bottle, now smashed into oblivion. His senses were keen like the blade in his hand, his single eye straining against the night and his blood thundering through every vein. 'Kill them! *Kill them!*'

Sterne Fassett knew he was beaten. He loaded and fired one of his pistols as the greencoats came on, and he suspected he might have clipped one, but there were simply too many, at least eight, he reckoned, and they were led by a snarling, one-eyed fiend with long, flowing hair and a face that was hard like granite and fit for the worst kind of nightmares. He could not stem the tide, so he fell quickly back on the hut, hoping to get inside its meagre shelter to reload. 'Get behind the walls!' he ordered Squires. 'Shoot through the windows!'

Squires nodded and went in, and Fassett followed, slamming the half-rotted door behind them. Tainton was nowhere to be seen, and Fassett wondered if the sanctimonious bastard had managed to hide the wagon in the time they had bought him. He understood that he and Squires had ultimately failed. Stryker's party would overwhelm them eventually. Revenge, after all, was a sharp spur, and the Royalists would never give up. Fassett would not see his cut of the reward, and he suddenly liked the idea of Tainton's plans ending in failure.

Squires was back near the cold smear of ash that had been their fire. His thick jaw worked frantically, spittle foaming at the corners of his mouth, a mangled stream of syllables spewing over his lips.

'They'll not offer quarter,' Fassett replied, guessing his comrade was entertaining the same thoughts. 'Stryker will murder us.' He darted to the window, fired one of the pistols, tossed it aside and primed the second. When it was ready, he took a huge, lung-scouring breath, and went to the door. 'Unless we murder him first.'

Stryker was twenty paces from the front of the hut, his men fanning out in an arc around him, when the door burst open. Sterne Fassett stepped out, a cocked pistol in hand, and he pulled the trigger, flame and smoke exploding in a great gout around his head. Stryker heard the ball whistle past, felt the punch of sliced air near his ear, and raised his sword. Fassett cursed viciously, then seemed to move away, vanishing behind his smoke cloud like a wraith, half spinning, half flying, movements fluid and viper-fast.

Stryker went after him, even as Locke Squires charged out of the hut like an enraged bear. Squires brayed to the waxing moon, words lost upon the stump of his tongue, and threw his pistols at the nearest greencoats, advancing on one with hands brandished like vast claws. Stryker did not look back, but he heard three or four muskets cough, and then the bear howled, a lingering, despairing sound that tailed off as the soldiers closed in, hammering down with the butt-ends of muskets and slashing with swords.

Fassett was at the back of the building when Stryker caught up with him. He already had a dagger in one hand. It was a long thing, as long as a man's forearm, with a decorated pommel and forward-facing quillons above the hilt that were designed to ensnare an opponent's blade. Fassett's face creased in a grimace as he beckoned Stryker on, and he delved into his waistband, producing an identical weapon in his opposite hand.

Stryker attacked, careful of the speed he knew the professional ravilliac possessed. He flicked his sword out, meaning to batter one of the blades from the mulatto's hand, but Fassett was lightning quick, quicker even than Stryker had feared, and he managed to step out with the agility of an acrobat. The thrust avoided, he danced back in, letting one of his daggers slide down Stryker's extended blade until their hilts met. He twisted savagely, intending to wrench the sword from Stryker's grip, but it was the Royalist's turn to spring out of range, and they faced one another again, turning a wide circle in poised stalemate.

Some of the greencoats appeared round the corner of the hut. Their muskets were spent, reversed like clubs to batter and bludgeon. 'Get into the trees, damn you!' Stryker snarled. 'Find that wagon!'

They knew not to interfere, and spread out, plunging into the copse.

'I'm going to cut you up, you ugly bastard,' Fassett said, his tone calm, considered. 'Rip out your guts and chuck 'em in the river.'

'That so?' Stryker answered, careful not to let his guard down for a moment.

Fassett's dark eyes flickered away for the briefest second. 'Then I'll have your slattern. My cock's hard as a dagger for you, lass.'

'Easier for me to slice it off, then,' Lisette Gaillard said. She was concealed in the black abyss that was the left-hand side of Stryker's vision, but he sensed she was close.

That made Fassett chuckle coldly. 'I shall hale up those britches and swive you till you moan.'

'A tired threat, I must confess,' Lisette retorted witheringly. 'But kill Stryker, by all means, it will save me the task.'

'Jesu, Lisette,' Stryker rasped.

Fassett cackled. To Stryker, he said: 'Do not test me, Captain.

You'll get pricked, and she'll get my prick. Unless you let me go now. It isn't me you want, it's that treasure.'

Stryker shook his head, dipping the tip of his sword so that the cool moonlight drifted up its length, the large garnet set into the pommel winking blood-red. 'You first, Mister Fassett. Then the treasure.'

Fassett rushed him. Again, Stryker was stunned at the speed of the man, and he found himself wondering who could possibly have got close enough to lop off the tip of his nose. He stumbled backwards, parrying slash after slash, astounded that Fassett could outmanoeuvre his long blade so easily with just the twin daggers. They reeled out into the field, careening across the grass. Stryker could feel his strength ebbing as he went, muscles still not as they had been the month before. He was barely able to keep from stumbling as he twisted and blocked, hoping against hope that Fassett would make a mistake.

Fassett spat oath after oath, his breath hardly faltering as he came on. Stryker deflected one dagger blow, offered his own darting riposte, which pushed the momentum back on to the smaller man, and he felt as though he had gained the upper hand. Suddenly he slipped. Unbeknown to him, he had reached the bank of the stream. He toppled back, scrabbling for purchase, but it was no good, and he was tumbling before he could find his balance. He hit the bank on the way down, mouth crammed with dirt, and collided with the water hard, the wind punched out of him. He was up on all fours as the icy stream rushed over his hands, but he could not seem to gather his wits enough to stand. He gasped, desperate to haul air into lungs that felt cored out and raw. And then he saw Fassett, or, rather, he saw Fassett's reflection. The killer had followed him down the bank, and he advanced, quillon gripped tight in each fist. Stryker's sword was nowhere to be seen, tossed away in the fall to languish somewhere amongst the stones of the riverbed. Stryker spat a mouthful of grit and spun about. The stone was the size of his palm, smooth at the surface but weighty for all that, and he hurled it as hard as he could. It would have cracked Fassett's skull as sure as a hammer against an egg shell, except that it missed. But it forced Fassett into an unexpected crouch that saw him stumbling on the loose stones underfoot, his balance betrayed.

'Stryker!' a woman's voice shouted. He turned as Fassett was scrambling to his feet. Lisette was there, ankle deep in water. She had his sword, and, with a wink, tossed it to him.

Fassett launched himself at Stryker, but the captain wrenched his shoulders round like an uncoiling spring, swinging the blade in a powerful arc. For a moment it looked as though Fassett had made it inside the range of the razor edge, but just as he flexed his elbows to stab at Stryker's chest, the broad steel scythed his shoulder. It was not a killing blow, but it cleaved deep into the flesh, severing skin and muscle in the blink of an eye, and slamming into Fassett's shoulder-bone. He was felled like a great oak, and he brayed at the stars as he collided with the water.

Above him was Stryker, blood dripping black and thick from his sword. Fassett made to move, but he only had one quillon left and Stryker kicked it out of his grip. Then Stryker stepped on his former torturer, pushing his boot down on Fassett's windpipe, pinning his head back in the stream so that the water just managed to slip over his cheeks and pour into his stunted nostrils. Fassett's face was a rictus of terror, wide-eyed and beseeching beneath the glassy surface, an evil spirit from an old folk-tale, a glowering apparition in an enchanted mirror. Stryker stared back, held his foot firm, and in the moonlight his eye turned from grey to quicksilver, glinting like an evil orb.

Roger Tainton cursed William Trouting as he whipped the nag with a spiked branch, compelling the downtrodden beast into the dense inner sanctum of the copse. The man had betrayed him not once but twice, evidently deciding to send his sin-drenched crew to capture the gold. Well, Tainton thought with relish, he would get a nasty surprise. Fassett and Squires would give the party a bloody nose and Trouting's would-be footpads would slink back to the *Silver Swan* with their tails thrust firmly betwixt their legs.

He slashed the branch down again, raking it hard across the horse's ribs. If he could just get it moving at speed, he might be able to press on beyond the copse and west, towards the road. With God's guidance Fassett and Squires would join him soon, or he could find somewhere to hide the glittering bounty while the sailors plundered the hut. At worst, they would kill the mute and the mulatto and stay at the decrepit shack for some time, but he was confident they would not chase him far to the north. They would be lost without their ship, after all.

'On!' Tainton snarled. The nag juddered forwards with difficulty, its cargo heavy and the terrain near impassable. Gunfire rattled behind. Shouts rent the darkness. He looked back, seeing nothing. 'On!'

Then he heard the rustle of bushes, the snap of twig and branch thrust roughly aside. There were voices – loud, close – but he recognized none. Tainton clamped shut his eyes, knowing there was no time to waste, but utterly confounded as to what to do. How had the seamen come through Fassett's trap so quickly? But the voices kept coming, and they grew in volume, and Tainton harangued the heaving pony, calling down the Holy Spirit to invigorate the pathetic beast's limbs. He reached into the voluminous depths of his cloak and plucked his secret pistol free. He had loaded it before taking the wagon into the copse, and now he jerked back the hammer.

A shout rang out, clear as a bell and triumphal as a hunting horn. They were behind him. He twisted back to see a face push through a thick knot of dying bracken. It was a small, round face set upon the tiny shoulders of a dwarf. The skin was grey in the gloom, but the eyes shone. They were yellow, bright like the eyes of a cat, narrowing to crescent moons as the man grinned. Tainton might have thought it some kind of demon, a forest-dwelling creature sent by Satan to test his faith. Except that he recognized the face all too well.

'Hold, you rebel bastard!' the little man croaked. He clutched a sword that he now twitched out in front. 'Jump down, there's a good soul.'

Roger Tainton did alight from the wagon, but fired his pistol. The dwarf went down, wheeling away to crash back into the mouldering bracken, and Tainton ran to him, acutely aware of the other calling voices, men who had evidently spread out across the breadth of the copse. The diminutive soldier was not dead, for his moans emanated from the bracken, but Tainton had not the time to finish the job. He wanted the sword, sweeping his arms through the big, curled leaves until he caught the glint of metal against the darker stems. He stooped to grasp it, spinning back amid a jangle of spurs and a rattling heartbeat. It hurt to run, but he did it nevertheless, reaching the wagon just as three, perhaps four, greencoats came into view between the trees. Tainton considered a charge. One last, magnificent attack for King Jesus, but he wanted to live, to fight another day for the cause of righteousness, and for his inspirational master.

So he abandoned the wagon. He went to the harness and snapped the sword up through its leather fastenings so that the palfrey stepped smartly away. It shook, suddenly aware of its new freedom, and he jumped up on to the bare, skeletal back and roared in its pricked ear. Mercifully, gloriously, the animal responded, galloping into the trees and away.

'*Merci*, Lisette,' Stryker said as he and the Frenchwoman clambered up the bank.

She reached the summit first, looking back with a face tight with renewed anger. 'I hate you yet.'

'I do not blame you,' Stryker responded through heaving breaths.

'Good.' She looked past him at the corpse of Sterne Fassett. The water had pushed him to the side so that his shoulders were wedged in the undergrowth at the foot of the bank, while water gently lapped at his feet. 'But I hated him more.'

'Good.'

Skellen appeared behind them. His bald head glowed with a sweaty sheen from the fight. 'All well, sir?'

Stryker shrugged. 'I vowed I would drown him in the sea.'

Skellen went to the edge of the high ground to stare down at the body. 'Near enough, sir.'

'Aye,' Stryker acknowledged, wiping his sword on the grass. 'Tainton?'

Skellen turned to face him with an embarrassed grimace. 'Got away, sir.' He waited for his captain to unleash the inevitable fountain of oaths. 'Shot Jack Sprat to boot.'

'Barkworth?' Lisette replied quickly. 'Does he live?'

Skellen nodded. 'Just winged him.' He sheathed his own blade now, arching his back so that the spine released a series of cracks. 'We've found something worth a look, though, if you'd like to follow me?'

They spent the rest of the night putting the scene of the killing to rights. There were four dead on Stryker's side, plus Squires and Fassett, and a group sent to retrieve the rotting corpse of Clay Cordell had brought him back to be lined up with the rest. They had nothing with which to dig a pit, and Stryker was unwilling to risk garnering any more attention from Pagham or Selsey by lighting a pyre, so the bodies had been carefully arranged in the forest, covered with branches, soil and stones, and left to feed the beasts of the wild.

Stryker was painfully aware of the dangers the gold would bring. They were a small unit now, just nine men, plus himself and Lisette, and they could not afford to run into rebel patrols or even risk the prying stares of hungry country folk. They were trapped in rebel territory; isolated in the enclosures and forests that formed the land between the coast and the city of Chichester to the north. They had enough strength to brave the night, for the footpads would not take on such a well-armed group, but that was scant encouragement, for Tainton had vanished, and there was every chance he would return with a party of soldiers from one of the local garrisons. They would have to march during daylight, staying off the roads and pushing as far west as was possible. But first they needed to head north, for the westward coast road was immediately fractured by the four harbours at Chichester, Emsworth, Langstone and Portsmouth, and Stryker was not about to take his chances in those rebel-held places.

'We'll go east,' he told Lisette, Skellen and Barkworth as they watched the rest of the men hitch a horse to the heavy wagon. A trio of his most reliable men – devoid of their green coats – had just returned from a nearby farmstead where they had traded one of Sir Alfred Cade's golden rings for the animal.

Lisette's chin tightened a fraction. 'East is further into Roundhead land.'

'And north is Chichester.' He shrugged. 'We must go round.'

She nodded. Skellen blew out his cheeks at the prospect of a march that seemed to be getting longer and more arduous by the minute.

'The horse looks strong,' Stryker said. It was hardly a French destrier, but it carried a great deal more meat on its bones than the poor nag Tainton had been using. 'We move north, away from the coast, for a mile or two,' he continued, 'Then swing east, for another few miles, and north again. We'll be quickly into the hills, avoiding Chichester entirely.'

'The hills?' Barkworth croaked. He had a hand clamped over his shoulder where Tainton's bullet had sliced the flesh. Fortunately the wound looked clean enough and had no errant scraps of cloth attached. He fiddled absently with the makeshift bandage fashioned from strips of Sterne Fassett's shirt. 'Then what? Barely a road up there, I'd wager.'

'Cap'n knows it like the lines of his palm,' Skellen answered, glancing at Stryker.

Stryker nodded. 'I grew up on the Downs. I'll get us through.'

'Then what?' Lisette asked dubiously. 'We cannot hope to walk all the way to Oxford with this bloody treasure.'

'Winchester,' Stryker said, the strands of a plan coming together after hours of private deliberation. He, too, had wanted to take the gold where it was safest, and that, without doubt, was Oxford. But it was too far, through the most dangerous territory outside of London itself. 'Basing is our only other garrison in the region, but it is under constant threat. Even if we reached its walls, we would never make it out again. We could take ship, sail round to Bristol, but from where? And from which port would we find help this far to the east?' Besides, if he ever set foot on another ship, it would be too soon. 'Winchester is our only course. It has men enough to provide a forward escort, and lies far enough west that we may reach friendly lines more readily.'

'But to get there,' Barkworth said, his noose-ravaged voice made all the more rasping by teeth gritted against pain, 'we must walk the high downland. That is a long way to trudge without running into the enemy.'

'We will make the march in two stages,' Stryker advised. 'I come from a town called Petersfield, twenty miles short of Winchester. If we reach it, I will find places in which we might keep concealed.'

'Laney is there,' Lisette said.

Stryker looked at her quizzically. 'Laney?'

She rolled her eyes. 'Benjamin Laney, the rector at the big church. He was the man who assisted me when I was there a year ago. He is staunch for the King.'

'Petersfield it is,' Stryker said. 'We find Laney. With his help, we might discover if the way to Winchester is clear.'

CHAPTER 17

Southampton, Hampshire, 20 October 1643

Wagner Kovac let the stick take his weight as he gingerly crossed the threshold. He did not strictly need the walking aid, but he had grown used to it during his recuperation, and, if he was honest with himself, he was keen to demonstrate the sacrifices he had made on behalf of his colonel. This was to be their first meeting since his return from the ill-fated hunt, for Norton had been away, cultivating his growing influence at Poole and Blandford and taking a view of enemy forces in the north-west of the county. Now he was back in the city he had found himself governing, and Kovac had been summoned from the infirmary as soon as morning flooded with light.

'The prisoners,' Colonel Richard Norton said, without looking up, 'have been rounded up, branded like cattle, and locked in their pens.' He was seated at the large table in his usual office, the surface scattered with scrolls, scratching noisily at a pale piece of paper with a large quill. 'I feel like a farmer, Wagner, truly I do.' Now he looked up. His face was set firm, eyes unmoving. 'And yet every farmer needs his helpers, his drovers and his farmhands. If a farmhand cannot do his job correctly, then the farmer must replace him, would you not say?'

Kovac stared at a mark on the wall behind his colonel. 'We killed one, sir. A sergeant from Rawdon's.'

Norton set down the quill and leaned back, forming a steeple with his fingers at the tip of his red beard. 'And yet you lost two men and three horses. You yourself are wounded.

Remind me,' he glanced pointedly at the Croat's bandaged thigh, 'shot with?'

Kovac felt his cheeks burn. 'A pricker, sir.'

Norton slid his hands up his face to rub at the blotchy skin near his temples. 'And your remaining trooper has a shattered wrist and will probably be of no use to me for the remainder of this war.'

'I am sorry, Governor.'

'I should hope so,' Norton said, peering through his fingers as though they were stakes in a fence. 'What happened?'

'He is good,' was all Kovac could think to say. He did not wish to regale his master with the story of his risible attempts to bring a fugitive to heel, or the way he had been tricked in to attacking so rashly, only to find himself sprawling in the mud of some nondescript forest. 'Very good.'

'Must I presume you speak of our dear Captain Forrester?' Norton asked, folding his arms.

'I do.'

'Curious, for he looked a soft sort, did he not?' Norton smiled, a gesture that did not touch his eyes. 'A penchant for the playhouse and a passion for pie.'

'He has a penchant for a fight, sir. A passion for trickery.'

'Either way, he bested you, and humiliated me.' Norton pushed himself from the chair and walked to the room's big window. 'You say he went back to Basing?'

Kovac shuffled his feet awkwardly to face the colonel. 'That is what he claimed.'

'I am an ambitious man, Wagner,' said Norton, his tone almost too bright. Kovac knew he fought to conceal a bubbling anger. 'I would subjugate this county for the Parliament, as you know. But have you considered what my reward will be if I were to succeed?' He turned now, meeting Kovac's gaze. 'And what reward might befit the men who helped me realize my ambition? Forrester's escape will be whispered among our prisoners and through the ranks of your own troop. Soon it will be out there, in the world, a tantalizing morsel of heroism and guile to be chewed and savoured by all. It will tarnish my reputation and limit my ambition. We must curtail such an outcome. Cut off the limb before the wound festers. Do you understand?'

'I do, sir.' Kovac answered. 'I go to Basing Castle?'

Norton nodded slowly, taking his seat again. 'You go to Basing Castle. You may rid us of our mutual enemy, while instigating the reduction of that vile hive of Papists.'

Kovac had half expected the order to come. He straightened, setting his jaw, pleased, despite his injury, to have the opportunity to put right the wrongs of recent days. 'How many men do I get?'

'Two hundred.'

'Two hundred?' Kovac repeated. 'Not enough, sir. Scouts say they are putting up earthworks.'

'Then find help,' Norton replied coolly. 'This is your dung heap, sir, and I expect you to wade through it. I will provide a letter of introduction, requesting assistance from our garrisons in the region, and you can prove your worth to me. Just get in,' he leaned forwards suddenly, '*Major* Kovac.'

Petersfield, Hampshire, 20 October 1643

Stryker entered the workshop alone. He and Skellen had walked down from the hills together, striding on to High Street with the story that they were two itinerant labourers, their weapons left with the rest of the group on the verdant chalky slopes overlooking the town. They had discarded their coats too, much to the sergeant's obvious chagrin, but his complaints against the cold fell on deaf ears, for the matching green would surely mark them out as soldiers. It was just past noon, and Skellen had gone into the White Hart, the sprawling inn at the eastern extremity of Petersfield's main thoroughfare. He would take a cup of spiced wine and sit below the window at the front of the building, watching the road for troops while Stryker went to the modest complex of shops on the far side.

The workshop was well lit and tidy, though it carried the ripe stench of wood shavings, salad oil and raw sweat. There were tools of all kinds hanging from various placements along the walls, various wooden trinkets and vessels were arrayed on shelves, and, he noted with interest, a large number of powder boxes hung from bandoliers that were looped over hooks in the ceiling beams.

The wood-turner was oblivious. He was standing in the middle of a large oaken frame, bent over a mandrel that spun frenetically, a sharp tool poised in hand. Behind him a huge wheel, bigger than a full-grown man, was being turned by a dark-haired youth who bobbed up and down with the crank handle. There was a leather strap running in a figure-of-eight between the large wheel and the turner's machine, and its slow revolution spun the mandrel at an astonishing speed. The focus of the wood-turner was such that, when Stryker cleared his throat, he wondered if the man would expire of fright.

'My apologies, Master Webb,' Stryker said as the wood-turner extricated himself from the frame with a stream of obscenities. 'I wondered if I might speak with you.'

'You are speaking already, it seems,' the wood-turner snapped. He dismissed the smirking apprentice with an irritable wave. 'What is it you want, sir, for I am dire busy?'

Stryker waited until the boy was gone. 'You are George Webb, are you not? Master wood-turner?'

'Are there any other master turners in this town?' But as the man searched his visitor's face the rigidity of defiance began to visibly thaw. He swallowed thickly and billowed a heavy sigh. 'Aye, I am he.'

Stryker nodded. 'I need your help, sir. Your advice.'

Webb wiped the sweat from his hands against his breeches. 'You are turning wood, sir? I would hope not, for such a thing is illegal, as you must know.'

'Not that kind of advice,' Stryker said. 'I wish to know,' he glanced around the workshop quickly, making sure they were alone, 'of soldierly dispositions hereabouts.'

Webb swept a hand through black and silver hair. He was suddenly nervous. 'Why would I know such things?'

Stryker dropped his voice to a whisper. 'Because you are an agent for the King, sir.'

'Preposterous,' Webb blustered, turning away.

'Hold,' Stryker ordered, reaching out to grasp the turner's elbow. He forcibly compelled the spy to come back to face him. 'You are for the King, Master Webb, as am I. And I require your assistance.'

'I do not know who you are—' Webb stammered.

'My name is Stryker.'

The wood-turner frowned suddenly. 'The wool merchant? Too young.' He chuckled mirthlessly. 'And too alive.'

'I am his son.'

Webb's cheeks coloured. 'My apologies. But your heritage does not make you Cavalier, any more than it makes you Roundhead.'

'I have visited Thomas Rowe, the tapster at Harting,' Stryker ventured. 'He is an old friend of mine, and, as you know, one who shifts for the Crown. One of your brother spies. He sent me here. Told me you could help.' He was rewarded by a flicker of recognition in Webb's eyes. 'I see that turns your wheels a touch.'

Webb seemed to be considering matters for a moment, but his face suddenly tightened and he shook himself free. 'I have work to do, and—'

'I grow tired of this, Master Webb,' Stryker hissed, angry now. 'If you speak plain with me, I will be on my way. If you do not, I'll be forced to treat you more harshly.' He saw Webb's Adam's apple bob as the man swallowed thickly. 'Now mark me well. I possess something important . . . vital . . . to our mutual cause. I travel over these hills with it, and require guidance by one who knows the lie of the land. Thomas Rowe tells me you are such a one.'

Webb gnawed the inside of his mouth, but eventually he nodded. 'Rowe is in the right of it.'

'First, tell me of this town.'

'Petersfield? Are you not from hereabouts?'

Stryker let his mind drift to his childhood home out on the rich pastures to the east of the town. The house was substantial and warm, built of flint and thatch beside the junction of the River Rother and its tributary, Tilmore Brook. Sheep grazed all day and he played in the river and in the trees and up on the chalky hills; he had never wanted it to end. But it had ended. 'Not for many years, Master Webb.'

Webb considered his words for a moment. 'It is a town divided. We had two members of the Parliament, and each sided with a different cause. That alone should tell you how frayed our old friendships have become.' He rubbed his eyes as if the thought exhausted him. 'Many in the marketplace will denounce a man for so much as a bawdy jest, such is their zeal, while others, like me, would have things put back to the way they were before the Puritan faction found their voice. Even our priest, a Godly man by the name of Benjamin Laney, has been driven out for his Laudian sympathies.'

Stryker nodded. Lisette would be sorry at the news. 'Rowe told me as much. That is why I am here. It was Laney I had hoped to find.'

Webb shook his head. 'Long gone, I regret to say.'

'But what of soldiers, Master Webb? Are there rebels operating in the town?'

'No, sir, not for several days, but they pass through.' He spread his palms to show that he had no real answers. 'You are safe enough for the moment, but I would not tarry if I were you.'

'But where do I go? I would make for Oxford, but the roads through the Thames Valley are too dangerous. I must reach the nearest garrison of strength, so as to collect an escort for the remainder of my journey, and my guess thus far has been Winchester, but I seek your guidance on the matter.' Stryker stepped closer. 'Tell me, sir, is it Winchester, or should I look elsewhere? Alresford? Or further afield. Reading, perhaps?'

'Basing.'

That caught Stryker by surprise. 'Basing House?'

'The King's forces took Reading at the beginning of the month,' Webb said, 'but I hear Waller is at Windsor with the beginnings of a new army.'

'Too close for comfort,' Stryker said, imagining a vast enemy horde mustering so near to the Royalist garrison.

'That is what I would suggest. We hold Winchester and Alresford, but the latter garrison is too small and will offer you no help, while Winchester is under constant threat from Southampton. Colonel Norton has been elevated to governor there, and he has busied himself in the spreading of his influence. Go to Basing; send a messenger to Oxford. If what you carry is so vital, they will dispatch men to escort you back.'

Stryker considered the advice. It seemed reasonable enough, but he was unwilling to abandon his original plan so readily. 'Winchester is but twenty miles from here. It is really so fraught with risk?'

Webb shrugged. 'Try it. Get yourself a fast mount and chance your arm. But I would wager a great deal that you would not cover the distance without running into Norton's troops.'

Stryker blew out his cheeks. If Webb considered it a dangerous proposition for a lone rider, then a heavily laden wagon escorted by eleven people on foot would find the journey impossible.

'Why,' Webb went on, 'his men were here just ten days ago.'

'Norton's?' Stryker asked. 'They strike this far from Southampton?'

'Aye. His force is predominantly cavalry. Such men move swiftly, but I'm sure I do not need to tell you that. Besides, they were in search of a particular man.'

'A spy, no doubt.'

Webb nodded. 'An officer out of Basing. He carried a warrant calling for the raising of the county for the Cavaliers. Norton got wind of it.' Webb's creased brow furrowed deeply. 'I am wretched to confess that he was taken here, in my very own shop.'

'How did they discover him?'

Webb looked at his shoes, evidently crest-fallen. 'I know not.'

Stryker thought about the implication of the spy's capture. 'If the marquess is rabble-rousing, then he makes his house a target. Parliament will wish to bring him to heel as a matter of honour.'

'Either way,' Webb said, sensing Stryker's reticence in trusting his advice, 'I would yet recommend you make for it in the first instance. You may pick up men. And it is quite the haven.'

Stryker offered his hand for Webb to shake and made for the door. 'I was there a year ago, Master Webb,' he said over his shoulder. 'And I can tell you it is more palace than fortress.'

'The marquess's man Forrester told me they have spent a good deal of time and money on new defences,' Webb replied, moving back to his lathe.

Stryker already had his hand on the iron handle, but he let it fall. 'Hold, Master Webb.' He turned to regard the wood turner. 'Repeat that name if you would.'

'The marquess's man?' George Webb asked, frowning. 'Why, Forrester was his name. Lancelot Forrester.'

Roger Tainton pulled the knife free. Even in the darkness he could see blood welling like spilt ink over the flesh, coursing over the curves of the neck in black rivulets to bloom on the sheets. The woman lay on her back in the feather bed, her sightless eyes wide, straining in her final panicked moments, glaring at the beams. Tainton's blade had severed her wind-pipe even as she slept, so that her wakefulness had been brief and violent. Her eyes had snapped open as he pushed the wickedly keen steel through skin and tissue, she had bucked and writhed as he felt the tip crunch against her neck bones, and her lips had worked silently as he held it fast, pinned deep, waiting for the life to seep from her body. It had taken longer than he had expected, and he had prayed the husband would wallow in his slumber.

He slid away from the newly made corpse and wiped the knife on the edge of the bed. It was a good weapon, he reflected.

A long, thin length of double-edged steel, with a thick medial ridge for strength and a fluted, octagonal grip that was carved from oak. He had relieved a pilgrim of it following a short altercation on the road near the border between Sussex and Hampshire, exchanging his weary nag for the traveller's fresh pony to boot. It had allowed him to press on through the wooded escarpments and grassy slopes of the Downs in the wake of his quarry, tracking their distinct wheel ruts in the soft earth but always staying a suitable distance behind. In the hours after his breathless flight from Pagham, he had thought to ride to Chichester in order to raise the alarm. But his mind had turned the consequences of such an act like a plough through soil, digging up images of a city mired in its own civic and regimental politics, of officers suspicious of a newcomer with a seemingly tall tale, and a governor who, even if he agreed to grant Tainton an audience, would not necessarily be disposed to assist. Tainton had, therefore, resolved to follow Stryker himself.

The pursuit from the Sussex coast had taken him up into the South Downs, climbing the ancient bridleways and weaving through blocks of dense woodland that had once been the haunt of wolves. He had traced the route of his enemies along the summit of a high ridge and down a steeply winding hill, finishing in a sleepy backwater named South Harting. There he had watched as Stryker visited a taphouse, and then the whole group took the north-westerly road back into the wild expanse, following its meandering journey past stream and valley and copse, until finally descending into this unassuming little place set deep in a depression in the hills. But it was here, in the fields skirting the town, that the trail had suddenly gone cold.

He eased himself off the bed. Mercifully, the husband yet slept, and he padded smartly round to the far side. He glanced out of the window through which he had climbed, hoping it would not rain, for his boots and their relentlessly noisy spurs had been left out there below the sill. He could see the buildings of High Street, their roofs silhouetted against a bright moon in a cloudless sky. It was another cold night, another step towards a bitter winter. He was glad at the thought that soon this ordeal would be over and he could return to London and her great and welcoming hearths.

Tainton rested the knife point just above the sleeping man's right eye. He held it there, poised and still in a steady hand, watching the fellow's chest rise and fall with each gentle snore. His free hand he slithered over the man's mouth. The eyelids shot up, head jerking forth, but Tainton pressed firmly on the man's face so that he could neither move nor scream. He saw the knife too, fear lighting up his gaze, and immediately he was still.

'Have a care,' Tainton warned, still pushing down upon the man's lips. 'I will remove my hand if you pledge to remain still and quiet.'

The man shifted his terrified stare from the blade to Tainton. He wiggled his brow in an evident attempt to acquiesce.

'Good,' Tainton said. He slid his hand away, though the knife remained. 'Stay on your back, there's an obedient fellow. Sit up quick and there'll be metal in your brain before you can close your eye. Understood?'

The man nodded mutely.

'You are George Webb, are you not? Wood-turner.'

Webb nodded, eyes on the knife.

'And you are a Royalist spy,' Tainton added. It was a guess, but why else would Stryker have paid the man a visit? 'Come now, sir, I haven't all night.' Tainton had followed the captain and his languorous sergeant down from the hills, and witnessed Stryker sneak into the wood-turner's premises. When he had returned to fetch Skellen from the tavern across the road, he carried no items one might find in such a place. No boxes or flasks or anything turned by an experienced hand. It was information Stryker sought, Tainton felt sure of it.

'Who are you?' Webb managed to blurt.

'No concern of yours.' Tainton put a hand to his cowl and push it back. He waited while the prone man absorbed the face that peered down upon him. The featureless skin, the hairless skull, the ice-blue gaze. 'Now, you are a Royalist spy, sir. Do not waste your breath in the denial. Speak plain, answer my questions, and you will see salvation this night.'

Webb's ashen face quivered as he nodded assent. 'Ask, sir, please, and be gone, I beg you.'

'I follow a man named Stryker. My horse threw a shoe, and when I had seen it repaired, he was gone.' He turned the blade slowly, letting the moonlight skim along the medial ridge. 'You saw him earlier this day. Where did he go?'

Webb swallowed thickly. 'N—north, sir.'

'North?' Tainton echoed. He frowned at the idea, feeling the antagonism of the taut skin around his forehead and temples. North took him towards a cluster of Parliamentarian towns. 'To what end? What destination?'

'Basing House, sir.'

Tainton gazed into the wood-turner's bulging eyes. 'Basing?' It took a moment for him to register the implication. Once behind the Marquess of Winchester's walls, he would be difficult to dig out. But they would not leave the gold there for the marquess and his family to plunder. They would look to move out for Oxford as soon as the way was safe. Tainton could not stop Stryker reaching Basing, but he could certainly arrange matters for when the one-eyed thief dared to leave its protective embrace. 'Where is the nearest Parliamentarian garrison?'

'To Basing?' Webb asked. 'Farnham Castle, sir.'

Tainton nodded, finally contented after the brief loss of his quarry. 'Then it is to Farnham with me, Master Webb. And you have my thanks.' He stood. 'Now I will set you upon the path of salvation, as promised. In that, you may join your goodwife.'

George Webb looked sideways then, staring at the woman by at his side. Even in the darkness he could see the blood staining her throat and breast, running into the sheets and seeping into the compacted feathers beneath them. A look of sheer horror crawled over his face, his neck convulsed as though he would vomit, and he drew breath to scream. Tainton stabbed him twice in the chest, forcing the dagger up between the ribs so that the air immediately hissed from the wound. Webb's jaw worked frantically, but no sound came. Tainton yanked at the blade, which required substantial effort and a knee in the turner's midriff. Eventually it slid free. He left the man to flounder in his own blood beside the corpse of his woman, and climbed out through the window, all the while thanking God. The trail was cold no longer.

CHAPTER 18

Farnham Castle, Surrey, 22 October 1643

Colonel Samuel Jones, a thin, elegant and pinch-faced man in his late thirties, stood in the courtyard of Farnham Castle. He was watching his greencoats as they ran through manoeuvres taken from the manuals of pike and shot. Sergeants and corporals bawled oath-laden orders as the tight squads pivoted around them, pikes were charged and shouldered by turns, and muskets snapped crisply from one position to the next. He was proud of them, for they were a good, solid, loyal body of men. But more importantly, he was proud of their home. The castle was set high on a wooded hill overlooking the clustered houses far below, and it was a supremely defensible place, but Jones also delighted in the ease with which he could keep his fighting men from the corrupting influence of their followers. Society's dregs. The hunched, foul-mouthed crones who attached themselves to the soldiers, turning regiments into itinerant towns. There would be children too, the sly, filthy little urchins whelped on their unholy unions. An army in the field was a melting pot of disease and sin as far as Jones was concerned. The thought made him shudder.

He waved to a young officer – a strapping, golden-haired youth who was overseeing the drill – privately noting the shapely curve of the lad's calves. When the officer moved out of sight, he glanced sideways at the fearsome creature who had come to his beloved garrison. 'I cannot spare the men, Mister Tainton.'

The man at his right flank wore a heavy cloak, the hood permanently drawn up to conceal his head. 'What do you mean,' the man grunted, blue eyes gleaming from within the sepulchral depths, 'you cannot spare the men?'

Jones produced a handkerchief from his sleeve with a flourish and wiped the running tip of his red nose. The afternoon was cold, and he stamped his feet. 'I mean precisely what I say, sir.'

'Your corporal tells me you have four companies of foot within these walls.'

Jones twisted to his other side, where a meek-looking fellow in the regiment's distinctive green coat peered back at him through thick-lensed spectacles. 'My corporal has no business discussing garrison strength with a stranger.'

'No stranger, Colonel Jones. I am an agent sent direct from Whitehall, on the business of Pym and of God.'

'And I,' Jones retorted icily, 'am commander of Farnham Castle, sir. I may discuss matters with you, but my minions may not.' He rounded on the corporal. 'Get out of my sight, Ingram, before I have the skin flogged from your spine.' He wiped his nose again as he waited for the ashen-faced subordinate to skulk away, then looked at the man who had introduced himself as Roger Tainton. 'Now, as I have said, I cannot spare any men for this escapade.'

'Escapade?' Tainton spluttered indignantly. 'There is a large consignment of gold and silver within Basing House, Colonel. It is not a few trinkets, sir, but a hoard. It is my commission to secure said hoard for the Parliament, and I require your assistance.'

Jones shook his head. 'I cannot do it, Mister Tainton. Not, and with the utmost respect, for mere rumours spread by men I do not even know.'

Tainton seemed to bridle at that. 'My masters will—'

'Your masters,' Jones broke across him harshly, 'may do as they wish, for *my* master has ordered me to gather my full strength.' He wagged a long finger in Tainton's face. 'Not diminish it.' The very idea was absurd as far as he was concerned. 'A lone rider, sir, gallops into my castle and orders me . . . a full colonel . . . to simply hand him my force so that he might traipse down to an enemy stronghold and dash them against its walls. I find it astonishing that you would even ask, Mister Tainton.'

'Not dash, Colonel, not dash! It is not Basing House I seek to attack, but a small party hidden within. That quarry will not tarry, sir. They will move out from Basing any day, I have no doubt. I simply require enough men to accost them when they take to the road.'

Jones shook his head. 'You are not heeding my words, sir. No soldier leaves this garrison.'

'Why, Colonel Jones?' Tainton persisted. 'What is the reason for this bullock-headed obstinacy?' He lowered his voice. 'The reward will be more than you can imagine.'

'I—' Jones began, but his stinging retort withered before it could form. Instead his attention turned to the main gates, around fifty paces to his right, where the grinding of metal heralded their opening. He glanced back at his unwanted guest, thankful for the interruption. 'Good-day, Mister Tainton.'

Roger Tainton saw his grand plans melt like winter's last snow as he stared at Jones's lean back. The colonel strode quickly across the courtyard, green-coated musketeers and pikemen capped in rounded morion helmets dipping their heads in acknowledgement as he swept by. Tainton had crossed the hills to Farnham with renewed hope after the wood-turner's timely flurry of information. He knew he would probably not catch Stryker's group before they reached Basing, for he had given them a head start of several hours, but, even if he had hunted them down on the winding country tracks, he had no idea how he would wrest the gold from their avaricious claws. But then God had ignited a spark in his mind, as Tainton had prayed He would. Webb had mentioned Farnham, and Farnham, Tainton knew, had a castle that was garrisoned by a highly respected unit. He had been convinced that Jones would be ambitious enough to see the potential in the venture, imagine the lofty commissions the successful capture of the Cade gold would secure, but the man's obstinacy had ruined everything. Now Tainton watched the arrogant colonel strut up to the castle gates and pictured daggers flying back across the cobbles to bury themselves deep between his shoulder-blades. Because the plans had gone catastrophically awry, and the gold was forever lost.

Tainton drew the cloak tighter about his torso, feeling the cold air more keenly than before. At the gate a force of cavalry streamed under the stone arch, filling the yard with their wheeling mounts and pushing the disgruntled greencoats to the sides. Their leader, riding beside a cornet of blue, black and white, was bulky of frame and looked to be of some significant stature. He scanned the cobbles until he noticed Jones, then kicked towards the castle commander, circling him once in a display of remarkable haughtiness. He removed his helmet as soon as the horse had come to a halt, revealing eyes that were pale and hard, cheeks pitted deeply and a chin furred with thick white hair. He called down to the colonel, presumably making his introductions, though it was difficult to hear from this distance.

Tainton quickly skirted the edge of the open space, making for the place where the two officers spoke. The soldiers had instinctively formed two halves of the same circle around their superiors, troopers behind their man, greencoats behind Colonel Jones. The air was tense but calm enough.

'I have papers from Colonel Richard Norton,' the white-bearded horseman was saying in a deeply guttural accent. 'Governor of Southampton.'

'Finally rid themselves of that wastrel Murford, have they?' Colonel Samuel Jones replied.

The German fellow nodded. He tossed his helmet to one of his nearest troopers and dismounted, finally discovering his manners. 'Aye, sir, they have indeed. And Colonel Norton would challenge Basing Castle.'

Tainton felt a knot form in his throat, as it always did when the serendipitous nature of the Holy Spirit worked in his life.

He forced calm into his breaths, moved past a cluster of musketeers, and found himself at the inner edge of the circle.

'Does he now?' Jones was saying.

'He looks to reduce Hampshire's malignants for good an' all,' the white-bearded cavalryman went on. His eyes were pale and hard, and he raked them over the groups of infantry like a man choosing a prime bull at market. 'I require men. Fighters for the cause.'

Jones was fiddling with his handkerchief again. 'These are Surrey folk, Major,' he replied levelly, but in the same superior tone that had so enraged Tainton. 'Hampshire is not their concern.'

The major tugged at the strands of his beard. 'Sir, I beg of you,' he said, his voice growing more contrite with each moment, 'Governor Norton would—'

The handkerchief jerked up to cut him off. 'Besides, and as I have told this gentleman already,' without looking he swept an extended finger round to point directly at Tainton, 'we do not have leave to send men into the countryside. Sir William Waller comes hither. We are expected to muster with the rest of his army. It will simply not do for me to dispatch much needed resource on your private errands.' Now he turned, glancing between Tainton and the major. 'Either of them. Now good-day, gentlemen. General Waller will be here within the week. Should you wish to take the matter up with him, please feel at liberty to wait within my walls.'

Basing House, Hampshire, 22 October 1643

The room was lined with stout candles of fine beeswax, each little flame tilting forwards as the man swept past, as if bowing to acknowledge the Earl of Wiltshire and Fifth Marquess of Winchester.

Stryker stood up, bowing along with the candles. He and Lisette had been invited to dine with Sir John Paulet and his military governor, Colonel Marmaduke Rawdon, in the Great Gatehouse, but the queen's agent had declined, preferring instead to visit the estate's private chapel with Paulet's wife, Lady Honora. He could not begrudge her that right, for the opportunity was rare in a land where overt Catholicism was a privilege reserved and tolerated only for society's elite. In fact Stryker was secretly pleased; he hoped the time apart would heal their mutual wound.

'I am deeply grateful for your kind welcome, my lord,' Stryker said as Paulet and Rawdon approached. The table at which they now found their seats was a huge slab of polished walnut, dark in colour, bright in sheen, like a muddy puddle turned to ice. It was full of salvers, ornate and solid like the ones, Stryker mused, forming a significant portion of the Cade fortune. They were piled with various sweet meats, breads, an array of cheeses and colourful fruit. The array was interspersed with more candles, a tall-necked decanter made of delicate glass, and three silver goblets. At the table's centre was a plate carrying a shoulder of mutton that looked utterly succulent and had already set Stryker salivating. After his days aboard ship, in prison and trudging over hill and down valley, such luxury was a veritable poultice for the senses.

Paulet was swathed in a cloak of red trimmed with dark fur and embroidered in thread of gold. Beneath he wore a blue and yellow doublet, a silver gorget and a white shirt that carried a fringe of lace in a nod to an old-fashioned ruff. He was thinner than Stryker remembered, gaunter of face, though his brown hair was still neat and his beard sharply trimmed and waxed. He took his chair, leaning back so that it creaked loudly, and watched as the others followed suit. 'I am pleased to offer respite to so revered a fighter, Captain. Your message is dispatched, you will be pleased to hear. The escort will come forthwith, and you may be safely away. But for now, please take your ease. The gold is securely hid.' One of his thin brows flickered just perceptibly. 'Though I confess I am unable to fathom why, dear Captain, you would refuse the offer of my vaults.'

Stryker had wondered whether Paulet would take offence at his selection of an underground store-room that had once formed part of the stabling of the Old House, and he took a moment to choose his reply carefully. 'I would simply keep the wagon and its contents in one place, my lord,' he lied, 'so that it might be retrieved with ease when my escort arrives.'

Paulet pursed his lips, putting Stryker in mind of a pouting child. 'It would be safer in Basing's deepest foundations, Captain, nestled secure beside my own coffers.'

This was exactly what Stryker did not want, for he half suspected it would not be easily separated from the dwindling Paulet family fortune when the time came. However, he simply nodded his thanks again. He had arrived at Basing just hours earlier, after an uneventful slog over the open pastures of the South Downs, and immediately set his men to their ease. They had disappeared into the sprawling complex of the Tudor mansion, while Stryker had seen the wagon put securely under guard in the empty store-rooms that had been carved out of the ancient motte. He had spoken briefly with Rawdon, who had come to greet them at Garrison Gate, and the evening audience with the marquess had been swiftly arranged. It was strange to be back in the grand house after a year of war. The buildings were the same, but the defences had changed drastically. There were staked palisades and ditches, high earthworks, jutting bastions and artillery batteries, all linked in a vast ring around the fortress. A formidable place indeed.

'I could not lose any more men, you understand,' Paulet said apologetically, shifting to the side so that a servant might fill his cup with wine. 'Not now that Waller is waking from slumber.'

Stryker thought back to the information he had gleaned from George Webb. 'I hear he raises an army at Windsor, my lord.'

Paulet nodded, snaking bejewelled fingers around the goblet. 'Where he'll march is anyone's guess, but I'll not be without my men.' He lifted the cup, taking a delicate sip. He grimaced, but not as a result of the wine. 'Still, that weasel at court would be pleased if William the Conqueror marched south.'

'My lord?'

Paulet twisted his face again. 'He plays games with me, Stryker.'

'He?'

'Rupert's creature,' Paulet answered sourly. 'Killjoy.'

'Killigrew, my lord,' Stryker said. 'Ezra Killigrew. I know him well. A toad, if ever there was one.'

'A schemer, sir,' Paulet persisted. 'A game player. He would sacrifice me at a damned altar if he thought it would aid the cause. He sent your acquaintance, Forrester, down here from Oxford with the express purpose of stirring Basing to action.'

'That was what Forrester was here to tell you?' Stryker asked. He knew Forrester had gone, captured in Petersfield by Norton's roving cavalry, but he felt duty-bound to discover what on earth his friend had been doing away from Oxford. 'To attack the rebels hereabouts?'

'Aye,' Paulet said, though the word was uttered in something akin to a growl.

Stryker cast his eye down at his plate as the servant set several chunks of mutton upon it. 'Is that not a noble aim, my lord?'

'Not when it is purely to take Westminster's malicious gaze away from Hopton,' Paulet snapped.

'Baron Hopton of Stratton,' Colonel Marmaduke Rawdon interjected upon seeing Stryker's nonplussed expression. Rawdon was a straight-backed, square-shouldered officer who carried a perpetual air of sensible sobriety. He was dressed entirely in black, though his coat was slashed along the sleeves to expose radiant yellow silk beneath. 'He raises a new army to the west.'

'Our esteemed high command,' Paulet cut in bitterly, 'order me to sally out from here, harass the enemy. Make certain they are not looking west when our newest baron makes his move. In short, Killigrew would happily see my estates destroyed if it served his design. And now that might very well happen, for, as you so rightly state, there is rumour of a second force readying for the field.'

'Essex and Waller must have set aside their differences,' Stryker said.

Paulet nodded, his face sullen. 'More's the pity. I believed my actions would enrage one monster, but not two.' He took a longer draught of wine, the breaths from his nostrils echoing within the goblet. Eventually he set it down with a small belch. 'Killigrew and his ilk. We are but pawns in their grand game. But what can I do? I must obey, for it is in the name of our dear sovereign that each of us shift.' He offered a twitch of a shrug. 'Suffice it to say we have done as instructed.'

Rawdon was cutting into his meat, but he looked up at that. 'Indeed, your friend has been instrumental in our struggles. Led my men to war, no less.'

Stryker smiled. 'I am not at all surprised, Colonel.'

'I confess, however,' Paulet said, 'That I misused him. Came to rely on his skill. We are not blessed with seasoned warriors within these walls, you understand.'

'Misused, my lord?' Stryker asked.

Sir John Paulet used his thumb and forefinger to smooth the triangular point of his beard. 'Sent him on an errand, Stryker.' He winced. 'A dangerous one.'

'That was how he was captured?'

Paulet nodded. 'It was.'

Stryker blew a gust of cool air through his nose as he glanced at the high beams above. After all the suffering of recent times, he had reached a degree of safety he had barely thought possible, only to find his friend and comrade in mortal peril. 'Do you have any knowledge of his whereabouts, my lord? Anything at all?'

'Much,' Paulet nodded, too happily for Stryker's taste. 'He was taken by Norton's scouts, imprisoned in Southampton, before achieving a dramatic and glorious escape.'

Stryker's jaw dropped in surprise. 'My lord?'

'I have lately been accosted in the most despicable manner,' a loud, aristocratic voice rang like a bell from the doorway. 'A willowy sergeant and a yellow-eyed dwarf, firmly in their cups, stumbled into my person like a pair of old soaks in an alley. When confronted, they simply let fly a barrage of foul oaths and bawdy laughter.' Captain Lancelot Forrester grinned, stepping into the room. 'Their commanding officer must be the very devil himself.'

Farnham Castle, Surrey, 22 October 1643

The brazier played its crackling tune as the two men regarded one another. They were either side of the iron grate that stood waist high at the edge of the courtyard, embers pulsing brightly within, each holding palms up to absorb the heat. The night was cold and crisp, and similar fires lit the entire castle grounds, infantrymen mingling warily with their cavalry counterparts as they clustered about these places of welcoming warmth. Sergeants patrolled, grim and menacing, weaving between the groups to ensure friendly exchanges throughout, but they did not venture close to this pair.

'You rode with troop?' newly promoted Major of Horse, Wagner Kovac, said across the brazier, his words turning to tongues of roiling vapour.

Roger Tainton nodded slowly. 'I was a captain in my father's regiment.'

'See action?'

Tainton reflected upon his short career with the Parliamentarian cavalry. Only days before his terrible wounds, he had led his men to a glorious and bloody rout of a Royalist unit, and the memory brought new sense to his dulled skin. 'Plenty.'

Kovac gazed with seemingly morbid fascination at Tainton's face. 'This was in battle?'

'Brentford,' Tainton said, beginning to regret the removal of his hood.

'Thought that was all infantry.'

'Then you were mistook.'

Kovac's head twitched to the side to show that he did not care. 'And now work for the Parliament?'

'That is what I said,' Tainton answered. He did not enjoy being questioned. He leaned into the fire. 'Waller comes hither.'

'William the Conqueror,' Kovac said sourly.

'He is preparing to protect the south-east against Hopton.'

'General Hopton?'

'The same,' Tainton confirmed. 'You were not aware?'

Kovac shook his head, gnawing his bottom lip as he did so. 'My colonel governs Southampton for the Parliament.'

'Then you had better send a rider back to inform him. Hopton will march east any day now, and I am certain Norton will wish to know.' He paused briefly as a green-coated sergeant paced past, using the butt of his halberd as a walking stick. 'And yet,' he said when the sergeant had moved out of earshot, 'you are unconcerned with such things, Major Kovac. Like me, your sights are set upon Basing House.'

'My mission is one of revenge,' Kovac replied with eyes made narrow. 'No more, no less. There is a man inside I need to kill.'

'But you cannot hope to reduce Basing with, what, one hundred and fifty men?'

'Two hundred,' Kovac corrected brusquely.

Tainton turned his head to study the courtyard. Troopers milled amongst the garrison men, spurs marking them out. 'Still—'

'No,' Kovac grudgingly agreed. 'I have letter from Governor Norton. Orders help from rebels hereabouts.'

'And you hoped to borrow some of the Farnham greencoats.'

'Aye.'

Tainton nodded understanding. 'I had the same ambition, Major, but it seems we are both thwarted by this order from General Waller. We need troops; he needs troops.' He shrugged. 'We cannot possibly compete.' A group of Jones's junior officers gathered about one of the nearest braziers, chattering and laughing like yapping dogs. Tainton lifted his hood, unwilling to give the pups any more inspiration for their jests. He took a deep breath, praying Kovac's ears would be open to the Word of the Lord. 'But I wonder. Perhaps we might coerce matters a touch.'

Kovac's hard face furrowed. 'Coerce?'

'Work things to our advantage, Major.' Tainton kneaded the air with his fingers. 'Together, God willing, we may fashion our mutual failure into a mutually beneficial success.'

'How?'

'There is gold in Basing.' He waited a second, making sure their eyes were locked upon one another. 'Help me destroy the great house, and you will get your share.'

'Of course there is gold,' Kovac replied derisively. 'If the house falls, there will be much to go around.'

Tainton gritted his teeth. 'Not the trinkets of a wicked peer, Major.' He blew out his cheeks, peering through the billowing cloud his breath had created. 'I do not mean candlesticks and goblets to be plundered shoulder to shoulder with our grubby musketeers.'

Kovac looked nonplussed as he teased the straggly ends of his beard with a thick thumb and forefinger. 'What then?'

Tainton leaned closer, lowering his voice further still as he glanced around the busy yard. 'I speak of a large hoard,' he said, 'already packed in the back of a wagon, ready to be removed without fanfare or the need to share. If Basing falls, you may leave your men to fill their pockets with baubles, while you and I take the real prize.'

'How do you know the gold is packed in this wagon?'

'Because a man named Stryker has it, and he would not be so stupid as to let a greedy peer get a sniff.'

Kovac shook his head. 'Jones will not give us men. And Basing is too strong for me alone.'

'Waller,' said Tainton. It took a few moments to let the name sink through the pottage-brained German's skull, but eventually he saw a glint of understanding in the pale eyes. 'The conqueror comes to Farnham,' he went on. 'Forget Jones and his craven greenbacks. We shall have an entire army. You help me, Major Kovac, and you will be a rich man. Moreover, you will be afforded the chance of the vengeance you so crave.'

Kovac sucked his teeth in thought. 'And how do we find the gold?'

Tainton smiled, because the glint he had seen in the cavalry-man's eyes had transformed from one of understanding into one of greed. He tapped his nose with a finger. 'Leave that to me.'

Basing House, Hampshire, 22 October 1643

'A pricker?'

Lancelot Forrester laughed as he lifted the wooden pot to his lips. 'As God is my witness, Stryker!' He tilted back the pot, neck quivering as he drank.

'How does such a thing come about, sir?' As he dipped his own cup into the barrel they had prized open, Skellen paused to ask his question. He stood protectively over the slopping vessel as though the Cade treasure were contained within.

Forrester wiped his upper lip with his sleeve. 'Hadn't the time for a musket-ball, so I stuck a pricker in his thigh.'

Stryker and Forrester had finished the feast in good spirits and bidden the masters of house and garrison goodnight. They had made their way through the winding corridors, and gone to make sure that the men were behaving themselves in the laby-rinth of red-bricked buildings. They had discovered Sergeant Skellen about to retire for the evening, ordered him to join them, and the three men had walked down to the Grange. The agrarian facility, with its stables, pens and granaries, was quiet in the main, but Forrester had insisted they make their way down to the Great Barn. He inveigled his way past the guards, invok-ing fire and brimstone on any man that dared keep the door barred, and soon they were inside.

'A pricker, sir,' Skellen went on. 'If you was a recruit I'd have your ballocks for that.'

'Indeed, William, it was hardly a regulation manoeuvre, I grant you.' Forrester was perched on a stack of stakes intended for the palisade. The beer kegs, dozens of them, were all around, and he had assured Stryker that a single barrel would not be missed. 'But needs must, when the devil drives, eh?' He looked blearily at Stryker. 'And what of your escapades? Parliament knew all along?'

Stryker nodded, cradling his own cup in both hands. 'They knew enough. Knew that the gold existed, that it was on Scilly. But they did not know where.'

'And Tainton was already on St Mary's, waiting for you?'

'Not waiting. He and his men had been seeking the treasure. They had been warned that we were on our way.' He drank deeply, relishing the heady vapours of the ale, but still, somehow, tasting the acrid salt water that seemed to have left an indelible mark upon his tongue. 'Tainton would have gladly taken the gold and sailed for London before we even arrived. As it transpired, we reached Scilly before he could locate it.'

Skellen snorted. 'If you can call that reached.'

Stryker's mind raced back to the wreck: the sucking tumult of black waters; the flotsam pulsing up to the surface around them; spars and sails and corpses. He nodded, catching the look of horror that ghosted like a veil over Forrester's face.

'Christ's kneecaps,' Forrester exclaimed, staring into his drink. 'I am sorry, Stryker. You have my sympathies, truly.' Glancing at Skellen, he added: 'All of you.'

Stryker, sat on a dusty three-legged stool. He leaned forwards as he spoke. 'Tainton had papers, Forry. Royalist credentials. He was able to convince the garrison . . . a *Royalist* garrison . . . that we were rebels.' Stryker shrugged. 'We had no credentials after the wreck.'

Forrester frowned in thought. 'How did he discover the whereabouts of the gold? I do not believe Lisette would have betrayed Cecily. They grew close before she died.'

'I told him,' Stryker admitted, sensing Skellen shift his feet in discomfort. 'They threatened Lisette.'

Forrester's mouth twitched in the suggestion of a wry smile. 'Has she forgiven you yet?'

'No.'

'But you recovered it, thank God.'

'The price was high.'

Forrester grunted ruefully. 'Ain't it always?' He reached out to Skellen, handing him the cup, and watched in silence as the sergeant dipped it into the barrel before returning it, replenished. He lifted it in salute before quaffing several gulps in a single breath.

'And you were here,' Stryker said, 'to suggest the marquess leave the safety of this place?'

'To rattle the bear cage, so to speak,' Forrester said. His chest heaved as he stifled a belch. 'While Hopton readies to strike into Wiltshire, Dorset and Hampshire.'

'And then on to London.'

Forrester nodded. 'That's the general idea. Though things might not be so simple. We were aware of Essex's army, the danger they posed, but they were hurting after Newbury Fight. We had hoped they would be spread too thin to engage Hopton with any degree of efficacy, especially after our sallies from Basing gave them something to consider.'

'Yet now we must contend with Waller,' Stryker mused.

'Precisely,' Forrester agreed. 'The Cropheads will imminently have two independent field armies in the south-east. One of them is bound to engage Hopton, regardless of what nuisance the marquess makes of himself. Which means my recent efforts have been rather wasteful. I was ordered to draw the rebel fury to Basing in order to distract them from Lord Hopton, yet I suspect the enemy will engage him regardless.'

'And war will come 'ere too,' Skellen said.

'You have it, William,' Forrester agreed. 'I rather think we should return to Oxford as soon as circumstance allows.'

Stryker drained his cup. 'As soon as my escort arrives.'

CHAPTER 19

Windsor, Berkshire, 25 October 1643

The mount, a dun-coloured mare with tufty brown fetlocks and a white patch between her eyes, tore up huge wads of grass with docile indifference as one of the rebellion's great men clambered ungracefully into her saddle. Sir William Waller adjusted his rump, moved his scabbard out of way so that he could place a dangling foot in its stirrup, and straightened to his full – if rather modest – stature. He wore armour, considering it proper and pertinent when welcoming new units to his army, but the day was cold, bitterly so, and the polished plate was concealed beneath a heavy, wool-lined riding coat. The irony was not lost on him, and he said as much to the man who drew up alongside.

'Get to use it soon enough, General,' Colonel Jonas Vandruske replied.

'God willing,' Waller said. The experienced Dutchman had become a valuable source of advice since the humiliation at Roundway Down, and he was well used to the man's sombre frankness. 'I do not wish to remain at Windsor all winter.'

Vandruske fished in the bags hanging at the flanks of his white-eyed stallion, but his gaze never left the road. He was watching a brigade of three regiments march into Windsor town. The lead regiment was clothed in red and followed a huge red standard. 'Now our Trained Bands have arrived, we go to Farnham?'

Waller tilted his head to the side as he totted the newcomers,

284

mentally adding this complement to his total strength. There were dense blocks of pikes, row upon row of musketeers, a long train of baggage and camp followers, flamboyantly scarfed officers, ensigns hefting regimental and company colours high in the chill breeze, and squads of drummers pounding like an orchestra of thunderclaps to herald their arrival. 'We await the artillery train. When word reaches me of their arrival, we will march south.'

'His Excellency will look north, then?' Vandruske said, having taken a pipe from the bag. He began to pack it with a wad of rich brown tobacco.

Waller nodded, still counting the files as they marched past. 'My lord Essex will deal with the Oxford Army; we shall engage Baron Hopton, who, we are told, advances from the west. His army amounts to near four thousand in all, half horse, half foot.'

Vandruske had lit his pipe and now he sucked at its mouth-piece in a staccato rhythm that sent a stream of tiny clouds about their heads. 'His aim?'

'Aside from sacking London itself?' Waller chuckled. 'Winchester, so the spies tell us. Parliament grows anxious, as you might imagine.' He unhooked a water flask from his saddle and took a sip. Baron Hopton of Stratton, he thought. He would have to write to congratulate Sir Ralph on his new title. His old friend truly deserved the accolade, despite earning it in the defeat of Parliament's army in Devon and Cornwall. He pushed the thought from his mind while the last of the red-coated ranks came by, replaced immediately by men in green. Vandruske was a pragmatist, but even he might find Waller's enduring friendship with the enemy general a little hard to stomach. 'Farnham will be our base, Colonel, for the castle is robust and the terrain well known to me.'

Vandruske patted his horse's neck. 'Best keep these men in reserve, sir, should we see action.'

Waller nodded. The London Trained Bands were the regiments raised from the City to protect the City, mustered by local grandees to defend their own streets and property, a force intended to keep the peace rather than prosecute prolonged war. And yet Newbury Fight had changed things. The London recruits so hastily sent out to the relief of Gloucester had found themselves facing the might of the king's Oxford Army, and the bitter gunfights and hand-to-hand murder that followed had tested the Trained Bands like the very flames of hell. Yet to the surprise of even their own commanders, they had not been found wanting. Now Parliament were keen to repeat the experiment, dispatching three more regiments to form the bedrock of Waller's new army. None had seen active service, however, and that fact weighed heavy on their new general's mind. They had not yet received wounds, nor marched through snow or slept in the rain. They had not yet buried their friends. 'Still,' he said, producing a scroll from the folds of his riding coat and scrutinizing the spidery handwriting within, 'the Westminster Liberty Regiment boast 1,084 musketeers, 854 pikemen and 80 officers. Not a terrible offering, wouldn't you agree?'

The corners of the Dutchman's thin mouth turned down exaggeratedly. 'And the others? The Cripplegate Greens and Tower Hamlets Yellows?'

'The Green Auxiliaries – let me see – 1,200 men, all told.' Waller looked up and squinted further down the road to where he expected the green-coated column to end. 'The Yellows a clean thousand. And Colonel Sir James Harrington, of the Reds, commands the combined brigade. I rate him highly.'

'Let us hope they deserve your faith, Sir William,' Vandruske intoned dryly, returning to his tobacco.

'See them quartered,' Waller said. 'Plenty of villages hereabouts. The rendezvous at Farnham will be the first day of November. They may take their ease until I give orders to march.'

'Very well, sir,' said Vandruske, sucking the pipe in long, deep drags. 'There is one more matter, however.'

'Ah, yes,' Waller said. 'Now, let me clap eyes upon this ne'er-do-well.' He waited for Vandruske to summon a subordinate, who in turn ordered two grim-looking soldiers to come up.

Between them, battered and bruised, was a young man of thin frame, lank, greasy hair and mottled-blue lips. Waller peered down at him along the length of his nose. 'Where was our game snared, Colonel?'

'Caversham, sir,' Vandruske answered.

'And what were you about?' Waller asked the boy.

'Now't, Your Highness,' the blue-lipped lad bleated in abject terror. 'Pickin' apples was all.'

Waller looked at the Dutchman. 'Jonas?'

'He was eating an apple, General,' Vandruske answered from the far side of his sotweed cloud, 'but he also carried a most interesting letter.'

'From?'

'Sir John Paulet.'

Waller felt his eyebrows shoot up. 'The Marquess of Winchester, no less. And what did it say?'

'Requested men from Oxford. A large cavalry escort.'

'An escort?' Waller echoed. He drummed his fingers against his thigh as he mused. 'To ride from Oxford to Basing House,' he said absently. 'I wonder what it was intended to protect.'

Vandruske shrugged. 'Refers to the Cade matter, whatever that may be.'

'Cade?' Waller said. 'There was a lawyer named Cade, I seem to recall.' He stared hard at the captured messenger. 'Well?'

A dark stain suddenly bloomed over the boy's breeches. 'I know not, Your Highness!'

'He's a spy, General,' Colonel Vandruske said. He shot the prisoner a nasty smirk. 'Let us see him dance a jig from the castle battlements.'

'*No!*' the boy wailed, falling to his knees in the mud. A foul stench poisoned the air suddenly. 'I'm a messenger only! No more! I beg you, sirs!'

Waller shook his head. 'There is no duplicity in those eyes. Tell me, lad, are you a God-fearing Englishman?'

The boy nodded as though he shook demons from his skull. 'I am, Your Highness. That I am.'

'But you are from Basing. A hive of Popery. Do you adhere to the old, corrupt faith to which the Paulets so infamously cling?'

'No, Your Highness! I am for Canterbury, not Rome, upon my life!'

'And will you fight for your rightful Parliament?' Waller asked, though he already knew what the answer would be. 'Will you bear arms against the King's insidious advisers, risking your life to liberate his royal person from the shackles of those wicked men? Or does your conscience tell you to spend a spell in our dungeon?'

'I'll fight, Your Highness! I shall fight with all my heart.'

Waller nodded, glancing at the Dutchman. 'Make it so, Colonel Vandruske. Perhaps the auxiliaries will have him.'

Jonas Vandruske nodded and snapped orders at the boy and his captors, while Sir William Waller coaxed his mare into a gentle walk. He rolled the parchment back into a tight tube and inserted it into his coat, letting the horse take him back towards the castle. Men nodded to him, doffed their caps, even bowed, but he barely acknowledged their respect. His mind, instead, was considering a man called Sir Alfred Cade. A man long dead but whose name, for reasons he could not fathom, had been invoked by one of the most powerful personages of the old regime. He could not help but wonder why.

Basing House, Hampshire, 25 October 1643

The din of the stables was almost deafening. The buildings were large rectangles, solid and well set in red brick, ripe with the pungent aromas of horse dung, straw, sweat and leather. They met at right angles, forming one corner of the New House, the triangular wedge of space between made up of well-swept cobbles.

Perkin Yates, one of the senior farriers in Sir John Paulet's employ, had led the way under the woodwormed lintel of one of the buildings, and now stood, hands on hips, survey-ing the chaotic scene. 'Folk are twitchy. You're fortunate they let you in.'

His companion nodded. 'I convinced them of my allegiance.'

Yates pursed his lips thoughtfully. 'As I say, they're twitchy,' he said in the broad accent of the northern counties. 'Nervous. Rumours of rebel armies reach Basing daily. People do not trust easily.'

Roger Tainton bobbed his head like a pious monk. 'Then I thank God they believed my truths.' He looked around. Young lads ran to and fro, carrying tools for the farriers and food for the horses, while the beasts themselves whinnied and brayed from behind their stalls, hooves clattering, dung steaming in the cold.

'You had better know your business, friend,' Perkin Yates said, 'or you'll be out on the road a'fore you knows it.'

Tainton had altered his appearance at Farnham, rolling his cloak up with his tall boots and stuffing everything into a sack. Now he wore simple latchets on his feet, stolen from Colonel Jones's stores, and a thick woollen cap, akin to the Monmouths often issued to infantrymen, covered his head. As he spoke, he tugged it further down to ensure that it covered his ruined ears. His face could not be helped, the missing eyebrows and sheer lack of definition in his features was something beyond conceal-ment, but the hat, at least, took the edge away from his freakish appearance.

He fastened one of the cloth buttons of his rough cassock as he watched an elderly man with taut, sinewy forearms hammer a shoe on to an irritable stallion's hoof. 'Thank you for your faith, sir.'

'Well, good hands are scarce,' Yates said brusquely. 'Mister Bryant, our Gen'leman of the Horse, commands the stables, mews and kennels. Though we have no use for the mews, these dark days.'

'How many hands do we have?' Tainton asked of his new superior.

Yates breathed heavily through a long nose. 'Had twenty down at Hackwood.' He shrugged. 'Now we survive with a skeleton complement. Rest are off to war or diggin' our earthworks.'

Tainton closed his eyes. 'May the Lord smite this devilish rebellion soon.'

'The Lord or Prince Rupert. I doesn't mind which.' Yates cackled maniacally and turned away, pacing past one of the urchins he had spoken of, who was busily sweeping huge clumps of faeces into a pile. 'Bound for the drain,' he said. 'Fishes gobble it up.'

'Where do I sleep, sir?'

Yates tilted up his bald head suddenly. 'Hayloft, Mister Chivers. Up in the rafters.' He looked back at Tainton, jabbing the air between them with a finger. 'I'll be watchin' a week, got that? If you proves yourself by then, you're in. If not—'

Tainton nodded rapidly as Yates made a thumbing motion over his shoulder. 'I understand, sir.'

The corners of Yates's mouth upturned. 'Call me Perks. Where did you say you was from, Mister Chivers?'

'Coventry, sir,' Tainton said, affecting embarrassed laughter as he added, 'Perks. And my name is Tom.'

'Never been m'sen,' replied Yates, 'but I'm sure it's a fine place. And you're a proper Christian?'

Roger Tainton tugged down the sides of his cap again. 'Catholic as Maffeo Barberini.' He offered a wink. 'Almost.'

'Ha!' Yates cackled again. 'Very good, Tom.'

'That is why I am here, in truth,' Tainton said. 'The country is not safe for a man of the old ways.'

Yates hawked up a wad of phlegm and deposited it noisily into a tiled gutter than ran through the room's centre. 'There ain't nowhere outside m' native Yorkshire that is safe for God-fearing men like us, young Tom. That's the grievous truth of it.' He crossed himself as he watched the spittle mingle with a fresh stream of horse piss and float away, a white raft on a yellow river. 'Basing Castle's not just a bastion for loyal men, it is a bastion for pure believers. The rebellion is not kind to the old religion, and that's the nub of it. Why, they say the French ambassador were lately at Westminster. His confessor, an Englishman, was arrested and will shortly be quartered at Tyburn.' Perkin Yates stared into the middle distance as his eyes became glassy. 'No, sir, it does not serve to be a Catholic with a Parliament so rife with demons as ours.' He blinked suddenly, staring hard at Tainton. 'You've come to the right place, Tom.'

Roger Tainton felt sick. He closed his eyes so that Perkin Yates assumed he was giving thanks. Instead he prayed for gold.

Cowdrey's Down, Hampshire, 25 October 1643

The horsemen trotting along the crest of the bare hill could see the clay-red sprawl of the great house below. Its structures and its walls, its crenellated towers and modest outbuildings, cluttered the landscape, nestled like a den of vipers between the plateau of Basing Park and the broad River Loddon. Basing House and its adjacent farm, split by a road of churned earth that had been barricaded at either end to form a secure defensive ring, appeared more formidable a site than Wagner Kovac had ever imagined. He had gone to Farnham with the purpose of gaining an infantry arm for his core mounted force, but always he had envisaged his ultimate assault would be against a palatial facade with grand memories and little substance. Now, as he cantered at the head of his armoured column, he understood that a detachment of greencoats would not have sufficed, regardless of the pig-headed Colonel Jones's obstinacy.

Cowdrey's Down loomed over Basing to the north-west, the Loddon carving its glistening route at its foot so that Kovac's view of the fortress took in the busy agricultural complex first, then the two houses beyond. A stone wall encompassed the estate, higher than he had imagined, and even from this distance he could pick out the black scars where loopholes had been scored in the brickwork for defensive musketry. On the north side, where the ground sloped down towards the river, a second wall was set with formidable towers.

'Fortunate Colonel Jones declined,' a lieutenant, face bisected by the single sliding nasal bar of a helmet in the Dutch style, shouted over the rumble of hooves.

Kovac glanced right to shoot the man a rueful smile. '*Ja*. We'd have failed.' He narrowed his eyes as the wind began to swirl into their faces. Tainton's plan was truly the only viable option open to him. He did not like sharing glory with such a man, but without Tainton he would be forced to return to Southampton with nothing to report but failure. Norton would immediately strip him of his majority, and ignominy would follow.

The wind was strong up on the hill, bitter against the skin of the horsemen, who wore helmets with vertical metal bars that would protect against a sword slash but not the elements. They shrunk into their horses' necks as best they could, pinching closed their mouths, breathing in shallow fashion through the nose, watching for the movements of the trooper in front when the wind prevented them from discerning shouted orders. Kovac stood in his stirrups, the pain in his thigh searing from groin to knee, reminding him of why he had come to this cursed place, but he kept his nerve and waved his charges on. They had languished at Farnham for three days, these warriors, and he understood the irascible humours that built in a man forced into such lethargy. Mutterings of disgruntlement had begun to be heard, fights had punctuated the evenings as troopers and greencoats clashed in angry exchanges, and he had resolved to take his men away from the castle while he waited for his part of the plan to swing into action. They wanted to see Basing – Loyalty House, as it was known by the Cavaliers – and Kovac, in the end, had acquiesced. They would hack out, terrorize the local villages, pound the highways and infest the lanes. They would eradicate the cobwebs of inertia and parade before their enemy, daring him to send his own horse-borne warriors to challenge them.

Kovac twisted back to look at his thundering troop. They

were resplendent in their bristling metal, creatures of slaughter, half man and half beast, martial, terrifying, and beautiful for all that. Some had curved sabres at their sides, others long, single-edged cleavers. Many were scarfed at waists and chests, and some had tawny ribbons tied at the shoulder or wrist. They were the colours of Robert Devereux, Earl of Essex and Lord General of Parliament's armies, and he knew they revelled in the association, for they had earned it under Stapleton's command at Newbury Fight. But it mattered not to Wagner Kovac, as long as they rode beneath his banner this day. He looked to his cornet, a young lad with a rebel heart and a wealthy father, cantering clear at the wing, gleaming in black and gold armour worth more than his steed, the black flag snapping madly above his head. A fitting standard for so strong a unit.

It started to rain. The droplets came at them like a volley of miniature bullets from the west, sleet-cold and stinging. Kovac dipped his helm into the torrent, letting the polished metal take the brunt, and gave the order to wheel about.

Stryker was with Forrester on the flat summit of one of the Great Gatehouse's imposing corner towers. They were looking north, over the tiled apex of the Great Barn, squinting through perspective glasses borrowed from the marquess at the cavalry-men on the crest of Cowdrey's Down. Save for the smattering of saplings in the park to the south and in spite of the rain, the view was clear all the way past the river and up to the escarp-ment that was now full of horses and men. They leaned into the rampart, propping elbows on the crenellated masonry, and trained the glasses from rider to rider, officer to trooper, reading the terrain and deployments as only a veteran could.

'What are they about?' Forrester said through the side of his mouth.

Stryker had lowered the glass to wipe the lens on the hem of his coat. It took time, for he wore a full-length buff-coat over the top, purloined by Forrester from Paulet's stores, but he was in no mood to grumble. The oiled hide kept him warm and dry in the stinging drizzle. 'Taking in the view.' He raised the leather tube again. 'Gauging the worth of an attack.'

He watched as the Roundheads began to file away, noting the tawny sashes that had been the Earl of Essex's mark, though they were now almost ubiquitous with any rebel unit in the south. A cornet of horse carried the colour on a hefty staff, and Stryker could see that it was black, but that hardly differentiated them in a war when new regiments, even whole armies, seemed to be raised and deployed with every passing season.

It was only when Forrester muttered a soft curse that he looked round at his friend. 'What is it? What do you see?'

Lancelot Forrester swore again. He kept the glass up, as though it had been nailed to his eye, his mouth flapping like a gasping fish in the hold of a boat. 'I know that colour. It is Kovac.' Now he lowered the glass. He looked at Stryker. 'It is Wagner Kovac.'

'Norton's man?'

'He is not here for Basing,' Forrester whispered darkly. 'He is here for me.'

CHAPTER 20

Farnham Park, Surrey, 1 November 1643

Beneath the batteries of Farnham Castle, on the sprawling expanse of green parkland identified as the long-awaited Parliamentarian rendezvous, Sir William Waller, supreme commander of the newest army in Britain, reviewed his troops. It had rained overnight, leaving the ground sodden and the air chilly and vaporous, and he walked before the assembled throng swathed in a long, fur-lined cloak, his wide-brimmed hat tilted slightly over his face. Before him was arrayed a formidable force, units clustered in dense blocks, their colours bobbing on the breeze.

'We hear Hopton is at Andover, Sir William,' Colonel Jonas Vandruske said. The tall Dutchman held his own hat beneath his armpit so that he could sweep a gloved hand through his short fair hair as he talked.

'They found no resistance in Dorset, then,' Waller said, pausing to look up at into the colonel's dark blue eyes. 'Do they march?'

Vandruske shook his head. 'Not thus far, sir. They muster around Salisbury and Andover in the main.' He shrugged. 'Some are at Winchester, of course.'

Waller resumed his progress. 'Then we have time. We must strike Sir Ralph before he can coordinate his efforts. Smash through Winchester, drive into his army at Andover, and push him westward until we may force his hand in the field.'

'You would risk open battle?'

'After Roundway?' Waller shot back wryly.

The Dutchman coloured a little, the large scar running horizontally across his cheek appearing paler against the blushing skin. 'No, sir. That is not what I meant. Not at all. Simply that our army, for all its size, has, at its core, divisions from the Trained Bands.'

'They'll fight if I ask them, Jonas,' Waller replied, though he felt far from sure. Did he really think that they would fight, or was some part of him driven by a desire to exceed the feats of his superior and nemesis, the Earl of Essex? The Lord General had relieved Gloucester and held Newbury with an army of hastily raised apprentices, and Waller would be damned if he could not match the achievement with exploits of his own. He turned his head to the massed ranks to prevent Vandruske reading the concern in his eyes. 'I mean to wait another day or two. More men and arms come to Farnham, and I would not leave them behind purely for haste.'

Vandruske grunted agreement. 'And the families of our new city folk are sending a train of provisions, I understand.'

'We will be well supplied, I am pleased to say,' Waller muttered, though in truth he was wondering what exactly he would face in the coming days. Rumours filtered from the north that the armies of Essex, Rupert, Byron, Newcastle and the Fairfaxes were again in the field, while in the south Richard Norton's men were engaging with Lord Crawford's Cavaliers. And in front of Waller, not thirty miles due west, Baron Hopton's forces were gathering like a winter storm. The nation was in a state of flux. The uncertainty made his heart race and his chest feel tight.

Waller had led his army out of Windsor two days earlier, the bristling column trundling through the countryside like a vast serpent, its spine made of men and horses and wagons and artillery, baggage carts, women, children and supply wagons. En route they had met up with more detachments from his own regiment, and when his ranks had almost completed their growth, they had streamed south into Farnham town. There was not the space in the castle to house such a multitude, and so the general had named the wide park as the place where they would muster. Now, with a straight back and swelling pride, Waller walked slowly across their front rank. There were redcoats and bluecoats, yellows and whites, the green–coated garrison from Farnham itself, and various gentlemen troopers in their own civilian clothes. The metal of helmets and pikes, muskets and swords, ornate pommels, swirling hilts and spinning spurs glinted in the weak sunlight. Huge squares of taffeta hung from poles above the infantry brigades while smaller cornets flapped to mark out cavalry, each with its own colour and devices: stars, diamonds, circles, fearsome beasts, tracts of Latin, biblical verses. Waller now commanded sixteen troops of horse, eight full companies of dragoons and thirty-six companies of foot. Almost five thousand men in all. In addition, he had ten large fieldpieces, drawn stoically by teams of harnessed working horses, and half a dozen cases of drakes, enclosed wagons of war with guns protruding from their loopholes that were capable of deadly fire in open terrain. And there was a large cache of black powder, though it was kept well away from the main carnival of colours, escorted by bluecoats armed with firelocks, for the handling of lighted match near barrels of powder was sheer suicide. Waller shuddered privately at the thought of an errant spark.

'Sir?' Colonel Vandruske prompted.

Waller smiled sadly. 'I was reflecting upon the safety of our powder train. Baron Hopton fell afoul of an explosion after Lansdown Fight.'

Vandruske's face creased sourly. 'A pity it did not put an end to him.'

'Have a care, sir,' Waller snapped brusquely. 'Sir Ralph may oppose me in war, but he remains my dearest friend.'

'My apologies, Sir William,' the Dutchman said, not sounding entirely contrite. 'Thoughtless of me. Yet you must soon engage him.'

Waller walked on steadily, nodding to Colonel Jones,

commander of the Farnham greencoats, who stood at the head of his men, their white banner draped from a pole behind him. The thought of fighting Hopton again weighed heavily upon his mind. 'I must shift for my conscience, and he must shift for his,' he said eventually. 'And we will be friends once more, when this lamentable business is done.'

'Sir William!' an officer shimmering in blackened armour astride a huge black stallion called down from his perch. He was positioned at the head of a dense block of heavy cavalry.

Waller beckoned to the horseman, stifling the image of jousting knights that his mind had conjured. 'Sir Arthur! Well met! Fare you well?'

Sir Arthur Heselrige was the forty-two-year-old Baronet of Noseley and the commander of Waller's Horse. A staunch Puritan, firebrand critic of the king, and good friend of Waller, he had led a regiment of cuirassiers since the beginning of the war, seen them distinguish themselves at Lansdown, receive a shattering rout at the disaster on Roundway Down, and now, with the grace of God and despite injuries received on that fateful day, had somehow made the Farnham muster with a reborn force of which he could be proud. He let his mount walk slowly out of the line. 'Well indeed, Sir William, well indeed.'

'And the leg?'

Heselrige was a lean, spare man with long auburn hair and a full moustache. He was noted for his irascibility, but now, patting his plate-caged thigh gingerly, he flashed a brilliant smile of small white teeth. 'Festered. Blood went bad, I'm fearful to report, and it stank some, I don't mind telling! But it healed, thank King Jesus.'

'It is providence keeps you breathing, sir.'

Heselrige nodded. 'Providence and proper armour.'

Waller smiled. 'It pays to ride to battle in an iron shell.'

'I was shot thrice at Roundway, Sir William, and all bounced clean away. It was only when the craven malignants cut my horse from beneath me that they caused harm.'

'And how are your dashing lobsters?' Waller asked,

deliberately employing the term the common soldiery used for the heavy cavalry, so encased were they.

Heselrige grinned again. 'Pious, brave and eager to follow William the Conqueror.'

Waller touched a finger to his hat. 'Touché, Sir Arthur.' He noticed another horseman rein in just behind the leader of his heavy cavalry. The man looked to be an officer, for a voluminous orange scarf was tied about his waist, but he only wore the accoutrements of the harquebusier – simple plate on back and breast, thick hide beneath, and a three-barred pot on his head. 'You appear to have a cuckoo in the nest, Colonel Heselrige.'

Heselrige glanced back briefly. 'This man sought an audience with you, General, but was denied. He came to find me in your stead. He has a message of some import, sir.'

Waller stared at the horseman, who removed his helmet to reveal a face pulpy from a legacy of pox, and a white beard tainted by yellowish streaks. His eyes were startlingly bright, almost mocking. 'I see you are not one of mine, sir, for you wear the colour of His Excellency, the Lord General.'

The horseman slid a hand instinctively to his broad scarf. 'My regiment fought with him at Newbury, sir. Under Sir Philip Stapleton.'

Waller mothered his simmering annoyance, glancing at a nearby aide. 'Get him another, Andrews. Blue or yellow, I care not which.' He looked back at the harquebusier. 'Sir Arthur evidently considered your message worthy of the telling. But first,' he said as the man urged his horse forwards, 'who the devil are you?'

'My name is Wagner Kovac, sir. Major, Colonel Richard Norton's Horse.'

'He was a clerk,' General Sir William Waller said as the four men passed, on foot, by the gently swaying corpse dangling from a gnarled oaken bough. 'From my own regiment, no less. A good man, so I thought. Regrettable.'

Major Wagner Kovac was at his side, staring at the

purple-faced clerk as the rope softly creaked with his weight. 'What was his offence, General?'

'Mutiny,' Waller said. He glanced up at the body of the man he had that morning condemned, a lesson in leadership for the others. 'The inactivity irks them, the weather enrages them. It was always thus.'

'We must watch the Trained Bands in that vein, Sir William,' Colonel Vandruske muttered. 'They do not relish leaving London.'

'Mutineers, the lot,' Sir Arthur Heselrige, heavy-footed in his jangling armour, added sourly. It was at his insistence that they had convened this meeting away from prying eyes and flapping ears.

Kovac grunted. 'In my country we—'

'And where exactly,' Waller interrupted, 'is your country, Major Kovac?'

'Croatia, sir.'

Waller raised his brow inquisitively. 'You sound rather Germanic, sir. I spent some time thereabouts, many years back. Fought for the Venetians first, then served with Vere in the Palatinate.'

'Father was Carniolan,' Kovac said. 'I spent much time there, though Croatia is my heart's home.'

'Even so,' Waller persisted, eager to test this man of whom he knew so little, 'The common tongue is Slovene, is it not?'

'The common tongue, sir, *ja*.' The cavalryman smoothed a fistful of white beard in his gloved palm. 'The better sort of folk speak German.'

Waller nodded, satisfied, and began a slow stroll along the adjacent tree-line as crows began to circle overhead. 'And what word were you to bring me, Major? Your commission is with Richard Norton, lately Governor of Southampton, yes? What, therefore, brings you to Farnham?'

'Basing Castle, sir.'

'Basing?' Waller echoed. 'That den of miscreants has been playing on my mind of late. Why, only a matter of days ago the

Marquess of Winchester's putrid warrant was read before the Commons.'

'His warrant to raise funds?' Kovac asked.

'The same,' Waller said, surprised. 'Seized, thank the Lord, before its damage became too great.'

'Seized, Sir William, by me,' the big Croat replied smugly. 'By my troop, down in Petersfield.'

'Then you are to be commended, Major Kovac, truly. Basing House must be reduced as soon as is opportune.' Waller found himself reflecting upon the note his own patrols had intercepted some days earlier. One requesting an armed escort to march down from Oxford. The marquess was evidently busy working against the Parliament.

'It is opportune now, General,' Kovac said.

Waller shot him a caustic expression, unhappy with the man's terse temerity. 'I do not follow.'

'I have waited at Farnham for you this past week, sir. Waited to tell you of the riches to be found within Basing's walls.'

'Sir John Paulet is a wealthy man.'

'No, sir,' Kovac replied. 'I speak of a large hoard. A trove in plate and gem. The personal fortune of the late Sir Alfred Cade.'

Waller stopped in his tracks. Now he knew why those additional soldiers were needed. 'You know this for certain?'

Kovac nodded eagerly. 'I do, sir. A Parliamentarian agent is within the walls even now, working towards the gold's liberation.'

Sir William Waller had his orders, and it would take more than the rumour of gold to capture his attention. And yet Paulet's warrant had indeed been read at Westminster, and they had called for him to be hauled to London in chains, his retainers pressed into the rebel armies and his estates confiscated. It would not, Waller suspected, take a great deal of persuasion to convince them that Basing House should be the real target for his new army. He blasted cold air through his nose. 'Hopton is on the horizon.'

'His ranks swelling like stinking buboes,' Vandruske piped at his back.

'Charming, Jonas,' Heselrige admonished, though without vehemence.

'They cannot be allowed to spread,' the Dutch colonel went on unabashed. 'We must lance them to draw out the poison.'

Waller nodded. 'He is in the right of it, of course, despite his unsavoury choice of words.' He fixed Kovac with a level expression. 'Much as I would like to strike at Basing, and as much support as we would doubtless enjoy in the Commons, it simply cannot be justified at this time.'

'At this time, sir?'

Waller spread his palms. 'It must be taken sooner or later, I grant you that much.' Inwardly he was imagining the riches they might discover somewhere in the palatial mansion's vaults, picturing the delivery of the Cade fortune to Parliament in a blazing triumph that would see his star rise higher than that of the supercilious prig, Essex. 'But Baron Hopton is the greater danger. He simply must be the focus of this army, until such time as the situation has changed.' He raised a hand to stem Kovac's intake of breath. 'You have my gratitude for the information, Major, and I will see that it is relayed to our mutual masters at Whitehall, but Basing is not where I will presently march. This army goes to Winchester.'

Basing House, Hampshire, 1 November 1643

Roger Tainton was not enjoying his new-found role as assistant farrier. It was not the hard work, nor the filth, the lack of pay or the paltry victuals. What he hated was the bowing and the scraping, the doffing of his itchy woollen cap to all and sundry, the way even the grooms sneered as he skulked past. He knew they would be watching him, judging his wounds as well as his skill; knew that no amount of headwear could conceal his face. In his heart he was still a Tainton, eldest son of the powerful Sir Edmund. His blood entitled him to sit at the highest table, in times of peace a guest of the likes of Sir John Paulet, not one of

302

society's maggots. But war had made him Paulet's enemy, faith had compelled him to sacrifice his standing, and this most difficult mission had demanded his slide into the gutter. On the surface he assumed the persona of the commoner, Tom Chivers, but underneath he was a raging sea.

'Hither, old cock!' a voice yapped from the far end of the stable. 'Tack this'n up well.'

Perkin Yates was not a hard taskmaster but he demanded a good job done, and Tainton was glad of his time in the cavalry. He had had grooms most of his life, of course, and ostlers had taken care of the horses at any inn his troop had passed through, but on campaign, riding out into hostile country and sleeping under the stars, the commanding officer had shared the privations of the men and been left to fend for himself and his mount come sunshine or storm.

Perkin Yates greeted him with a slanted grin. 'Done well, Tom.' He slapped the bay mare to which he had tended, indicating for Tainton to take the halter. 'Well indeed.'

'Pappy was a groom, Perks,' Tainton said, deliberately roughing the edges of his syllables. 'I listened well.'

'Indeed an' you did,' the Yorkshireman chimed. 'You'll be happy here, I've no doubt. Now I'm to have a clinch wi' the finest love ever I did have.' He patted his breast with a mischievous wink. 'Sotweed from paradise.'

Tainton nodded. He had forsaken the drinking of smoke since his enlightenment, but he could not help the tingling in his mouth at the memory of fine Chesapeake Bay leaf. 'Take your ease.' He surveyed the empty stable. 'I'm well on my lonesome.'

'Just so, Tom,' Yates replied, performing a smart about-turn.

'Oh, and Perks?' Tainton said.

'Aye, Tom?'

'I've to put some tack in one of the sheds along the way, but I believe the place to be locked. Perchance you'd have the key?'

Yates jammed his clay pipe between his lips. 'Half the bastard keys in this place go a walkin', never to return.' His eyes darted up to a shelf behind Tainton. 'Up there you'll find the skeleton key. Turns every stabling door in the New House, and a few in the Old House, I'd wager.'

Tainton reached up and took the key down with a handful of dust and cobweb. 'Thank'ee indeed. I'll finish up.' He waited until Yates had vanished through the doorway that led out into the cobbled courtyard, and then quickly completed his work with the horse. When it was tacked and tied by the halter to a stout rail, a trough of food within easy reach, he made his way out of the side door that connected the room to another stable. It was his eighth day in Basing, the seventh of active searching, and he was beginning to struggle to keep his frustration in check. He had always known the gold would be locked away somewhere in the bowels of the fortress, but there would be people who knew its whereabouts. Stryker and his woman were two such targets; some of the one-eyed fiend's adherents would doubtless hold the information too. And yet there were simply too many people crammed into the sprawling site. Men, women and children, horsemen and infantry, gunners and their mattrosses, labourers, engineers, physicians, artists, priests, displaced aristocrats and their retainers. In the crowds, Tainton had found that he could move without fear of being accosted by someone who would recognize him, but he had not been able to track those same people down, especially given the poor state of his eyesight. All he could do was keep searching and pray that Kovac would be able to convince Sir William Waller to bring his army to Basing House before Stryker made his next move.

The stables were set into the north wing of the New House, and Tainton weaved his way through the adjacent block, past the trough beneath which he had stuffed his expensive boots and cloak, picking between barrows, pitchforks and busy broom-wielding stablehands. Soon he was into the next block, and this, like the first, was empty, so he made for the main doors that opened on to the courtyard and plunged into the flock of people that thronged between the various buildings. He would, as he did every day, make his way from New House to Old

House making sure to keep his head covered and his eyes awake to faces he might know. He had about half an hour before Yates would wonder where he was.

Stryker pressed his fingers into the bruises at his ribs. His strength had almost entirely returned in the days since he started indulging in the robust diet available to Basing's inhabitants, but his face and chest had been badly battered, and he suspected he would feel tender for days to come. He was waiting for a pair of halberdiers to unlock the broad double doors at the foot of the stone slope that plunged steeply into the foundations of the Great Gatehouse. Behind him the Old House sang with the sounds of the day, and he closed his eye, revelling in it.

'She fares well, Stryker.' Colonel Marmaduke Rawdon's stentorian growl crashed like a thunderclap as he strode out from below the stone archway. 'Though she declines to leave her chamber.'

Stryker nodded his thanks. Lisette's association with the queen had seen her granted quarters within the most comfortable part of the estate, and she had promptly vanished from Stryker's company. For his part, he had kept with the remnants of his whittled party. But as the days wore on, Lisette's absence ached more keenly. He understood her feelings, but that had not stopped him asking Rawdon to look in on her from time to time in return for his advice on certain aspects of the burgeoning earthworks. Thus, he had found himself casting his eye over gun emplacements and powder magazines, new bastions blooming like grim petals from the loose-soiled palisades, and even the positions of picket teams, sent into the outlying countryside.

'I am glad she is safe,' he said, following the colonel down the slope. 'I would leave this place, sir. Take—' he glanced warily at the guards '—the wagon—back to Oxford.'

Rawdon went through the wide doorway and plunged into darkness. 'You are free to go as soon as your escort arrives.'

'You've heard nothing?' Stryker said as he stepped into the gloom.

'Nothing,' Rawdon's disembodied voice rumbled back. 'The messenger went out, that is all I can tell you.'

'Direct to Oxford?'

'Direct, of course,' was the snapped reply, Rawdon's perpetually level-headed demeanour fraying a touch. 'Time will resolve.'

'I trust so, sir.'

They were at the rear of a dank chamber that had been excavated from the chalk. Once a storehouse attached to the old stables, it was now hardly more than a bare cave, its unadorned walls moist and floor rough underfoot. There was no illumination, and they were forced to leave the doors wide open to allow the day's watery light to seep in. Stryker's eye gradually grew accustomed to the dense murk, and he saw Rawdon glide to a black lump at the very back of the room.

'Waller is at Farnham,' Rawdon said, standing beside the object that looked to Stryker like a huge pile of raw coal.

'So the rumours have it, sir.'

Rawdon began fiddling at the undulating surface of the pile. He walked steadily backwards, peeling it away as if some magic tore the very shadow off the wall. Stryker saw that it was a large, black sheet. Beneath it, twinkling in the feeble light with every inch revealed, was the treasure of Sir Alfred Cade, piled high in its wagon. The colonel dropped the sheet and plucked one of the trinkets from its place amid the salvers and chests. 'More than rumours, Stryker,' he said as he turned the solid golden cross in his hands. 'He is at Farnham.'

The red garnet set into the object's base winked at Stryker as he spoke. 'And this new army he is supposed to have?'

Rawdon whistled softly as he gazed at the heavy cross. He placed it carefully back with the rest of the hoard and looked up. 'With him this very moment.'

'How many?'

'Some say five thousand, others as many as eight. Pray God he does not think Basing a large enough fish for his supper.'

'Or pray,' Stryker said, 'Hopton advances beyond Winchester to take him by the collar.'

Rawdon grasped the sheet and dragged it back across the wagon to snuff out the glimmering gold. 'There, Captain, your bounty is safe, as promised. Kept in the wagon, ready to move as soon as your escort allows.'

Stryker nodded his thanks. 'I am grateful, sir. And the guards will remain?'

'They will remain,' Rawdon confirmed. 'They know not what they protect, naturally.' He followed Stryker out into the daylight, walking up the broad slope after the pair had overseen the locking of the double doors. 'Have you seen the German fellow again?'

'Kovac?' Stryker shook his head.

'Perhaps they were simply scouting.'

'Perhaps.' Stryker paused as a man pulled a precariously wobbling dog cart past, its load of earthen clods rising far too high than sense would allow. 'Captain Forrester is convinced he seeks revenge. He is one of Colonel Norton's officers, out of Southampton. Unlikely to scout this far, would you not think?'

Rawdon spread his palms. 'Not something of which I am expert, I confess. But what is the fellow thinking? That he can ride direct through our gates and run Forrester through? Seems peculiar, to my mind.'

'Peculiar indeed, Colonel,' Stryker agreed. He too had ventured the idea that nothing more sinister than coincidence was at work, but Forrester had been uncharacteristically adamant. Yet Kovac could not have hoped to scale Basing's walls with two troops of light cavalry, which begged the question: what did his arrival presage? Stryker knew its portent could not be good.

Roger Tainton was in the Old House. He moved, as was now something of a routine, around the circumference of the Norman ring-work, skirting servants' quarters and a bakery, a row of storehouses and the infirmary. He reached the northern section of the complex, keeping to the shadows. A group of small boys skittered past like sparrows, the leader screaming with delight as he kicked a heavy ball through the crowds. Tainton reached out swiftly and cuffed one of the urchins, sending him reeling. His younger brother had been killed at one such game on Shrovetide when they were striplings. Stabbed in the guts while defending the goal. It had been a legitimate, if unfortunate, action by his opponent, and the training master had allowed the matter to drop without charge, but Tainton had ever loathed the game. He watched sourly as the grubby whelp wheeled away, flinging him a malicious gesture and a fountain of filthy oaths. The lad's friends laughed, the ball bounced off a cart and round to the rear of sheep pen, and the group vanished.

When he looked up he feared his heart might stop, and he was forced to stoop a little for air. He gritted his teeth, steeled himself, swallowing hard and praying harder. For there, coming from the direction of the Great Gatehouse, striding like a pair of cocks on a dung heap, were two men. One was old, slate-grey and garbed in a slashed doublet and wide, feathered hat. The other was lean beneath a coat of mossy green, his hair long and black, face clean-shaven and hard as a granite cliff-edge. He had one eye that was bright like quicksilver, the other gone, its socket buried deep beneath the tentacles of a terrible scar.

If conspicuousness was of no concern, then Roger Tainton might have dropped to his knees in worship there and then. As it was, he took a step back, held his breath till his lungs burned, and stared so hard his eyes began to ache. Because, by the grace of God, he had found what he was looking for.

Farnham, Surrey, 1 November 1643

If there was one thing that Wagner Kovac had learned in his years of martial service, it was that guile, mixed in the right proportions with tenacity, was a powerful brew. Inwardly fuming, he had nonetheless bowed to the general, expressed his gratitude at having been blessed with the brief audience, and thanked Waller for the grace to even consider his plea. But when he had been dismissed, his mind had gone to work.

Convince Waller, Tainton had said. Make him fall upon Basing with the full might of his fresh brigades. Wagner Kovac wanted the gold; how could a man deny such a windfall? But that was not his driving reason for reducing Basing House. Above all, Kovac wanted Captain Lancelot Forrester, trussed and pleading for his life, tied to the back of his horse and dragged all the way to Southampton, where vengeance would come together with the rehabilitation of Kovac's own reputation.

The big Croat was seated on a damp, rotten tree-trunk that had been upended and left to moulder in the scrub fringing Farnham Park. He took a moment to flick specks of mud from his boots and fold the tops down to his knees, then looked up to stare across the park. There were thousands of figures moving in the fire-lit dusk. The new army, rumoured amongst the men to soon be dubbed the South-Eastern Association, had been told to prepare for an advance into the west – first Alresford, then Winchester, and then a move against Hopton's main force. They had bivouacked in the parkland below the castle, camping in the open around their flickering fires, clustered in groups with their families. Wives and mistresses chattered as they scolded children, cooked pottage or stew, mended or washed clothes. The men recounted stories and bawdy jests, played at dice when the more puritanical officers were not about, or drank smoke from tooth-worn pipes. The rasp of sharpening steel cut through everything, a constant companion to the chirp of voices and the crackle of flames. Kovac's troop had been evicted from the relative luxury of the castle, their billets given to more valued men such as gunners and engineers, and he had taken them out to the farthest part of the park so that their mounts could be tethered to trees and, more importantly, so that he could meet his contact away from prying eyes.

'I ride on the morrow, Major Kovac,' a voice spoke in hushed tones from the trees to his right.

Kovac looked round to see a moon-faced man peering through the branches. His eyes were black slits, his hair covered by a woollen cap that was tugged over his ears, and his torso was wrapped tight against the cold. 'You understand?' he said, turning his attention back to the bustling camp. 'Be certain, Lieutenant Budge, lest you wish your neck stretched like a Christ-tide goose.'

'I will take my patrol to watch the enemy, sir.'

'And what will you look for?'

'Lord Hopton's army, sir, as per my orders from General Waller,' Lieutenant Budge replied. 'His strength and disposition.'

Kovac bent down to the leather bag between his feet. It had not left his side since his departure from Southampton, for, apart from his personal effects, it carried a purse made heavy by Richard Norton. Without looking round, he plucked a solid gold coin from within the pendulous pouch. He looked at the double crown with a smile. The single piece was worth ten shillings, a worthwhile sum for a junior officer of horse. He tossed it cleanly over his shoulder.

'You will look for Hopton's army, Lieutenant,' he said after a moment, giving the purse a gentle shake. 'But what will you see?'

'Whatever you wish me to see, sir,' Budge replied thickly. 'Say the word, and it shall be seen.'

CHAPTER 21

Basing House, Hampshire, 5 November 1643

Stryker had finished overseeing the emplacement of the last of the guns out on the earthworks when the scouting party, led by Frederick Lawrence to scour the country to the north and east, returned to the fortress. He left the gun captains and their mattrosses – foreigners in the main – scuttling and squabbling about their iron beasts, considering elevations, checking and rechecking touch-holes, and strode quickly back up to the house's inner sanctum. There he found the dismounted horsemen making report of a vast army that numbered, they estimated, up to two thousand horse and almost double that in foot. Lawrence himself confirmed the rumours just before noon, thundering through Garrison Gate to bring news that he had personally spotted the standard of Sir William Waller bobbing in the van. 'They marched out of Farnham at dawn. Now mustering around Alresford.'

'Alresford?' snapped Sir John Paulet, Marquess of Winchester. He had tried to keep his voice hushed, for the Old House was busy with people, but anxiety seemed to lift the volume unconsciously. 'Then what think you their destination?'

'Winchester, I shouldn't wonder,' Lawrence answered, his face twitching. 'He will engage Hopton.'

'But Hopton has fallen back upon Andover,' Paulet said dubiously. 'What is his will here?'

Colonel Marmaduke Rawdon raised a hand to garner the attention of the group. 'I understand Baron Hopton means to rendezvous with a contingent from Salisbury and Colonel Gerard's brigade down from Oxford. Only then he will advance westward.'

Paulet drew a lingering breath, letting it trickle slowly through his nostrils. 'Then perhaps we are safe. Waller passes us by.'

'I pray it is so, my lord,' Rawdon said, his sentiments echoed in murmurs by the others. 'But let us stand ready, regardless.'

Paulet nodded. He looked at Stryker for the first time. 'Is my ordnance in place, sir?'

'It is, my lord,' Stryker said. 'There is little we may now do but watch and wait.'

Chilton Candover, Hampshire, 5 November 1643

The tavern was stifling in the heat of its two deep hearths, and the air was thick and fuggy, pungent with the stench of tobacco smoke and ale. Outside, spread wide over several patchwork fields all around the village, the army of Parliament made their fires for the night. They had no tents, very little shelter save a few farm buildings and the branches of bare trees, and the crackle and spit of flame was accompanied by the incessant griping of soldiers unaccustomed to life on campaign and unhappy with billets so exposed. In the tavern the officers were warm and dry, and they laughed and chatted, drew on pipes, imbibed the local brew and reminisced of home. Some stood by the windows, staring out at the blackness, a persistent drizzle speckling the dirty glass, while some simply leaned over rough-hewn tables and let their pots take them to places they would rather have been. One group, though, were huddled in a rear corner of the flint building, careful with their words lest the very beams themselves harboured Royalist ears.

The gathering, half a dozen in all, fell silent as a man in a thigh-length buff-coat approached. He stood over the large table and smoothed down his auburn whiskers. 'Sir William, what has happened?' he asked in taut tones. 'My horse ride for the Alresford muster, only to discover you have come north at this late hour.'

Waller leaned back in his chair and folded his arms. 'I am glad you could join us, Sir Arthur.'

Sir Arthur Heselrige's cheeks reddened and he offered a begrudging bow. 'Forgive me, Sir William. It has been a long ride.'

General Sir William Waller regarded his irascible cavalry commander coolly. It always surprised Waller how slender the colonel was without his armour. 'Winchester is no longer my prime objective.'

'No longer?' Heselrige spluttered. 'Hopton is not yet prepared to march. His force musters around Andover. We must press our advantage while he teeters on his back foot!'

'Would that were possible, Sir Arthur, but news reached me at Alresford.' It had been a hard journey south and west. The Farnham muster had been blighted by rain and wind, their drills increasingly difficult to perform as the weather turned against them. Waller had resolved to make his move the day before, but his army had heard the trumpeted reveille on a chill and wet dawn that had rapidly been consumed by a wintry blizzard, rendering a march next to impossible, and he had been forced to dismiss them for another day. Eventually they had been afforded an opportune window by the elements, but the roads were wet and the going cloying at best. They had reached Alresford early in the afternoon, and it was there that Waller's mind had been changed.

'News, sir?'

Waller nodded, curling his fingers about a worn-looking pot of spiced ale. 'News of the direst nature. Our scouts report a strong body of enemy horse moving south from Oxford. They mean to strike us in the rear, I am certain. If we move upon Winchester, we are liable to find this new enemy snapping at our heels.' He lifted the pot and took a long, heady draught, leaving Heselrige to digest the information. 'We will be caught between the pincers of Hopton and his ally,' he said after a time.

'We risk destruction, for we do not possess the strength to fight them at once. That is why we are here. I will not reach any further west until I am certain of the Cavaliers' plans.'

'But we must engage the enemy, General,' Heselrige pressed as Waller had known he would. 'For morale, if nought else.' He shot a caustic glance at one of the commanders of the Trained Bands. 'The London men mutter of home. They will not tolerate—'

Waller hit the table. 'They will tolerate whatever I desire them to tolerate, damn your eyes!' It was not a hard blow, but his fist was clenched tight and the uneven legs rocked violently, slopping drink and food across the surface. The assembly looked down, unwilling to meet their general's gaze, and to Waller's gratification even Heselrige had the decency to avert his eyes. 'Am I understood?' he asked, softly now.

The others nodded mutely. 'My apologies, Sir William,' Heselrige murmured.

'Accepted,' Waller said, 'and your comments are duly noted, Sir Arthur. Indeed, I have turned our endeavours over in my mind ever since the scouts came in. That is why we shall not sit idle. We will occupy ourselves with the reduction of a different target, gentlemen. One that will keep our new brigades busy, but one close enough to the safety of Farnham, should reports of this new threat prove correct.'

Heselrige looked about the faces with renewed curiosity. 'A different target, sir?'

Sir William Waller nodded firmly. 'On the morrow, my friends, let us make an assay upon that den of Papist iniquity loathed so keenly by God Himself.' He raised his pot in offer of a toast. 'Let us destroy Basing House.'

Andover, Hampshire, 5 November 1643

Sir Ralph Hopton, Baron of Stratton and General of King's Charles's western forces, tugged the long sleeves of his leather gloves further up his forearms. He was mostly recovered, yet he was still self-conscious of the wounds that made his limbs thick, their senses dull, and his face strangely lopsided, as if the skin on one side had slid down his cheek-bone a fraction. The result was this unfortunate worrying at his clothes, and he inwardly cursed himself for the failing.

'Colonel Gerard,' he said, forcing a jauntiness he did not feel into his tone, 'how now, sir?'

Colonel Charles Gerard rode his grey stallion to the cross-road that was their agreed rendezvous. At his back, arrayed in the depths of darkness, were the packed lines of horsemen that made up his cavalry brigade, and they sat, implacable, upon their mounts as he doffed his hat to his superior. 'Well met, my lord, well met. And I bring you a brigade of horse for the protection of Hampshire!'

Gerard was the twenty-four-year-old heir to a powerful Lancashire dynasty, and his confidence overwhelmed any weakness that might have been engendered by a lack of years. He was the antithesis of Hopton – where the general was sober in dress and sombre in humour, the colonel was the very model of a Cavalier, adorned in silks and lace, with long hair cascading beneath a huge felt hat – but Hopton liked him all the same. Gerard was a professional soldier who, like Hopton, had learned his trade in the Low Countries and had served with distinction at Edgehill, Bristol, Lichfield and Newbury. 'Let us move to quarters, Colonel,' Hopton said, steering his mount about.

'Quarters, my lord?' Gerard asked. 'Do we not take the war to Waller's doorstep? He has gone, I hear, to the fields north of Alresford for the night. Perhaps Basing is his design. Might we not engage him before he slights their loyal walls?'

Hopton shook his head. In truth, he had been caught out by the speed at which Waller, his particular friend and formidable enemy, had moved into the south. Perhaps it was the residue of Lansdown that made him hesitant, or an inherent mistrust in his army, now that his Cornish stalwarts were no longer with him. Either way, he would not act rashly. The army needed time to prepare; Winchester, too, required time to put itself on an adequately defensive footing. 'I would wait a while,' he said eventually. He looked up at the sky. There were no stars, for the clouds were thick and low. 'Let us witness Sir William's next move, and act accordingly.'

Gerard clenched his teeth. 'And Basing, my lord?'

Hopton turned his back on the colonel. He knew the young blades in his retinue would whisper cowardice, but his grand scheme had been put at risk by Waller's return to the field. 'I will not jeopardize Winchester for the sake of Basing House, sir,' he called over his shoulder. 'The marquess, for the time being, must look to his own safety.'

Near Preston Candover, Hampshire, 5 November 1643

Wagner Kovac found Lieutenant Matthew Budge in a barn that had been turned to stabling for the night. Budge's troop had returned from their distant patrol that afternoon, during which time Waller's army swarmed in the fields about Alresford, their tentacles stretching out to farmsteads and hamlets in a wide arc, stripping the common folk of whatever winter provisions they had managed to squirrel away.

Budge, sitting on a low bench, bare feet stretched out in front, was barking commands at a hapless local lad who was clumsily picking muddy clumps from the officer's boots with a blunt knife. Boy and man looked up sharply when Kovac limped in, and the latter dismissed his new servant with an irritable wave.

'I told you I would find you, Major,' Budge hissed, throwing a furtive glance at his troopers at the far end of the barn. 'I cannot be seen with you.'

Kovac tugged at the strands of his beard. 'Try speak to me like that again, Lieutenant. Just try it.'

Budge's round face coloured. 'I beg your pardon, sir, but I am right to be wary, am I not?' He rose, padding over the dusty floor to the Croatian. 'They would kill me if they discovered my duplicity.'

Kovac shrugged. 'You work for the rebellion, Budge, not the malignants. It is no terrible thing to arrange the destruction of an enemy citadel.'

'But it is indeed terrible to deceive a general of Parliament, sir.'

Kovac smiled. 'Is it done, Lieutenant?' He took the heavy purse of double crowns from the snapsack across his shoulder, holding it up for the scout to see.

Budge glanced around again before nodding. 'It is done.'

'You reported?'

'I did,' Budge cut in with a teeth-gritted rasp, 'what I said I would do. There was a brigade of horse riding south.'

'Truly?' Kovac asked, thrown by the concept that Waller had not been treated entirely to lies.

Budge rolled his eyes. 'I could hardly concoct a threat from nowhere, Major. My entire troop bore witness, do not forget.'

Kovac let the insult wash over him this time. There were more important matters now to consider. A scrawny young stripling, sent from Tainton, had slithered over Basing's earth-works the previous night and come to find Kovac's unit. His message spoke of a particular place within the fortress; a place containing riches, to which Kovac must bring his entire troop as soon as the stronghold was breached. The pieces were moving into place, just as Tainton had foretold. He narrowed his gaze all the same, so that Budge could see his annoyance. 'What, then, was reported?'

'The brigade was bound, I believe, for Andover to meet with Hopton, that is the truth of it. But I have informed Sir William that they sweep east, intending to come about his rear and crush him between their hooves and Hopton's muskets. That is why we have come north. Waller will now abandon Winchester, lest he be caught too far from Farnham.'

'All is well, then,' Kovac said. 'He is timid, as we thought. Fears another defeat.'

317

Budge held out a palm that trembled slightly. 'Now give me the money.'

Kovac tossed the purse to Budge and gave him a low bow. 'Good work, Lieutenant.' He backed towards the doorway. 'Perfect, in fact.'

Basing House, Hampshire, 5 November 1643

Stryker and Forrester entered the room to the sound of raised voices. The chamber was one of opulence, the dark wood of its floor and walls polished to a high sheen, the ceilings painted with elaborate frescoes of biblical scenes, winged cherubs and impossibly beautiful women draped in flowing, daringly immodest robes. They paced quickly, accompanied by the clatter of their own boots, until they reached the far end of the room.

'And where is Hopton in this?' Sir John Paulet, Lord St John, Earl of Wiltshire and Fifth Marquess of Winchester demanded in a voice that seemed frayed at its edges. 'Tell me, Colonel Rawdon, for I am confounded beyond my wits!'

Marmaduke Rawdon was one of a trio of soldiers in the marquess's presence, and he glanced at his two colleagues before answering. 'I know not, my lord. Last we heard he was at Andover.' He caught sight of Stryker and Forrester and offered a tiny nod. 'Good of you to join us, gentlemen.'

'Damn it all, Rawdon!' Paulet exploded. 'This is my land, my home, and my chamber! I shall welcome them, and none other!'

Forrester shot Stryker a meaningful glance. Stryker edged closer to the group. 'And we have responded to your summons, my lord.'

'You have my thanks, Stryker,' Paulet said, bringing his temper under control. 'My apologies for the outburst. You understand matters have taken a dire turn.'

It was only two hours since the rider had come, roaring out of the grey dusk to bring news not of an army moving steadily west on an inexorable collision course with Winchester, but one that had veered to the right at Alresford and gone, initially inexplicably, north. But, of course, it had been all too explicable when the reality had struck the minds and hearts of Basing's tense population. Sir William Waller was not, after all, marching on Winchester. He was headed for Basing House.

The news had spread like flames in a dry forest, coursing unchecked from senior officers, down through the ranks and into the quarters of grooms and bakers and gong-scourers, inciting panic and leaving chaos in its wake. While Rawdon's yellow-coated regulars spent the early evening bringing order to the estate, Lord Paulet had convened a council of war.

'And what does the craven charlatan do in Andover, save cower?' Paulet asked Rawdon. 'You told me only this very morning, Colonel, that he would rendezvous with other detachments and strike west. So where is he?' He rounded on Forrester. 'I was told to harry the rebels hereabouts, was I not? Ordered by that snake, Killigrew.'

Forrester could only nod. 'Aye, sir, you were.'

'Distract them, you said,' he went on, wide-eyed and relentless, 'so that Lord Hopton might advance into Hampshire.' He turned to the others, playing to the crowd with spread palms, the jewels twinkling at his fingers. 'And I did as I was asked, would you not say, Colonel Peake? Colonel Johnson?'

Lieutenant-Colonel Robert Peake, an Oxford engraver and print-seller who had shown himself an adept leader of men during his time at Basing, nodded his balding head quickly. 'Aye, my lord, of course.'

'And our good baron duly invaded the county, did he not?' Paulet continued, his ankle-length robe of crimson swirling as he swept his arms about. 'So why, when Sir William Waller marches to engage him, does he skulk back to the border, leaving the man they call *Conqueror* clear sight of my walls?' He waited for an answer, but none was forthcoming. 'For my efforts,' Paulet pressed, quieter now, 'efforts intended to aid Hopton's advance, I am repaid with a direct threat from Waller himself. This is not how it is supposed to be, gentlemen.'

Rawdon cleared his throat. 'I can only agree, my lord. The design was to take Parliament's eye from the true threat, not draw its full fury to our walls.'

'Our walls?' Paulet echoed, almost spitting the words back in Rawdon's face. 'These are *my* walls, Colonel Rawdon, and I'll thank you not to forget it. I did not ask for a curmudgeonly Protestant to interfere in matters here, as you would do well to recall.'

Rawdon's cheeks flushed. 'I recall it clearly, my lord.'

Paulet's simmering gaze fell on Stryker. 'What is happening, Captain? You are the most experienced soldier among us. Tell me exactly what game Waller plays.'

'I suspect there is no game afoot, my lord,' Stryker said, feeling cornered. 'Lord Hopton was sent to invade the south-east and Sir William Waller has been dispatched to stop him. Hopton has been waylaid at Andover, and Waller has decided to blood his troops in an attack upon Basing House. I know not the reason for either decision, my lord, but that is the nub of it.'

Sir John Paulet's shoulders seemed to slump. He gnawed his lower lip. 'Thus, we must face this new army alone.'

'Aye, my lord,' Stryker agreed solemnly. 'I fear we must.'

Stryker asked Forrester to go to the men as soon as they were dismissed. His greencoats had come so far these weeks since Gloucester and Newbury. Marched and fought, sailed and survived. They had buried friends and taken beatings, lost a fortune and won it back. Now all that the remnants of Captain Stryker's Company of Foot wished to do was return to their regiment with the prize so dearly bought. 'They are restless, Forry,' he said in the corridor outside Paulet's capacious chambers. 'Stand them to arms. Put them up on the walls. Let them watch for the enemy.'

'I will,' Forrester agreed, making for the spiral staircase that would take him to ground level. 'And you?'

Stryker followed him, descending in his wake as far as the floor below. 'I would tarry here a while.'

Forrester raised his brow in amusement. 'Is that what you call it?'

Stryker laughed. 'Hardly. I hope only for her to open the damned door.'

'Then your hope is not a forlorn one, old man,' Forrester said, nodding towards the door at Stryker's back. As Stryker turned, he grinned and continued down to the courtyard.

'*Canard*,' Lisette Gaillard said, a pale wedge of her face visible from beyond the door.

'Duck, is it not?'

'Duck, *oui*,' she answered, beckoning him inside. 'I have duck.'

'Does it not wish to be near the river?'

'A poor jest,' she muttered witheringly, closing the door behind him. 'It is roasted. A gift from his lordship.'

Stryker went further into the room, stepping on to the first of several large pelts that brought warmth to the hard timbers of the floor. It looked comfortable, with expensive furniture and a large, four-poster bed. There was a huge window facing out to the north, and he went to look down, though he could see little in the darkness. There were a couple of braziers flickering near the Great Barn, but they seemed blurry and obscured, and he realized mist was drifting off the Loddon. 'Paulet must like you.'

Lisette wore a long, flowing gown of silver and blue. It seemed an age since he had seen her dress in anything remotely feminine, and he stood admiring her until she made an irritable sound at the back of her throat. 'I am Catholic.'

'Most people in here are Catholic, Lisette. I think he is pleased to have a beautiful woman in his company, not least one with the ear of the Queen.'

Lisette went to a polished table of walnut wood and began carving strips off a trussed duck sitting on a plate. The juice pulsed in russet rivulets where the steel had punctured the flesh. 'Will you eat?' She looked back at him, suddenly concerned. 'How do you fare now, *mon amour*?'

Stryker's guts still griped with every morsel that crossed his lips, but he cared nothing for his ills in that moment. 'It has been too long since you have addressed me so.'

Lisette laid down the knife. 'You should not have told Tainton, Stryker.'

'I disagree.'

Her gaze sharpened, pupils tightening to pin-pricks. 'I am still angry, Englishman. Cecily died for that bloody secret.'

Stryker steeled himself for an argument, though he could already sense that the searing fury she had harboured on Scilly had abated. Now it seemed more like grief, and he knew the feeling well. 'Cecily died, aye. You will always mourn her, however you may rage. Nothing will close that hole, Lisette, believe me.'

She shook her head. 'You should not have told that bastard.'

'I had no choice. You are too dear to me.'

She planted her hands on her hips in exasperation. 'I am your weakness, Stryker. It is not good for a warrior to have such a thing.'

Stryker moved closer. 'On the contrary, I believe it is what makes a man fight harder than other men. He has something – *someone* – he would protect with his life.'

She shook her head angrily. 'But I am not someone, *mon amour*. I am a warrior, too. I cannot be sheltered and shielded and coddled. I am not your bloody goodwife, tending to children and waiting by the hearth for your return.'

He laughed at the image. 'And I would never ask it of you.'

'Which is why I am such a danger, don't you see?' She went to him, gripping his arms tight as though she might shake him. 'My presence turns you foolish. Compels you to make stupid choices that, if I were any other woman, you would never be forced to make. You cannot be the soldier you were meant to be when I am near.'

'Do not speak so, Lisette,' Stryker replied, touching his fingertips to her mouth. He wanted to kiss her, but feared her forgiveness would not extend that far. 'We have the gold. We took it back! I regret what happened, but I will never regret my reasons.'

Lisette stepped away, her face strained by a sadness that stole his breath. She returned to the table and the steaming meat. 'What now?' she asked. 'The escort should have arrived. I hear Waller is near.'

'He is.'

'Will he attack?'

'I believe he will.'

Now she looked back. 'So our escort is too late.'

Stryker nodded. 'We are here for good or ill.'

CHAPTER 22

Basing House, Hampshire, 6 November 1643

Stryker woke when he felt the tremors. At first he had assumed it to be part of some vague dream. Often he slept fitfully, assailed by old battles and vengeful enemies, and he guessed the vibrations crawling along his legs and spine were recollections of some explosion or escalade in which he had once taken part. Except that they persisted. He lay still, hearing only his pulse, and let the almost imperceptible sensation reverberate through his limbs, all the while blinking at the billet's low ceiling to ensure he was truly awake. After a minute or so, he sat bolt upright. Across from him, also sitting up in their beds, were Forrester and Skellen. Both men turned to him, eyes wide. 'I feel it,' he said.

After the news reached Basing of Waller's change of plan, they had almost expected to see a vast horde appear immediately over the horizon. The lookouts had not left their posts, the gun-crews had doubled their drills, and the scouts prepared to ride out in larger numbers to scour the hills and roads for a rebel vanguard. But the fog had descended. It had lain thick through the night, blanketing the land in clouds so bilious and white that it seemed God Himself had wanted to shield his eyes from the wickedness that had befallen England. Basing's defenders had clambered on the walls, straining their eyes through perspective glasses to snatch a look at the roads and the park and the river, but the fog had confounded them and prevented their scouts from negotiating the treacherous countryside. And so, much to

324

their vexation, the Marquess of Winchester and his five hundred or so fighting men had been forced to wait and watch, wonder and fear. Stryker had returned to quarters desperate for rest. A large part of him had wished to stay with Lisette, to feel the warmth of her against him, but she had not invited his touch, and shame had kept him from broaching the subject. In the end, he had had to console himself with the knowledge that hatred no longer festered between them. It would have to suffice for the time being.

Stryker went to one of the windows carved into the side of the long building, and pushed open the shutters as his men roused themselves from their cold slabs of compacted straw. A freezing gush of air hit him square in the face, and he took an involuntary step back. It was still foggy, the courtyard wreathed in thick white, as though twenty feet of snow had fallen during the night, but already he could see the ghostly outlines of figures moving within the cloud. A bell rang somewhere, though it seemed strangely muffled by the fog, and he realized an alarm had been raised. He touched the window pane. The low thunder that had woken him was vibrating still, ominously building with every passing minute.

He and his greencoats left their quarters to find Colonel Rawdon while the tremors thickened in the misty air. It was as if some great storm raged off the coast or up in the rebellious metropolis. The sensation penetrated the walls and ramparts, the soaring towers and the deepest cellars of the fortified mansion, and soon every person within the ring of defences was wide awake and perched high on wall or tower, palisade or roof, staring into the drifting fastness that yet enveloped them.

Stryker left his men at the foot of the Great Gatehouse, telling them to make ready their weapons, and climbed up the spiral staircase. As expected, Rawdon was there along with the marquess and the lieutenant-colonels Peake and Johnson. 'They're here, sir.'

Paulet rounded on Stryker. 'You cannot possibly be sure, Captain!'

Stryker wondered how the place was to survive with Paulet and Rawdon vying for command, but he stifled his concern. 'I know the sound of an army on the march, my lord.'

Paulet, who was wrapped in a luxurious robe, pulled a sour expression and turned back to the crenellated rampart. 'Piffle, sir.' He raised his highly polished brass perspective glass. 'And I'll thank you not to scaremonger down in the house.'

'Scaremonger?' Stryker answered. His tone approached disrespect, but he went on nonetheless. 'My lord, the alarm is raised. The people are aware of what awaits this day. The trembling you feel is that of hooves and of gun carriages, of supplies and of thousands upon thousands of feet.'

Paulet let the glass drop a touch as he peered into the mist with his naked eyes. 'I had prayed—'

'You are certain, Captain Stryker?' Colonel Rawdon said, finally finding his voice as Paulet's faltered. 'Should we call the garrison to arms?'

Stryker stared down into the mist and then looked from Paulet to Rawdon. 'Aye, sir, we should. General Waller comes hither, and if we are to save Basing, we must give him a fight.'

An hour after noon the mist began to clear to reveal an army. Stryker had remained with the group on the Great Gatehouse, waiting for the inevitable, but when it finally happened, even he found the breath punched clean from his chest. The road into Basing village – the Lane – came into view first, its broad muddy band resolving slowly from the thinning shroud, and then the farm buildings of the Grange edged through, their rooftops like brown spines on a vast white beast. Beyond were sudden glimpses of silver of the River Loddon, and then the green of the lower slopes of Cowdrey's Down. The sun was bright, burning away the mist with every passing moment, but it was only when a sudden gust of chill breeze swept across the hill that the first colours were revealed. There was a huge red standard spangled in stars as silvery as the Loddon. There was a banner of deepest green and brightest gold, and another of yellow, its blue decoration jutting defiantly through the lingering wisps. Behind the colours were row upon row of infantrymen. Dense forests of pike and neat ranks of musketeers, some of which were already beginning to move out of file and stream down towards the river. To the flanks were the horse. Vast swathes of grassland were entirely obscured by men in helmets and breastplates, arrayed behind their cornets, armour and weapons glimmering with ominous beauty. Stryker saw cuirassiers too, completely encased in their iron shells like knights of old. Their presence worried him little, for horsemen were entirely ineffective against fortresses, but he felt a building sense of unease all the same. The cuirassiers had been shattered and humiliated at Roundway, and now here they were, reborn before Basing House. A statement of sheer Parliamentarian determination, if ever there was one.

'Christ Jesus,' Sir John Paulet whispered as he stared, slack-jawed, at the revelation. 'Holy Mother protect us.'

'Look there,' Rawdon was saying. 'The colour marked by a tree in full leaf.' He was pointing at one particular standard that flew at the very front of the horde.

'*Fructus Virtutis*,' Robert Peake said, using a glass to read the motto inscribed beneath the device. 'Fruit of valour.'

Rawdon nodded. 'It is Sir William Waller's personal standard. There can be no more discussion, gentlemen. We must act.' He indicated the section of yellow-coated infantry that was already deploying down towards the river. 'Get some of our musketeers down to the Grange,' he said to Johnson. 'If the enemy strive any closer, give them very hell.'

More important than any luxury was the fact that from her rooms set high in the Great Gatehouse Lisette could look northwards through her large windows and watch for the enemy. Like every other man and woman in Basing, her view had been hindered by the fog, but as the afternoon slipped by, she found herself ideally positioned to watch the firefight that now erupted in the marshy land immediately north of the Royalist defences, played out between the racing river and the outer wall of the Grange.

The Parliamentarian musketeers, in yellow, had crossed the Loddon by a narrow, raised lane, and fanned out on the southern bank, their match-tips glowing like beastly eyes in the murky sunlight. They kept up a brisk rate of fire, diving behind the hedges and shrubs that hugged the watercourse, the plumes of their powder smoke rising and rolling to replace the fog. Opposing them were Rawdon's men, also in yellow, and they swarmed along the breadth of the lower walls that separated the Grange fish ponds from the rushing river. Soon, with return fire rippling out from those outermost defences, the whole area around the marshy banks was enveloped in smoke as the rebels edged inch by inch towards the Royalist positions.

Lisette was seated on the edge of the window-sill, skirts bunched so that she could draw her knees to her chest. It was a strange experience to witness the bitter contest through the tessellated glass diamonds that somehow removed her from reality; an experience made more strange because she herself had wandered with Stryker in the wild land beside the river just a year earlier. The mood of the house had been optimistic then. The walls had echoed with musket fire, but it had been recruits practising for a war they still hoped would pass them by. She and Stryker had slipped into a tangled copse and made love as the guns roared out. Now those trees had gone, the copse cleared mercilessly away, and the guns worked in furious anger. The world had been turned upside down.

After two hours it was clear to Lisette that there were not enough of the rebels to make a true inroad. They had barely advanced a matter of twenty paces beyond the Lane, and, though casualties were thin, they would soon expend their ammunition. It seemed a strange opening gambit for a man as experienced as Waller, but then she noticed the movement on Cowdrey's Down. The hill loomed immediately to the north-west, and it was there that many of the Parliamentarian units had appeared when the first mist had burned away. But they had moved down and away during the afternoon, gone, she presumed, to make camp and set up their own siege-works. What was left, she now noticed, was the train. She could not tell exactly what pieces Waller had at his disposal, but the black barrels appeared huge beside the crews that busily unhitched them, their muzzles gaping from the side of the hillock like so many sharks, intent on biting chunks out of Basing's walls. She counted ten in all, guessing the majority were demi-culverins that would make little impact. But two seemed bigger than the rest. Demi-cannon, perhaps. Castle-killers, capable of hurling a twenty-four-pound shot that would eat away at all but the very stoutest defences. She had seen one – named Roaring Meg by the men –at work on Hopton Heath. Meg had carved a swathe so wide and bloody through the rebel ranks that day, they had been too afraid to fill it. The Cavaliers had held the field as a result. Lisette leaned in closer to the diamond-shaped panes, although the leadwork impeded her view. She could see the gunners scurrying like ants. A few of the heavy pieces were on the move, trundling on their huge wheels to the west, and she guessed they were destined to hook round towards the southern flank, to be ultimately placed on the plateau of Basing Park so that the fortress might be pounded from both sides.

Six big pieces seemed to be static on the hill. Wicker sheets were being tossed from the back of a wagon and laid out to make a platform at the rear of the gun carriages to allow the heavy ordnance to recoil without sinking into the wet soil. It was a mark that they intended to bring the iron monsters rapidly to bear.

Lisette rose from the sill and wrapped herself in a riding cloak she had been lent by the marchioness. Fetching up the knife she had used to carve the duck, she went down the spiral stairs to the inner yard of the Old House. The crackle of musketry seemed louder out here, spitting in desultory clusters as the distinct scent of sulphur drifted up from the discharging weapons. Lisette was well accustomed to the sounds and smells of war, and yet still she flinched, for the noise was achingly close.

'Warm work, Miss Lisette,' a familiar voice came through the gunfire. She turned to see the tall, languorous form of William Skellen.

'It is, Sergeant. Where is Stryker?'

Skellen was sucking a pipe, his perpetually carefree manner reassuring. He took it from his mouth and pointed up at the Great Gatehouse roof with the stem. 'Up there, Miss Lisette.'

'They mean to bombard us.'

'I'm sure they do.'

'Now, William,' she added, more urgently this time. 'They are making ready the heavy cannon. I saw it from my window. Will you tell Stryker and the others?'

'Think they'll 'ave seen for 'emselves from up there.'

'Please,' she pressed, 'just to be certain.'

Skellen nodded. 'Of course, Miss Lisette.' He made for the arch and the entrance to the staircase, pausing to look back. 'Do not return to your chamber.'

She rolled her eyes. 'I am not stupid.' All at once she regretted the retort and offered him a smile. 'Thank you, Sergeant, for your concern. I shall take a stroll past our treasure, I think.'

He nodded. 'Very good, miss.'

Roger Tainton was shovelling dung from beneath a skittish cob when he heard the first musketry ripple across the afternoon. The noise itself took little toll on him, for he was well used to such things, but he quickly realized that the rest of the house was in uproar. Just as cooks left the kitchens and gong-scourers clambered out from the latrines, so every member of the stable block, from senior men like Perkin Yates right down to the lowest boys, abandoned their posts to find a place at the walls, all clamouring for a sight of the skirmish that had rent the afternoon in two.

Tainton duly left the horse to complain and kick and pull against its tethers, for, now that he was alone, he had business elsewhere. He pulled the woollen cap down over his withered ears and went out into the open. As he suspected, there were whole families gathered on the roofs that formed the northern rampart of the New House. They chattered and gasped, pointed out things to one another that both terrified and excited, and cheered heartily when the Royalist forces down in the Grange loosed a volley against the assailants. Men began chants in support of the monarchy that were taken up by the others with gusto, putting Tainton in mind of a crowd witnessing a controversial theatre production. He half expected ale to be served along with their sport.

'Go on!' one woman jeered, shaking her fist at the spectacle below. 'Ger'off back to London, you bastard Cropheads!'

'Where's your King Jesus now?' the man beside her bawled, sketching the sign of the cross over his chest.

Tainton left them. He could neither see what they witnessed, nor cared to. He went at a half-run for the Postern Gate, the guards ignoring him as they called up to their comrades on the rooftops, and hurried over the bridge that led to the Old House. Now was his time, he told himself. Kovac had kept up his side of the bargain, for he had brought an army to Basing House, and, as Tainton had prayed, the inhabitants' attention was now firmly fixed elsewhere. He passed unhindered through the small gatehouse on the far side. The circular courtyard, like its newer counterpart, was devoid of people, for they were all up on the ramparts, and he was able to reach the cover of the brick-built well at the centre of the Norman motte in a matter of seconds. From behind the curving masonry he surveyed the Great Gatehouse and the slope that led down to the subterranean vault within which, he was certain, Sir Alfred Cade's treasure was secreted. He had watched the twin doors at intervals for several days, noting that they were never left unprotected, and had resolved to get inside as soon as opportunity allowed.

The guards remained at the foot of the slope, grim and impassive, halberds in hand, but Tainton fancied his chances against them. He had brought a long chisel from Yates's tool chest, one that would puncture right the way through to a lung if delivered by a man who knew how to kill. He looked left and right, summoning the courage to make his move.

It was then that he saw her, cloaked in ermine, the hem of a silvery blue dress sweeping out around her ankles as she walked through the archway towards him, her long, golden hair falling in tendrils over her shoulders. She was beautiful and yet all he felt was disgust. It was as though invisible hands had crammed rancid meat into his guts so that bile bubbled up in acidic jets to singe his throat. He loathed Lisette Gaillard, and in that shocking, heart-stopping moment of incandescent hatred, the gold slipped from his mind like sand through a sieve.

Tainton bolted from behind the well, ignoring his aching hip as he passed the slope and the disinterested guards, and plunged into the short tunnel running through the foot of the Great Gatehouse. Lisette was caught unawares as he clattered into her. She struggled and thrashed as he clamped his hand across her mouth, spinning her round so that she faced away from him, her arm bent savagely up between her shoulder-blades. She tried to cry out but the scream was muffled by Tainton's fingers, and he drove his knee into the back of hers, her leg instantly crumpling so that her body slumped back into his arms. He pulled hard so that she lost all balance, dragging her backwards, her heels scoring long ruts in the earth, and then they were in an empty alcove set half-way along the tunnel. On the far side was the fan-shaped outer yard, but the folk out there, milling at its edge, only had eyes for the fight down at the river and the rebel manoeuvres up on the hill.

'So much company,' Tainton rasped in her ear, 'yet so alone.' The chisel was in his waistband and he yanked it free, lifting it to her throat. Her whole body seemed to spasm. He clenched her tighter. 'Should have done this back on Scilly, *mademoiselle*. Still, the Lord is faithful to his servants.'

Just then the ordnance up on the hillside erupted. Startled, Tainton loosened his grip for a moment, but it was enough, and Lisette brought her elbow up into his sternum. It was not a heavy blow, but her bony joint felt sharp as steel in the epicentre of his chest, and he released her with a yelp. She stepped away, but instead of fleeing she immediately turned, a knife in her white fist. It seemed too large and crude to be anything more than a kitchen utensil, but she blurted a stream of pledges in her native tongue and lurched at Tainton, slashing at his face like a woman possessed.

Roger Tainton screamed and lunged at Lisette Gaillard, not caring about her blade, but his screams were drowned by the crescendo of a second volley from Waller's batteries. This time a shot hit home, smashing into the brickwork of one of the turrets immediately above them. Masonry, ornately carved chunks of alabaster and a score of tiles rained down to shatter on the outer courtyard. The Frenchwoman ducked instinctively, and Tainton saw his chance. He darted left through the inner arch and into the warren of buildings that was the Old House, not daring to glance back.

—⁂—

'I am come from Sir William Waller himself, my lord.'

The trumpeter had been sent out from the Parliamentarian lines on the north bank of the River Loddon. The rebel general, after his short harassment of Basing's defenders, had called a halt to both the infantry assault and the bombardment, demanding a parley with the garrison. Trumpeters were often used for parley, which meant those chosen for the role were necessarily cautious, cunning and observant. He had been led blindfolded through the earthworks and into the palace, boots crunching over the rubble the round-shot had caused to shower from the Great Gatehouse. Now, with dusk on the way, he stood just inside the Old House, surrounded by a party of angry Royalists.

'Come, sir?' Sir John Paulet, Marquess of Winchester, barked. He and Rawdon were at the very front of the crowd, dressed deliberately in their finery. 'To say what?'

'General Waller,' the trumpeter went on, 'sends me to demand the castle, for the use of King and Parliament. He offers fair quarter to all within these walls.'

Stryker stood close to Paulet. He heard mutterings from within the crowd at his back, whispers that spoke of Waller's evident desire to broker peace, and he held his tongue for fear of shatter-ing the frightened inhabitants' resolve. Privately he suspected the cessation had more to do with dusk's increasingly vice-like grip. The gathering gloom was stealing targets from the musketeers and the gunners, and soon the assault would be forced to a pause regardless of Waller's intentions, good or otherwise.

'Come!' Paulet commanded, his haughty tone exaggerated. He led the rebel representative into the wide rectangular form of the Great Hall, the very heart of his grand house, now turned into a centre for storage. A gaggle of senior men followed leaving the massed population of Basing to gossip in their wake.

Stryker moved towards the temporary structure near the Postern Gate that served as his billet. Inside was Lisette, perched on the end of his palliasse. Skellen, Barkworth and Forrester were all there, standing in various places around the room, each wearing an expression etched with concern. Two of his green-coats, the Trowbridge twins, immediately moved in behind him, guarding the doorway with primed muskets. 'What is it?' he asked Lisette.

She kept her head bowed, looking up through her lashes. 'I was attacked, *mon amour*.'

Stryker felt sick. 'Attacked?' He glanced at the others, but the men in the room stared down at their own feet, so he looked again at Lisette.

'I am unharmed. Shaken, perhaps, but unharmed.'

Skellen cleared his throat. 'I found her in the Gatehouse arch-way, sir. Was on my way down from speaking to you. Brought her here.'

Stryker swallowed, his throat suddenly itchy. 'Who was it?'

Lisette straightened as if summoning courage enough to speak. 'Roger Tainton.'

Stryker had been expecting to explode in a welter of rage and vengeance, but on hearing the name he could do nothing but gape. 'You—' he began, immediately tripping on his own tongue. 'You have been through an ordeal, Lisette.'

Lisette stood suddenly. 'Do not *ordeal* me, Stryker, you bloody fool,' she hissed. 'I know what I saw.'

'Tainton?' Stryker said incredulously.

'Tainton, damn you!' Lisette snarled, advancing on him. 'It was he.'

'Here? In Basing?'

'How many times must I say it?'

Stryker rubbed his palms through his hair and over his tired eye. 'Why now? If he followed us from the coast, why did he not act before?'

'Act?' Lisette laughed bitterly. 'In what manner? Attacked us on the road? All eleven of us? If you know one thing about Roger Tainton, Stryker, it is that he is a patient man. He inveigled his way inside this place so that he could steal the gold from right under our noses.'

Stryker blew out his cheeks. 'He's been watching us. Biding his time. He wants the gold, you are right, but I'd wager he saw you alone and took a chance to make an end of you.'

Lisette nodded. 'I dare say you are right, *mon amour.*'

Stryker looked to the pair of greencoats at the door. 'Jack, Harry. Stay with Miss Lisette. Keep her safe.'

'No, Stryker,' Lisette cut in, though not unkindly. 'It is the treasure you must look to.'

'Guard the cellar, then,' Stryker conceded, knowing Lisette well enough not to waste his breath on fruitless arguments. 'Let us have our own men at the door.' He watched the twins disappear into the courtyard and turned to Lisette. 'For Christ's sake, woman, keep yourself behind doors.'

Lisette Gaillard's expression told him she would do nothing of the sort, and he opened his mouth to protest again when a cannon fired from up on Cowdrey's Down. It was a lone shot, with no agonized scream or juddering impact to tell of anything but a whistling miss.

Stryker quickly stood, going with the others for the door and the outside world. Even as he cast his gaze about to locate someone who might provide an answer, Sir John Paulet stormed out of the Great Hall, almost kicking the door off its hinges, and rounded furiously on the trumpeter who had trailed out behind. 'What is the meaning of this, man?'

'I—' the trumpeter seemed as baffled as all the others within Basing House, and his jaw worked wordlessly.

'Then I shall tell you!' Paulet fumed, his face almost as bright as his robes. He stared, bulging-eyed, up at the gentle hill, where a thin finger of smoke still lingered to betray its provenance. 'It is treachery, pure and simple! Your master employs parley as a mask for his murderous duplicity!' He spun on his heels, pointing a jagged forefinger first at a group of his personal guards, then at the trumpeter. 'Arrest this man at once!' While a quartet of bulky men hefting halberds pushed through the throng to take the Parliamentarian emissary in hand, the marquess summoned a drummer. 'Take this message to our unwanted visitor. Tell Sir William that I understand very well his words "King and Parliament". Understand the betrayals they mask. "King" is but one thing; "King and Parliament" quite another yet. Tell him that Basing is mine own house, held lawfully by my family, and kept against any man. More particularly, it is now commanded by His Majesty, for it is his garrison that dwells herein, and, as God is my witness, it shall remain thus.'

The knock on Lisette's door just after midnight made her almost leap out of bed with fright. She sat bolt upright, wondering if she had dreamt it, but then it rattled a second time, soft but persistent. She hoped it was not Stryker, for, though her fury had mellowed in the days since leaving Scilly, she had no intention of letting him warm her sheets. It was cold out, bitterly so, and she was already wearing a full-length robe for warmth. She tugged it tighter about her midriff and padded across the pelt-strewn floorboards. There were sentries in the corridors of the Great Gatehouse, and she doubted whether Tainton would be brazen enough to try another attack so soon and in so public a place, but she snatched up a knife from the dresser all the same, edging open the door tentatively.

The woman who came into the room was probably in her thirties, with dark hair that was dappled with grey. She was thin and wiry, but blessed with the steady gaze of one entirely confident in their own self-worth. Lisette doubled in a low bow as the voluminous lavender nightgown swept past her, the scent of rose water just detectable in her wake.

Lady Honora Paulet, mistress of Basing House, possessed a shrewish face of permanently pursed, thin lips and a sharp nose. Her eyes were dark in colour, but their gleam was bright with intelligence, and they peered with interest from above high, delicate cheekbones. 'Mademoiselle Gaillard.'

'My lady.'

The marchioness regarded Lisette coolly, but something in the twitch at the corners of her eyes spoke of a woman intrigued. 'They say you have the ear of Queen Henrietta Maria herself.'

'They are right, my lady.'

The narrow, mousy brows rose a touch, pushing into the creases at her forehead. 'An intelligencer, no less.'

'When called upon, my lady, *oui*.'

Honora Paulet produced a folded triangle of vellum and gave it to Lisette. 'Then you may consider yourself called upon.'

CHAPTER 23

Basing House, Hampshire, 7 November 1643

It was just before dawn and Stryker was in the Grange with Colonel Rawdon. They were in the northernmost section, beyond the long, narrow fish ponds. There was danger here, for they skirted the line of the outer wall that formed the very first obstacle for any attacker once they had reached this side of the river, and every so often the report of a musket would crack from the encroaching rebels in warning. They were safe enough for the time being, for the wall was as high as eight feet in places; nevertheless, the shots reminded them that the enemy was frighteningly close. Some of Waller's detachments had stolen across to this side of the waterway during the night, and the Royalists had woken to barriers almost within pistol shot of their walls, the rebel intent clear as crystal.

'I have placed teams all along this wall here,' Marmaduke Rawdon was saying, his bushy brows twitching with each gruff word. 'They knock loopholes, see?'

Stryker peered between the shoulders of a group of musketeers who were busily working with hammers at the lower part of the wall. They were making holes wide enough for a musket to be inserted, but were careful not to smash too much of the mortar because a larger hole would create a weakening breach or be too enticing a target for the men behind the enemy breastworks. Already some of the holes were beginning to be used, and pot-shots cracked out sporadically along the line. 'Like arrow slits of old,' he commented.

Rawdon nodded. 'They'll be at us soon. We must make their work warm.'

Stryker looked back at the Barn. 'You will need to cut positions there too, sir. This wall is too low to hold for long. If we are to make a stand at the Grange, it must be in there.'

Rawdon said that he had already ordered such a course, and they went back to their tour of the defences, all the while heckled by disembodied voices from the far side of the wall. Stryker looked to the east, watching for light on the horizon, wondering what horrors the new day would bring. The night had been brutal and sleepless. Waller had, at least, apologized for the rogue cannon shot during parley. Two hours after the drummer had been dispatched with Paulet's angry response, he had been sent back from the rebel lines with a message from Sir William excusing the rudeness of his gunners, and explaining that the shot had been loosed by accident. Furthermore, and to highlight his contrition, he had offered free passage to all the women and children, including Marchioness Honora and her brood. The offer had been robustly rejected by Paulet's stern wife, a decision outwardly applauded inside the beleaguered stronghold, though Stryker wondered how the ordinary folk felt. Either way, the die was cast, and the guns had shouted once more. Waller had six heavy pieces on the hill to the north-west, and each one belched its fury six times during the night. Stryker was no stranger to a besieging army's use of artillery, but even he had found the thirty-six thunder claps a difficult thing to bear. In the end, he found himself simply pacing the yards and alleyways of Basing House, listening to the occasional shower of rubble or earth as one of the balls hit a mark, and staring into the darkness as if Tainton's pale, ruined face would lurch forth from the shadows at any second.

Sometime during the small hours, he had found himself down towards the half-moon rampart that protected the southern side of the house. The sentries walked the line behind their earthen palisade, matches glowing in the blackness, puffs of vapour marking each breath. Out to the south, on the flat expanse of the Park, small fires betrayed the enemy positions. They had come full circle about the estate, closing it off, and the Park, Stryker guessed, would soon become home to another gun battery. It was as he climbed up to the rampart to take a better view, knees and toes scrabbling for purchase against the sodden soil, that a familiar voice had broken out somewhere behind.

'You inspect our work, Captain?' Colonel Marmaduke Rawdon had asked.

Stryker slid half-way back down the slope and laughed when he saw who the speaker had been. 'It is the enemy's work I inspect, sir.'

'Even so,' Rawdon had said, sweeping his arm out to indicate the line of the ditch, 'will you indulge me? I would value your judgement.'

The pair had walked the defences for the rest of the night, progress aided by the ceasing of the rebel bombardment at around four o'clock. They nodded to orb-eyed sentries as they went, passing along the newly deepened ditch that skirted the Old House and down into the road that had once run between the twin mansions and the Grange but which was now barricaded and guarded by musketeers at either end. Judging by the fires, it seemed that the lion's share of Waller's army was still concentrated on the northern front, encamped on the higher, drier ground on the far side of the swollen Loddon, and it was from that direction, Rawdon surmised, they would launch any major assault. That was why, as the first dreary chinks of light began to filter over the hills to the east, his yellowcoats were busily making the farmyard properly defensible.

'We should get the supplies out of the Barn, sir,' Stryker said as they moved back towards the huge brick structure that dominated the farm.

'I have already ordered some corn and oysters taken up to the house,' Rawdon replied. 'But what carts and horses we have are

destined for the infirmary, should there be an attack. The chirurgeon will need transportation for the wounded.'

And the dead, Stryker thought. 'I will bring my men down
to the Grange should a fight break out.'

Rawdon glanced at him dubiously. 'Are they ready to be
thrown into the fire again, Captain?'

Stryker smiled. 'I do swear my sergeant grows mildewed if left
to languish for long.'

'You and your men will be welcome wherever you feel they
are needed, Stryker.' A group of soldiers crouching against the
wall of the Barn stood pike-straight as their colonel went by,
and Rawdon touched a finger to his hat in acknowledgement.
'My lads are good and brave,' he said, keeping his voice low, 'but
they lack real experience. We have sallied hard these last weeks,
and many have bloodied their swords, but that is no substitute
for real battle.' He grumbled a rueful chuckle. 'Do you know to
what I put my time before the war, Captain?'

'No, sir,' Stryker lied.

'I dealt in cloth and Canary wine. My life was rich and easy,
sir, rich and easy.' He laughed again, more heartily this time.
'At the age of sixty, when I have led a full life and should, by
all natural rights, be looking towards my legacy, I find myself
governor of a fortress in the midst of divers foes.' He shook his
head. 'Providence is a strange mistress, Captain Stryker. Strange
indeed.'

'You may still look to your legacy, Colonel,' Stryker said.
'Though it will no longer speak of a great merchant, but of a
great military leader.'

'You mock me, sir,' Rawdon said, suddenly looking ancient
to Stryker.

'I do not, sir,' Stryker said. As he finished the words, the artillery up on the hill severed the morning's peace like a vast
earthquake. He looked up at the hill, wreathed thickly in powder
smoke. A sizeable body of infantry, perhaps five hundred strong,
seemed to be moving at pace down towards the river. He
touched a hand to Rawdon's elbow. 'I fear you will soon have

the chance to make certain your legacy, sir,' he said, nodding towards the approaching force. He turned away, breaking into a run and only glancing back to shout, 'I go to fetch my men, Colonel! We've to fight this morning!'

Stryker found his men on Basing's north wall. They were fifty paces to the west of Garrison Gate, perched high on a wooden scaffold, and from here, with only the road to divide the main estate from the Grange, they could easily see the fight raging in the Marquess of Winchester's agrarian complex. He went to join them, the planks clattering under foot as he ran along the platform, and conducted a quick head-count. Just seven without the Trowbridge boys, assigned, as they were, to guarding the gold. It would have to do.

'You have your weapons?' he shouted.

They held up muskets and some blew on their coals for effect. Skellen stepped forth. He had found himself a halberd, the mark of his rank and his weapon of choice. 'Down there is it, sir?'

Stryker followed his gaze. The sergeant was staring balefully at the walled rectangle that was the Grange, its small outbuildings almost invisible within the false mist of powder smoke. 'It is, Will.'

He turned abruptly away, leading the group along the wall and down a rickety ladder that bowed alarmingly under the combined weight. When he hit ground level he paused to snatch a glimpse of the Old House, its grandiose gatehouse already looking as though it had aged a millennium under the ministrations of Waller's heavy cannon. Even as he stared, a high-pitched scream tore the air above their heads and a ball slammed into the brickwork. The distance was too great to do any significant damage, but a shower of splinters flew out in a wide stone fountain. Stryker looked at Skellen. 'Tell me she is not in there, Sergeant.'

Skellen shook his head. 'It's been evacuated, sir. She goes to the infirmary, so Cap'n Forrester says.'

Stryker's blood ran chill. 'She is hurt?'

'She assists the chirurgeon,' a new voice sounded at his back.

Stryker turned to see Lancelot Forrester. 'Oh?'

'Mademoiselle Gaillard is not adept at fighting at range,' Forrester said. 'She feels more useful tending to the wounded,' his face twisted in distaste, 'until such time as the scrap reaches close-quarters.'

Stryker nodded. 'Care to join us, Forry?'

Forrester drew his sword. 'A man can die but once, old man.'

Captain-Lieutenant Jedidiah Clinson was a man with much to prove. At twenty years, he was young to be the lieutenant of General Waller's own company, and he felt the pressure like a knife between his shoulders. The other officers undoubtedly – if grudgingly – respected him, for his skill with sword in hand would match any man, but he also sensed they were watching his every move, waiting for a mistake that might dislodge him from the general's favour. Every task he undertook, therefore, required the utmost dedication and zeal, and that was why, as he moved through the narrow lane and over the swollen Loddon at the head of the five-hundred-strong forlorn hope, he braced himself for a storm of bullets from which he did not dare shrink.

The fire from the defences was thick; the stink of burnt powder instantly ripe in his nostrils. Clinson had to jerk at his boots with every pace, for the ground was a saturated morass. His knees screamed in lancing pain and his hips ached as he used his sword to hack a way through the undergrowth hemming the southern riverbank, taking a moment to pray and to pat his commission, which was folded into a tight square in his breast pocket. The leaden hail pelted them as they spread out, and they half turned by instinct, like men striding into a gale, but Clinson raised his sword, ignored the sound of a ball as it whistled past his ear, and charged straight at the walls that were just twenty paces away. They screamed like madmen, their comrades hunched behind the hastily raised breastworks on either side cheering them on, offering steady covering fire. All around men fired at the defenders, whose frightened faces peered through crude loopholes in the brickwork, while the artillery raged over everything, battering the Old House at the same time Clinson battered the Grange. It was a living nightmare, the like of which he could never have envisaged, and every sinew in his lean frame seemed to beseech him to turn tail and run, but he could not. He had a force of good men, and they were ample to take the Grange from the relatively few malignants poised on the far side of the seething wall. Clinson screamed and crowed and twirled his blade high so that all could see him.

Stryker and his men had gone as far as the fish ponds when they realized the rebel detachment had crossed the raised lane. More shots rattled out, this time from within the perimeter of the Grange, and Stryker saw that the wall was almost entirely hidden by smoke as the yellowcoats poured their fire through the loop-holes. Some of the braver souls had fashioned fire-steps out of planks of wood, hay bales and hogsheads, and they leaned over the top of the wall, spitting their leaden venom at the oncoming rebels. But the officers on the walls were already bawling at their charges to fall back, and a steady stream of Royalist defenders flowed towards the Barn. The huge double doors were flung open by screaming sentries, and the men bolted inside. Stryker and his greencoats went too, rushing into the vast building even as shouts were heard from the walls. He looked back just as the doors were being swung closed, catching a fleeting glimpse of glowering faces and clawing hands as men scaled the wall, drop-ping unhindered into the Grange.

Inside the Great Barn, the Royalists were hurriedly pushing Basing's winter supplies to the walls. There were two sets of opposite doors, split by a brick and flint threshing floor, and they rolled barrels of beer and milk to the north-facing entrance, stacking them against the barred timbers for reinforcement. They could not afford to block the rear door, for fear of entrap-ping themselves, but cases of pork and dried peas, small carts loaded with hay, and even a pile of feather beds were heaved over to the walls all around in order to provide extra cover. The musketeers threw themselves against their incongruous buttresses, thrusting muskets out through the ragged holes and picking off targets as the rebel force flooded over the north wall.

Stryker climbed a precarious tower of metal-banded chests. He reached a point almost a third of the way up the wall where the mortar was visibly crumbling, and kicked out one of the bricks with the heel of his boot. He peered through just as the Barn's defenders began to fire in earnest, the reports of so many muskets utterly deafening as they echoed about the oaken timbers of the trussed roof. The stench was almost unbearable, the acrid pall stinging his throat. He bit back the bile that climbed up from his fragile guts and blinked the tears from his eye, forcing himself to brave the incoming flow of bullets to scan the outer wall. The Roundheads kept coming, men crouching on the far side with cupped hands were boosting their confederates over the low summit to drop beside the ponds and join the attack. It was not just to the north, however. Now that he had a good view of the assault, he could see the Parliamentarian front widening, as more units skirted east and west, evidently intending to come around the sides of the Grange.

Stryker turned away from the spy-hole, the stacked chests creaking and teetering precariously beneath him. He saw Rawdon down beside the huge doors, barking orders with drawn sword, the bright silk of his slashed coat a beacon for men to follow. Stryker sheathed his weapon and made a funnel of his palms around his mouth. 'Colonel Rawdon!'

Rawdon looked up. 'Captain Stryker?'

'They advance on both flanks, sir! We shall soon have them at our rear!'

The colonel spun, impressively for a man of his age, orders tumbling from him in a series of hoarse syllables that had men scuttling to the rear doors. They gathered in clusters against the frames, unwilling to close the thick shutters but ready to meet any threat. Stryker dropped from his perch, sliding haphazardly down the swaying stack so that his rump smarted by the time he reached the rammed chalk floor. His men were lining the walls between the barrels and cases, firing upon the exposed Parliamentarians as they edged closer to the vast building. A large number of Rawdon's musketeers were gathered to his right, firing through holes knocked in the Barn's eastern gable end, and he guessed the outbuildings of the Grange must now be swarming with enemy soldiers.

Skellen was close, face screwed up against a loophole, and he thumped him gently on the shoulder. The sergeant leaped up, shouldering his pole-arm as he followed, and the pair ran to the rear doorway. Now Stryker drew his sword again, holding it up for the anxious yellowcoats to see. 'We're going out there.'

'Out?' one of the men said, barely able to squeeze the sound from his dry throat.

Stryker nodded. Behind them the northern doors were juddering and shaking on their huge iron hinges. Despite the steady defensive fire, the Roundheads had reached the Barn. Without petard or ram they would not force the doors easily, but the splintering cracks told of at least half a dozen axes that would soon tear new holes in the stout timbers. Besides, their very presence was sufficient to send a shiver of alarm through the smoke-choked Royalist ranks, and curses and prayers rang out between the shots.

Colonel Rawdon's stentorian tones growled out above everything now, and Stryker was thankful for his presence. He could not be sure that any of the fearful yellowcoats would follow his lead, but he looked back into the smoke-filled interior, squinting for a glimpse of Rawdon, and saw Basing's grey-haired governor pointing directly at him.

'Fifty men!' Rawdon bawled, singling out groups of defenders with an outstretched finger and a snarl. 'Fifty! You! You! You there, Corporal!'

The sally party began to form at the open rear door, where Stryker waited with sword held high. It comprised about half the defending force, the rest being needed to keep up the covering fire, and Stryker nodded his thanks to the colonel before stepping out into morning air. It stank of sulphur.

The group – Stryker in the lead, followed by Skellen, twoscore of yellowcoats and a smattering of men in civilian clothes – charged with a great, ear-splitting roar. They ran round the corner of the Barn, muskets levelled or turned about to use as clubs and swords brandished. Some had pistols cocked ready to empty into the faces of their foes, and then they were at the north doors, where the most advanced rebels had reached to beat on the timbers and fire directly through the Royalist loopholes.

Smoke had turned dawn to dusk, and it was difficult to see exactly what they faced, but men were there sure enough, with their own muskets and hangers, dirks and partisans, and Stryker slammed headlong into the first, flattening him with just his shoulder, kicking him in the face as he stepped into the next opponent. The Cavaliers howled like blood-scenting wolves, and tore into the clustered rebels, hacking and slashing like men possessed. A rebel sergeant, waist swathed in a wide blue scarf, twirled like a circus tumbler, swinging his huge halberd at chest height in an irresistible arc that would cleave a man in two. He came at Stryker, his war-cry unintelligible, and the long staff with its triple blade of axe, hook and point sliced the air as Stryker ducked low, only just out of its murderous range. Skellen appeared as his captain stumbled back in the face of the rebel's rage, and in his huge grip he clutched his own halberd. He whipped the pole-arm up, jabbing it into the face of the screaming Roundhead. It took little toll, simply nicking the man's chin, but the move had made the rebel catch his stride, lose his balance just a fraction, and Skellen's boot was up in his crotch before he knew what had hit him. The enemy sergeant brayed and kept coming, but he was winded and his swing had lost its momentum, and Stryker stabbed low, cutting a deep gully just above his knee. The halberd clattered out of his grip and he collapsed over the compromised leg, and then Skellen's halberd was racing down from on high, butchering the side of the blue-scarfed sergeant's shoulder, a spray of dark blood speckling his own face and that of his enemy. And then he was down, face buried in the mud, and the Royalists were over him, beyond him, looking for more men to cut down.

Stryker ploughed on, ramming one man on to his back with a dropped and driven shoulder, kicking another hard and low so that he could feel the testicles mash against the bridge of his foot. There was always the chance that he would be stabbed from below, lanced by a blade wielded by one of those he had felled but not killed, yet he cared nothing. He felt the battle-rage in his veins, the gut-twisting, heart-pounding, muscle-tightening excitement and the stink of sweat and vomit and blood and powder smoke, ripe and heady in his nostrils. A concoction loathsome and enticing all at once.

An enemy officer, dressed elegantly and cutting in precise diagonal lines with a long, single-edged sword, seemed to be snapping orders as he fought, and Stryker made for him. The man, a young fellow with a fair, wispy beard and slender nose below a wide hat that was tilted back away from his eyes, jabbed with snake-like speed at a Royalist throat, missing by fractions, and brought the hilt round for a punch to the face. He kicked the dazed man out of his way, dancing past in the graceful manner of a trained fencer, and caught Stryker's eye. Stryker pulled back his cracking lips in the most hideous grimace he could manage, brandishing the teeth broken by Locke Squires and feeling the ugly scar tissue around his left eye twist and contort. He lunged ferociously, hacking at the stylish officer without pause for thought. The young man parried the first and second blows easily, gritted his teeth as he offered a half-hearted riposte, then jumped back nimbly, bringing himself out of range. He issued a flurry of orders that Stryker could not discern in the melee, and then he was gone, vanished amongst the bodies and the smoke.

It was with shock that Stryker saw the Roundheads retreat. He had thought perhaps twoscore had reached the doors, and that they would be a challenge to clear away, but the sally, unex-pected as it had evidently been, had served to stun Waller's vanguard, and many had fallen back to the fish ponds and the smaller shacks and pens that dotted the eastern half of the Grange. He swung his sword above his head, crowing as loud as his parched throat would allow, and the others followed suit, their challenge carrying up to Waller on Cowdrey's Down and to Paulet in the Old House. Somewhere more artillery was raging, rolling like thunder to the north and east, and Stryker guessed that the Roundhead ordnance had shifted its attention to the New House. Perhaps, he dared dream, it was a move of desperation on Waller's part, for the general had seen his great attack fail, his best men unable even to take the Grange, let alone Basing House itself, and Stryker grinned at the men who gathered around, cheering one another and spitting curses at the cowering rebels.

The wind was up, and it caught the man-made fog, gathering it up in an instant and whisked it away from the farm to reveal the north wall. Stryker saw the enemy properly. There were hundreds of them, maybe as many as a thousand, pouring over the wall and amongst the outbuildings, marching forwards in an inexorable wave. They had not saved the Grange, after all. They had merely stalled the tide. The Roundheads were coming again.

Captain-Lieutenant Jedidiah Clinson had seen a demon. A living, breathing, screaming devil in a green coat with half his face missing and the other half lit by a silver eye that seemed to look right into Clinson's soul. They had been doing well, his unit, scaling the wall in the face of spiteful return fire, and he had sensed glory when a group of his best men had followed him all the way to the heavy double doors, their axes going to furious work. Even when the enemy had sallied from what he now guessed had been an unknown rear entrance, Clinson had seen enough vigour in his stoic charges to feel confident of sweeping the stubborn malignants away. But into the melee the demon had cut a path the like of which he had never before seen. Clinson was a gentleman, the son of a minor aristocrat, a confident, intelligent individual, Waller's rising star, a man born to lead. But in a heartbeat, peering into the demon's dread gaze, he was a child again, and he had simply not known what to do.

Muskets still fired from the Royalist positions as Jedidiah Clinson rallied his men. His party were largely untouched, miraculous though it was, and he yet had a force strong enough to take the Grange and everything in it. He looked to his left, to the eastern section of the farm complex where the smaller buildings dotted the mud. Over those walls and amongst the pigsties and chicken coops, the pens and the carts, came more blue-scarfed fighters, more detachments sent down by Sir William when he had seen the initial attack beaten back. Yet he felt no succour, no joy and no relief. It was as though he had been punched square in the stomach, such was his shame.

Clinson levelled his sword at the Barn. 'I return to that hellish place.' The demon had frightened him, and he could not deny it, but the fear of the one-eyed man was as nothing compared with the disgrace of this failure. The reinforcements still streamed over the Grange's low perimeter, and already they were pushing from the buildings in the eastern end to threaten the Barn's right flank, and then, once the defenders had fled, all would know that Captain-Lieutenant Clinson had finally proven his naysayers right.

Clinson shook his head. 'Not this day,' he whispered as he walked. And then he was running, feet sliding and slopping in the filth. Nothing would prevent him reaching the Barn this time. He did not look back, though his heart soared as the sound of hundreds of mud-slapping footsteps filled his ears, and he knew his men were with him. The Barn erupted in response, flashes of flame and white clouds pulsing in bilious gouts from the rough-hewn holes through which the black muzzles of muskets pointed, but Clinson would not be cowed this time. He gripped his sword tight as he ran and screamed to God for the victory he so craved.

After the briefest council of war Stryker could remember, he and Rawdon had agreed to abandon the Great Barn. The fighting front was now all the way along the outer margin of the Grange, with soldiers flooding in waves from Parliamentary positions beside the Loddon and out towards the village, so that Rawdon's beleaguered defenders were in very real danger of becoming isolated from the house. No man would be driven out of the Barn without a fight, and they lined the wall, some crouching low, others high on scaffolds constructed out of provisions. Colonel Rawdon paced at their backs, barking commands and steeling their resolve.

Stryker sent a dozen yellowcoats out of the rear doors, half of them to go round to the western gable of the Barn, and half to the east, so that their fire would prevent the enemy from flank-ing them. He had his own men cluster beneath the apex of that open arch, facing the barred north doors with muskets primed and matches hot. He left them to dart over the narrow causeway of the threshing floor and leaned into the timbers, now pocked by lead, of the closed doorway, pushing his eye into one of the splinter-edged holes. He saw the rebels gather in a dense pack; then, behind their leader – a man he recognized as the elegant officer from the melee – they began to surge forwards. Soon they were at a run, some faltering in the sapping mire but most keeping pace with the foremost men. A few had loaded muskets, which they held horizontally so that they might blow on their coals as they moved, but most had swung the long-arms about to present the solid wooden stocks as clubs. The officers had pistols and swords, and they used them as if they were colourful ensigns, holding them aloft as rallying points for the howling rebel tide.

'*Fire!*' Marmaduke Rawdon's authoritative tone bellowed out from the far end of the Barn, his single word crashing like a cannon shot and echoing in the beams. In the time it took to blink, the world was shattered as the Royalist muskets juddered back, kicking like disgruntled mules at shoulders and spitting fire and fury out into the Grange.

Stryker watched through his spy-hole, its frayed edges grinding at his skin, and when he saw the oncoming horde sheer instinctively towards the doors he fell back to join his greencoats.

'*Get out!*' Rawdon brayed. He was waving frantically at any man who thought to tarry. 'Fall back to the house, damn your hides!'

The yellowcoats did not need telling twice, and they ran to the rear doorway, filtering between Stryker's group, who remained gathered beneath the arch with muskets poised. The barred doors at the northern face of the building shook and groaned as men slammed into them from outside. Axes split the timbers in frantic flurries, and this time they worked with frightening efficacy now that the Royalist guns were no longer jutting from their loopholes. The crackle of musketry was steady outside, and Stryker hoped the units at either end of the Barn yet prevented the enemy from striving round to encircle them, but the continued battering at the closed doors told him the rebels were content to keep their losses low. Holes gaped suddenly in the timbers, and light burst through in blinding shafts. Stryker's men braced themselves. He heard Simeon Barkworth mutter something behind his carbine – he preferred the shortened cavalry weapon to a musket that was as long as he was tall – and knew the Scot was daring his enemy to come forth. Arms groped through the tattered axe breaches, hands clawed at the bar, and then it was off, clattering on the flint path, and the door was opening, its great hinges creaking above the exultant shouts.

Stryker's men fired their muskets as the Roundheads piled into the Barn, flinging them back as if plucked by the fingers of invisible Titans. The wave seemed to break against an immovable cliff, and they faltered, bunching on the threshing floor, spilling sideways on to the rammed chalk. Stryker backed away, the last defiant blow delivered, and his men went too, calmly but quickly, pulling shut the rear doors and gathering the teams at the gable ends.

'To the house!' Stryker ordered. Everyone sprinted for their lives across the smoking yard, over the wall and into the road that divided Basing House from its farm. Behind them the rebels were flowing out, a few taking pot-shots that fell well short and wide, and all, save one, crowing to the gathering clouds. The Grange had fallen.

CHAPTER 24

Jedidiah Clinson had survived. He did not rightly know how, for the demon had appeared again, the last out of the Great Barn, and with him had come a small but compact volley of musket shots that had taken a searing toll. But Clinson had been to the side, squashed with the massed bodies against the wooden frame, and now, as the light slowly began to dim outside and the air was filled with delicate, persistent raindrops, he sat down to enjoy his success.

The Barn was a massive victory. Much more than the first line of Basing's defences, it was a foothold, a bridgehead from which to launch the next wave of attacks that would now focus on the fortress itself. Moreover, the huge stone edifice and its smaller outbuildings provided much-needed shelter from the increasingly foul weather, and from Royalist sharpshooters. But best of all, the Barn was full. It was crammed with provisions. Food and drink, bedding, linen, enticing palliasses and feather beds. The end bays were stacked with straw and the walls buttressed by countless boxes and barrels and cases and chests, all waiting to be explored. It was a wonder, a treasure trove, and, as Jedidiah Clinson delved into a case of salted pork, he considered it the most marvellous reward he could imagine.

He stared around the room, its atmosphere thickened to a gritty miasma by the battle. It was a tall structure, solid and strong, though ragged now that its slit windows – made for ventilation – had been joined by more makeshift gaps battered by the defenders. High up in the gable ends there were owl holes, intended to let the birds in to hunt rats, but now a valuable escape for the choking smoke. About him, his men finished laying out the dead and wounded against the hay at each end. There were streaks over the chalk floor where corpses had been dragged. The men began to take off snapsacks and set down their weapons. They sheathed their tucks, snuffed out match-cords and checked powder boxes. Some pulled beds from tall stacks and slumped down to rest, while many began to crack open the intriguing barrels and crates. Clinson snapped an order that no ale should pass any man's lips, and set about cleaning his blade.

A runner appeared with a snappy bow and doff of his Montero. 'Compliments of General Waller, sir.'

Clinson looked up wearily. 'Well?'

'And you're to press our advantage, sir.'

Clinson gaped. 'My men have been at warm-enough work, I think. They require rest.'

The messenger shrugged. 'Should I give Sir William your answer, sir?'

Clinson stood. 'No, you should bloody well not.'

'Very good, sir.'

Clinson stretched his back, squared his shoulders and sheathed his blade. He went to the south doors, where the Royalists had made their final, spiteful stand, and from where he could look up at Basing House. The huge expanse of the New House stretched off to his left, a palatial pit of excess that simply called out from its walls to be crushed by God-fearing folk. But between grange and house there was a road, and beyond the road, lined with soldiers, lay the first of the fortress's formidable outer walls.

Clinson called to his men to follow. He may have taken the Barn, but the rest of the muddy Grange had fallen to other detachments, and out in the gathering gloom the smaller structures were swarming with men seeking plunder. Some of them were from the Trained Band units, the Londoners lending their might to the occupying force, and the clusters of musketeers who heeded the call to arms were milling forwards in the wake of their commanders, the lure of loot not quite as strong as the fear of punishment. They had each seen the clerk hanged at

Farnham, after all. Clinson wondered how effective the raw recruits would be when faced with Basing's stubborn Papists. Still, he felt encouraged by the presence of his victorious five hundred, and he turned to repeat his orders.

Stryker's men were on the outermost wall of the Old House, which bordered the road that cut between the estate and its farm. The land was raised by a few feet, so that they looked down upon the south wall of the Grange, and they pushed up against the rain-soaked bricks, ducking low to load their weapons and swinging over the top to fire. The enemy were coming in droves, pressing all along the northern front like a swarm of angry bees, their glowing matches dancing in the dimming afternoon light. Some leapt from the Grange to push into the road itself, but they were caught without shelter, coming immediately under a shower of lead from Basing's rampart. Most huddled into the low wall that hemmed the farm, cutting loopholes through which to fire, just as the Royalists had done.

Marmaduke Rawdon was ever present. He raged as he paced behind the stone curtain, screaming encouragement at the men of his regiment, at the private gentlemen who had joined the marquess's household for politics or faith, at the dismounted cavalrymen, at the soldiers brought in the summer by Lieutenant-Colonel Peake, at Stryker's green-coated veterans, at the stablehands and bakers and brewers and thatchers and grooms and chandlers who had been handed a musket and told to defend their home. His blade shone, speckled with water and reflecting the wan light with each slash cut into the air, his eyes bulged and his lips were pared back as he snarled hoarse commands.

Down at the Grange a trumpet cried above the gunfire, shrill and haunting, and the deep percussion of drummed orders rumbled out from command posts back at the Loddon. At once the Parliamentarian units moved, they clambered up and over, landing on the road, boots splashing, heads cringing into chests for fear of being plucked to oblivion by Royalist sharpshooters. They were making their move now, braving the defences before night stole the opportunity away. More and more groups of men, some in red, some green, some yellow, tumbled out of the Grange and into the road, thrusting at the backs of their comrades, bunching in a dense mass as they surged towards the limits of the Old House.

The men on the wall responded. The rain was heavier now, blurring their eyes and numbing their fingers, but it did not dampen their resolve. They had oiled rags bound tightly over the musket locks so that pan and serpent and powder would stay dry, and they loaded, fired and reloaded with methodical, almost mechanical repetition. Most did not possess the experience of Stryker's small group, and shots were loose, prickers dropped, scouring sticks fired by accident. Many made their weapons ready with impressive speed and dexterity, only to see their ball roll clean from the muzzle as they swung the barrel down to point at the road. But the attackers were no better. The Parliament men had vast numerical superiority, but the wind and rain turned the road to slush, and they found it impossible to pick out targets from an enemy protected by a rampart and obscured by smoke. Their progress across the road was sporadic, ebbing and flowing as the ragged Cavalier volleys harried them, but they had enough fire-power of their own to keep Royalist heads down and, with every brief lull, they covered a few more paces.

Stryker dropped low, covering his head with his arms as a bullet ricocheted off the top of the wall. The man next to him screamed, toppling back, hands clamped over eyes enfiladed by a spray of splintering mortar. Stryker crawled to him, ignoring the screams, and tore off the man's bandolier, ammunition pouch and primer flask. The man had dropped his musket and match, but the hemp cord still smouldered stubbornly on the wet soil, and Stryker snatched it up, blowing gently at its tip and managing to liven the bright coal. He thumbed open one of the powder boxes, upended the charge and added a ball from the pouch. He fixed the match to the serpentine, touched a measure of fine priming powder to the pan, and rose to the edge of the rampart. What he saw when he looked over snatched the very breath from his chest. The Roundheads had not bolted straight across the road to attempt a foolhardy escalade of the outer wall. Instead the drums had sent them east, to his right, where, at the far end of the rampart, Garrison Gate loomed tall and inviting.

He stood, ignoring the couple of hopeful shots that spat up at him. 'To the gates! To the gates!'

Colonel Rawdon had evidently foreseen the danger, for his men were already filing along the wall to where the storming parties converged. They were at the main gates, a tight wedge of men and steel, gathering for one final push before darkness fell.

Jedidiah Clinson was half-way back, lost amongst the clamouring tide of men who pushed at the enemy gates. He had taken something like two hundred and fifty – half his original force – out of the Grange and against the fortress. The other units had come too, and now, by his reckoning, there were significantly more than a thousand bodies surging around the barred arch that protected the inner approaches to Basing House, a melting pot of coat colours, banners and accents. Above them, New House and Old House drifted in and out of focus as the mist of the cannons scudded around windows and towers, curling between crenellated roofs and twisting like talons about the spires. Soon, Clinson thought. Soon he and his men would be running amok inside the sprawling cathedral of sin, tearing down its tapestries, smiting its smug opulence and digging out its Popish priests. He peered through the bunching shoulders, through hefted muskets and glinting swords, to stare at the gate. Soon it would fall. There would be a great explosion as a petard blew, making a gaping maw of the arch and frightened mice of the men behind it. He glanced down at the single-edged backsword in his hand, tightening his grip. Soon.

Stryker could not believe what he saw. He was on the wall just twenty or so paces down from Garrison Gate. The road below was teeming with Roundhead soldiers, all milling in anticipation of the archway becoming a chasm through which they would pour. But none on that sloppy expanse of mud seemed to have the means to achieve their aim. From up on the wall it was easy to see the sheer number of Parliamentarians, but not a single man, from common musketeer up to dandy officer, came forward with anything but cries of outraged impotence. There were no ladders ferried to the foremost ranks, no granadoes lobbed at the stonework, nor petards attached to the gate itself. Nothing.

A low murmur climbed out of the roadside. It was like the bleat of frightened sheep, but deeper, for the noises came from the throats of men who understood that they were trapped like cattle at a stile. They had striven so far under fire, bolstered by their gains at the Grange, and yet no one seemed to have prepared them for the moment when they actually reached their goal. Now they were like ducks in a pond, milling helplessly as hunters began to take aim from the wall above.

'Give them flame, my lads!' Colonel Marmaduke Rawdon bawled. 'Give them very hell!'

Stryker, like the rest, did as he was ordered. He still had his loaded musket, and he rested it on the rampart, keeping it level while he picked a target and letting the muzzle drop at the last second. He pulled the trigger quickly, not giving time for the ball to topple out, and the space around him went from damp to bone dry as the shot seared the air about his face. He had no idea whether the ball had flown true, for the rain and smoke and sheer number of Roundhead bodies made for an impossible search, so he dropped down to his haunches and began the laborious process of reloading. All along the wall men cheered, even as the enemy guns continued to pound from their far-off batteries, and he knew they were saved. He primed the musket all the same, clambering to his feet and looking for another chest to pick off. But there were none. The road had emptied in a matter of moments. All that was left were the bodies, dashed in the mud like twisted mannequins, pale, shocked faces staring up at the clouds, rain rinsing the powder grime from their cheeks. The rest had gone. The huge, exultant storming party had scurried from the road like rats from a sinking ship, throwing themselves over the wall and into the Grange to seek shelter, lick wounds and ponder upon what exactly they were doing at a gate with no means of breaking it down. Inside Basing House, while the heavy artillery continued to roar, the Royalists cheered.

—·⚏·—

It was growing dark as Sir John Paulet, Marquess of Winchester, found the men commanding the defence of his magnificent house. They were standing on the wall beside Garrison Gate, yards from where the desperate Roundhead attack had faltered an hour or so earlier. Rawdon had picked up a wound just below his eye, a horizontal nick from a shard of brick that gaped red, winking in a macabre parody of the lids above as he spoke. He peered down into the Grange through his brass-bound perspective glass, muttering to his subordinate colonels, Peake and Johnson. Stryker was there too, with Forrester and Major Lawrence, and together the five had formed a hasty council of war to decide just how to proceed. They had successfully cleared the civilian members of the garrison, those, at least, unable to bear arms, back to the buildings on the south side of both houses, installing the chirurgeon in the wine cellars beneath the Great Hall so that he might tend to the wounded without fear of careening iron shot. The single heavy artillery piece positioned on the north side of the Old House had been adjusted so that it would point directly down into the Grange, lest a renewed attack come from that quarter, and the walls and towers had been inspected by teams of musketeers. Now they had to wait and watch. The fighting continued, lambent tongues of flame licking the darkness as shots burst from each faction, but the determination for a concerted escalade seemed to have been dowsed by the rain. Groups of Parliamentarians sallied out from the various farm buildings, or from the village church to the north-east, but they reached only far enough to discharge their muskets in a desultory volley that achieved little.

'How now, gentlemen, and a splendid fight it was!' Paulet announced gleefully. He was enclosed against the weather in a coat that reached to his ankles and was crusty with wax. A large, thick pelt swathed his neck and fur gloves warmed his hands. 'They run back to the *Conqueror* with tails firmly betwixt legs, do they not?' He moved to the rampart, leaning elbows against its bullet-chipped summit. Half a dozen shots rang out from the enemy positions below, but the reports were strangely muffled, and none so much as reached the wall. 'And now their powder's damp!'

'Ours too, my lord,' Colonel Rawdon observed wryly.

Paulet pulled a sour expression, then squinted up at the black mass of Cowdrey's Down. 'Tell me, sirs, what game does Waller play? The man has five thousand troops out there, on the hill, at the river, in the farm, the village and even the churchyard. Yet they tarry where they stand. Our men put them to flight . . . *huzzah* for their bravery . . . but why does Waller not come again?' Paulet shook his head. 'I cannot fathom it.'

It was as if the rebels had been so embarrassed by their ineptitude at Garrison Gate that they had not the stomach for another attempt. The rain would add to their reticence, of course, and the fall of night too, but it had still been something of a surprise. As Stryker stared down at the Great Barn watching the men walk in and out carrying sacks and crates to some of the outbuildings, realization dawned. He cleared his throat, awkward in the company of so many high-ranking men. 'Vittles.'

All eyes went to him, but it was Paulet who spoke. 'Stryker?'

'The Great Barn, my lord, is fat with supplies.'

'And ale,' Lancelot Forrester added.

'And ale,' agreed Stryker. 'A lot of ale.'

It took a moment for the meaning to sink into the marquess's mind, but slowly his jaw dropped. 'Good Christ, Captain Stryker, you do not suggest the rebels have stopped for supper?'

'Waller has not, sir,' Stryker replied. 'His colonels have not.

His men?' He glanced up at the inky sky, feeling the fresh pricks of rain flutter over his face. 'The night is cold, and we gave them a hot fight. They've stumbled into a paradise of oysters and meat and beer, my lord. Beds, sheets, pewter goblets and warm hay. Why would they vacate such a home?'

'Why fight, my lord,' Forrester chimed, 'when you may feast?'

'Would you expect your men to behave thus?' Paulet argued.

Stryker shook his head. 'But my men are not a parcel of pie-sellers and cobblers, newly enlisted and prodded down from the City.'

'The scoundrels,' Paulet blustered, utterly incensed at the notion. 'The villains!'

'Sir?' Stryker said, unsure if he was more surprised by the marquess's naivety or by the fact that the opportunity for plunder had waylaid the rebel advance. 'It has curtailed Waller's attack.'

'Aye,' Rawdon seconded his words. 'This is a good thing—'

'Good?' Paulet cut the colonel off, face as red as Rawdon's wound. 'Good? Protestant drivel, as ever, Marmaduke! Is it a good thing that the rebel knaves thieve my hard-grown, hard-reared, hard-reaped provisions?' He slammed his fur-mitted fist on the parapet. 'That they gnaw their way through my meat and corn like an infestation of voracious vermin?'

'What would you have us do, my lord?' Robert Peake, military chief until Rawdon's arrival, ventured gingerly. 'We cannot very well claw those supplies back.'

'And yet?' It was Lieutenant-Colonel Johnson who spoke. All eyes went to him, and all saw that he was looking at Stryker.

'And yet,' Stryker said, 'might we deprive the enemy of them?'

'Sally out, Stryker?' Rawdon asked. He shook his head vigorously. 'An absurd notion. We cannot risk such a thing. Waller's army is vast.'

'It is vast, Colonel, aye,' said Stryker, his pulse beginning to quicken with the fermenting idea. 'But it is tired, it is damp, and, in the Barn, I'd wager it is firmly in its cups.'

★　★　★

Stryker checked his borrowed pistol. It was primed, sitting safely at half-cock, with the frizzen pulled back over the pan. The weight in his grip felt reassuring. Lancelot Forrester came through the group. He held a pistol too. In his other hand he gripped a cup, and he lifted it in salute. 'Drink today and drown all sorrow, you shall perhaps not do it tomorrow. Best, while you have it, use your breath, there is no drinking after death.'

'Shakespeare?' Stryker asked.

Forrester took a long sip and handed it to Stryker. 'Fletcher and Johnson.'

Stryker drank from the cup. It contained strong wine, and he gulped it back. 'Are you ready?'

Forrester blew out his cheeks as Stryker passed the cup to the next man in the group. 'Never more so.'

The sally party was small, because Rawdon was determined that he could not afford the loss of any more men. What he agreed to, therefore, was an act of stealth and guile. One not designed to hurt Waller's main army, or even to dissuade him from his objectives, but simply to deny to Roundhead stomachs what had been intended for Royalists.

Sergeant William Skellen loomed over Stryker. 'You reckon they're bumpsy, sir?' he said quietly, halberd in one hand, blazing torch in the other.

Stryker nodded. 'You saw how many beer barrels there were, Sergeant. What would you do?'

Skellen grimaced. 'Nothin', sir.'

'Why?'

'Because you'd shove this halberd up my arse.'

The thirty men gathered behind Garrison Gate amid the glow of flaming torches. Twenty-five were chosen men, sergeants and musketeers, hard, gallant and itching for a fight. Before them, swords bared for a night's slaughter, Basing's council of war almost in its entirety readied itself for the off. Only Frederick Lawrence had stayed behind, for his crooked spine limited his effectiveness out of the saddle, but Colonel Rawdon had insisted upon leading the charge, and he had been joined by both Peake and Johnson. Stryker went too, his men forming the left flank of the twenty-five, and Forrester could not be dissuaded. Now they waited as Rawdon's best shots clambered to the north wall and prepared their muskets, poised for the command to give covering fire.

'But what of the rebels?' Stryker said, his voice deliberately soft. 'Did you see their officer?'

'Down in the Barn? Aye, a young peacock.'

'Indeed. A good swordsman, granted, but a stripling. You think his hard-faced lads will keep sober after the fight we gave them?'

'Reckon not,' Skellen muttered.

Stryker slid his basket-hilted broadsword a few inches up and down its scabbard, ensuring it would not stick in the moist conditions. 'The whole garrison could not best Waller's army, for it is truly vast, but the rebels in the Grange will be enjoying the comforts therein.'

A heavy clunking sound emanated from the gateway itself as the locks were turned and bars lifted. Rawdon hissed something to an aide, who scuttled up to a man on the wall, and the long row of musketeers blew in unison on their match-tips. Stryker fought to catch suddenly hasty breaths. He looked at Skellen. 'Godspeed, Will.'

'An' to you, sir,' the tall sergeant intoned. He said the same to Forrester, turning the halberd shaft in his palm so that the triple-headed blade glimmered in the torchlight. 'Let us crack open a few skulls.'

'Traitors!' Captain-Lieutenant Jedidiah Clinson raged. 'Rotten-hearted, copper-nosed, scrofulous knaves! I shall—I shall—'

'You shall drink with us, Cap'n, sir, and make merry,' the corporal crooned from his perch on a pile of feather beds. The side of his black-gummed mouth was crammed to bursting with salted bacon, and in his hands he cradled a pewter goblet, beer slopping over its rim as he raised it for a toast. 'For we have this day bit a chunk out o' the Markiz of Winch'ster's ignoble fackin' arse!'

364

'Aye!' another soldier cheered. 'And a pox on him!'

'A pox on him an' his Pope-buggerin' posse!' the corporal exclaimed. He quaffed his beer and dunked the cup into the barrel that had been crudely torn open. 'We've won us this day, sir, and we shall all enjoy it!'

Following the abortive assault against the north-east gate, Clinson had fallen back with the rest for shelter in the Grange, and he had waited for orders to come down from Waller. But nothing had been forthcoming. What he found in the Barn was drunken, shameful chaos. The men, it seemed, were more loyal to their stomachs than their Parliament, and they had poured into the huge chamber to loot and eat and drink. There was plenty to go around, enough to have supplied Basing for weeks, and they went to the kegs and boxes like slugs at a vegetable garden, devouring their way through whatever they could find. Most, however, stayed near the beer barrels. They imbibed the welcome brew like babes at the teat, taking their fill without pause, and Clinson was left to simply watch with growing disgust.

'We have been ordered to pursue the attack,' he bleated, though he knew his words sounded ridiculously small in the high-trussed space. 'Make again for the walls. Storm the castle.'

The corporal shook his head. 'We've no ladders, sir. No ram, no explosives. It is a worthless escapade. One to which Sir Billy will toss our wretched skins for nought but his pride.' He took another long draught, belching hard. 'Well I ain't goin' no more. Not till the morrow, leastwise. Soldiering treats a fedary worse than scouring latrines back 'ome, sir. Six days o' shit till Sunday. Not tonight. Tonight we drink, eh lads?'

The others cheered. Clinson silently took names for the dawn hanging that would surely follow. And outside, from the Royalist positions, a huge volley of musketry ripped into the night.

—✠—

The man known in Basing House as Tom Chivers ignored the sudden spike in musketry while he skulked from the rain under the eaves of the Great Hall. It had been an impressive building once, but it had been long superseded by the more palatial spaces of the Tudor mansion. As such, it was a good place to hide, for Basing's residents rarely went near.

Roger Tainton watched the Great Gatehouse. Or, rather, he watched the low-set doors at the foot of a slope that led into the Gatehouse's foundations. He watched the guards, new men since his unfortunate tangle with the French witch. Stryker's men, he knew, for he recognized them from Scilly. These were not the brawny apes in Paulet's employ, but had been hand-chosen by Stryker himself, and he would not chance his arm against such men with just a chisel or blade. What their arrival had confirmed, however, was that this, without the shadow of a doubt, would be where he would find the Cade trove. All he had to do was wait and watch.

God, of course, and as ever, had provided the answer. Waller's guns had continued through the night, focussing their dead-eyed anger against the Gatehouse, which meant very few civilians had remained in this sector of the complex. Only the infirmary seemed to be using one end of the hall, for the wounded were being ferried up and down stone steps that led to the old wine cellars, and that posed little concern for him. Moreover, a trio of heavy guns had since been brought to bear upon the New House, which had necessitated the evacuation of the stables, meaning Tainton's presence there was no longer required. It was all perfect. Nearly perfect.

Tainton stared at the guards. He shifted his weight from one snug and dry foot to the other, pleased with the retrieval of his beloved riding boots, their spurs chattering to him softly. He kicked the bulging snapsack gently between them. His provisions would last a good while yet. Time was on his side. Now it was left only to pray.

When the cannon fired Tainton knew he had been heeded. It exploded up on the rampart, the only piece in Basing's armament able to be trained upon the Grange, and a huge cloud of dirty white vapour bloomed into the sheeting rain. The guards, almost identical in their tall frames, pinched faces and blond locks, ran out from the slope, crossed to a ladder close by on the Old House's ancient wall, and clambered up the worn rungs. Theirs was an action borne only out of inquisitiveness, but they would be gone long enough. Roger Tainton collected his snap-sack and moved out into the courtyard. As the rain pelted his wool-hugged pate, he remembered a verse from the Book of Proverbs. 'In his heart a man plans his course, but the Lord devises his steps,' he whispered softly, plunging a hand into a coat pocket. When he pulled it out, the small object felt cold in his grip. Slim and rusty, it was hardly a tool of glory. And yet tonight it would do the very work of God.

—⁂—

The volley had had the desired effect. It had torn out from the northern perimeter of the ring-work, rippling all along the rampart of soil-buttressed stone, bright tongues lapping the night, smoke billowing in unison. The musket-balls whistled across the narrow divide of the road and slammed into the Grange wall, behind which many of the Parliament men were huddled, and a shower of shards sprang up as the rebels sheared away from their loopholes.

As those foremost Parliamentarians cringed from the volley, the sally party raced out of the Garrison Gate. They sprinted over the sticky road, muskets, pistols and blades ready for blood-ing but mouths firmly shut until the time was right. Stryker was near the front, between Forrester and Lieutenant-Colonel Johnson, and he felt his senses sharpen with every pace. There were a lot of soldiers in the Grange, but they were spread out, at rest and enjoying their unexpected repast, and it was that ill-preparedness that the Royalists were relying on.

The big gun fired from up on the battlements. It was the only piece pointed northwards, for Rawdon's belief had always been that any attack would come from the Park to the south-west, but it would be useful all the same. Stryker caught a glimpse of a large, filthy puddle up ahead, its surface shivering at the booming report of the cannon. He jumped it, pulling the pistol to full cock as he landed, and then they were at the Grange.

The iron shot careened over their heads. It punched into the Great Barn, smashing a large hole in the brickwork just below the roof, and Stryker could hear the frightened screams from within even as he hurled himself over the wall. He stood quickly, staring into the darkness of the farm. There were buildings all across the eastern half of the complex, while the Barn dominated the west, and already Rawdon and Peake had taken some of the sally party into those mud-spattered shacks. Bellows of alarm and rage rang out and shots crackled. From the black abyss came sudden light as the first thatched pen was consumed in flame.

Stryker looked to his left, down the line of the outer wall, and saw that the Parliamentarian musketeers, having shaken themselves from the covering volley, were frantically making their own weapons ready.

'*Charge!*' Stryker brayed without hesitation. He drew his sword, levelling it at the startled enemy, and bolted forth. He heard the howls of the men at his back, could discern the familiar cries of Skellen and Forrester and Barkworth, and then they were at the first Roundheads. A man in a blue coat sprang out from the shadows of the wall immediately to his left, and Stryker emptied the pistol, shooting him square in the face. The man vanished in a bloom of smoke and blood. Another came on almost immediately, so Stryker threw the pistol at him, clattering his temple in a sickening crack. Then they were into the Roundheads, tearing like a hungry pack of wolves, their swords whirling and slashing and cleaving, the air alive with the sound of swords and the cries of men. Stryker's group contained perhaps ten musketeers, and their shots roared beneath the torch glow, snatching men to their deaths at no range at all. Johnson was there, he now realized, and the colonel – a man Stryker reckoned to be in his early thirties, with auburn hair and a sharp triangle of beard thrusting from his bottom lip – was bawling for the sortie to veer right, away from the wall and towards the Great Barn.

Captain-Lieutenant Jedidiah Clinson knew he was in trouble. From his position in the south doorway of the Great Barn he could see that the Royalist counterattack was small in nature, for the torches did not number more than a score, but the bulk of Waller's army were bivouacked outside the Grange, out at the churchyard or up on the hill. The cavalry had ridden down to the plateau of Basing Park. It left a good number of men in the Grange – three or four hundred – but only a fraction of those had continued the fight. Most were looting the outbuildings, sleeping in the haystacks or gorging themselves amid the Barn's plentiful stores. They were not expecting such an attack, and now they drew swords with bleary eyes and unsteady legs. Half were drunk, with many more well on the way, and they staggered and stumbled as they formed a fighting front behind him, tripping on their own scabbards and fumbling with muskets they had no hope of loading in time. Clinson prayed aloud, at the top of his lungs, and he held up his sword to present a model for his pathetic charges to follow. And he prepared himself for death.

Stryker made straight for the Barn doors. To his right the fires were licking high in a dozen places where Rawdon's group had scoured the outbuildings. Torches had been raked across the thatches, touched to beams and wagons and boxes and barrels, and then, finally, jammed hard into hay and straw so that deep, red, angry flames leapt out, hot enough to defy the rain. The Parliamentarians were running. He could hear their cries, and he knew that their weight in numbers did nothing to counteract the shock and fear. They would rally eventually, of course, when a stoic and level-headed officer finally corralled enough of them to form a coherent fighting group, but for the moment it was anarchy, a confusion of labourers and weavers and tapsters who had forgotten that they were supposed to be soldiers. Now was the time to enact their plan.

Stryker almost tripped on a discarded musket as he ran, and, catching the match-glow in the corner of his eye, he guessed it was primed. He jabbed his sword, point down, into the mud, stooped to snatch up the long-arm, levelled it at the gaping mouth of the doorway, and pulled the trigger. The ball exploded away, and beneath the arch a soldier in a red coat and morion helmet, stood briefly, as if fighting against a sudden squall, and then toppled face-first into the mud. Stryker tossed the weapon back into the morass, plucked free his sword and reached the entrance, barrelling into a man whose own sword shattered as it parried Stryker's superior Toledo steel. They fell. Stryker was on top of him, smashed the man's hooked nose with a butt of his head, and scrambled to his feet. The defenders were running, pouring out of the north doorway as if their breeches were aflame, and Stryker's men gave chase. Some of the men with torches paused to fire the crates and hogsheads that were left in the huge building, then followed behind, pursuing the Roundheads into the open space below the fish ponds. Already drums and trumpets called out from the north and it was clear that Waller had dispatched a force to snuff out the audacious assault.

'For the Church and the law!' a deep voice boomed like a Cannon Royal to Stryker's right. 'For good King Charles, and a pox on the Parliament!'

Stryker squinted into the darkness to see Rawdon, and he nodded quickly to him. The team who had fired the outbuildings had converged, as planned, in the Grange yard and now they engaged the last, desperate group of rebels who had been too slow or too brave to fling themselves over the northern wall to safety. There were ten or eleven Parliament men in the gloom, their swords drawn, and Stryker saw that one was the elegant officer he had faced before. He shouted a challenge to the man, calling him on.

Clinson saw the demon and understood that his star had finally fallen. He could not run, but only stand and fight, and he went to the one-eyed man with a prayer on his lips. To his surprise, an auburn-haired officer stepped between them.

'He's mine,' the man said. He was an officer, a senior one, by the look of his gold-laced buff-coat and blood-red scarf, and Clinson met his sword blow with a deft parry. His prayer had been answered, and he thanked the good Lord from the very depths of his being, for this high-ranking Cavalier was the kind of man with whom Clinson liked to fence. He danced out and in, keeping his elbow flexed and his left knee bent, turning the Royalist's blade away with agile ease. Hand-to-hand duels had broken out all around, but his men were outnumbered. Many corpses had been left in the Grange, many men had fled, and Waller's reinforcements would not arrive in time. The sally party, all snarls and crows, knew they would win this small skirmish, and they grinned wickedly as Clinson's last few men were cut down. He could at least show the arrogant malignants how a real swords-man went to work. Clinson darted forwards, forcing a desperate parry from the gold-laced officer, then retreated, tempting the sweat-sheened soldier into a grunting lunge. He let the man come, drawing him off balance, and flicked the point of the blade away, then whipped his own sword up to jar at his opponent's breast. It hit hard, but the man's coat of buff hide was thick and of good quality, and it absorbed the riposte impressively. But the officer could not regain his balance and he sprawled away from Clinson with a shrill yelp, Clinson hooking his ankle with a well-placed boot. The officer went down, sliding on his side in the slick mire, and Jedidiah Clinson went to him.

Stryker thumped the swirling hilt of his sword into the thickly bristled face of a rebel sergeant, and battered the man's reeling body away with a gloved fist. In one movement he was over the prone Roundhead, jumping into the path of the expensively dressed young officer, and he swept the sword up to meet the man's blade as it came down to dispatch Lieutenant-Colonel Johnson. He had wanted to teach him a lesson for taking the Grange from the Royalists in the first place, but Johnson had interrupted him before he could engage. Stryker had watched in horror, blocked as he was by other desperate rebels, as the Parliamentarian set about tutoring Johnson in the fineries of single combat, and it was only at the last moment, as the fellow delivered what had been designed to be a killing blow, that Stryker had finally cut his way through.

The young man spun away as his single-edged sword jarred with a thunderous clang against Stryker's weapon, his face a sudden mask of fear. Johnson spluttered and writhed in the mud below them, trying to stand, but Stryker ignored him, stepping quickly past. He hacked, battered and cleaved at the young swordsman. There was no finesse in his movements, only rage and strength, and he knew his enemy did not know how to respond to an attack such as this. It was like fighting a boy. Stryker felt strangely sorry for the officer, whose skills were polished but woefully inadequate against a murderer. He did not stop, could not stop, and soon the lad was slipping, stumbling in the grime, able only to parry and whimper.

Clinson did not know what to do. The demon, half his face torn away, the other half a creased and granite-hard manifest-ation of fury, was simply too strong, too implacable, utterly relentless. Every block sent ripples of pain up through his palm and wrist, jarring his shoulder and shoving him back. He was being bullied out of the duel by a man chillingly comfortable amid the flames and the mud and the powder-stink. Clinson tripped on the body of one of his men, slipped with his standing foot in a patch of waterlogged slurry, and toppled back. His sword was gone, vanished in the filth, and then the demon was above him. He did not even see the killing blow, just felt the pressure at his throat above his silver gorget, heard the crunch of his own sinews as they were severed, felt the bubble of blood rise into his mouth. For a second the dancing orange flames that raced and hissed throughout the Grange appeared before his eyes. Then everything became black.

★ ★ ★

Stryker jerked his sword from the dead officer's windpipe and wiped it on the man's breeches. He sheathed it quickly, offering a hand to the breathlessly thankful Colonel Johnson while Skellen knelt to rifle through the pockets of the fresh corpse. All around them the fires raged, raindrops hissing on the white-hot embers. In one of the outbuildings the powder boxes strung on a wounded man's bandolier began to ignite, his shrieks piercing the night.

Marmaduke Rawdon and Robert Peake were gathering the men. They had lost two of Rawdon's yellows. Skellen held up a square of paper. 'Captain-Lieutenant Jedidiah Clinson,' he read aloud, shaking the paper between thumb and forefinger. 'His commission, sir.'

'A brave fellow,' Stryker said. He thought of Andrew Burton, his young protégé who had met his end on a blood-soaked hill in Cornwall. He felt suddenly wretched. 'Brave lad.'

Rawdon gave thanks to the sally party. 'We may not have this place,' he added, 'but nor shall the enemy. Now it is time for us to depart.'

As they turned south, the screams of men caught in the yard's many outbuildings erupted, rising over the crackle of flames and the drums and trumpets. Men who had fallen asleep in their cups were woken as their skin roasted, ensnared by steel and blaze. The Royalists made their way back to Garrison Gate in silence.

—◆—

General Sir William Waller watched in utter disbelief as the flames enveloped the farm. His horse twitched beneath him as if it shared his consternation. The screams of roasting men carried up to his positions – distant, almost ethereal wails – like a wind through a narrow gorge, and he grimaced as he tasted bile in his mouth.

'More, Sir William?' one of Waller's aides, mounted on a docile grey to his left, enquired in a well-bred voice that was pitched high and querulous.

'More?' echoed Waller.

'You have used but a fifth of your army, General. Send the rest, I implore you.'

'To what end?' Waller answered without taking his eyes from the blazing farm. 'We have no way of breaking the gates.' Now he turned to look at the aide. 'We have no way of breaking the damned gates!'

The aide swallowed thickly, fiddled with his grey's pricked ears. 'Of course, sir.'

'I had rested on the premise that our force, having taken the Grange, would frighten the fight out of the enemy. Their very presence at Lord Paulet's door would cow him into surrender. Clearly I was mistook in that. What is the butcher's bill?'

The aide's face screwed up in a maze of creases. 'Uncertain as yet, Sir William, but we have lost many. Clinson among them, I hear.'

Waller drew a lingering breath, tugged gently on his whiskers with a gloved hand. 'A pity. No more will be thrown at Basing this night. Our powder is damp and our will damper.'

'We retreat?' a new voice interrupted.

Waller looked to his right, where the irritating Croat, Major Kovac, had reined in. The blunt-speaking cavalryman had become something of a flea in his ear during the day, but before biting Kovac's white-sprouting head off, Waller reminded himself that the man's commanding officer, Dick Norton, was a powerful man in the county. To make an enemy of the Governor of Southampton would be unwise, even for a man such as Sir William Waller. 'No, Major, we do not. I have had a gutful for today. My britches are sodden, my feet like blocks of ice, and I would rest. We will withdraw a mile or so for the night, to return on the morrow.'

'But, General—' Kovac began to protest.

Waller lifted a flattened palm for silence. 'That is the long and the short of it, Major Kovac. Do not gripe, sir, for you will have your chance. That I can promise.'

CHAPTER 25

Basing House, Hampshire, 9 November 1643

The Grange fire blazed all night and deep into the following day, but it gradually cooled to a steaming ruin and by the next dusk even the greediest flames had been dowsed by the merciless rain. The Royalists pent up in Basing House spent the day after the battle simply staring northwards. The remnants of the Grange were a sad sight, to be certain, but it was the movement beyond that simmering charnel pit that so captivated the exhausted defenders. Waller's army had withdrawn. They knew it was not a retreat; not a real, lasting one, at any rate. He had bivouacked in the surrounding fields after the assault, licking his wounds and, no doubt, plotting a new escalade, but the weather had not been on his side. It had hammered the hills, filled the Loddon so that it burst its banks and flooded Waller's breastworks. It had bogged down their supply wagons and made their gun batteries subside as if they had been placed on sand. It had numbed the hands and feet of his men, dampened their powder and eroded their resolve, and Waller, so reported Major Lawrence's ebullient scouts, had fallen back upon Basingstoke to wait out the storm.

Stryker had stood to arms with the rest of Rawdon's beleaguered force all that day, even as rumour of Waller's retreat had filtered through to the ranks. They were hopeful, for the downpour was relentless, cold and pervasive, and it seemed reasonable to think that the enemy would seek proper shelter under the solid rooftops of a town rather than sit like an army of

375

bedlamites in the rain, waiting to freeze to death. And yet it was not until the second dawn that Garrison Gate had been opened and Stryker, Forrester and the few remaining men of Mowbray's Regiment of Foot streamed out to take stock of the Grange and ensure there were no ambushers lying in wait.

The outbuildings were gone, devoured by the inferno, and the supplies they had contained were now reduced to a mess of mutilated silhouettes. The ground still smouldered in patches, and in its toxic brew of mud and water and ash the remains of men could be seen, scorched and raven-pecked legs and arms jutting up like rocks on a low-tide shore. There might have been as many as a hundred and fifty souls out in the swamp that still carried the scent of cooked flesh, and only the crows chattered as the men waded through.

The Great Barn was all that remained. Its thick stone walls had been impervious to the blaze, its roof too high, and it stood now like a grim memorial to the bitter fight. Inside, most of the provisions had been incinerated, despoiled, pillaged for the Parliamentarian train, or simply eaten, but the men collected what little they could. The dead were sifted and lined up for burial once their pockets and snapsacks had been plundered of valuables. After that, it was a matter of waiting and watching. The Grange was no longer a defensible proposition, but neither was it an effective forward base for an attacker. Thus, Rawdon spent a number of hours bringing his northern defences back as far as the road. If Waller chose another assault from the north, then his forces would stream like a herd of frightened bullocks across the tattered farm, so Basing's stand, he decided, would be made on the outermost wall of the fortress itself.

'But would not the Great Barn make an ideal battery, sir?' Lieutenant-Colonel Robert Peake suggested to Rawdon as the council of war took advantage of a pause in the rain to tour the segment of wall that surrounded the mansion's gardens. It had not been intended as anything more than a decorative facade just a brick and a half thick, but now, like every other aspect of the great place, loopholes, earthen buttresses and gun emplacements had turned the once tranquil patch of land into what was effectively Basing's north-west bastion. 'God forbid they pound us from such a range.'

Rawdon walked at the head of his group while muttering orders at an aide. He glanced round at Peake. 'God forbid, Robert. But how shall Waller put his piece there? The ground near the river has become a swamp, the Grange a marsh at best.'

Lieutenant-Colonel Johnson was at the back, chatting with Major Lawrence as he dug grime from his fingernails with the tip of a jagged knife, and he gave a short snort of amusement. 'Took us an age to wade through there, Robert. Why, that haughty music almost drowned on his way back to the Conqueror!'

The others laughed. According to the Royalist drummer who was in the enemy camp delivering Paulet's furious rebuttal, the trumpeter had become lost in the vile mire around the river before eventually returning to Waller's lines. When finally he found his way to friendly pickets, he was caked in stinking mud and had lost one of his boots.

Rawdon even allowed himself a smirk. 'Nought so mighty as a music carrying a general's message, eh? I confess I was some-what pleased by the news.' He looked at Peake. 'So you see, Colonel, I cannot imagine Waller could get any kind of piece to the Grange without it being immediately swallowed, let alone one big enough to trouble our walls.'

Stryker smiled at Rawdon's reply. Any trace of self-doubt had been eradicated by the heat of war. 'Where, then, sir?'

Rawdon's sharp gaze swivelled round to regard Stryker. 'Captain?'

'We must consider General Waller's next move, sir. Put ourselves in his very boots, if you will.'

'And where do those boots march?' Rawdon asked.

'Not the Grange.'

Rawdon's bushy grey brows jumped a touch. 'No?'

'The place is a tomb, sir. And Waller's army look to be Trained Bandsmen in the main.'

'Meaning?' Peake chirped, his eyes darting rapidly from colonel to captain with a mixture of intrigue and impatience. Unlike the affable Johnson, he seemed uncomfortable with the influence the relatively lowly officer had come to wield in this elite group, and his good manners were beginning to fray.

'Meaning,' Forrester said in a wry tone that told Stryker he, too, had detected the tension, 'the buggers would rather be tending their shops and warming their wives than hurling themselves into a bloody morass.'

'Their fedaries,' Stryker agreed, 'have failed once already, and those raw recruits up on the hill were forced to stand and watch. They'll have no stomach for a repetition, sir. The attack will come from elsewhere.'

'The Park?' Rawdon prompted. 'The New House?'

'If I were Waller?' Stryker answered with a shrug. 'Both. And he will not make the same mistakes. This time he'll be prepared.'

'Ladders?'

'Ladders, petards, grenadoes, and anything else he needs. He shan't have been idle while he sits out the rain.'

Rawdon sucked at the matted bristles of his moustache. He glanced at the supercilious aide. 'I want the walls further bolstered.'

The aide, a bespectacled fellow with a spotty chin and fingers that were brittle and blue, bobbed again. 'Which, sir?'

'All of them,' Rawdon said. 'Earth, rubble, whatever can be found. The gates too. No weak points, you understand me?'

'Aye, sir.'

'And a new half-moon on the outside of Garrison Gate. Let them fight their way to our door this time.'

'Colonel Rawdon!' a voice, slightly nasal and pitched high, carried to them across the gardens from the east. 'Rawdon!'

The party looked as one towards the small gateway leading from the direction of the Old House. Rawdon bowed, the rest followed suit. 'My lord.'

Sir John Paulet, Marquess of Winchester, swept down from the higher ground, the hem of his cloak brushing the path's small stones to leave a wake like ripples behind a boat. 'Rawdon! My confessor has been humiliated!'

'Humiliated?'

Paulet's cheeks were a deep crimson, and Stryker wondered whether it was a result of chilly air or hot temper. 'My priest, Colonel. A gaggle of your heretical musketeers did kick up a muddy puddle at him this dawn.'

'A puddle, my lord?'

Paulet clenched and unclenched his fists. 'Kicked it, besmirching his robes in the most disrespectful manner! I shall not have Protestant blackguards behaving so ill within these walls, Rawdon, by God Himself, I shall not!'

Stryker saw his chance to slip away as governor followed marquess back up the slope, duty-bound as he was to assuage Paulet's prickly honour. He stayed with the group until they were in the Old House, then shook the hands of the others before making for the Great Hall. He had not been down to its cellars, but he had heard that they were cavernous and well protected from any shot flung over the walls, and they made a sensible choice for the temporary infirmary.

'Give me a moment to explain, old man. Does the Bard not say—'

'Do not dissemble, Forry, I have no mood for it. She was not in the damned infirmary, so where is she?'

Stryker had found his friend up on the fortified rooftops that formed the south wall of the New House. He was peering down at the deep ditch and the staked earthen rampart beyond. Forrester's initial grin had melted as he had looked into his fellow captain's eye, the colour draining from his cheeks. It had been enough for Stryker to know that he had been lied to.

'Very well,' Forrester said on the back of a deep sigh, leaning his elbow on the crenellated edge of the roof. 'She did not wish you to know of her mission.'

'Mission?'

'She delivers a message from the marquess.'

'To whom?'

'Lord Hopton.'

'What message?' asked Stryker, his eye narrowing.

'What do you think?' Forrester retorted defiantly. He looked up at the clouds, which were pregnant and threatening in vast banks across the hills. '*Dearest Lord Hopton, it is with great regret that I report of the impending destruction of Basing Castle, the slaughter of its inhabitants, and the utter ruination of the righteous cause of King Charles Stuart in the fine county of Hampshire. Yours in imminent defeat, Sir John Paulet, Marquess of Winchester*, or words to that effect.'

Stryker turned to stare outwards, to the fields and parkland that hemmed the estate on its south side. 'That scheming bloody stoat.'

'If you refer to the marquess,' Forrester interjected, 'have a care, for he has ears everywhere, I'm certain. Besides, you'd be wrong, in part at least. It is his note, but it was given unto Lisette's hand by the marchioness. She evidently does not trust in her husband's people.' He laughed without mirth. 'A shrewd decision, would you not agree, given the non-appearance of our much vaunted escort?'

Stryker did not, in that moment, care one jot for the escort. His mind whirled with Lisette's vanishing, with her deceit. 'Why did she not tell me?'

Forrester smiled kindly. 'Because she knew you would resist, and because you had a mountain of troubles on your heart already.'

'And because of what happened.'

'On Scilly?' Forrester would not meet his gaze. 'That too. She suspects the two of you cannot operate to the best of your abilities when each knows the other's work. I was only made privy so that someone in your confidence knew what became of her. She did not want you suspecting Tainton's blade in this.'

'How did she get out?' said Stryker.

Forrester glanced back beyond the high turrets to the broad rise of Cowdrey's Down. 'Waller's cordon was not so tight. And one so resourceful as Lisette? I imagine it was no strain. She went during the bombardment, before they took the Grange.'

'Then let us hope she made it through,' Stryker muttered, looking south and imagining her corpse swinging from one of the oaks that smudged the distant horizon. If she was captured with the marquess's letter, then it would be the worse for her.

Forrester nodded. 'For all our sakes, old man. For all our sakes.'

Amesbury, Wiltshire, 9 November 1643

'Waller launches an assay against Basing Castle.'

The speaker was Sir Ralph Hopton, Baron of Stratton. He was dressed in his usual sober attire, his hat slanted down to one side to obscure the scars across his temple and ear, and he sat in the corner of a taphouse on the Winchester Road. The newly-made lord was pressed into the join between two flinty walls as if he expected an assassin's bullet at any moment. His hands, as ever, were gloved, and in them, made milky orange by the glow of a sputtering tallow candle, was a sheet of vellum. He licked his lips, reading silently, then looked up. 'The Lord Marquess speaks of a veritable horde at his gates. Foot, horse and heavy ordnance. He desires my assistance forthwith.'

'He has desired your succour for days, my lord,' one of the assembled officers muttered, a little more loudly than was appropriate.

Hopton's eyes were not as keen as they once had been, but they were yet able to pierce the gloom when an insolent subordinate required chastisement, and he slammed a fist down on the table. 'Have a care, Sergeant-Major Allerton! Wish you a post commanding our latrine diggers?'

The officer, obscured by the shadows at the rear of the room, cleared his throat awkwardly. 'No, my lord, no. I did not mean to speak out of turn. Meant no offence.'

Hopton nodded. He would not accept such destructive

chatter, but that did not mean he was completely blinkered to the feelings of his men. This new army's task was to clear Dorset, Wiltshire and Hampshire of the Parliamentarian menace and then swing left, pushing north into London, to smash the rebellion right in its belly. The first part of Hopton's strategy had been as straightforward as he might have hoped, the majority of the territories falling swiftly to his threat, but now, as Hampshire was almost in his grip, Waller had come to stop him. Matters required more consideration than had been originally thought.

'I have awaited more men, more ammunition, more supplies,' he said, his voice measured and stern. 'I would not risk a repeat of Newbury Fight by wading headlong into a mire from which I cannot extricate myself. But we now have enough about us to pursue the enemy, 'tis true. Sir William has pushed his pieces across the board; now I may make my move.'

Another man stepped from a shadow. 'You will relieve Basing, my lord?'

'I shall,' Hopton confirmed, receiving a chorus of excited whispers in response. 'We may march in a day or so, should the rain ease. I will write at once to His Majesty, requesting further reinforcements. I believe we have a good body of men in Reading who might be spared.' He glanced to his left, where a clerk busily scribbled notes on scraps of parchment in a spidery hand. 'Dispatch riders to all divisions. We shall muster at Kingsclere.'

'My lord,' the clerk said, not looking up from his quill.

Hopton set down the sheet, flattening it with his palms. 'To your work, then, gentlemen.'

When the assembly had dispersed, he sat back, tugged at the fingers of his gloves, and called out to an aide. The door opened once more, and in strode a diminutive figure in a long cloak. 'Thank you for your bravery in this, madam.'

The woman scraped the hood from her head, revealing long, golden hair and a pale face. 'Duty done, my lord.'

'What is your name? You are not from these parts.' Hopton smiled. 'Nor, I suspect, are you the common apple seller you claimed to be when my outriders first found you.'

She returned the smile. 'My name, Lord Hopton, is Lisette Gaillard.'

Basing House, Hampshire, 9 November 1643

Roger Tainton had been worried. He had used Perkin Yates's skeleton key to slip his way into the musty, dank bowels of the Old House. He had waited, listening to the muffled crackle of muskets, the earth-shaking din of heavy artillery and the shouts of men, women and children, all witnessing the fall of the place they had come to regard as home. Except it had not fallen. Waller's attack, so successful in its early throes, had, it seemed, been thrown back, and the guns had lost their voices, the strained cries from out in the courtyard had fizzled to nothing, and then all was quiet. And now Tainton found himself locked inside this self-imposed prison.

He had felt the gold. He could barely see anything at all, but beneath the sheet had been the wagon, and there, crammed tight, had been the treasure. Even in the darkness, he had checked it, probing hands snaking over the ranks of cool plate, across the various bejewelled baubles and over the solid forms of chests that he knew were brimming with coin. He had expected Stryker to keep the trove in one place, for only a fool would trust the marquess not to skim the cream for himself, but it was still an exquisite feeling to have his instincts proved right. Yet he had not been able to fling open the double doors to the tune of Kovac's Teutonic tones echoing around the Old House amid a great Parliamentarian victory. He had not been able to hitch his compatriot's horse to the wagon and drag it out of the estate while Waller's victorious men rampaged in search of blood and loot and women. None of that had come to pass, and he had been left hoping and praying for a miracle.

Two days, he estimated, had passed since the end of the assault, though it was difficult to tell. Only the constant, tortuous drip of water down one of the slimy chalk walls gave him company as he sparingly gnawed his way through the snapsack-load of provisions. More worrying had been water, for the flask he had brought only contained enough for a couple of days, but the rain had kept the slick walls well irrigated, and he had found he could syphon enough to survive. At his lowest moments, when his mind played tricks and his ears echoed with hollow voices whispering promises that this place would be his tomb, he wondered at the audacity it had taken to steal the gold from under Royalist noses. Mocked himself for the very hope that he might relieve Stryker of his great prize a second time by hiding here, locked away, awaiting a rescue that had not materialized. But the mission, from conception to the coast, from stormy seas to the search of Scilly's windswept islands and all the way back to the mainland, had been fraught with risk and danger and cost. Diving into this clammy hole on the chance that General Waller could reduce the Marquess of Winchester's estate to rubble was just one more risk upon many. One more leap of faith. And that was the crux of it. Tainton still had, albeit in an oblique way, possession of the treasure, and his faith was undaunted and undeterred. Tainton had come too far for the King of Kings to abandon him now. So he prayed, sitting in the darkness, gnawing on salt pork, sipping gritty water from the excavated chalk, and waiting for Sir William Waller to arrive.

CHAPTER 26

Basing House, Hampshire, 12 November 1643

The Parliamentarian army returned just before noon. It was Sunday, and Stryker's men had joined the soldiers commanded by Rawdon, Peake and Johnson in the fan-shaped entrance-yard outside the Old House for a sermon delivered by a dark-browed preacher who seemed intent on describing hell's torments in gratuitous detail. The men had formed up in ranks behind their colours, flanked by sergeants and officers, as a strong breeze buffeted them, and they had dutifully kept their silence as their mortal souls were harangued. In the panelled luxury of the New House, a similar but very distinct service was undertaken as Basing's Catholic contingent reflected upon their own salvation, Sir John Paulet's priests – the men with perhaps most to lose were they ever to be taken by the rebels – performing their tasks as God's anointed conduits.

It was as both sides of the religious divide filed out into the daylight to become one again that the men on the precariously damaged towers of the Great Gatehouse began to ring their bells. The rooftops and walls, turrets and bastions were quickly lined with folk all staring northwards, searching the skyline as unit after unit of infantry, cavalry and dragoons swarmed over Cowdrey's Down, along the River Loddon, and into Basing village.

Paulet himself was amongst his people, beseeching God for strength and calling orders that, though superfluous given Rawdon's fastidious preparations, served to bolster the morale of the frightened population. The marchioness was there, too, skirts whirling as she swept through the nervous crowds with words of encouragement and fortitude. They looked to the sky, prayed for rain, but, though the sun was entirely cloaked in a murky grey miasma, no merciful droplets fell.

—— m ——

Sir William Waller rode his horse along the crest of Cowdrey's Down, letting it follow the camber so that, when he was twenty yards off the summit, he drew up and dismounted. He could feel the earth tremble at his feet. All around, to the east, west and south, dense blocks of infantry were on the move. From up here, a little way along from where his ordnance were already being unhitched from their teams of horses, he could see the brigades shift in and out of formation as they found their places within the trio of divisions that would encircle the house. It was strange being back here, in almost the exact spot from which he had witnessed the crumbling of the first attack, and yet now, on this windswept Sabbath, with the words of morning sermons still fresh in their ears, his men would right the wrongs of five days ago. There was no option but to persist in the enterprise; Waller had a reputation to rebuild. He had been Parliament's shining light in the early days, its dynamic alternative to the lethargic caution of the Earl of Essex. But Roundway Down had changed all that: Waller was no longer the rebellion's star, his brilliance eclipsed by the man he despised most in the world. He badly needed a victory, and quickly, for Hopton's new army was said to be on the move somewhere to the west.

'Beef, Sir William?' an aide was saying. Waller heard the words, but was not truly listening. Instead he laughed. 'Sir William? Would you like beef or chicken?'

Waller looked at the aide. 'I am sorry, Harold. A thought took my mind elsewhere.'

The aide looked nonplussed. 'General?'

'It is no secret that I do not share friendship with His Excellency.'

The aide's eyelid fluttered gently. 'No, General, it is not.'

'And nor is my friendship with Lord Hopton a matter of concealment.'

'No, sir, nor is it.'

Waller laughed again. 'Does the irony not amuse you? I must defeat Hopton in order to regain my position at Westminster, a position begrudged by Lord Essex.' He shook his head at the wonder of it. 'I must thrash my friend to confound my enemy.'

The aide nodded sagely. 'But you must reduce Basing Castle before you may engage your friend in battle.'

'Aye,' Waller said. It was not strictly true, for he could abandon Basing altogether and march directly upon Hopton, but his troops were raw, untried, and their only experience of warfare thus far had been the inept failure to hold the Grange, followed by days and days of rain-sodden inertia. Mutiny, he suspected, was not far from their minds, and he needed a resounding victory at Basing to bolster their resolve. 'We will break the malignants this time, Harold. Are the siege items dispersed amongst the brigades?'

'The supplies you requested from the capital have been sown like seeds, Sir William. Each of the three divisions possesses ladders to span ditches and scale walls; they have petards aplenty and certain units were given grenadoes. The reserve dragooners have also arrived.' He held out a hand, palm flattened to the grey skies. 'We are ready for the escalade, Sir William, so long as the weather holds.'

They watched from the escarpment for another hour as Waller's cavalry deployed around the ruin of the Grange. They drew close to the long line of walls hemming New House and Old House, staying just out of musket range, and began hurling abuse at the defenders lining the works. If the threats served to dampen Royalist spirits, then God would surely forgive.

A man in civilian clothing, golden hair sprouting beneath a felt hat, came up from the direction of the ordnance, sweating atop a piebald pony that seemed to struggle with both the gradient and his vast weight. His jowls and midriff wobbled alarmingly as he reined in a dozen yards from Waller, sliding ungracefully out of the saddle, and waddled the last paces to his general. He bowed low. 'Sir William.'

Waller touched a finger to his hat. 'Larsson. What news?'

'The big gatehouse, Sir William?' Larsson asked in heavily accented English as he swept back an arm to point down at the fortress.

'You are my chief gun captain, Mister Larsson,' Waller replied, raking his gaze over the enemy earthworks and mentally gauging its weak points. 'I did not bring you all the way from Stockholm to ignore your advice. What say you?'

Larsson rubbed his fleshy chin. Blue eyes, deep-set within puffy sockets, swivelled round to regard the Royalist target. 'Took its lashes well the last time, did it not?' He shrugged. 'Still it stands.'

Waller nodded. 'My thoughts, indeed. And it'll be empty now, if Lord Paulet has a grain of sense.'

'So?'

'So the marquess and his Romish court will be in the New House, I shouldn't wonder,' Waller said. 'Concentrate your fire there.'

Larsson's many chins trembled in acknowledgement, and he fished in his pockets for a pair of woollen balls. He shot the general a wry smile, promptly inserting them into his ears. 'As you wish, Sir William.'

—m—

'Where's your Hopton?'

'I heard he had his eyeballs singed out at Bath Fight!'

'God put 'em out for consortin' with Papists!'

The cavalrymen down in the village erupted in furious laughter. They had come from the north-west, a poison-tongued vanguard to soften the resolve of Basing's beleaguered inhabitants before the real business got underway, and they trotted out in groups from the protection of the timber-framed homes to within earshot of Garrison Gate, amusing themselves with ill-natured jibes and an assortment of colourful taunts.

Stryker stood with Skellen and Barkworth on the rampart to the east of the gateway. Below him, to his left, was the road from where the unfortunate forlorn hope had launched their abortive charge before the rain had come to interrupt the conflict, while to his right, protecting the corner of the New House, was Rawdon's new ditch and staked earthen palisade, curving in the shape of a half-moon. The ongoing Parliamentarian manoeuvres made it difficult to know exactly where troops were best placed, and the defenders were spread ominously thin all around the walls and works.

'Too scared to fight us, you lubberly gang o' piss-a-breeches?' a trooper on a speckled grey shouted through funnelled palms.

'Prince Robber too busy swiving his poodle to help?' another of the riders bellowed, causing a ripple of raucous jeers from his comrades.

The chest-rattling din of an artillery piece broke the taunting. Its booming report shattered the early afternoon, sending rooks and blackbirds skywards from an autumn-stripped copse at the side of the village, flapping and wheeling and squawking in terror. The inhabitants of Basing House collectively held their breath. Together with the horsemen outside and the infantry still shuffling around the fortress perimeter, they looked up at Cowdrey's Down, to where a tell-tale pall of dirty vapour pulsed up and out. The shot, when its arc took it out of the murky ether to plummet on to the sprawling estate, did no damage at all. It screamed as it came down, slicing the air with cruel intent, but the aim was high, the trajectory off, and it slammed into the belly of the ditch on Basing's south-eastern fringe. Waller had ten heavy guns on the hill, and now they all followed the leader; nine more guttural belches spewing racing smoke from the black barrels, nine more cacophonous eruptions. Two hit home, both thudding into roofs within the New House. Someone screamed. Dozens of unarmed individuals, corralled and put into teams by Marmaduke Rawdon during the rainy interlude, went immediately to work clearing rubble and seeking casualties, while the officers issued orders to their men, preparing them for what the day was sure to bring.

Stryker noticed that the shouts from down on the road had ceased with the opening of the bombardment. Indeed, it looked as though Waller's cavalry were mustering further back, as if preparing to clear the way for something more meaningful. He caught Skellen's eye. 'They will storm.'

'Made a swine's ballocks of it last time, sir,' Skellen said, staring up at the hill where the gun-crews scurried like so many ants as they reloaded their pieces.

'He is nae treadin' the same path,' Barkworth's croak answered for Stryker. He was pointing directly east, where, even as the artillery roared into life once more, a large body of musketeers were slowly marching, heading south. 'They're surroundin' the place. Doin' things properly.'

'Sounds like you're pleased,' Skellen grumbled.

Barkworth shrugged. 'If I'm gonnae fight someone, I want to respect him.'

The bulk of the Parliamentary force was still concentrated on the north flank, around the river and the village, but they had formed two distinct bodies of men. The third group, a thousand or thereabouts, were moving at pace towards the Park via the east. 'He leaves two divisions on the north side,' Stryker said, 'The others circle to our rear. This is no dash across the Grange, but a planned advance.'

'Jesu,' Skellen muttered. 'We ain't got enough lads to cover the walls, sir.'

'It'll be a hard day's work,' Stryker agreed bluntly. 'Unless Hopton appears on the horizon.'

'Do not hold your breath,' a woman's voice cut in suddenly, making all three turn in surprise. 'No, *mon amour*, do not hold your breath.'

—⚬—

A rider on a big mare, its head lashing irritably to the sides, cantered down from the top of the hill, past the rearguard troops, the grim pikemen in their dent-crumpled morions, and beyond a bank of artillery pieces that seethed gently as their crews reloaded. The wet ground splashed the beast's straggly fetlocks, a stream of sodden soil clumps flinging out behind. He veered left, away from the booming pieces, and headed towards a group of horsemen who examined the outline of Basing House through perspective glasses, mutters and nods punctuating their study. The bay drew up a few feet from the party, lifting its tail and defecating hugely as it stooped to champ at the churned grass.

Waller lowered his glass, lifted his face a fraction to see out from beneath the tilted brim of his hat, and eyed the newcomer coolly. 'Are your troopers ready, Major Kovac?'

'They are, sir,' Wagner Kovac said. His voice was calm enough, but inside he was in turmoil. It had all taken too long, he was sure. He had brought Waller, as promised, to Basing's walls. Had manipulated the general into an attack, and had watched with smug satisfaction as the forlorn hope had reached all the way to the main gates. But they had failed, the rain had come, and all had been lost. Yet now they were back, returned for another bite of the juiciest apple in all England. It was miraculous, wonderful, and, to Kovac, terrifying, for this time they simply had to succeed. 'My men will be with the rest of the horse, General.'

Waller nodded. 'All is well, then. And I shall thank Governor Norton personally for your service here.'

'Unnecessary, sir,' Kovac intoned piously, 'but appreciated.'

'The artillery will soften the place a while, then the foot and dragooners will storm,' Waller went on. 'The horse are to follow up. Pick off any fugitives as they run.'

'What of Hopton, sir?' a man spoke to Waller's left. He was saddled on a vast, muscular destrier, and was so encased in metal that he looked like a medieval knight.

Waller pursed his narrow lips, his moustache lifting in unison. 'Scouts report of a concentration of men at Kingsclere.'

'But that,' the iron-clad officer responded in surprise, 'is but eight or nine miles to the north and west of this place.'

'Stone's throw, Sir Arthur, aye,' Waller agreed. 'But it is not Hopton in person. Not his whole army. He is not yet ready to make his move. Thus, we must reduce the marquess before we are compelled to deal with the baron.'

Kovac cleared his throat. All eyes turned to him. It was an impudent thing to interrupt a council of war, but he could not bite his tongue when so much was at stake. 'What if we are delayed?'

'Then we shall withdraw,' Waller answered slowly, as if inviting his subordinate to challenge.

'You cannot.'

Waller's eyebrows climbed up to his fringe. 'Cannot, Major? Again, you seem to possess no control over that mouth of yours, sir.'

Kovac felt the collective stares like hot needles. He looked away. 'I apologize, General, but I am keen to reduce this Papist hovel.'

Waller picked at something in his teeth before turning back to watch his troops move below. 'See that you remain courteous in my presence, sir, or you will find I am less forgiving in future.'

Kovac could not help himself. Talk of withdrawal was simply too much to bear. 'Merely—'

Now Waller eased his mount round to face the Croat. 'Oh?'

Kovac breathed deeply. 'Merely, Sir William, I would urge you attack. Forget the bombardment, it wastes valuable time. We cannot retreat under any circumstance.'

Heselrige's gauntleted hand went to the hilt of his sword. 'How dare you, sir!'

'Hold, Sir Arthur,' Waller said calmly. He addressed Heselrige, though the knowing smile he gave was aimed at Kovac. 'The good major, here, is unconcerned with military tactics, Sir Arthur, for he believes a cache of gold lies under Paulet's floorboards.'

Heselrige frowned. 'Then why have we not been informed?'

'That is my quandary,' Waller said. 'It cannot be so important if Whitehall has not informed me of its presence.'

'They do not know it is here, Sir William,' Kovac argued, though he knew he convinced no one.

Waller shook his head. One of the batteries further along the escarpment opened up, shaking the earth, and he was forced to hold his peace until the shots were away. 'We shall pound their walls until two of the clock. That is the long and short of it, Major Kovac. Only then will we unleash the foot.'

Kovac had come to understand that calm delivery of an opinion went a long way with the sanguine Waller. But now he could see that his plans risked unravelling for the sake of rank idleness. He balled his hands into fists. 'We must attack now, General.'

Heselrige went so crimson it looked as though his eyeballs would fill with blood. Waller set his jaw tightly. 'You overstep, man.'

'Now, General, I beg of you,' Kovac persisted. If Hopton's forces were truly gathering so close, every hour was crucial. 'We already let slip the morn for the sake of sermonizing.'

'I will not deny the men their chance to make peace with God, Major,' Waller retorted acidly, 'and I would warn you to keep a hold of your runaway tongue.'

But Kovac was too desperate to have his voice heeded. 'Now we bombard when we ought to scale their cursed works.' He pointed to the huge bodies of men that were slowly inching round the house to the steady rhythm of drums. 'Send them at the castle now, sir. Break it down.'

There was silence for a time. Kovac and Waller regarded one another coldly, while Heselrige seemed to boil within his suit of heavy plate. The rest found themselves staring uncomfortably down at Basing House.

'I am to lead the assault,' Waller said eventually. 'My regiment is down there, and I will be at their head when they march to battle.' He pointed at Kovac. 'You will be there too, Major.'

'Sir?'

'You are a good fighter, so I am led to believe, and you, it seems, have the hottest blood when it comes to talk of a storming.' With a jerk of his chin he indicated the infantry divisions on the other side of the river. 'Down there you will find the London Trained Bands. They are green as grass, inexperienced. They would welcome good officers. You will join them forthwith.'

That startled Kovac, and he found himself scrabbling for a reply. 'Sir, I—'

Waller's raised palm cut him off. 'I care not the brigade to which you might attach yourself, but attach yourself you shall. They will be first into the breach, Major, first to wet their blades and first inside Lord Paulet's opulent warren. It is what you have been yearning for, sir, so get down off that horse and get to work.'

—◇◇◇—

The bombardment continued as the rebel divisions edged their way into position. Not all of Waller's troops were involved, for, from their vantage point on the north wall, Stryker and his men could see well enough the pikemen waiting in rows on Cowdrey's Down, turning the hillock into a vast, spiked beast. At the foot of the hill, on the far side of the river, were several troops of horse and dragoons, and these, with the carefully arrayed pikes, served to remind the defenders just what awaited them should a breach be made. But the men who would first exploit any cannon-ripped hole, or, indeed, tear down the rampart with their own hands should Waller give the order, were musketeers. Their banners danced and snapped in the wind, rising like colourful sails from the deep rows of soldiers who gradually took up places at what were evidently three designated points. The first and second divisions, as expected, had remained on the north and north-east, and would, it seemed, put their vigour into assaulting the New House and the main gate that they had previously, and impotently, reached. The last division curved all the way round to the high, flat land of Basing Park, and they looked to be preparing themselves to make an assay against the Old House. Colonel Rawdon, with Paulet relentlessly barking instructions, demands and questions in his ear, soon found himself a mount and went about the home turned castle at almost a gallop. Stryker wondered if the decision to command from the saddle was purely military in nature, or whether it was simply a relief to be away from the marquess's haranguing voice. Either way, it was a fruitful choice, for Rawdon seemed to be everywhere at once, organizing the men on the earthworks, checking on fieldpieces and ensuring the walls were covered as well as could be.

Stryker and Lisette left the men near Garrison Gate and went down to the Old House to check on the gold.

'Have you seen Tainton?' she asked him as they picked their way through the rubble that still littered the archway through the Great Gatehouse.

'Not a trace.'

He sensed her staring up at him as they walked, trying to catch his eye. 'You've been searching?'

'We have,' Stryker lied. In truth he had barely had time to think, so embroiled had he become in the defence of the house. 'Where have you been?'

'Amesbury. Disguised as an apple seller.'

'To Hopton?'

She nodded. 'To Hopton.'

'And?'

'And now I stink of apples, while Hopton ponders.'

Stryker stopped. They were almost at the slope that led down to the abandoned vault they had claimed for the Cade fortune, but now he held her shoulders, hope surging through his veins. 'Ponders?'

'He comes hither, *mon amour*, but not until he can rendezvous with reinforcements.'

The word hit Stryker like a punch in the jaw. He felt dizzy, sick. 'Reinforcements?' he spluttered. 'Jesu, Lisette, he must have enough men to frighten Waller off. To lift this damned siege.'

Her mouth curved down at the corners to suggest that his questioning was foolish. 'He does not wish to. Not to the detriment of his shiny new army. So he awaits reinforcements from Reading. Only then will he save Basing.'

Stryker released her, stepping back and rubbing a dirty hand over his eye. 'If they take too long there will be nothing to save.'

'I do not think Hopton loses sleep on that matter. He has fear in his eyes.'

'He had no such fear at Stratton Fight.'

'Injuries alter a man.'

Stryker had already drawn breath to launch another bitter diatribe, but her shrewd thrust pushed the words back down his throat. How could he argue with one of the few living people to have witnessed Stryker's own horror, to have held his hand as the chirurgeons pieced together what was left of his eye socket, to have nursed him and cradled him and changed his dressings and whispered that everything would be just fine. The attack that had taken his eye had left an ineradicable mark on Stryker. It had changed him, and, for a time at least, he too had been ruled by fear. He stared at his boots, unable to hold Lisette's hard blue gaze. 'Did you tell him of the gold?'

She nodded. 'When finally his fawning bloody advisors gave us peace, and that is why he has promised to lift the siege, but he will not risk defeat, not even for the treasure.'

'Then we truly are alone.'

She nodded. 'For some days, I think. That is why we must help Rawdon, Stryker. Basing must hold if we are to take the gold to Oxford.'

Stryker almost laughed at the notion that they alone might change the course of the impending tribulation. But she was right, he saw. There was no option but to fight, so it was imperative that they fought well. 'When did you return?'

'I slipped in just after dawn.' She clearly read his irritation, for she allowed herself a tiny smile. 'You begrudge me passing Hopton's reply to Lord Winchester?' she chided. Then she crossed herself. 'And it is Sunday. I have been at my devotions.'

He could hardly argue with that, so he led her to the slope instead. 'I am glad you are well, Lisette.'

She shrugged and nodded down towards the wide doors set into the Gatehouse foundations. 'The gold?'

'Safe.' He lifted his hat to acknowledge the sentinels that stood with primed muskets at the foot of the slope. 'The twins stand guard.'

'*Bon*,' she said simply, waving at Jack and Harry Trowbridge. 'I should like to go in. Take a look at what it is we have struggled so hard to protect.'

Stryker was about to agree when shouts came from the looming towers above them. The Great Gatehouse had been abandoned as a residence after Waller's first attack, but lookouts maintained their vigil from the turrets, the views unassailable in all directions. Their voices were strained, urgent, and Stryker immediately left Lisette where she stood. Because, finally, Waller's infantry divisions were on the move.

Near St Mary Bourne, Hampshire, 12 November 1643

General Sir Ralph Hopton could hear the gunfire. It sounded like very distant thunder, ebbing and flowing on the wind, distorted by hill and vale. He sat on a low stool within his campaign tent drinking smoke from a pipe decorated with holly-leaf motifs. A clerk with blackened fingertips and rheumy eyes was hunched over an adjacent table waiting for the next dictation. But Hopton could not think of anything but the bombardment that raged just a few miles to the east. He hated himself for not intervening.

The tent flap rustled as a sentry hauled it back, and Hopton looked round to see the youthful face of a man he knew well. 'Lord Percy.'

Henry Percy was dressed in a suit entirely cut from thick buff hide, the breeches trimmed with white lace and mud-spattered from a hard ride. His helmet, in the crook of his arm, was of the Dutch style, with a single, sliding nasal bar, and around his waist a lavish red scarf was fastened with an enormous knot at the small of his back. Percy's face was narrow and sharp, his chin cleanly shaven and his eyes turned down slightly at the corners in a manner that made him seem always to be amused. 'How now, my lord?'

Hopton stood to offer the usual pleasantries. 'I thank you for answering my summons.'

'Dispatched by His Majesty's word, General.' Percy shook himself rapidly, as if he were a dog, to shake the tangles from his curled black hair. 'My horsemen are ready and willing. We will teach that villain Waller a few lessons.' He cocked his head to the sound of the cannon fire. 'And are we to follow our ears?'

'We are, sir,' said Hopton. 'We must relieve Basing House as soon as is opportune.'

Percy frowned. 'Is it not opportune this very moment, sir?'

'We await one final piece for our board.' Hopton paused to suck gently at his pipe, easing the fragrant smoke out through his nostrils. 'Sir Jacob Astley. He brings nine hundred foot from Reading to Kingsclere. My vanguard awaits him there already. The rest of the army shall march thither on the morrow.'

'We have not the numbers without Sir Jacob?' Percy pressed.

'Not quite,' Hopton said, and he was forced to turn away lest the young Cavalier read the doubt in his face. He returned to his seat. 'With the nine hundred I will be sure of victory. Basing is well defended, it will hold a while yet.'

'So be it, sir,' Lord Percy said, though his disquiet was evident.

Hopton forced himself to smile in an effort to show the supreme confidence he had lost at Lansdown. He needed it back if he was ever to challenge Waller in the field again, which meant he needed a victory, however small. And that meant making certain that he had enough men to relieve the siege. He would wait for Astley, no matter how long it took, and pray that the defenders of Basing House could hold out just a little longer.

CHAPTER 27

Basing House, Hampshire, 12 November 1643

A ll three Roundhead divisions attacked at once. The batteries up on the hill fell silent for the first time in two hours,
to be replaced by musketry rattling along Basing's north and
south-western flanks. It was a mass escalade, comprising a trio
of densely packed wedges juddering forth from both sides of the
estate, striding towards the Royalist stronghold simultaneously
like three leviathans, ensigns rippling like so many horns at the
snout. The leviathans roared as they crawled to war, chants of
God and Parliament rising in crashing waves to drown out the
defenders' sporadic shots, drawn blades held aloft by officers,
glinting like bared teeth.

Stryker had gone straight back to Garrison Gate. It was
effectively the fortress's chief entrance, and it seemed logical
that at least one of the three enemy divisions would concentrate their efforts on its destruction. When he reached the
rampart, he saw that he was correct. One body was further to
the west, surging through the charred remains of the Grange,
but another had gathered its men and guns amongst the leaning stems of the copse that formed a hedge between Basing
House and its attendant village. Their fieldpieces were small –
sakers and drakes, Stryker guessed – and not powerful enough
to make a practicable breach in the defences, but the latter
were mounted on timber-shielded wagons so that they could
be brought up at very close range to harry the walls. This they
did as the division shifted and morphed in and out of line, the

399

ranks organized into attack formation by screaming sergeants. Stryker could see Waller's personal standard in the pulsing lines of men, and he wondered if the general himself was joining the fray. The bulk of the division, however, was made up of men in red and yellow coats.

'See the colour?' Colonel Marmaduke Rawdon's gruff voice rumbled.

Rawdon had climbed up to stand next to him, and now he used his sword tip to point at a vast square of red taffeta in the van of the division. 'Spangled with silver stars, yes?'

'Aye, sir.'

'That is the Westminster Regiment.'

'Trained bands,' Stryker said.

'Indeed. I once served with them.'

Stryker was taken aback. 'And you're happy now to kill them?'

'I am, Captain. For my king, I most certainly am.' He indicated the yellowcoats. 'Those men are the St Katherine's Regiment. Better known as the Tower Hamlets Auxiliaries.'

Stryker drew breath to speak but paused as one of the wagons carrying the drakes erupted its flame, its shots splintering brickwork at the side of the gateway. 'They're raw.'

Rawdon nodded. 'And they've been out in the rain for days. Keep at them, Stryker. Hammer them as hard as you may, for they shall not stand.'

'Me, sir?'

The colonel was already half-way down the ladder, and he looked up briefly. 'I go to consult with his lordship. Colonel Peake holds the north-west corner, and Johnson the south. You command Garrison Gate, Stryker. Keep the bastards out.'

'You have heard the news of Hopton?'

'He comes hither!' Rawdon shouted as he resumed his descent. 'But not quick enough to change this day, Captain. So we must keep them out!'

With that, Rawdon was gone, and Stryker reviewed his new command. Garrison Gate was a brick archway, the doors built in solid oak. Rawdon had cleaved a half-moon earthwork around its outer face, from which a dozen musketeers were already firing into the copse, and had used the spoil to buttress the gate on its inner face. The walls on either side were only a brick and a half thick, but they were lined with musketeers who added their own fire to that offered from the half-moon. He looked left and right, counting his contingent in groups of five, and quickly understood that he had around a hundred men, Rawdon's yellows in the main, interspersed with his handful of greencoats. It was not many to withstand a thousand, but they had the defences and the height, while the Londoners would be forced to plunge into the open ground if they wished to scale the walls.

The drakes blasted into life again, their collective recoil sending the armoured wagons rolling back by ten yards or more. The Parliamentarians in the copse cheered. Away to his left, Stryker saw that their sister division was on the move, surging through the Grange to swarm on to the road. He silently prayed that Lieutenant-Colonel Peake's men knew what they were about. Now the massed ranks in the copse came at a swift walk, their banners unfurled, jutting from the front of each company and regiment like the figureheads of flamboyant privateer frigates. Stryker ordered a volley, and his men obliged, the wall opening up in a rippling cascade of flame and smoke and noise. One or two Parliamentarians in the foremost rank fell, snatched back with spraying blood and gnashing teeth, but the range was too great to take a heavy toll. Stryker did not care, and he bellowed for his men to reload. It was enough to pour lead into Waller's advancing force in the hope that they would begin to think twice about this deadly march.

'Give 'em hell, lads!' he screamed. He crouched, making his own musket ready. Skellen and Barkworth were on either side, and they did likewise. 'Shoot the bastards! Send them back to Parliament with lead in their bellies and piss in their britches!'

He stood, fired his musket, and waved the smoke away so that he might see the enemy more rapidly. It was then that he saw the ladders.

'What is it, sir?' Skellen was saying as he thumbed open a powder box hanging from his bandolier.

Stryker nodded towards the column's right flank. 'As we feared, they are prepared.'

Skellen squinted down on to the enemy. They were close now, perhaps thirty paces from the half-moon, and he too saw the group of redcoats who hefted about a score of ladders between them. 'Shit the bed.'

'Look at the greys further back,' Stryker said. 'Dragooners, perhaps.'

Skellen swore again. 'They've got petards.'

So Waller had truly resolved to conduct matters professionally; there would be no chaotic milling beside Garrison Gate this time. They had the means to blow breaches in the walls and, failing that, to climb right over them. He went to make ready his musket, for there was no alternative but to fight.

Tainton wondered if his eyes were ruined. They were far from perfect following the slow cooking in hot tar, but now, after so many days in a dark chamber, he wondered whether they might cease to function at all. At least, he reflected, the dried beef smelled appetizing as he gnawed his way through the tough shreds, his rump numb on the damp, uneven chalk of the floor. At his lowest ebb he had let doubts assail him, barrack him, bully his resolve. Would Waller come back? Would he be trapped in this God-forsaken hole for ever? But he had heard the booming salvos of heavy artillery, and his soldier's ear told him that the echoing reports came from outside, firing in. In that moment he knew that Kovac had succeeded, Waller had returned, and nothing about this place was forsaken by God.

He finished the last scraps of meat, stood up so that the spurs jangled satisfyingly, reminding him that he had once been a warrior, and went to the door. It was time to find out if his eyes still worked.

The half-moon fell quickly. Simply overwhelmed, Stryker's dozen men in the curving earthwork scrambled free after their last shots were discharged, bolting back to the walls and heaving each other up to the safe embrace of hands dangled from the rampart, a stream of bullets smacking into the wall around them, flattening to leaden discs as splinters showered in all directions. The fire was deadly now. They were still undaunted on the ramparts on either side of Garrison Gate, but two Parliamentarian divisions had reached the ring-work and were offering volley fire all across their fighting front so that it was difficult for the Royalists to so much as show their faces to fire back. All along the rampart they were crouched low, backs flattened against the damp bricks, hurriedly reloading muskets and easing them through the crenellated parapet to shoot without aiming. But the attack had stalled, for the rebel fieldpieces had failed to make any real breaches and they were reluctant to charge directly at the walls. Instead they milled out in the open, their sheer weight of numbers forcing Royalist heads down for protection, but they were unable to make ground.

Stryker risked a peek over the rampart. The road to his left was teeming with Roundhead soldiers, while at the north-east corner, his corner, they had occupied the half-moon, firing at almost no range up at the gate. A regimental standard had been planted there, on the half-moon, and the case of drakes had been dragged up beside it. All the while ladders were being shifted to the front, passed from hand to hand through the dense ranks like buckets of water from well to fire. Stryker ordered more muskets to be trained on the men at the ladders in order to pick them off and slow their passage to the front, but not enough were loaded and primed. The defensive fire was sporadic at best, lone pot-shots offered as thick volleys flung in response at a frighteningly constant rate.

'There's too fuckin' many!' Skellen was shouting away to his left. 'Too many!'

Stryker had no answer. 'Hold! We hold this damned wall or we die trying!'

The shrill cry of a horse came from below and behind, and Stryker twisted round to see an officer canter to the base of the wall. He hurriedly dismounted, not bothering to tether the handsome white beast, and scrambled up the scaffolding. 'Here to help!'

'You are?' Stryker asked, crouching again.

'Lieutenant Hunter, sir. Colonel Rawdon asked me to lend my pistol, which I do with gladness!'

The officer was young, no more than sixteen or seventeen, and his expensive clothes and ostentatiously feathered hat sat well with a fresh face and brilliant white teeth. Stryker laughed at the absurd courage that came with youth. 'Then get to it, Mister Hunter!'

Hunter beamed, reminding Stryker with a sudden pang of sadness of Andrew Burton, and jerked his pistol from his belt. He stood, cocked the piece and pulled the trigger. Hammer and frizzen met in a bright spark, but the pan fizzed pathetically, no ball issuing from its black maw, and the lieutenant frowned. 'Damned flash in the pan, sir. What rotten luck!'

The bullet took Hunter in the jaw, tearing half of it away and leaving the other half ragged and lolling. For a moment the lieutenant seemed to sway, his eyes wide in pure disbelief, his grin left in place in a macabre parody of what it had been a heartbeat before. He seemed to be trying to speak, but nothing but scarlet bubbles came from his throat. Stryker was left to stare up at the gaping mess, blood dripping on the boards between them, and then Hunter crumbled. It was as if the bones had melted within his legs, his torso caving in above, and he toppled back without a sound, only narrowly missing his horse as he hit the ground.

'Jesu,' Stryker whispered, but he was immediately ripped from his morbid reverie by a rough shake of his shoulder. He looked back to see Skellen squatting against the stone, just allowing the top half of his head above the rampart.

'They're blowin' the gates, sir.'

Stryker turned and inched up to see for himself. Sure enough, two men had scrambled beyond the half-moon and approached Garrison Gate. Under the protection of a fierce covering fire from their red and yellow comrades, they were hurriedly fixing the bell-shaped explosive to the doors. The fuse would be lit in moments.

'Water, sir?' Skellen asked. 'Dowse that bloody match?'

'No time,' Stryker replied. Then a thought struck him. The gates were heavily packed with earth on their inner face, a fact unbeknownst to the storming party and their petardiers. He dropped the musket, cupping hands around his mouth. 'Leave them!' he screamed along the inside of the wall. 'Leave the petard! Load your weapons! Load your weapons and mark me well!' Rawdon's men were slow to respond, for the order to cease fire seemed so incongruous in such a hot fight, but they did as they were told nevertheless. Stryker looked at the nonplussed face of his sergeant. 'They've picked the wrong place, Will. The wall is thin, the doors thick.'

The petard exploded in a shower of earth and timber, a bright tongue of flame licking up at the arch and back towards the half-moon. Smoke billowed in crazed jets, rounded and rising in every direction like a crop of mushrooms, and a thick pall settled around Garrison Gate. Stryker was lying on his front, belly scraped by the rough wood, looking not at the doors but at the earthen buttress. As he had predicted, it was too high, too deep and too dense for the petard to destroy. The soil, wet as it was, simply absorbed the power, and though the outer wooden slats of the doors had almost certainly fractured, they did not cave inwards.

He stood now. The fire from the roadside had ebbed, for all Parliamentarian eyes were on the gate, desperate to see through the gritty miasma left by their petard, eager to witness the breach that they so dearly needed. And so he fired. His bullet killed an officer in the half-moon, making men tear their eyes away from the misty doors and towards the rampart, and he bellowed a challenge. His greencoats, joined by Rawdon's men at the same instant, rose to their feet as one, and as one they fired. The volley ripped down upon the half-moon, the road and the copse further back, mud spurting as balls hit the earth. It enfiladed the

Londoners, who were already realizing that their petard had failed. There was no breach. They had far superior numbers, but now they would have to use the ladders, pushing them up against high walls that were lined with killers. Even as the Royalist volley ebbed away, Stryker was ordering his charges to reload, because now the day turned on courage, or the lack thereof. He knew that the petard would have worked perfectly had it been fixed to the wall, but luck had been on his side, and the explosion had done nothing except dampen Roundhead hopes. These were not seasoned troops, and he wagered that the failure of the petard would have a greater effect than any number of defenders on the smoke-wreathed rampart.

His men were quickly ready. They stood again, emboldened now, for still the shots from down on the road were desultory and ill-timed. The Parliamentarian storming parties had come up to the walls again, and again they had failed to find a way into the fortress. They were uncertain, shoaling tentatively before their braying officers like trout beneath a looming shadow, and then, step by step, they began to move backwards.

The Royalists jeered. They kept loading, kept firing, chanting always for the King and for God, and their enemy, so vast and unstoppable, kept inching away from the walls. One of Rawdon's yellows was hit, toppling over the rampart to crunch sickeningly on to the road below, but the rest seemed impervious to the hurried and poorly aimed shots that came their way.

'*Fire!*' an officer on the wall shouted, a dozen muskets rattling at the call.

'*Fire!*' someone further down towards Peake's section screamed, perhaps a score of shots tearing out in answer.

Stryker's musket was ready again. 'Fire, you bastards! *Fire!*' He pulled his trigger as men on either side of him did the same, smoke slewing in bitter gouts all around them.

The great wave had smashed against rocks that had proved immovable, and it was rolling back now, retreating to the sea even as orders came to stem its flow. Drums hammered hard, issuing commands to renew the assault, but the division that had failed at Garrison Gate was not to be coerced any further, and, to rapturous cheers from the ravaged rampart, the second division seemed to be following suit. All along the northern wall the tide was turning, and so long as the men in the front ranks were refusing to fight, their comrades further back could not be brought into the fray. Thus the huge fire-power the division possessed was rendered utterly impotent.

Captain Lancelot Forrester had been asked to lend his experience to the men defending the south-western approach. There were two guard towers set into the wall along this section, flat-roofed but defended by crenellations that jutted like a gap-toothed grin, and it was from one of these higher platforms that Forrester watched the enemy advance. He was with two lieutenants, a Captain Le Saux, Major Lawrence and a handful of yellow-coated musketeers. Rawdon's men were Londoners in the main, and they knew the colours of the rebel regiments almost as well as they knew their own. They named the companies as they came up before the house, spitting malice towards the attackers with the distilled venom only ever reserved for those who had once been neighbours.

The shape of the attack quickly became clear. From his vantage point, Forrester could see the column, perhaps a thousand strong, trundle to the heavy rhythm of their drums in two distinct groups. The first, half the total complement, formed a vanguard, and he guessed these men would be the forlorn hope. One of Rawdon's corporals, on the rooftop beside Forrester, identified the largest colour – green, with wavy golden rays – as that of the Cripplegate Auxiliary Regiment, the inexperienced men and boys of Waller's new army, the cannon-fodder who would be first into action, sacrificed to allow the second section, the veteran companies, to scale the walls in relative safety. The second group marched, but they were fifty paces behind. They would be the assault troops when the dirty business of crossing the earthworks and pushing ladders against the wall had been done by men Waller could afford to lose.

As on the north-eastern corner, a half-moon ditch and staked palisade protected the wall, with a second ditch – the ancient castle's dry moat – immediately below the high brick facade. The Cripplegates came on, the crackle of musketry and ordnance vibrating down from the north, seemingly heralding their arrival.

'Christ,' Frederick Lawrence hissed at Forrester's side. He wore his armour, as if he were ready to mount his horse at any moment, though of course this fight was not for Paulet's harque-busiers. 'Hear it?'

'I hear it,' Forrester responded brusquely.

Lawrence twisted back to look towards the opposite corner of the embattled estate, but he could see nothing beyond the New House rooftops and the thick swirling smoke that seemed to shroud everything. 'Will they hold?'

Forrester ignored him and bellowed at the men on the walls to make ready. He looked at Lawrence. 'Where is the gun-crew?'

'Gun-crew?'

'Major,' Forrester snapped. He pointed to the tower to their right, thirty yards along the ring-work. It was lower than their own platform, still twice the height of the wall, and on its summit sat a small fieldpiece, its black barrel pointing skywards between its wheels. 'That falconet. Where is its crew?'

Lawrence turned to descend the spiral steps behind them. A torrent of shrill shouts replaced him, coming up from the stair-case, and it sounded to Forrester almost as if a flock of gulls were flying up from the ground below. He turned away from the advancing Londoners to see Lieutenant-Colonel Johnson appear on the rooftop, flanked and followed by almost a dozen women, the chief of whom, to Forrester's astonishment, was the Marchioness of Winchester herself, Lady Honora Paulet.

The marchioness was petite, her frame seemingly brittle, but her green eyes blazed beneath a fringe of black and silver ring-lets. 'Not possible? I'll thank you, Lieutenant-Colonel, not to tell me what is and what is not possible in my own home!'

Johnson's attention to his beard became more hurried still. 'I cannot permit you to remain on the wall, my lady.'

'Tripe!' she retorted, lodging her hands on the voluminous skirts at her hips. 'My ladies and I will remain here, on this very spot, sir, and you will have to carry us down one by one.'

Johnson could see that he was beaten, and he shook his head wearily. 'Please keep your heads down. His Lordship will have my skin for a scabbard should any harm befall you.'

The Marchioness of Winchester swept past him with an imperious wave, beckoning to her attendants. The women followed, lining the edge of the tower at either side of Forrester and the other men, who all bowed to Her Ladyship with barely concealed smirks. Forrester noted some of the women dragged large, lumpen cloth sacks, obviously heavy with whatever bounty was inside.

'Forrester,' Johnson said. He was still back at the hatch that led down to ground level. 'You'll join me.'

Forrester tore his gaze away from the formidable marchion-ess. 'Sir?'

'They'll be at the half-moon in moments. I would drive them off.'

Forrester felt himself tense. Johnson, he recalled, had been the man who had challenged Clinson to personal combat in the fight for the Grange, and would have lost his life were it not for Stryker's timely intervention. Not only was the man clearly reckless, but he had a reputation to restore, and the two ingredients made for a dangerous brew indeed. 'Drive them, sir? A sortie?'

'The same!' Johnson barked, his voice excited now that he had abandoned his ill-advised quarrel with Honora Paulet. 'My men are assembling below.'

'Is that wise, sir?'

'It is invaluable, sir! I have sent for support from the north wall, where the fight, by all accounts, goes well.'

Down below, a great cheer rose up as the forlorn hope reached the half-moon. The few Royalists left manning the earthwork scrambled away, fortunate that their enemies were more concerned with bringing up their cumbersome ladders than with flinging lead shot at their backs, and they dived into the dry moat, scrambling up under covering fire from the wall and squeezing through a small sally port that was quickly reblocked with wicker sheets, rubble and bits of old furniture. The Cripplegate Auxiliaries took up positions along the half-moon's palisade. They would use it as a breastwork from which to launch their escalade. They moved the ladders up quickly to the front rank, all the while supported by musketry that rang out from the rank behind. An ensign in a wide blue scarf stood on the half-moon, in full view of the Royalist sharpshooters, and called his men on, swirling the huge green banner above his head. More colours joined. Reds and yellows, smaller ones with various devices to denote each company, flooded the earthwork, hurling insults and lead at the section of wall that sat between two squat towers, and preparing for the final assault.

—⁂—

The Westminster Liberty Regiment was the largest of Waller's Trained Bands, and he had carved them up, placing most on the northern two divisions, spread evenly across the fighting front, while two companies had been ordered to the division at Basing Park. There, they had been ordered to the flanks of the greencoated auxiliaries, providing covering fire while the Cripplegate men moved their ladders to the fore.

It was with one of the Westminster companies, striding in the wake of a captain's red and silver banner, that Major Wagner Kovac was now positioned. He did not know what hurt him more; the fact that he had been reduced to a plodding infantryman, the dangerous reality of being ordered to storm a castle, or his enforced membership of the woefully under-trained and audibly disgruntled Trained Bands. The only poultice to his slight was the possibility of getting inside the fortress. There was gold in Basing, and he wanted it. But, far more important, a man named Lancelot Forrester was in there somewhere, and Forrester had a debt to pay.

Kovac's new red-coated unit came round to the eastern end of the captured sconce, making ready their muskets. Shots coughed from up on the wall. One man was torn back, bullets clattered off helmets and holes were ripped in the wind-flapped ensigns. The captain commanding the flanking unit ordered his front rank to fire, and a huge, rolling volley erupted all along their foremost line, sending the Royalists ducking low behind their brick shield. The men on the west flank fired too, just as the first men from Kovac's company peeled away to reload at the rear, the second rank stepping up to fire. Kovac was in the fourth rank. He scolded himself for his own idiocy. For his runaway mouth he had paid with a place in what the Dutch called the *verloren hoop*, and there was no option but to kill or be killed. He drew both his pistols, pulling them to half-cock, and waited his turn.

Stryker was overseeing steady, rolling volley fire from Basing's north-eastern corner as a party of musketeers edged out to retake the half-moon. There were casualties down amongst the storm-poles, and the Royalists dragged them back, plundering valuables, blades and ammunition before leaving them in a groaning line flush against the wall. They had time, for the threat had dissipated in a matter of seconds. The twin Round-head divisions had retreated to the village and Grange, recovered their order and formed neat ranks once more, but although drums rumbled throughout the flag-marked units the attack seemed to have completely run aground.

'A grand fight,' Colonel Marmaduke Rawdon decreed as he paced smartly along the rickety platform to shake Stryker's hand. 'Have we the beating of them, d'you think?'

Stryker rubbed soot from his stinging eye. 'Not yet, sir, but they're not comfortable out there.'

'*Ha!*' Rawdon brayed. 'We've put the fear of God into 'em, my boys!'

The men on the rampart gave a parched huzzah as ladders were dropped over the side for pairs of musketeers to set about collecting the casualties. Dead and severely wounded would be left until the gates could be safely opened, but Rawdon wanted the enemy's walking wounded taken inside for use at the bargaining table should parley be requested.

A runner reached the colonel as the first injured Roundheads were gathered up and cajoled at sword-point up the ladder. He doubled over, panting hard and bracing hands against his knees, only looking up when Stryker and Rawdon clambered down from the wall. 'Compliments of Lieutenant-Colonel Johnson, sir,' he said breathlessly.

'Well?' Rawdon prompted impatiently.

'The third division has taken the Old House half-moon, sir. The colonel would sally out, seeks reinforcements.'

Rawdon looked to Stryker. 'Can we spare the men?'

Stryker nodded. 'For now, sir. A score, or so.'

Rawdon nodded, pushing thick fingers through the matted grey of his hair. 'See to it, Mister Stryker. Take them down to the Old House. You'll need a dozen of mine to make up the numbers. Pick whomever you will.'

—⁂—

Roger Tainton unlocked the door carefully. He could hear the two guards muttering outside, their voices were only just audible above the din of battle that seemed now to come from all fronts. The skeleton key clicked as it turned, and then a deep clunk echoed about the chamber as the lock was released. He froze, jaw clenched, hearing his pulse rush in his ears. But no shouts of alarm rose shrill above the gunfire. He was only wearing one boot, the other was in his hand, and he let go of the key, taking the long, thin, double-edged dagger he had stolen near Petersfield from his waistband.

He could have rushed out, played upon the element of surprise, but the flinging doors might force them to retreat out of range, and it seemed better to go to work away from prying eyes. So he simply rapped his knuckles on the door and stepped back into the darkness.

The double doors opened almost immediately.

'Who's here?' a voice called from below the lintel.

'Just your imagination,' another man replied, his accent and tone remarkably similar to the first. Tainton remembered that the men were twins.

'Who unlocked the bloody door, then?'

Tainton tightened his grip on the dagger's octagonal handle. 'Help,' he whimpered.

The light at the doorway framed the two guards, making them seem gigantic. They walked gingerly into the room. 'Hello? Who's here? Show yourself.'

Tainton could only see one match-tip aglow, which meant they were not both able to give fire, and he thanked God for it as he leapt from the gloom. He went for the silhouette with the lit match, stabbing up at the musketeer's throat as he lunged, jamming the blade as hard as he could manage into flesh and muscle and sinew. He released the oak handle without another look, and brought his other arm up in a diagonal sweep before the second, stunned sentry. The man rocked backwards, and might have avoided the boot heel itself, but Tainton's bright, jagged spurs sliced through the middle of his face. His weapon clattered on the solid floor, hands sliding up to his face, and Tainton kicked him on to his haunches. Then he dropped the boot, picked up the discarded musket, and smashed down at the blood-blinded soldier with its solid wooden stock, bludgeoning through protective hands and wrists until he felt the softer crunch of nose and cheeks and eyes. It was over in seconds. The doors were wide open, daylight flooding the darkness, and Tainton ran to ground level, blinking in the unaccustomed brightness. There was no one.

He took a knee, hissed a prayer, and went back to close the doors. By now he had hoped to have seen Parliamentarian troops pouring over the rampart like a plague of rats. The note had been specific, his location clear. Kovac was to bring horses and soldiers to Tainton and together they would take the hoard out of the fortress in the chaos of the inevitable sack. He went back to the top of the slope, turning a circle on the spot, blood-drenched palm shielding his eyes. Nothing yet, though there seemed to be a fearsome exchange of fire down between the two towers on the south side. Perhaps the breach would be made there. It was irksome, but not problematic. He would simply have to await the inevitable victory.

Lisette was on one of the rear turrets of the Great Gatehouse and from here, with the lookouts and sharpshooters, she had jeered the advance of the divisions against Garrison Gate, and cheered their defeat. From this distance, with the smoke shroud thick and constantly scudding, it was difficult to make out individuals amongst the teeming soldiers on the rampart, but occasionally she was half-certain that she glimpsed Stryker amongst the men near the gate.

Perhaps half an hour had elapsed since the first assault, and the fight still spluttered on that northern front, but the twin rebel divisions had failed with their petard, and they were ensconced in the village and in the Grange. The real conflict now seemed to have shifted to the south, and from her lofty platform Lisette had watched the third enemy division trundle up to Rawdon's carefully excavated earthworks. The whole area had vanished in gun smoke as the battle began to rage. It was time to move, she decided.

Lisette saw Roger Tainton on her way to the top of the stairs. As she went to take the first step, she glanced out on to the courtyard below. Some of the sharpshooters had also decided to leave the tower, and in deep shock she moved out of their way, clinging to the bricks. It was him. If he had not attacked her, she might never have noticed him amongst the hundreds of inhabitants, but their brief duel six days before was as fresh in her mind as the battle she had just witnessed. His bald head, his strangely lopsided gait; even from up high she was convinced. She steadied her breathing, and turned for the stairs.

CHAPTER 28

'Glad you could join us!' Johnson exclaimed brightly. 'They hold the sconce at present, thus I expect an escalade imminently.'

'They have ladders?' Stryker asked, having galloped south ahead of his group on the unfortunate Lieutenant Hunter's white gelding.

'They do.'

Stryker nodded. 'Then let us give them pause for thought.'

'My sentiments exactly, Captain!'

Stryker's party appeared in moments, their faces drenched in sweat despite the chill of the day. Seven wore the green coats donated by a contrite William Balthazar, while the rest bore Rawdon's yellow. They were quickly ushered into line, all loading muskets except for William Skellen, who had abandoned his long-arm in favour of his beloved halberd. Johnson ordered the sally port open, and the piled debris was quickly hauled back, exposing a breach in the wall that was big enough for a single man to squeeze through if he ducked low. The men shuffled forwards muttering prayers and encouragement to each other.

Stryker moved to Johnson's side and peered out through the hole. What he saw snatched the breath from his lungs and the moisture from his mouth. 'Jesu, Colonel, there are hundreds of them.'

Johnson nodded. 'We have a surprise or two, Captain, do not fret.'

Fret, Stryker thought ruefully, was an astonishing understatement. Out on the half-moon, edging forwards now that their ladders had been shuffled to the front, were dozens of men preparing to charge at the Old House. On both of their flanks, musketeers following red ensigns were already firing a steady stream of bullets up at the rampart, forcing Royalist heads to keep low, and to their rear was another wedge of musketeers, who, Stryker supposed, were being kept back for the time when the forlorn hope had broken the back of the defences. Stryker pulled the dagger from his boot and drew his sword. His bowels had turned to water and his jaw felt iron-tight. He knew it was madness, and yet nothing would make him turn back.

'They're coming!' a familiar voice bellowed from above.

Stryker looked up to see the red-cheeked face of Lancelot Forrester peering over the edge of one of the two guardhouses punctuating the run of the wall. Forrester nodded briskly to him, but addressed Lieutenant-Colonel Johnson. 'The Cripplegates are advancing!'

Johnson went back to the sally port, squinted through the small gap, then stood back so that he could see Forrester's disembodied head. 'Let them reach the ditch, then give the order!'

A great cry went up from outside. It began as a low grumble before rolling and building to a visceral howl of rage as the men of the Cripplegate Auxiliaries bounded out from the half-moon, ladders carried at the front, and raced over the few yards of land that divided the outer-work from the ancient moat. That moat, which lay immediately beneath the Old House wall, was now a dry ditch that had been staked and deepened at Rawdon's instruction, but it did nothing to stop the swarm making it to the other side. The men on the rampart shot at the enslaught, winging a couple of men and killing one outright, but there were just too many to stem the tide, and the ladders clattered and scraped on the bricks as they were hurled up against the walls. The ensign with the blue sash was in amongst them, and he stabbed his huge colour in the foot of the ditch, planting it in the freshly turned soil, and the men surging around it cheered as they went to begin their climb.

A little way along the foot of the wall the sally port remained open, and, between the shoulders of men firing out into the ditch, Stryker witnessed the crushing charge. The noise was deafening, the terror within Johnson's poised raiding party palpable, and every fibre of his being begged him to challenge the rash lieutenant-colonel's orders. Forrester's voice rang out again, the smooth, educated accent frayed by urgency, but Stryker could not discern the words. It was only when he heard screams of a different kind that he understood what had happened. Up on the guardhouse, he now realized, were women. Lots of women. And their shrill cries spoke of rage and vengeance. He looked up but could see nothing, so he pushed nearer to the port, only to discern glimpses of rubble falling like massive hailstones amongst the green-coated attackers. There were tiles falling like huge snowflakes, bricks spinning down on to the heads of the Parliamentarians, and stones too – large and small – clattering off helmets and into the faces of those trying to scale the ladders.

Johnson was grinning maniacally at Stryker. 'Lady Honora!'

'Sir?'

'The marchioness, d'you see? She has her ladies up there, aiding our cause!'

The men all along the inner wall cheered, the women up on their raised platform continued to pelt the assault troops, and then, just as Stryker felt they must surely exhaust their stony ammunition, Forrester's voice shrieked again and a gun fired. It was a falconet, he supposed, or something similar. A small gun, not capable of taking any kind of toll on wall or earthwork. But this one fired from the second guardhouse roof, at painfully close range, and the screams of the men in the ditch told him all he needed to know. It had been loaded with case shot, a wooden cylinder packed with musket-balls, and that cylinder had split as the charge spewed it from the barrel, the balls scattering in a wide, murderous arc that whipped mercilessly through the Roundhead ranks.

'*Now!*' Johnson brayed, drawing his sword as he went to the sally port. '*Charge!*'

Then they were outside, exposed on the southern edge of the wall, plummeting into their own ditch and the chaos of the shredded greencoats. Stryker's men were all around him. 'Loyalty!' he screamed, for it was the field-word they had all agreed, differentiating his own green-clad troops from the Parliament men. 'Give 'em a salvo, boys!'

The Royalist party, up on the far side of the ditch now, let rip with a ragged volley that pulsed in a shattering crescendo, and then flipped their weapons about, using them to club their stunned enemies. The men of the Trained Bands now panicked. The auxiliaries abandoned their ladders and went for their swords, but their front ranks, flensed by the case shot, were too frightened to press on, and they turned into the men clamouring behind, causing a melee amongst themselves while Johnson's thirty Royalists slashed and snarled at their backs. There was a scramble up to the half-moon, through the fence of sharpened stakes and headlong into the second half of their own division. It was anarchy; the reserve troops could not move forward, the city men were not willing to regroup, and the whole division began to cave in on itself.

Johnson was on the man-made lip of the half-moon, whirling his blade high and beckoning his men on. Stryker was deeper still, and he battered a man's hanger from his hand, kneed him in the crotch and smashed his face to a bloody pulp with the heavy guard of his own sword. He ducked a desperate swipe from a reversed Roundhead musket butt, drove his dagger up into his assailant's belly and shouldered him out of the way. Men swirled on all sides like moths at a flame, careening into one another, hacking and snarling like rabid dogs. He could feel wetness on his face but could not tell if it were sweat or blood. He was deaf to all but his own pulse, revelling in the heady stink of blood and dirt and smoke that invaded his nostrils. He crowed to the darkening skies, feeling the wild, rushing, heart-searing joy of a battle won, of an enemy mauled, and spun on his heels, the mud sliding like ice as he searched for the next opponent. But not all the Parliament men had cut and run.

'How do you plan to escape?' the woman said.

Roger Tainton looked up, startled. He had been seated, fastening his boot when the doors had eased open. There, standing beneath the lintel, framed by the grey afternoon, was the silhouette of a woman. He could see that she was short, wrapped in a long cloak, the hood bunched at her shoulders to allow freedom for her golden hair. One of her hands emerged from the folds of the cloak. White, delicate fingers were curled around the handle of a slender dirk.

Tainton eased himself to his feet. 'Escape? I will stroll from here like a conquering hero.'

The glint of teeth showed briefly in the gloom as Lisette Gaillard smiled. 'You were expecting Basing to fall?' She made a tutting sound with her tongue. 'Alas, but the waves break against it, *monsieur*. And Lord Hopton is on his way.'

Tainton tasted acid in his mouth. He swallowed it down. 'You lie.'

She laughed, a dry, mocking cackle that made him want to draw the entrails from her. 'Try it. Fetch a horse, take the gold down to the gates and see what happens.'

Tainton had his own knife in his hand, but he moved to the side, carefully placing his feet so that he did not trip on the bodies of the guards. He leaned against the wagon, pushing his free hand up under the heavy sheet. 'This paltry bastion cannot stand against Waller.'

Lisette had seen the corpses. She stopped, a ghastly horror contorting her features. She looked at him, eyes bright with hate. 'Murderer.'

Now it was Tainton's turn to laugh. He made it scornful. 'One more murder to commit, *mademoiselle*.' As he hoped, she rushed at him, pouncing like a cat in the darkness. He pulled the solid gold crucifix from the wagon and tossed it at her as hard as he could. It caught Lisette on the side of the head, a glancing blow but enough to crack hard on her skull. She lost her footing, stumbled the last few yards, and sprawled in a mangled mess at his feet.

—◠◡◠—

Kovac was in the front rank of the Westminster redcoats, and he levelled his twin pistols at the men rushing out of the ditch. The assault had stalled, the feeble Cripplegates scattered by a single cannon shot and a gaggle of harridans armed only with stones, and he hoped each of the pathetic cowards would see the end of a rope by nightfall, but his flanking unit had survived. The officers at the front had held them firm, the sergeants and corporals on the sides and rear had issued the right threats, and the men, nervous as they were, had not capitulated. Their sister unit, on the west flank, had gone, it seemed, their carefully ordered rows dissolved and already mingled with the greens pushing back on the reserves. But Kovac's unit was still strong, and it could obliterate this paltry sortie with a single, well-delivered volley.

He pulled the pistols to full cock, aimed at the men jeering the failed Cripplegates, and waited for the order to give fire. It was then that Captain Lancelot Forrester came into his sights, as if gifted by God Himself. He emerged from the tiny sally port, sword brandished and glinting, and scrambled down into the ditch. In moments he was back up, bellowing with the rest of the vile malignants, and Wagner Kovac laughed because he no longer cared about the faltering escalade. He would have his man after all.

Stryker caught Forrester's eye. 'There!'

Forrester looked to their left, to the half-dozen lines of redcoated musketeers still arrayed in good order on what had been the right flank of the enemy division. 'At them!' Forrester snarled. 'Get at them!'

The sally party seemed to veer as one, coming off the halfmoon and bolting straight towards the Parliamentarians. Stryker was there, Skellen too, Barkworth's Gaelic war-cries hoarse and chilling somewhere behind. There was no use running away now, for their backs would be carved by lead, so they kept going forwards as the officer commanding the Roundheads held his blade high, pausing for the briefest moment. With a shout that was drowned by the screams of the oncoming Royalists, he swept it vertically towards his boots.

'Down!' Stryker bellowed. Johnson's sally party dived forwards, sliding in the filth just as a furious volley roared out from the front rank of the redcoats. Dirty smoke slewed on the wind, forming a barrier between the two groups, but the Royalists were up, none hurt, and their bared teeth gleamed white against faces smeared in mud. Stryker knew that they must have seemed like demons rising from the depths of the earth, wild-eyed banshees that could not be killed, and he brought back his blade just as the second rank opened fire.

Wagner Kovac cried out. Not because his first pistol ball had missed Forrester, but because the man at his back had shot him in the shoulder. All along the line of Westminster Liberty musketeers, men fell. But they did not fall back, shot by the enemy. Instead they fell forwards, smashed in their heads and spines by a second rank in sheer disarray. The redcoats had panicked, Kovac realized as he dropped his pistols, one still cocked, and sank to his knees. After the front rank fired, the men behind should wait for their comrades to retire, then step forth to bring their own muskets to bear. But they had not waited. Frightened by the charging Royalists, they had discharged their weapons too soon, and now the bodies of their comrades dropped all along the line, slumping face-first in the sloppy morass.

Lancelot Forrester hit the redcoats at speed, slamming into the first man and cleaving a glistening gash down the side of his neck. He could hardly believe what had happened. They had charged at this large body of men, only to see perhaps four-score of the enemies killed by their own. The men at the back were already running, bolting like deer before so many hounds, the will to fight gone from them. Two mad-eyed soldiers leaped out of the broiling melee to cut off his advance. One, a thickly bearded sergeant toting a blood-wet halberd, jabbed at Forrester's face with its razor point, while his comrade, a short fellow with pocked skin and a bulbous nose, swung a musket butt low, meaning to shatter his shins. Forrester vaulted the musket and parried the halberd aside. He turned like an acrobat inside the range of the staff and slammed his head into the sergeant's nose. The sergeant recoiled, blood cascading over the bristles of his beard, but Forrester sensed his pock-ravaged confederate lunging from somewhere to the right. There was no time to respond, and he braced himself for the blow. It did not come. The man to his right screamed, a querulous, skull-splitting noise, and Forrester took the moment to hew open the belly of the sergeant with a horizontal slash of his sword. He turned to see that the second man had been skewered on a long blade, his jaw still working furiously like a landed fish. Forrester looked up to see Major Lawrence standing over the hapless rebel.

The major's face was a mask of anguish, for his hunched spine evidently complained at this unnatural employment, but Lawrence shot Forrester a wolfish, blood-spattered grin and jerked his sword free of the red-coat's neck. 'I'll be damned if I miss another battle.'

Forrester made to thank him, but Lawrence was gone, screeching like a hawk in a shrill battle-cry. Forrester stepped on, waded haphazardly over the new-made breastwork of bodies, and then an irresistible strength hauled at his ankle. He fell, plunging on his side in the mud, sword skittering away. He twisted on to his front, pushing up, but something still grasped his boot tight. He kicked hard, feeling a crack as he did so, and then he was free, sprawling away. He clambered to his feet, barely keeping his balance, and snatched up a discarded pistol. The man who had tackled him was caked in mud, his left shoulder and arm entirely soaked in blood, but in his right hand he held a filthy pistol that he now raised. He had a beard that was matted with yet more grime, and it might have been impossible to know his identity except for the eyes that peered out from the black mask like two nuggets of ice.

Forrester nodded at Kovac's thigh. 'How fares the leg, Captain?'

Wagner Kovac patted it gingerly. 'It hurts, you dandy arse-licking Papist. And I'm major now.'

'My apologies, *Major* Kovac,' Forrester said. 'They promote men for failure in your army, it appears.'

Kovac spat a gritty globule of phlegm at Forrester, jerked the pistol out with whip-crack speed, and pulled the trigger. Nothing happened. He looked down at the spent short-arm in astonishment, and Forrester lifted the pistol he had grabbed and shot the Croat between the eyes.

—⁂—

What if the French whore had spoken truthfully? Tainton had made his pact with Wagner Kovac on the premise that Waller would reduce Basing to a steaming ruin. Never had the possibility occurred to him that the tenacious little general could fail against so meagre a stronghold. He still prayed for victory, but still the walls held, still the Parliamentarian colours were not hanging from the battlements. So Tainton had decided to find a horse. The whore, unconscious and bleeding in the chalky vault, had challenged him to take the gold to the gates and see what might come to pass. She evidently had considered him a fool. But Tainton was no fool. He would go to the gates, but he would not be stopped.

Tainton left Lisette in the darkness. Outside, the carts used to bring the wounded back from the walls were still gainfully employed. He waited as two, each drawn by a skinny mule, trundled off towards the south of the circular bailey, where the noise of battle remained loudest. As they disappeared a similar little vehicle came up. This one, drawn by a sturdy piebald horse and driven by a lad of perhaps eight or nine, carried three men on its rear platform. Tainton watched as the chirurgeon's assistants emerged from the Great Hall, each smeared in the blood of other men, and hurriedly lifted two of the three men down. They conveyed them in turn to the wine cellars, while the third man, evidently only nursing a flesh wound to his forearm, was able to find his own way down for treatment.

As this group vanished, another team of stained and red-fingered attendants emerged. There were six men this time, working in pairs, and between each, lolling like a rolled carpet, was a corpse. They swung them on to the cart, gave the lad a wave, then went back inside. The boy clicked his tongue sharply and the horse was immediately compliant as it turned a circle, the cart jerking into life. Tainton ran to stop it, grasping the bridle, holding the piebald firm.

The boy, his wide, freckled face looking perplexed beneath a shock of red hair, frowned deeply. 'Sir?'

'Rebel dead?' he asked.

The boy nodded. 'Givin' them back, sir.'

Tainton smiled sweetly, released the bridle and clambered up to the driver's bench. He hit the boy once, sharp and hard on the nose, and the brittle little body crumpled rearwards in a heap on the back of the cart.

—m—

Captain Innocent Stryker was back at the sally port. The Roundhead division had ruptured, imploded, and was now in full retreat back up to the plateau of Basing Park. He supposed they would come again, but not yet. All along the Old House curtain wall, men, women and children cheered. The Marchioness of Winchester was offering a regal wave to any who looked up at her tower, as if she alone had won the day, and Johnson was busily hauling his small detachment of heroes into the ditch and up to the wall. Stryker manned the port, watching warily for an enemy counter-attack as he ushered each man through until eventually all were accounted for. The last man in was the colonel, who ordered the hole closed and then stretched out his hand.

'You came on horseback, Captain, yes?' he asked as Stryker shook the proffered palm.

'Aye, sir.'

'Then I'd ask you to recover your steed and locate Colonel Rawdon and His Lordship. Convey my regards and impart detail of what has transpired here.'

'Pleasure, sir,' Stryker said, striding along the base of the wall to find the tethered gelding.

'And Stryker?'

Stryker paused, turned. 'Sir?'

Johnson slammed home his sword with a rakish grin. 'Glad to have had you with me.'

The heavens opened as Stryker clambered up on to the skittish white. He guided the snorting beast up to the centre of the Old House, the Great Gatehouse looming immediately up ahead. He veered right at the imposing stone fountain, guessing Rawdon and the marquess might be inspecting the damage done to the huge Tudor mansion by Waller's artillery. Already the rain was hard, the droplets huge and chill, and pools began to glisten in the ruts made by the wagons carrying dead and wounded back and forth from the infirmary.

His glance was only a fleeting one. So obscured was it by the rainfall that at first he ignored it for a trick of tiredness. But he looked again at one such vehicle. It was trundling towards the arched tunnel at the base of the Great Gatehouse. Somehow, its wheels seemed strange. Almost as though the bottom few inches had been cut away by some magic. He pulled the gelding to a slippery halt and stared more intently. The wheels, he saw, were cast abnormally low at the rear, sunk so far into the mud that it was a wonder they moved at all. It seemed strange that one wagon would be loaded with so many casualties, given the fleet the marquess had made available for the task. It made no sense.

The battle seemed to have waned. Exultant cheers replaced the cacophony of gunfire, cannonade, screams and drums. Tainton prayed yet. He beseeched the Lord to harden Waller's resolve, give courage to his men, instil fear in the hearts of the Romish Paulet and his minions. Only when he coaxed the piebald, hitched now to the gold-laden wagon, to the far side of the Great Gatehouse, did the lone, mournful trumpet cry out from the direction of the village. Tainton had been a soldier, a good one, and he knew the call to retreat when he heard it. Waller had lost his nerve.

He pressed on. In the open, on the large, empty fan-shaped space that served as the Old House outer-yard, the rain hammered in chilling, diagonal sheets. The wagon slewed to the side, threatening to become mired, but the stolen piebald struggled stoically, maintaining enough momentum to plough through. He coaxed the animal to the left, making for the small gatehouse that guarded the bridge over the ringwork ditch. It would take him out to the grass-lined road between the house and the walled gardens, and from there he could move with relative ease on the better terrain, following the slope down to Garrison Gate.

'Stiff 'uns!' he called up to the pair of sentries at the window of the gatehouse, tugging his hat down over his shrivelled ears. 'Expired on the chirurgeon's slab!'

'Theirs or ours?' a man with heavy jowls shouted a reply. His whole face, thrust out into the rain, wobbled beneath a battered morion helmet.

'Theirs!' Tainton answered. 'Givin' 'em back! Colonel Rawdon says why use our pits when they can dig their own?'

The fat man in the ancient pot cackled a laugh that ended in a wet-sounding cough. 'Right you are, cully!' He waved Tainton through and ducked back from the driving storm.

Tainton whipped at the horse. The wagon lurched through the archway, mercifully sheltered from the rain, hooves clopping on the flint path that lead towards the bridge. Suddenly Lisette Gaillard groaned from under the thick sheet, giving him a start. Her moans were indistinct and slurred, and he was not concerned that she posed any threat, but a man carrying corpses would arouse suspicion if one of them moved, so he hauled on the reins. He slid down from the seat and went to the rear of the vehicle, peeling back the sheet far enough to reveal the French-woman. She was slumped over the chests, her left temple caked and dark with drying blood, but the movement of the sheet seemed to wake her and she gradually sat up.

'Where?' she croaked, swaying. Her pupils tightened as she caught a glimpse of the blade in his hand. 'You. *Fils de pute.*'

Tainton licked his lips. 'I had hoped to keep you for later, where our final conversation could be more—leisurely.' He tightened his grip on the octagonal knife handle. 'But you are more useful to me as a cadaver.' Tainton stood on the tips of his toes to grasp Lisette by her collar, and dragged her yielding body down so that her bloody face hovered just above his. 'You destroyed me, woman. Robbed me of my body and my future. I have waited a long time for this moment.'

Lisette spat in his face. '*Va te faire méttre, connard.*'

He grinned, bringing the knife up to her windpipe. 'For it is written. Vengeance is mine; I will repay, saith the Lord.'

Her blue gaze twitched away. She was staring back at the Old House yard. Her purple lips turned up at the corners. 'And behold,' she whispered, 'a pale horse. And he that sat upon him, his name was Death.'

Stryker clattered on to the flint runway under the arch, hauling the mud-smeared gelding to a whinnying halt just a few yards to the rear of the covered wagon. Tainton was there, leaning against it, a long dagger in his hand.

'You did not need to concern yourself, Captain,' the rebel agent said, remaining stock still as he spoke. 'All I ever wanted was the gold and the woman.'

Stryker swung his leg over the saddle and dropped to the hard ground. His hand was shaking and he drew his sword if only to occupy it. 'Murderer.'

Tainton made a show of sniffing the air. 'Stryker, you are the worst kind of liar. A man pretending noble intent when all the while it is you who kills for a corrupt king, you who thrives on

427

blood and death, you who swives your Popish punk without concern for the sins you commit. You lust and you deceive and you are destined for hell's purifying flames. *I did what was necessary.*' He tapped a foot so that his spurs gave their metallic rustle. 'You asked me why I wore these, remember? Rotating nine-point rowels, made from stamped sheet iron. Exquisite. Each point chiselled into a leaf effect, and devilish sharp. Proved their worth, would you not say?'

The ragged gash Stryker had seen on Jack Trowbridge's mutilated face came back to him. He had gone to the subterranean chamber first, checked for the gold. All he had found was his musketeers, carved and bludgeoned as though a wild beast had savaged them, and a cart empty of gold. 'My men I accept,' he said hoarsely, his voice echoing under the stone arch. 'But the boy?'

'Casualty of war,' Tainton said.

The youngster's deeply slit throat had gaped in that dark vault, causing vomit to bubble up to sour Stryker's mouth. 'Victim of a depraved bastard.'

'Spare me.' Tainton's voice dripped with scorn. 'The rebellion must have the gold to survive.'

'The Solemn League and Covenant,' Stryker said bitterly.

Tainton shrugged. 'The Scots are an avaricious tribe. The Parliament must do what it must do to secure their help.' He patted the wagon. 'This will do nicely.'

Stryker forced a mirthless laugh. 'You've lost, Tainton.'

'As far as your friends on the gate are concerned, I carry a cartload of Parliament bodies. We are honour-bound to return them for burial.'

Stryker shook his head. 'You'll die here.'

'If that is God's will, then so be it. I go to my maker, Stryker. To sit at the right hand of King Jesus. You cannot say the same for your own soul.' His eyes narrowed. 'And your demise will come, Captain, trust in that. You cannot win this war. We *know* you. We know everything you do, every move you make.'

The taunt pulled at threads in Stryker's mind, ones he had

forgotten still dangled. He took a step closer, twitching his sword in threat. 'How did you know the gold was on Scilly? Who gave you that information?'

Roger Tainton laughed, his teeth, so incongruously handsome in so foul a skull, gleaming like strings of pearls. He grasped a fistful of sheet and dragged the covering back, exposing the glittering bounty. But Stryker's eye saw only one thing. One prize. Curled like a still-born foetus atop the wooden chests, hair turned black and matted in her own blood, was Lisette Gaillard. Her eyes were closed, her face starkly white.

Roger Tainton threw his knife. It was intended for Stryker's chest, but it glanced off his upper right arm. Stryker yelped in pain, dropped the sword, and his enemy made a desperate lunge at him. Tainton hit Stryker hard in the midriff, both men careening backwards in a tangle of limbs. They were off the flint path now, collapsing together in the quagmire of the yard, their grunts smothered by the rush of the rain. Shouts, muffled by the storm, rang out from the windows above. Stryker's right arm was numb at the open flesh and stabbed by lancing pain down towards his wrist and fingers, so he groped for Tainton's eyes with his other hand. Somehow he found the soft target, pushing, delving, clawing with his nails until Tainton screamed. They rolled apart, slipping and sliding in the filth, standing at once to face one another. Tainton's hat was gone, his bald, patchy pate shining in the rain.

Stryker stooped to pull the dirk from his boot, but he swore viciously as he caught sight of his own sword in Tainton's hand. They circled warily, each feinting to force the other to move. Stryker darted inwards, closing the gap, but Tainton kept him at bay easily with the longer steel, and then the Parliamentarian had his back to the gatehouse, and he edged towards it, never taking his gaze from the Royalist. He reached the arch, then the vehicle itself, and clambered up so that he balanced on the rearmost edge next to Lisette.

'She lives, you know,' Tainton said with an expression of exquisite relish. 'You had a chance to save her.'

'Tainton!' Stryker pleaded, hearing the desperation in his own voice. He knew it would do no good, so he inched round the side of the vehicle in an attempt to reach the horse.

'Stay where you are!' Tainton ordered.

Stryker froze. He was still three yards from the animal. He turned back.

Tainton put the tip of the sword to Lisette's breast. 'With your own blade, Stryker. It could not be more perfect.'

Stryker dived. He went for the piebald's rump, stabbing it as hard as he could. The animal shrieked as though it were being gelded, kicked out at Stryker, only just missing his head, and reared with another shrill wail. It bolted, hauling the wagon over the flint runway and out on to the rain-harried bridge. Stryker scrambled to his feet as it slipped on the far side, crashing over its forelegs, the heavy cart skidding and veering in the saturated mud until it slammed into the hapless, braying beast. Then all was still. Lisette seemed to stir, woken by the mad, brief charge and the pulsating rain.

He looked back. At the far side of the gatehouse, soldiers had appeared. The ones, he supposed, who had hailed them from the windows. They were armed, one of them barked something at him, but Stryker ignored them. Instead, bleeding and exhausted, he crossed to Roger Tainton. The Roundhead agent moaned. He had been thrown clear of the wagon, landing awkwardly on the mortared flint so that both his arms seemed perversely canted at the wrong angles. He held them up, agony etching deep valleys around his mouth. 'Forgive me!'

Stryker thought of the torture he had endured at the orders of this man, of the stiff, mottled-blue bodies of the Trowbridge twins, of the red-headed boy whose reedy throat glinted in the dark like a ruby. He stooped, dragged one of Tainton's boots from his foot, eliciting a shrill cry from the former harquebusier. 'Only God forgives.'

He slashed the boot down and across so that the jagged spur tore a frayed line in Tainton's neck. It was not deep enough to kill instantly, but blood spewed, hot and steaming in the cold, to

430

pool around his hairless head. He gargled, tried to sit, eyelids flickering, shattered arms flailing. And then he slumped back, mouth agape, a look of pure amazement on his face. He twitched once, a last spasm of violence, and then he was still.

CHAPTER 29

'Home!' the single word erupted from the sodden faces arrayed in the fields just north of the village. There were thousands, brought up in their tight ranks, neat lines crafted expertly by sergeants wielding sharp halberds and sharper tongues.

Sir William Waller scowled as he rode across the front rank, chin dipped low so that his hat took the brunt of the storm. At his back the black edifice of Basing House loomed like a festering canker from the soil. A pestilence that refused to die. At his front was his army, so many regiments drawn up like toy soldiers in the lashing rain. It was a model piece of martial prowess, a lesson in drill and timing. And, he knew, it was all an illusion.

'Home! Home! Home!' the cry rose again, turning into a throaty chant that rolled like a wave, yet waning before it reached the foremost ranks, so that none could be singled out for having lent their voice to the mutiny.

Waller held up a staying hand, lifting his head against the rain. The city regiments had spoken. They had never wanted to be here, never wished to march so far from their families and livelihoods. After two shambolic attempts to take Basing, the rain seemed to have sounded the final death knell in their spirits. 'Night falls swiftly!' Waller shouted. 'Will you take this malignant castle for your general?'

'Home! Home! Home!' the regiments rumbled.

A rider encased entirely in armour thundered to Waller's side,

432

wheeling his horse about. 'This is the Devil's work, Sir William!' he called through his heavy visor. 'Hang every tenth man!'

Waller wiped water from his eyebrows and offered the cuirassier a withering smile. 'This is not Rome, Sir Arthur, and I am not Crassus. Tell me how we will renew the attack, if I have sent so many of my own men to the grave? Lord knows we have buried enough this day.' He spurred past Heselrige as the chant gathered momentum again, pulsing like a beating heart up and down the tight lines of men from Westminster, Tower Hamlets and Cripplegate. When he was close enough to see the whites of the nearest eyes, he drew a pistol from its saddle holster. 'The next man to use such base language will be shot by mine own hand! This will not do! Not do at all!'

The chant withered as quickly as it had grown, but the sentiment remained, etched on each and every face. Waller trusted his own men, the veterans forming his personal regiment, and most of the horse, dragoons and even the Farnham Castle greencoats. But the London Trained Bands were his core, the bulk of his army, and without them he was nothing. He pushed the pistol home, turning his mount. He was disconsolate. His ambitious attack had lasted no more than two hours. It had involved more than three thousand men, himself included for a short, unremarkable few minutes. They had been well armed, adequately kitted and equipped with brass petards and plenty of ladders. Yet on all fronts his army had been thrown back, humiliated by a rag-rag amalgam of Papists, peasants, aristocrats, artists and mercenaries. There were even unsettling reports of the garrison's womenfolk taking up arms. Before he could renew the attack, the rain had come. The thrum of heavy, ruthless droplets on the sodden fields and against the glassy surface of the River Loddon had replaced the noise of drum and cannon, and now, at dusk, his grand army was teetering on the verge of open mutiny.

An aide appeared from one quarter of the dusky field, and Waller instinctively knew the message he conveyed would be laden with doom. He unfolded the proffered parchment silently, the inky scrawl immediately blotting and blurring as raindrops pattered amongst the letters, but he only bothered to scan the smearing lines. It was clear enough. Lord Hopton, it seemed, had made rendezvous with Sir Jacob Astley at Kingsclere, and was ready to march. Waller's best friend and most formidable enemy would be at Basing House imminently, at the head of the king's new western army. The report spoke of nearly five thousand men, divided evenly between foot and horse, and, unlike Waller's hastily cobbled force, Hopton had several notable and experienced units under his command. Waller screwed the message into a tight ball and tossed it into the mud. He would fight Hopton, that much was certain. As he scowled into the driving storm, he made a private vow not only to engage the advancing Cavaliers, but to destroy them utterly. But not here. Not yet. He barked orders to his aides and officers, issuing a general withdrawal, and rode away, not knowing if the moisture on his cheeks was chill rain or bitter tears.

—m—

It was only when the light fully faded, oppressed by blue-grey clouds that pooled like immense bruises, that the inhabitants of Basing House finally believed in their miracle. They danced and sang, broke open the barrels of beer and claret they had rescued from the flames that had devoured the Grange, and jeered the distant torches that marked a retreating army on the black horizon.

Colonel Marmaduke Rawdon did not rest. He paced the perimeter, setting teams to bolster the earthworks, patch the cannon-pocked walls, reposition the storm-poles out on the half-moons and convey the dead to their graves. As promised, he had indeed sent out the Parliamentarian casualties, gathered up from the ditches to the north-east and south-west, and had already dispatched foraging parties to secure supplies. The task of basking in the glory of victory, therefore, went to Sir John Paulet, Lord St John, Earl of Wiltshire and Fifth Marquess of Winchester. He ranted and raved, toured every courtyard, every

434

arch, every room and every rampart, his formidable wife on his arm, a retinue of ebullient sycophants in his wake. He toasted King Charles, drank to the bravery of his garrison, and brayed to a sky still hazed with powder smoke that no rebel would ever breach the walls of Loyalty House.

'He says it's our Gloucester, sir,' Sergeant Skellen grunted as he went to stand at Lisette's bedside. Stryker had taken her to the infirmary, where the chirurgeon had done his best to stitch the gash on her temple, but she had not stayed there long. The old wine cellars were crammed full of wounded men often lying two to a palliasse, top-to-toe and crying out in tandem, and, upon hearing of Lisette's plight, the marchioness, Honora Paulet, had sent for her. She had been taken, still only semiconscious, to the more sumptuous surroundings of the New House, where a spacious and warm room had been provided, and it was here that Stryker and his men had begun to congregate. They could hear the sounds of celebration and relief outside, and each man clutched a goblet of fine wine, but none in the room made merry. Stryker was on the bed, cradling her limp body, smelling her hair and whispering tales of their unlikely victory. The others, Barkworth, Forrester and the rest, simply stood at the edges of the bed and watched. They had suffered so much to reach this moment that only solemn reflection seemed right.

Stryker looked up. 'I suppose it is our Gloucester, in a way. Massie's victory there was used by the news-sheets up and down the land. Rawdon's will be likewise.'

'I do not imagine,' Forrester said with a wry smile, 'that Rawdon will garner a mention.'

Stryker gave a rueful chuckle. 'Aye, well, the marquess was impressive in his own manner. It is his estate, after all. He is entitled to the victory.'

'Hopton is expected to arrive on the morrow,' said Forrester. 'Perhaps the day after, if the rain does not ebb. Will you entrust the gold to him?'

Stryker felt Lisette's hand squeeze within his. He shook his head. 'We will ask him for a company or two, and we will take the bloody treasure to Oxford ourselves. It is the least we deserve.' Her fingers compressed his again, and he knew she was content. He lifted his cup from a table at the bedside and raised it in salute. 'To our fallen comrades. All of them.'

They drank, long and hard, and they wept for their friends.

EPILOGUE

Near Oadby, Leicestershire, 1 December 1643

'Your man failed us.'

The speaker stroked his chestnut mare, urging it to be still, though he feared his deep uneasiness in the saddle would be obvious to the man he had come to meet. They were on a hilltop bare except for one tree, and that tree had been the agreed rendezvous. He hated riding, feared the roads, but knew there was little choice in the matter. He was an intelligencer, a good one, and he accepted that such irksome duties were necessary from time to time. The mare twitched again, making him start, and he covered his embarrassment by fiddling at the pewter buttons of his cassock. It had stopped raining, mercifully, but still he hauled the hood up over his heavily oiled hair, a gust of lavender billowing into his nostrils with the motion.

His companion was his very antithesis. A big, powerful soldier, clad in plate at back and ribs, legs swathed in expensive hide, left arm gauntleted, right arm gloved in kidskin. He adjusted his thighs a fraction, expertly guiding his grey horse forwards to a patch of long, luscious grass beneath the lonely tree. 'You know this for certain?'

The intelligencer nodded quickly. 'I have seen the accursed treasure with my own eyes. They paraded it through Oxford as though it were an Imperial Triumph. It will buy the King a lot of weapons.'

The soldier looked back as his horse tore up wads of grass,

437

green bubbles foaming at its bit. 'Regrettable. Tainton was a Godly man.'

'And the League?'

The soldier had removed his hat, ruffling sweaty auburn hair through fanned fingers as he spoke. 'The deal with the Scots will move ahead. Parliament will wring the money from the rapacious City worthies. We will do what we must if we wish to prevail in this war.'

'And Stryker?'

'What of him?'

'He killed your man. Told me so himself. What if Tainton mentioned me?'

The soldier shot his informant a derisory glance. 'You are an important fellow. He cannot touch you.'

'But if he suspects.' The intelligencer felt his bowels loosen a touch. He shook his head, feeling his fleshy face wobble. 'Stryker is like a wild beast, Colonel. The longer he gnaws on a bone, the sharper his teeth become.'

The colonel plucked the fine glove from his hand and scratched at the cluster of warts that sprouted like toadstools between his eyebrows. 'You fear him?'

'As I fear Lucifer himself.'

'Then perhaps we should take care of this troublesome fellow. Would that provide succour?'

The intelligencer rubbed a hand over his pudgy face, pressing palms into tiny eyes set deep beneath thick lids. 'It would, it would.'

The colonel's mouth twitched. 'And, while such arrangements are put into place, if I were to arrange a swelling of your remuneration?'

'I would yet fear him.'

'But you would cope.'

'Aye.'

The colonel stared at the horizon and watched the clouds scud on the freezing air. 'Then we shall proceed. Are you with us?'

The intelligencer sighed heavily, a great plume of vapour dancing around his head. 'Of course, Colonel. I take great risk riding this far from our lines. Does that not prove my loyalty? The information about the gold, about its whereabouts. Are they not proof enough?'

The colonel shrugged. 'I find men are weak-willed,' he said simply. 'You are important to us, Ezra. Vital to our righteous cause, never forget that. Now,' he added in a tone as brisk as the morning, jerking the reins to drag his grey from its blissful grass cropping, 'I have correspondence to see to. My old friend Dick Norton—'

'Norton? The Governor of Southampton?'

'The same. Idle Dick, as known to me, though he has not been so idle as the name might suggest. He works to secure Hampshire for our cause, and asks for my help.' He pursed his lips and picked at the warts again. 'I will speak to Vane, to the Parliament, if I must, though they irritate me with their vacuous chatter. We will see Norton succeeds.'

'And what of me, sir? What do you ask?'

The soldier returned his hat to his head and let his horse walk away from the tree and along the crest of the hill, heading north-east, back to Parliament territory. 'We must make our plans for the winter campaign,' he called over his shoulder. 'I require troop dispositions, the sensitivities and humours of the generals, the strategy to be employed by Newcastle and Hopton and Rupert. I need all these things, and I have faith that you are the man to provide.' He wheeled the horse about, cupping a hand to his mouth. 'Tainton is gone, but you remain Parliament's great hope. Can you bring me what I need, Mister Killigrew?'

Ezra Killigrew, aide to Prince Rupert, confidante of King Charles, and agent of the rebellion, waved at the horseman. 'I can, Colonel Cromwell! And I will!'

ACKNOWLEDGEMENTS

Thanks, as ever, to my editor, Kate Parkin, who persevered with me through the revision process, and to my agent, Rupert Heath, whose enthusiasm for the series has been a huge source of encouragement from day one.

Much gratitude to the whole team at Hodder, particularly Hilary Hammond, Swati Gamble and Emilie Ferguson, and thanks also to Malcolm Watkins of Heritage Matters, whose expertise has been vital in ironing out some of the historical inaccuracies that inevitably appear. As ever, all remaining mistakes are my own.

Last, but absolutely not least, much love and thanks to Rebecca, Joshua and Maisie, for everything.

HISTORICAL NOTE

Warlord's Gold begins just a few days after the First Battle of Newbury. The Siege of Gloucester – as described in Stryker's fourth adventure, *Assassin's Reign* – had been a disaster for the Royalists, who had abandoned their efforts in the face of a surprise Parliamentarian relief force under the command of the Earl of Essex. But, as Essex returned to London, Charles I rallied his beleaguered army and gave chase, overtaking the Parliamentarian army at Newbury and forcing them to march past the Royalist force to continue their retreat. The armies engaged on 20 September 1643, with the Royalists hoping to smash Essex's hastily raised force before moving east to take London. But far from delivering a final, decisive blow, the battle raged throughout the day, eventually petering out in stalemate as night fell. The next morning, low on ammunition, the Royalists were forced to allow Essex to pass and continue his march to London.

If the tide began to turn at Gloucester, then Newbury was the first stage in a building of Parliamentarian momentum that would never be stopped.

Around this time, an agreement was reached between the Scottish Covenanters and the leaders of the English Parliament. Known as the Solemn League and Covenant, it was a military league and a religious covenant, the purpose of which was overwhelming the Royalist field armies, who still by late 1643 looked likely to win the war.

The alliance came about because the English rebels, quite understandably, sought assistance from the highly regarded Scottish army. The Scots, however, were principally interested

443

in the religious union the agreement would bring about. They had been alarmed by the discovery of a plot by the Earl of Antrim to bring an Irish Catholic army into the conflict on the side of Scots Royalists, but, more crucially, they wished to unite the churches of Scotland and England under the Presbyterian system.

Negotiations – led from the English side by Sir Henry Vane – proceeded quickly, as both factions were keen to defeat the king in the field. The Scots agreed to send an army into England on condition that Parliament would co-operate with the Kirk in upholding the Protestant religion and uprooting all remaining traces of Popery. Although it was implied that Presbyterian forms of worship and church government would be enforced across Britain and Ireland, the clause was qualified to read that church reform would be carried out 'according to the Word of God'. This compromise would, eventually, cause deep divisions in the union, but by January 1644, Westminster's hopes were realized and the Army of the Covenant crossed the border into England, thus tipping the scales permanently and changing the course of the Civil Wars.

By the seventeenth century the Isles of Scilly consisted of four inhabited islands – St Mary's, Tresco, St Martin's and Agnes – and dozens more uninhabited islets. Lying in the Atlantic (the term Celtic Sea was not proposed until 1921) just twenty-six miles south-west of Land's End, Scilly had long been an ideal base, both for defending the Channel and for piracy. During the Tudor period this strategic importance began to be properly recognized, and the Crown appointed a governor to bring law and order and raised a garrison to secure Scilly for the realm.

The islands saw significant action during the Civil Wars. At various times, they provided shelter for Royalist privateers, gave sanctuary to the fugitive Prince of Wales, and were the setting for the first major amphibious assault of the wars. But those tales are yet to be told, and Stryker will doubtless play his part, so I will not go into detail here!

During the period in which *Warlord's Gold* takes place, the population of Scilly – about three hundred and fifty – had no more choice as to which side to support than the rest of the country's common folk. Thus, they were directed by their governor, Sir Francis Godolphin, a staunch Royalist. Godolphin was Sheriff of Cornwall, and he spent his time on the mainland, deferring power to his deputy, Sir Thomas Bassett. But Bassett, too, was bound for England, joining the Cornish army at the outbreak of the conflict and eventually (readers will remember him from *Hunter's Rage*, where he commanded one of the columns at the Battle of Stratton) taking a major-general's commission.

Who assumed command of the garrison in Bassett's absence? The most senior figure I can trace is Captain William Balthazar, so it seems likely that he ruled the islands during the early part of the war, his base being Star Castle, the star-shaped fort located on the south-western headland of St Mary's known as the Hugh. He is duly given his place in the book, and I hope I have not been too harsh on him.

The climax of *Warlord's Gold* takes place at Basing House, the seat of John Paulet, the Marquess of Winchester. During the Tudor period this property was transformed from a basic medieval manor into the sprawling palace that became a Royalist fortress within an area dominated by Parliamentarian forces. As described in the book, there were two main houses: the Old House, essentially a medieval motte and bailey castle; and the New House, a large rectangular mansion. A bridge and gateway linked the two houses. Beyond these were outbuildings, orchards and gardens, all contained within a boundary wall of approximately one mile in circumference, and to the north was the Grange, the farm complex that contained storehouses, animal pens and fish ponds. And, of course, the Great Barn. By the time of the events of *Warlord's Gold*, Basing had already been attacked once, in July of 1643, by local Parliamentarians under the command of Colonel Richard Norton. The assault had been held off by the marquess's small force until the arrival of a relief force led by Lieutenant-Colonel Peake. Shortly afterwards,

Colonel Marmaduke Rawdon arrived with the rest of his regiment and set about strengthening the fortifications. This was a timely move, for the autumn was to bring the first concerted effort to reduce Basing's walls.

As described in the book, Sir William Waller, having made peace with his rival, the Earl of Essex, had raised a new army of more than five thousand men. Initially it looked as though he would advance against Winchester, but he seems to have changed tack at the eleventh hour. Was it his plan to attack Basing all along, with the march towards Winchester simply a feint? Or did he change his mind after receiving exaggerated reports of a large Royalist force (Gerard's Brigade) marching south to rendezvous with Hopton? I have taken the latter view, giving responsibility for the report to the fictitious Wagner Kovac.

Arriving at Basing, Waller set up his artillery on Cowdrey's Down to the north of the house, and after his summons for the marquess to surrender was declined, he gave the order to fire, and the first siege began.

The events of November 1643 unfolded much as I have retold, though I confess I have condensed some of the action for the sake of the plot. A cannon really did discharge during the early negotiations, hardening Royalist resolve and compelling Waller to apologize for 'the rudeness of his disorderly guns during parley', and when the Roundhead messenger was finally sent back with Paulet's answer, he fell into a marsh and lost a boot!

On 7 November the first major assault took place, when a large detachment of musketeers under the command of Waller's captain-lieutenant, Captain Clinson, took the Grange after some fierce fighting. Though the battle raged all the way along the road dividing the farm buildings from the house, the Parliamentarian attack could not force a breakthrough. This was almost certainly not helped by the plentiful supply of food and ale they discovered in the Great Barn. The temptation to rest within the stone walls must have been irresistible. As night fell, the Royalists counter-attacked, compelled, I feel sure, by the thought of the enemy eating their way through vital supplies. In the fight that followed, the Grange was torched, with only the Great Barn left standing. A bitter hand-to-hand fight ensued, and, as described in the book, Lieutenant-Colonel Johnson really did engage Clinson in a personal duel. Accounts suggest that Clinson was having the better of the fight but was eventually killed by others who came to Johnson's aid. I have attributed the intervention to Stryker.

Waller attempted a second attack on 12 November, having spent the intervening (and very wet) days in Basingstoke. After a heavy bombardment, the Parliamentarians stormed the defences from three directions at once. While the London regiments mounted attacks from Basing Park to the south and west of the House, Waller led his main force from Basing village in the east. He planned to make a breach near one of the gates with a petard, but, as witnessed by Stryker, the petardier chose to blow the gate itself, which was heavily reinforced, rather than the thin walls on either side. No breach was made, and as the Parliamentarians looked on in horror, they came under heavy fire from the rampart and were eventually forced to retreat.

Elsewhere, the other attacks achieved little more. One group of Londoners reached the earthworks of the Old House, placing their standard in the ditch, but they were harassed by the women of the garrison, who hurled stones and bricks from the battlements, while a well-situated cannon enfiladed them with case shot. As the advance stalled, a sudden sortie led by Lieutenant-Colonel Johnson (probably with much to prove after his duel with Clinson) threw the inexperienced Trained Bands into chaos, with some of the rear ranks firing on their comrades before the foremost ranks had time to retire. With darkness falling and heavy rain setting in, Waller abandoned the assault on Basing House and once again ordered a withdrawal to Basingstoke.

During the next few days, Waller received intelligence that Lord Hopton was concentrating his Royalist forces to the west (Hopton did indeed receive a message from Paulet carried by a woman in a basket of apples). With his London regiments threatening to mutiny and scores deserting during the miserable nights, Waller had no choice but to withdraw to his base at Farnham Castle.

Basing House was saved, at least for the time being, and the Royalist commander, Colonel Rawdon, was knighted for his part in the defence.

Sir Alfred Cade's gold did not exist. Nor did the characters involved in its story. Roger Tainton, Ezra Killigrew, Sterne Fassett, Clay Cordell and Locke Squires are all figments of my imagination, as, sadly, is Titus Gibbons, though there were plenty of privateers at the time on which he is based.

But, as I've already mentioned, William Balthazar really was Captain of Star Castle, while Marmaduke Rawdon and his subordinate colonels, Peake and Johnson, did oversee the defence of the house during the first siege.

As for Stryker and his men, it is sure to be a turbulent winter. The company has been shattered, and the balance of power is looking ever more precarious. After Gloucester and Newbury, the armies of Parliament are beginning to gain confidence, and as the snow falls, the Scottish Covenanters are mustering north of the border. There are more struggles to come, and battles aplenty.

Captain Stryker will return.

HISTORY LIVES
at Hodder

From Anya Seton and Mary Stewart to Thomas Keneally and Robyn Young, Hodder & Stoughton has an illustrious tradition of publishing bestselling and prize-winning authors whose novels span the centuries, from ancient Rome to the Tudor Court, revolutionary Paris to the Second World War.

————

Want to learn how an author researches battle scenes?

Discover history from a female perspective?

Find out what it's like to walk Hadrian's Wall in full Roman dress?

Visit us today at **HISTORY LIVES** for exclusive author features, first chapter previews, book trailers, author videos, event listings and competitions.

🐦 @HistoryLives_

tumblr historylivesathodder.tumblr.com

www.historylives.co.uk